Levant Mirage

by

Oliver F. Chase

Copyright © 2015
Pearl River Publishing Group, LLC
EPCN Library of Congress pending
All rights foreign and domestic reserved
ISBN: 978-0-9861406-2-4
0-9861406-2-7

Cover art by Rick Schroeppel Elm Street Designs Studio
Nashville, Tennessee
http://elmstreetdesignstudio.com/

Pearl River Publishing Group
All rights reserved.

Dedication

For my dad, who refused to accept humble beginnings foisted upon him as a life's plan.

Acknowledgements

A small group of advanced readers treated my manuscript to a scrupulous review, correcting gaffs and suggesting alternatives. These wonderful folks included Dr. Clay Andrews, Elizabeth Calantoni, Jerry Baker, Ashley Sanchez, and Best Selling Author Gregory Lamb among others. This work is a far better product because you paid me the greatest tribute, your friendship.

Even though this isn't my first rodeo, there's a lot cowboys and cowgirls out there who always encouraged me … even when they didn't like how the hero got knocked off his horse, or took second place in a two man contest. The fact that you trusted our friendship enough to let your objections be known gave me encouragement and strength.

Editor Arlene Robinson used tact, facts, and thoroughness to bring this manuscript along. If you happen upon an error, only I own it.

Chapter 1

The computer attack began around one in the morning and went on for six hours. The Pentagon didn't get the word until nine. When the NSA confirmed some military servers had given up their secrets, the entire system was shut down—hard. The Pentagon's staff suddenly found itself looking for paper reports no longer available. Most didn't bother and wandered to the coffee shops to wait it out. Or, they just went home.

Adam sat at his desk with an unwashed mug and a single window open against a rampaging radiator. His index finger creased, then flipped an old perforated computer readout as he crossed off a number. As a college freshman, Dartmouth's student newspaper called him their best hope for a winning season. By his junior year, another bright star took his place and Adam went to second string. When a rushing lineman decked the new quarterback, Adam substituted and threw the winning pass against rival New Hampshire. After the game, he got drunk and got laid. With the football victory, the night became a trifecta for his memory banks. He would need it as a gray pall covered the world the next morning. Standing in his boxer shorts, he watched the second World Trade Tower come down while he and his fraternity brothers each wondered about their future.

"Hey, buddy."

Adam's dark brown eyes looked up from his work. "Good morning, sir."

The section's second-in-command grinned from the doorway. "You going to let me buy you that drink after work tonight? I've got dinner reservations."

Adam allowed his mouth to work a smile he didn't feel. "Sure. I'd enjoy that after hours of literally pushing a pencil." He let the yellow number-two drop. This job was his last in the Army. Failure at the lieutenant colonel's promotion board last summer had been a final, quiet revenge for bad publicity. "The hackers nailed us this morning. Maybe we should just let them have it, they want it so bad."

The tall man leaned against the doorjamb. "Did they ever say who got us?"

Adam rolled his shoulders. "Rumor control says it's the

Iranians, still pissed for blowing up their centrifuges at Natanz."

"That was the Israelis," Brad said. Both men smiled at the old joke. "When are those guys going to be satisfied with kicking our cyber butts?"

He wasn't looking for an answer. Adam's assignment to an Air Force colonel was a little unusual. Then again, so was their friendship.

"There's a fourth tonight," Brad said as he popped a uniform cap onto the back of his head and worked arms into an overcoat. With his blue eyes and salon-cut blond hair, he looked more bad-boy Madison Avenue than former helicopter rescue pilot. "She's an old friend. Introduced me to Lynn, so I kind of owe her." Brad's flavor of the month usually involved pretty, blond, and statuesque women.

Adam, however, knew Lynn, and she was smart and ambitious. He wondered if the colonel might have met his match. "That's fine, sir," he said. "Just fine. Any *old friend of yours* and all that stuff."

"You'll like Miranda," Brad said. "Everybody loves a celebrity. Besides, you need to get out more. She's visiting this week from New York City. Your old stomping grounds, the Big Apple, right?" Brad slipped into his folksy Georgia accent. "Y'all just be rounding out a threesome. I can't leave this other gal home all alone. Ain't that against the law, or something? You'll just be helping out a brother."

In the early days, Brad and Adam were renowned on Fort Myers tennis courts and the competition golf circuit. Salt and pepper, as the few less kind said. Even as the days grew dark and the controversy ugly, Brad never wavered. Adam owed the guy. Still, he hoped for a short night. This weekend was his to spend with Julie. "Sounds good, sir. I'm sure it'll be fun."

"Yep. You'll like her. All dark and mysterious. She'll be right up your alley."

Adam's mocha skin darkened. Until Marty taught him to left-jab twice and cross with a right, boys on the playground thought razing him great fun. The recollection of hazing and rejection, as well as the occasional adult slight, showed on his face.

Brad sighed and dropped his chin. "Ah, shit, Adam. I didn't mean anything by it. You know me, I'm always running my big mouth."

6

Adam smiled in spite of the adrenaline that bumped into his system. "I also know you're one of the good guys, sir. No sweat."

Brad resumed the grin. "Excellent. I'll call you with the details after I talk to Lynn." He hesitated. "Oh, yeah. General Miller called a briefing for this afternoon. Didn't want me, just you and Tom Connecelli. I'm headed over to the Hill anyway to have lunch with the senator. Dad's all excited, has something to tell me." He grinned at Adam. "Looks like we'll both have secrets."

"I'll be there, sir."

"Great. And be on time. It's never good to have Miller pissed at you. See you tonight."

With a shake of the mouse, Adam remembered the unplugged machine. He found his place on the endless column of figures and started again. As Brad pulled the door closed, he noticed his sergeant staring from the outer office.

The National Military Command Center occupied a large piece of the Pentagon's basement. Adam made the meeting with barely a moment to spare. One of the lowest-ranking members of several services in attendance, he found a seat in the rear of the war room's small amphitheater. He'd taken a phone call from an upset Katherine wanting to know why the child support check wasn't in her bank account. He spent extra minutes to explain the Army's system for paying, and had to run through the halls to avoid an angry General Miller and a disappointed Colonel Benchley. He settled into his chair.

"If I might have your attention, please. I am Colonel Hal Wilson, aide to Chief of Staff General Lowe. Each of you has been cleared for this briefing. Please note this is a US Top Secret and an EU Most-Secret brief. Sensitive compartmented information cannot be discussed outside this room. No one who isn't here now has a need to know." Colonel Wilson's grim mouth punctuated the words. A slight man wearing blue pinstripes and a knotted tie sat nearby.

"As you are probably aware from flash reports and CNN coverage, a few days ago the Islamic State of Iraq and Syria, or ISIS, took back control in several Iraqi cities and small towns." Wilson stood in front of a screen with a back lighted PowerPoint briefing displayed, and pointed at the map. "Qaim and Rutba were among them. A counterattack failed and the Iraqis were pushed back. During

7

the fighting, US spec ops captured an ISIS commander from a sect loyal to the radical Rahim Tajalli. Several Al-Qaeda leaders consider this jihadist offshoot too radical even for them. After transport to Baghdad, the commander underwent interrogation. He revealed knowledge of a Panamanian-registered ship under US contract, the *Morning Dawn*, sunk by Al Qaeda sabotage. Those of you who were around might recall this incident contemporaneous with the loss of seven CIA agents at our Camp Chapman base. Others died that day, too. This followed on the heels of and only days after, the infamous Christmas Massacre."

Adam stirred as his gut tightened.

Wilson continued. "The loss of the ship received little notoriety. There was a lot going on that week."

Wilson flipped to the next slide, showing an expanded satellite view of the Atlantic. "At the time, no one considered this anything but bad weather and bad luck. With the ISIS commander's information, all that changed. The NSA unearthed its archived NOAA GOES-12 pre-commissioning data that shows a disturbance, and the disappearance of the ship. The satellite was not geosynchronous at the time, was unmonitored, and no further data was gathered. There was no Mayday received. When the ship failed to report on time, a British P3 Orion out of Gibraltar conducted a search. After the ship failed to make port, the US Navy dispatched a destroyer, but two weeks after the sinking. They, of course, found nothing. No recovery operation was launched."

General Keith Miller cleared his throat, and Adam glanced over at him. Miller cut his red-brown hair into short, wiry bristles, like a mean and unruly pit bull, an image he encouraged. "Okay, so there was a lot going on that day and someone dropped the ball," Miller said. "Why don't you just explain why this is important so long after the fact? After all these years in salt water, I assume there's nothing usable on board."

"Yes, sir. What was not realized at the time, a second ship shadowed the *Morning Dawn* and in fact, hid in her wake. Only the newer NSA analysis techniques confirmed it."

"And?" said Miller, prompting Wilson with a glance to his watch.

"The NSA decided the ship was a submarine, sir. The GOES-

12 satellite was still in test status when the sinking occurred, so the sub wasn't tracked. For all this time, there's been no intelligence on the loss of the ship or its cargo. But now, if an ISIS field commander found out, the secret is no more. When soldier bees know, a lot of people know. Military Sealift Command rescue and salvage ship USNS *Grasp* is en route to search." Wilson glanced and received a nod from the man in civilian clothes. "The *Morning Dawn*'s first port of call was to have been Tel Aviv."

General Miller set his jaw. "Okay, you got my attention. Let's hear it."

"Yes, sir. The ship carried top-secret cargo to the Israelis. We don't know why it went to the bottom so quickly and without a Mayday. The Navy says sabotage or a torpedo could have done it. The *Morning Dawn* carried cruise missiles, the AGM-200 or as they're referred to now, the JSAM. The cruise missiles were operational. The variation here was a fire-and-forget command module in its first combat role before being deployed with the Navy's stealth X-47 Pegasus...."

"Still waiting, Colonel." General Miller's legendary lack of patience festered.

Wilson brought up a new slide with a jab of his finger. "The JSAM's guidance system was new at the time, an innovation that works without GPS or external targeting mechanics. A missile can make an undetectable surgical strike more than ten thousand miles away from any naval fleet. If it knows where it starts, the system's orders can't be changed, even if we lose our laser guidance, satellites, or human command and control."

General Miller set his jaw and leaned toward the speaker. "I'm still in the dark here. We lost a ship. The ship had some new missiles, now old technology. They haven't been fired back at us because they're sitting at the bottom of the ocean under a mile of salt water."

Wilson almost glanced at the civilian, but Miller's face squeezed into a single, angry wrinkle.

Wilson spoke. "It's the guidance system, sir. The design might be compromised. Only a few command modules were in existence at the time of the sinking. Many more have since been produced with upgraded components, but those were the first."

9

Miller blew out a breath. "And, could the sub recover any of our weapons? Do the containers float? Could a salvage operation have been staged without our knowing? Come on, Colonel. What's going on?"

Wilson squirmed. "Because the ISIS commander knows about the ship and the new, ah, the old JSAM's target locator command module, DIA declared the system compromised. We are to assume other nations, and possibly the enemy, has our system."

"That's a hell of a leap in logic." Miller's veined hands gripped the edge of the table in front of him, straining the heavy black plastic. "Come on, Colonel, what's the bottom line? The technology is obsolete."

"It's the submarine, sir...."

"No, no." Miller leaned back and gritted his teeth. "What you're trying to say is we've pulled the new systems out of the pipeline, haven't we?"

Wilson took a deep breath, knowing the general's ire might be the least of his problems. "The Joint Chiefs agreed the weapon command module is compromised and is now removed from the operational inventory. We'll inform the governments in possession of this system, and advise everyone to revert to less-than-stealthy technology. Our ability to hit over-the-horizon targets will return to a mix of Doppler, GPS, and human pilots. For the time being, our allies won't have a capability to strike deep into enemy territory from long distances."

General Miller's present position might be the acquisitions chief, but as Adam knew too well, the general cut his teeth leading soldiers on the battlefield. "Wait a goddamn minute," Miller said. "You're going to pull all these weapons, and you're not deploying the replacements first? This happened years ago, for Christ's sake. What you're doing is leveling the playing field *against* our guys. You don't know the JSAMs are compromised. You're guessing."

"The Joint Chiefs believe—"

"And, I'll follow the goddamn orders, Colonel. But what the hell?" Miller turned to the back wall. "Major Michaels?"

Adam snapped to his feet.

"You built this command module in college, right?"

Adam and General Miller shared a dark history, and Miller already knew the answer to his question. Adam said, "I was part of an MIT PhD team who replaced the old GOLIS, or go-onto-location-in-space system, with an unchangeable, geo-synchronized, bioorganic—"

"Jesus Christ, Michaels." Miller dropped his chin to stare at the tabletop. "You built it, right or wrong?"

"We built it, sir."

"Can the bad guys compromise the system after all these years?"

For the first time, Adam saw Tom Connecelli in the front of the room turn to look at him. Michaels, Perez, and Connecelli, the three amigos they called themselves, the PhD team who built the bio-organic prototype that became the command module for a thousand missiles. The two men locked stares. Adam said, "Yes, sir. They've had enough years to reverse engineer the system. They could do it." Connecelli closed his eyes, letting his shoulders sag. Adam continued. "It's unlikely the command module could survive any time immersed in salt water, but the theory could be compromised by now."

"God damn it." Miller rotated his attention back to the front of the room. "Continue, Colonel."

For the next thirty minutes, the briefing flashed on the screen and the talk droned. The small man in the blue pinstripe suit never spoke or introduced himself.

As the men filed out, Adam heard his name. He turned to General Miller. "Good afternoon, sir."

Miller spoke without preamble. "What the bureaucratic bozos didn't say is a drop-in replacement will ship to Fort Dix over the weekend. Did you know about this?"

Adam had used his pencil that morning and checked the entry. "Yes, sir. I knew."

"And you didn't inform Colonel Wilson in there?"

"I saw your endorsement before the IT system went into the toilet. I figured if you didn't want to say anything, I'd keep my peace, too."

"Good for you," Miller said, clipped and angry. A head shorter, but formidable as he pointed a finger. "I want you on a bird to Dix first thing Monday morning. Check the shipment and get it delivered.

11

Clear?"

"Yes, sir."

"When you see Colonel Benchley, have him call me. He'll be my personal envoy to meet with a few allies and explain this royal screw-up. I'm sure he'll make the most of it." Miller didn't like Brad's connections, and hence didn't like Brad. In fact, the general didn't like anyone since he was hurt by the political fallout from Adam's Christmas Day Afghanistan debacle. This morning, his anger found a new level with the Joint Chiefs' decision.

"You actually did build this system, right Major? You weren't a pencil pusher then."

"After my first tour in Iraq, I developed the graphene theory interchange for the command module from a NASA-funded DARPA project, sir. Sheila Perez grew the cellular structure and Tom … Commander Connecelli and I wrote the code." Adam had only been a first lieutenant then, and seemed to be on the fast track to career success. "I put the package together, and micro-wired the electronics to form the graphene and render them unchangeable. The three of us wrote it up and I presented the PhD paper behind closed doors. Munitions experts took it and made it work in the missile system. I returned to Iraq a month later."

Miller let his breath go. "All right. Our flanks are exposed, Michaels. More importantly, we're leaving our key Mideast friends open to an enemy attack. Iraq and Syria are only the first to feel the ISIS pinch. They won't be the last, and despite what those idiots at CNN say, ISIS doesn't need Baghdad or Damascus. Now, they've got a country the size of Virginia that can overrun Saudi Arabia, Israel, and Turkey. Even if this country had the guts to go in and kick the shitheads out, there're plenty of little countries that would rather wear burkas and stone women. You think we've got problems? Wait a couple months. Our world is about to change and not for the good."

"Yes, sir." Adam watched him walk back into the chamber and wondered if Miller was right, or just one more casualty from too much time fighting Al-Qaeda and Washington, DC.

Chapter 2

By five-thirty, the Pentagon's deserted corridors echoed Adam's footsteps. The first few months of navigating the multiple rings confused him. Now, he walked the near mile without seeing the dark wood paneling, concrete pillars, or plastic nameplates. A part of his trip took him to the rebuilt outer circle of the 9/11 attacks. The softened voices gave the passageway an ethereal breath. Adam signed his special clearance badge back into the daily log and crunched down the salted steps.

A confusion of tailpipe exhaust and cold gave the air an unpleasant alchemy accentuated by the high sodium-vapor lights under a gray sky. An early snowfall covered the parking lot, giving many in DC the excuse for a three-day weekend. Wind from the river found the unbuttoned top of his heavy coat as he stooped into his ten-year-old Corolla.

The key produced a single click, then nothing. Out of the car and under the hood. A passerby stopped. "Anything I can do?" The man saw Adam's rank and snapped off a salute.

Adam smiled. "Thanks, but unless you've got a spare battery or jumper cables in your back pocket, I'll be calling the auto club."

"Sorry, sir. Bad day for a dead battery."

"Thanks for stopping, Marine."

At least the problem of the evening was solved. He wouldn't make it to dinner. He slid into the passenger's seat to pull the mobile from the glove box. He'd known the power was low from his morning's call to Julie. At thirteen, his daughter had a lot to say about most everything. Now cold-soaked from a day in the car, the phone wouldn't even boot up.

"Crap." Adam rolled the device in his hand while he pulled the door closed against the wind. He remembered when Marty Callaway laid the little instrument on the table in front of Adam's former-socialite mother. Lillian accepted the gift and promised to use it. She never did, and likely never intended to. But she smiled up at Marty, the family's consigliore as she called him, with the fondness of a mutual history reaching back into her wild youth. One of McCaffrey

13

Shipping's many lawyers, Marty had been with the family since law school, and became the sole attorney privy to the family's secrets.

Adam locked the door and headed back into the building, reminding himself to buy a new phone battery, maybe even a new phone. Sentimental thoughts usually preceded any real search for new technology. He splashed his way through the slush, formulating the words for the message to leave on Brad's phone. Once I-270's traffic snarled, he'd make the call. After that, he'd wait for the wrecker to jump the Toyota and enjoy getting a little drunk in front of his small flat screen. Asleep by nine. Maybe he'd just have the car towed and take a taxi home.

His hand stopped short of the light switch in the office. "Colonel?" he said, surprised to see the man's back.

Brad spun from a half-seated position on the sergeant's desk, dropping the papers in his hand. "Adam? Jesus Christ!"

"Sorry, sir."

"Do you always sneak up on people like that?" They stared at one another as Brad picked up the sheets.

"No, sir."

Adam's boss wore his blue uniform overcoat. "You need to transfer to the DIA, Major. That's a hell of a talent you've got there, sneaking up on people. They teach you that in the Army?"

Adam closed the door. "I didn't mean to startle you, Colonel."

"Well, Christ-on-a-crutch, you did." Brad took a deep breath to regain the equanimity the evening would require. "I thought you'd already left?"

"Battery's dead, and I needed to call the auto club." He didn't add his plan to cancel the evening.

"Well, that's no good." Brad tapped an index finger on the papers. "I needed an answer. Dix called me looking for the parcel numbers for the JSAM shipment. Computers are still down, but I think Aberdeen has them."

Brad dropped his eyes first. Even as Adam's superior officer, the war room briefing needed to stay in the war room. Adam said, "I believe that's the paper you need, Colonel. Captain Rodriquez has the shipping invoices. I've got the electronic confirmation before they shut the system down. I'll get the parcel numbers for you."

14

Brad shifted his weight from foot to foot. "You know what? I'll wait. There's no rush."

"I can find it," Adam said. "It's really no problem. Did you happen to speak with General Miller?"

"Yeah, you're right. I'm headed to Tel Aviv on Sunday. And you're headed to Dix. Lucky boy." Brad grinned and clapped his hands together. "As long as you're without wheels, why don't you ride with me?"

Adam's evening slipped away. "Well … thanks. I can call a cab after dinner."

"This will work out. You call the motor club and arrange things." He glanced at his watch. "They'll take an hour, so there won't be enough time to change clothes. We can just go and grab a drink if we're too early. The public can stand to see us in uniform this once, right?"

"Yes, sir."

"It's after five. Call me Brad."

"Sure thing."

* * *

The Holiday Inn was thirty minutes away from the Pentagon in heavy traffic, but near where Brad's girlfriend lived. Lynn Kostunica and her friend Miranda from New York waited in the lobby when they arrived. Most patrons in the bar worked at Housing and Urban Development, the CDC, or NASA, all of which were less than a block away. The foursome managed the two-for-one special before the hour ran out and they could walk the few blocks to the Moroccan restaurant.

Brad finished his third scotch and leaned into the table. Smart, opinionated, and knowledgeable, he'd dominated their conversation with a firsthand description of the troubles in the Mideast. "When I was with NATO, we spent time all over Egypt, the Sinai, Lebanon, and Jordan. Can't do it today, since the war. Americans are high-value targets over there now. Did anybody ever give a thought to how the Arabs might feel when their homeland was given away? Their Levant?"

The couple at the next table glanced over. "Sir?" Adam said.

15

"Volume?"

"Right, right." Brad gave a quick wave of his hand. "Sorry ladies, I get wound up." Dishes clanked nearby as the waiter arrived with a narrow-necked amber bottle and four tiny glasses.

Lynn smiled at him. "You should run for office, Brad. For just another pretty face, you're a smart guy."

Adam understood Brad's infatuation. Lynn was striking, with long eyelashes over blue eyes and a low-cut dress one size too small.

"Run for office? Hey, great idea." Brad gave Adam a knowing look. "You'll love this drink. Anise, aniseed liqueur from Morocco. Not too sweet." He pushed his empty scotch tumbler aside for the moment.

"Licorice, right?" Lynn said and tasted with her lips. "I like licorice. It's good for so many things." The pink tip of her tongue explored the inside of the glass. Brad returned the leer over the top of his own.

Adam wondered how anyone at the Surface Transportation Board managed to get work done with Lynn walking their marble hallways. A few months ago when Brad first dated Lynn, he explained that as an émigré from the former Yugoslavia, she easily out climbed her native competition. She'd brought a master's degree in marine engineering and a lot of hard work to the STB. Adam pondered if she'd be the one to finally tame the mischievous Brad Benchley.

The fourth for the evening, Miranda Cinclaire, was lovely as well, with dark brown hair and brooding eyes. She turned to Adam. "What do you and Brad do all day in the Pentagon?"

Adam's drink burned his throat and he coughed his surprised reply.

"It's an easy question, soldier boy. I was just asking what you do with my tax dollars." A transplant to New York City, Miranda's southern accent was interesting, and like Brad's, optional.

"The cameras aren't rolling, Major, so feel free," Brad said, chuckling.

"Sorry," Adam said, making his recovery as artful as possible. "I wasn't expecting the really tough questions right away." He sipped his water and looked into deep, inquiring brown eyes. "Defense logistics, mostly."

16

Miranda scrunched her eyebrows.

He tried again. "It's the boring part of the Army. Like the world's biggest Wal-Mart. We make sure there're enough beans and bullets for the guys doing the real work. Not exactly sexy, but Napoleon would be proud."

Brad tipped up his anise and shook his head. Adam saw the gesture. "What?"

Miranda laughed. "Napoleon, huh? If that's Bonaparte, I think he's the one who ran off my great-great-granddaddy and stole the family farm we'd won in a crooked poker game."

Brad set the empty glass on the table, and gave Adam a quick frown. "It's a little more than just beans and bullets, Miranda. We handle everything, especially all those secret drones killing the ISIS leaders." He leaned in. "Most of those guys aren't the sharpest knives in the drawer anyway, but they do have a stranglehold on oil. Adam knows more about that than me though." He picked up his empty tumbler and rolled his ice cubes around, then flagged a waiter. "Another scotch."

Adam watched as the man nodded and walked away. "Let's drop it, okay?"

"Aw, come on," Brad said. "We're all friends here. What's the straight scoop from Damascus?"

Adam willed his CO to have a moment's clarity.

Lynn shifted in her seat, placing a hand on Brad's forearm. "Maybe this isn't the right forum. What do you think?"

Brad shrugged. "Adam's got family connections over there, right?"

"Too much information," Adam said. He knew the Internet made everyone an open book, but he never volunteered anything about the family.

Lynn squeezed. "Sure, sure."

Miranda turned to Adam. "Sorry. I didn't mean to start something."

Adam smiled. "No worries."

"Terrorism doesn't have borders, Adam. That's all I'm saying. Half those guys actually believe in that Levant Caliphate homeland stuff." His voice was low, but he glanced at the nearest table.

The waiter placed the scotch in front of Brad and glanced between the two men. Brad looked at the drink and pushed it away. "Sorry, buddy. It's a sensitive subject, and I was way out of line."

"No sweat," Adam said.

"Let's talk about something else," Lynn said. "Let's talk about my best friend, Miranda." She squeezed a smile across the table. "I demand all the dirt on the new leading man. He is *so* yum bucket."

Miranda smiled and surprised Adam by taking his hand. "I'd be happy to tell all his secrets, but don't let him know."

Adam liked her touch, and let the ladies fill the silence. Brad's remark hurt because Adam's Syrian connection was true. As a youngster, he wanted to know why he couldn't be a McCaffrey. After all, he reasoned, Grandpa was a McCaffrey, as was his mother, Lillian. When he asked, her story was pat and prepared, and Adam didn't catch on. His mother explained that as heir to the legacy of a deceased humanitarian physician, Adam should be proud. His father's name remained on the lips and in the prayers of the Kurdish refugees he'd saved. At the time, that seemed good enough. After an upperclassman razzed him about a tabloid picture of his naked mother romping in an Italian fountain, the story crumbled, much like the boy Adam had punched. The article accompanying the picture said Lillian had a baby out of wedlock and born in Switzerland. Adam knew the baby was him, and until college graduation, believed in and fought boyhood battles over the fictitious Dr. William Michaels and the hue of his skin. More than one family lie marred his twenty-first Christmas at the McCaffrey estate.

The waiter stood beside the table. "May I offer dessert, sir?" He recited the menu.

Lynn and Miranda declined. Brad ordered Halawa Mishmish, pistachio-apricot-date balls, for everyone.

Miranda tried one, but then tapped her glass indicating another drink. "If I'm going to have something with this many calories, it should contain alcohol. Are you going to make me drink alone?"

"No, of course not," Adam said, and signaled the waiter. Brad and Lynn sat with their heads together ignoring the other two.

Miranda turned to him. "The evening turned personal tonight. I'm sorry if I contributed."

"It's not that," he said, wishing Brad never broached the subject. "I don't usually share the family secrets until the second date."

She smiled. "Hmm, I like the sound of that."

Now he laughed, too. "You know what I mean."

"I think so. I hope so."

Lynn picked up her small handbag. "I think it's time for me to indulge in my nasty habit."

Miranda glanced over. "I thought you quit."

Lynn gave a small shake of her head and kissed Brad on the chin. "Interested?"

Miranda watched them for a moment as they left, then turned to Adam. "I've known Brad since I was a freshman undergraduate and he was a big-time fraternity alumni muckety-muck. I remember him as bit of a bad boy around the edges when the drinks are flowing. I don't think he meant anything."

Adam knew his boss fought an unfair reputation brought over from his early days. "He's a good guy, I agree. Maybe a little crazy, but then again, he is a pilot and a decorated one, so he deserves some slack."

"Loyal. Very nice."

Adam changed the subject. "You're living in New York, then."

She nodded. "I am. I just renewed my lease now that … I'm alone."

For a long moment, he could think of nothing to say.

She covered his hand with her own. "Please, Adam. Don't worry about filling the silence. When someone drops out of your life after three pretty wild years, the space they leave … hurts. I appreciate you coming out tonight, you know. Brad sort of told Lynn who sort of told me you live on a mountaintop in the Catskills."

He laughed and she joined him. "It feels that way sometimes, but really it's more like an apartment in Alexandria. I'm really happy about tonight, too. You're a terrific lady."

She blinked surprise. "Why, thank you, sir. I like you, too." Her hand stayed on his.

They talked as the music played and people moved around them. He learned that she took singing lessons from a famous voice coach that Adam had never heard of. Her life and social circles seemed

19

far different from his own, even when he'd courted society a long time ago.

When a grinning Brad and a disheveled Lynn returned, Adam called for the check.

Brad protested, and Adam waved him away. "My treat, please." The waiter glanced down at the card, and then eyed Adam. "Is there something else?"

"My apologies. Perhaps a driver's license?"

"No problem." Adam handed the man his embossed plastic card. He watched as the man read slowly.

"Thank, you, sir." The man left with a last glance, and took a long time. When he finally returned Adam scribbled a signature, added cash for a tip, and pocketed the receipt. The night would eat a big chunk out of a small checking account.

Brad grabbed up his overcoat. "Okay, after-dinner entertainment, and this time, it's on me." He scowled good-naturedly at Adam. "Any objections? I've got a great deal on the theater right next door. Miranda can't miss this."

Lynn turned to her friend before the protests could begin. "This is research, Miranda. The belly dancers are authentic from Tunisia. We won't stay long, I promise. It'll be fun."

"Research?" Miranda looked at her watch.

"For you," Lynn said with a laugh. "Aren't you a dancer, too? Come on."

"Okay, but I'm committed tomorrow. I'll need to get the late train back tonight."

"You can sleep all the way home." Lynn turned to Adam. "You'll get her back to the train, right?"

Three sets of eyes were on him. "Yes, of course," he said, forcing a smile, feeling somehow disappointed.

Miranda picked up her clutch bag. "Okay, then. A quick trip to North Africa, and then Union Station for the ten o'clock train."

Chapter 3

The foursome rounded the corner under the streetlights as an engine started a block away. Adam couldn't enjoy the show. His mind was preoccupied with the weekend he'd planned for Julie, and of course, the stunning woman enjoying the show next to him. Creosote timbers from the old tracks gave an odd, yesteryear smell from a time when small shacks and tiny vegetable gardens surrounded rural DC. No longer. Now the block was surrounded by government architecture.

Adam and Miranda slowed until they were a few yards behind the other couple's quicker pace.

"I have a question" said Adam, "Why—"

"Finally!" Miranda said with a laugh. "Belly dancers can be a distraction, I get it. But you haven't asked me a single thing all night."

"I'm sorry. It's just …" She waved him away and stopped. Brad and Lynn continued to walk and laugh. A whisper of snow joined the mist. "Okay, here goes. Why do I hear a southern accent now and then, if you're from Canada?"

She took his arm and pulled close. "You caught me."

An engine accelerated from behind them.

"LSU," said Brad, stopping to look back. "Ms. Cinclaire is Canadian, born an American citizen, returned to Quebec with her family, and became …" His mouth screwed up. "… a Tiger. Can you believe that?"

"Go purple and gold, and quit butting in. Keep walking," she said to Brad with a rah-rah fist. She squeezed Adam's arm as her voice rose to catch Brad's ear. "I was undergrad at LSU, but don't mind him. He's upset because no matter what he does, he'll always be a Dog."

"UGA. Go Dawgs …"

Brad's words were lost when a van pulled between the couples. The side door slid open and two men jumped out. One put a pistol into Adam's face. Both wore ski masks.

Adam's actions were instinctual. He slapped the pistol to the side and stepped in front of Miranda, knocking her backward. "Run," he yelled as a shot ricocheted off the concrete.

The other man grabbed for Miranda, but Adam's right fist sent

21

him to the ground. The first man recovered and whipped the steel barrel at Adam's forehead, rocking him backward. "Get in," the man said, his voice a raspy hiss. "Or, I'll kill you here."

Blood trickled down Adam's forehead. The second man rose, fury in his expression, and grabbed for Adam, for a moment blocking the pistol.

Adam took advantage with a knee to the groin and two quick jabs that sent the first man tumbling into the other. In the confusion another shot fired, this time followed by a scream.

The driver gunned the engine and stared at Adam with wide, frightened eyes. For a moment, the man reminded him of the restaurant waiter. The smaller of the assailants writhed in pain as he fell inside the van. A man yelled out from the other side of the street about calling 911. "You bastard," breathed the assailant, looking at the gathering crowd. "This doesn't end here. Go! Go!"

The van lurched forward and careened off a park bench and then, sped down the street. Brad barely leapt clear of crushing wheels as he ran back to join the fight.

"Jesus, Adam," Brad said. "Was that what I thought it was?"

Adam turned to Miranda. "Are you okay?" She nodded but stood motionless, wide-eyed and terrified.

Brad noticed the scrape over Adam's eye. "You're hurt, buddy. Come on and sit." The concrete bus bench was askew but upright. Lynn dialed her phone.

Adam's head swirled. Miranda sat down beside him, taking his arm. "My God. I think they tried to kidnap you." She took tissues from her purse and pressed them against his eyebrow.

"I'm fine," he said. "I look worse than I feel."

Lynn hung up. "The police will be here in a minute."

Brad laughed. "In DC? Give me a break." He looked at Adam. "Want me to get you a drink or something?"

Miranda turned. "No more alcohol. Coffee, maybe."

Several people from a late-evening BBQ place stood on the sidewalk watching. Brad yelled across the street. "Do they serve coffee in there?" A man waved and ran inside. "Give me a hand, Lynn."

Miranda and Adam sat in silence until he turned and said, "That was wild."

"No one will ever match this for a first date, blind or otherwise." She smiled and dabbed, but the blood already stopped. "Looks like it could use a stitch."

"Are you a nurse?"

She paused to gaze at him. "Three brothers on a Canadian cattle ranch. There was no end to stitching them up." She laughed. "Big, unruly, and regular Saturday-night brawlers, but I've never seen anyone take on two men before. And one with a gun."

He shrugged. "Just silly instinct involving no conscious thought. I'm sorry things didn't turn out better this evening. There's still time for the late train if we get a cab. You'll be home in a couple of hours."

Miranda dismissed his hurry with a wave. "I never imagined you were such a … fighter. You're so calm, quiet." She looked up and crinkled her nose. "Are you some sort of karate expert or something?"

Now he smiled. "*Or something* is closer. I probably had more than my fair share of fights growing up. Mostly because of my skin pigment."

"The men I know can't take of themselves. They use words. I've never met a man of action."

He smiled. "Sorry, that's not me. I probably could've gotten both of us killed because I wasn't thinking, just responding."

She closed the distance between them. "You're modest, too. I thought you were acting before." She smiled, embarrassed. "I Googled you, of course. You've got more press than me. Why is the *New York Times* mad at you?"

"Long story."

Brad and Lynn crossed the street. "He's a war hero, too. You mentioned that, right?"

Adam rolled his eyes. "Please, Brad. Colonel or not …"

The other man's eyes were shiny with mirth. "Silver Star. Saved his entire company from an ambush and got wounded in the process."

"My God," said Lynn. "My boss has one of those on his wall. He never stops talking about it."

"You should see Adam's citation …"

"Brad?" said Adam, the warning evident in his tone. "Don't.

23

No joke."

Brad shrugged and handed the cups over. "I hear you, brother. But one day I *will* tell the story, because you won't. It should've been more than a Silver Star. And it would've been except a bunch of Army generals got their panties in a wad."

They sat in silence waiting for the police to arrive. A city ambulance came and left, but the police were still missing. Brad and Lynn sat in his idling Lexus, but Adam wanted the air.

"My divorce was final this week," Miranda said into the night. "This was sort of my coming out."

"I'm sorry to hear that," said Adam. "Divorce isn't easy. Do you have kids?" She shook her head. Adam continued. "I've got Julie and she's a sweetheart. If it wasn't for her ..." He trailed away. "She's still young enough to like me. Katherine, my ex, and I get along better now. We'll never be friends like before, but it's an improvement over the last few years."

Miranda took his hand. "Julie's a pretty name."

"She's a great kid. We named her for my grandfather, Julius."

Miranda squeezed his hand. "I'm just glad to be out. I'm not sure either of us meant till death do us part. This thing had more to do with a photo op than love." She offered a small smile. "He's an actor, too. We sort of just used one another. Shallow people doing shallow things."

"That's not my impression. Did I know you were an actress?"

"Yes, Adam, unless you didn't listen to me brag all night."

"I'm sorry, I ..."

She laughed. "Kidding, kidding. I can't believe Brad didn't mention it."

Adam thought for a moment. "He might have. I've been sort of busy lately."

"I know. Saving damsels in distress, fighting street thugs, and trying to find the Superman cape you misplaced."

They both laughed. Brad pointed as the police car arrived. "Good," he called out. "We can get this over with."

Chapter 4

He awoke with his mouth's familiar chalk taste little different from many other Saturday mornings. The digital clock read five-thirty. Rather than the subdued morning sun, a subliminal smell of brewing coffee woke him. He rolled his feet to the bare floor.

"Good morning, sleepyhead," Miranda said from the doorway, her trim figure lost in an old Dartmouth T-shirt. She sipped a mug of coffee.

"Morning," he said, his voice raspy.

She smiled toward his nakedness, and returned to the living room.

He covered himself and felt muscles stiff from the fracas. He tried and still couldn't process the assault. Why the waiter, and why try to kidnap him? He would call the military authorities later in the day. All contacts with the police were reportable, so he must. They could do little other than read the police reports and he would not have his weekend ruined by sitting all day at Bolling Air Force Base. Besides, the police should easily be able to locate the waiter.

He found sweat pants and a pullover shirt, washed his face and touched a sore forehead. A tiny butterfly held the two edges of skin together. Both sides of his mattress bore evidence of the evening before.

She sat at the high, round Formica kitchen table, one foot tucked comfortably under the other, watching a few feathery autumn holdovers peck at brown and soggy grass.

"Hello again," she said. Her combed hair and touch of makeup left him with the impression she always looked good. Tender fingers touched his face. "Not too bad. Besides, scars look good on men, especially the leading-man types."

He laughed. "Oh, please. Any more coffee?"

"In your pot and not too bad, if I do say so myself."

He poured and sat opposite. She sipped the dark liquid and didn't rush to fill the silence. The glass sliding door looked over vacant land destined to be more housing when the economy came back. For now, the brown field and tangled brush offered an emptiness

25

in the gray day.

"Coffee okay?" she asked after several minutes. "Your machine was a little strange to me."

He nodded. "Uh, huh. Actually, it's a lot better than the coffee I make."

"Well good," she said.

They sipped.

She spoke first. "Can I get personal?" He looked up and nodded. "You don't have too many overnight visitors, do you?"

"Well, that's true, actually." He paused and tried to remember even a single one. Katherine probably didn't count. Besides, that night had been a disaster. "Since the divorce, there really didn't seem to be a reason."

"You know most men don't think about divorce like that. For them, it's more like a get-out-of-jail-free card." Her cup was empty and she moved a few dishes for a spot in the sink.

"I suppose you're right, but my wife divorced me. Not the other way around."

She watched him for a long moment, then said, "That will have to wait for later, because I really do need to catch the train."

Her abruptness shocked him. "Please, don't misunderstand."

She returned to her seat and leaned in a few inches from him. "What is it I'm not to misunderstand? You're still in love with your wife."

Her words took the breath from him. "I'm not an idiot, Miranda, and I'm not some soppy teenager. I'm pretty firmly in middle age, and I probably did as much to chase off Katherine as she did to get away from me."

She watched him cocking her head to one side.

He smiled. "And, I don't see anyone. I haven't wanted to see anyone. I'm not studying for the priesthood or anything. I have a big family who isn't pleased with me, and a daughter I don't see enough." He touched the top of her hand and smoothed her silk skin. "I haven't dated since the split. That was a couple of years ago. I don't go out, and there isn't anyone special. I have friends, but they're not … conjugal."

"Go on."

26

He gave a short laugh, and took a deep breath. "Okay. The few people I did hang with, the ones left over from my marriage are long gone. Most just transferred, but others didn't want any part of me afterward. The divorce was messy. Lots of bad things got out. Our two families are sort of … prominent. People talked. My work friends moved on with their careers and I stayed behind. So you see my reputation is sort of skewered. You know, like damaged goods."

Miranda said nothing.

He took a deep breath. "Geez, you want my whole life story in one sitting?" She nodded. "Okay. You might recall Brad talking about getting crosswise with the brass last night. I was involved in an Afghan police patrol that didn't go well. People died. And, like they say, once accused, always guilty."

He took a sip of the coffee and watched the same morning sparrow venture closer to the glass. The tiny bird pecked, then flew off. "No one in the Army wants to catch the failure disease. We're all like sharks. You keep moving up the ladder to breathe, and of course, we sometimes eat our young when things go bad. Only the strong survive."

"You know Lynn and I Googled you, right?"

"You mentioned that."

"We were just making sure you weren't a serial killer or anything." Adam gave a laugh. "Okay, maybe we were curious. I read about your wild days, the football hero, and about the battle and the court-martial. You were exonerated, Adam. They gave you back your medal, so I don't understand."

"It's the way of the world. I have a daughter and she lives here with her mom. I see her on weekends so I'm staying in the area any way I can, for as long as I can. The Army lets me do that. Another job might not, and I don't use my family's money—"

His mobile phone sat in the charger and interrupted. He checked caller ID and looked up.

"Daughter," he said.

"Take it," Miranda said and walked quickly into the bedroom.

"Morning, Julie. Report card week, right? Well, how did we do?" He listened. "Well, that's excellent in English. Still having trouble with Mrs. What's-her-name?" He laughed. "Of course. How could I forget that?"

They spoke several minutes more until he glanced at the kitchen clock. "Sure. By noontime, I can … wait." His voice trailed away as he remembered the complication sharing morning coffee. "Honey? Let me call you back. No, no. We won't be late. I just want to call you back." In a moment, he pushed the off button and replaced the phone.

Miranda returned to the living room. "Small apartment. Can't help but eavesdrop. Is it time for me to slink back into the woodwork from whence I came?"

"Not at all." He studied her face. "I try never to miss an opportunity to be with Julie. She didn't take the divorce too well. She … she's just starting to come back around."

"I'll call a cab, Adam. You call Julie back, make your arrangements." She headed back to the bedroom.

The clipped sentence stung his ears and yet he knew to discourage this now meant fewer complications later. "I'm sorry, Miranda."

"Oh Christ!" She whirled around. "Don't apologize. This is me being silly. You have a life. I know that." She walked out leaving Adam to stare behind her.

He rose stiffly and dumped the dregs of his cup.

She emerged wearing slacks and a sweater and pulling her weekend bag. "I was feeling sorry for myself," she said. "My bad."

"I'm the one who should be apologizing," he said and touched her hand. "I took advantage last night. I should know better."

"Maybe I took advantage of you."

He grinned. "Maybe. The point is …" He looked at her more closely, touching her nose. "Freckles?"

"Hush," she said, pulling both his hands down and drawling in the Louisiana accent, "Those are beauty marks." She grew serious. "I wanted to stay last night, Adam. I needed you to hold me. You seemed to understand what I was going through and I appreciated that." She smiled, an impish crinkle around her mouth. "In a lecherous sort of way, of course."

He laughed aloud. "Thanks a lot." He kissed her lips with a feather touch. "How about a personal question?" She nodded but

28

dropped his hands, crossing her arms. "How old are you?"

"I'm twenty-five. Almost over the hill in Hollywood speak."

"No way!"

"Way." She giggled.

"Good Lord!" He exhaled. "You *are* young."

"Boy, do you know how to charm the gals. And, before you get caught in a fib, I already know you're thirty-seven. Google. Not even a generation apart, and in the prime of your life. I'll vouch for that."

"Thank you."

"I'm glad I stayed," she said, moving close to his chest.

The intimacy swirled in his mind. "Me, too. All we've been doing is apologizing. Why don't we start again? Julie and I are going to drive into Maryland and see a friend of hers in Annapolis for crab cakes. Why don't you join us?"

Her face clouded. "I've got to get back to the City, Adam. Besides, you already told me how precious time with Julie is. Give me your phone."

He pulled the phone from its charger and handed it to her. She tapped into his starred contacts. "No excuse for not calling now. 'MC,' that's me. Don't forget."

He took her phone and tapped in his own number. "The invitation's open, if you change your mind." He handed back the phone as she kissed his chin. "No excuses, goes double."

Chapter 5

Julie ran down the stairs before he could even bring the car to a halt. "Wow, Dad!" She slid into the leather seat, all arms and legs, with a pretty face reminding him of a younger Katherine in family pictures. "Awesome car." Enterprise had rented him a red BMW.

He walked to the porch to pick up the overnight bag. In the house's small stoop, Katherine watched tight-lipped and arms crossed.

Willowy and athletic, his now ex-wife's star rose in the Department of Health and Human Services. He never doubted her eventual confirmation at one high government post or another. They met while preparing for DC's Marine Corps Marathon, and married six months later in Adam's family home in Bingham, New York. He'd promised to resign after a tour in Iraq, but with each challenge at home, found the Army's timing convenient. The second Afghanistan deployment brought the disaster that ended his career, and their marriage. Katherine's position as a senior government executive for HHS firmly cemented her in the hierarchy of Washington power. She grew in stature and reputation, as he stagnated, feeling neither envy nor jealousy.

"I see divorce is treating you well," she said. Her quick words hurt, even as he accepted her antipathy. Adam embarrassed her family, a transgression never to be forgiven, even if her personal career barely felt a speed bump.

"It's a rental, Katherine. The Toyota's in the shop."

"Whatever," she said, and closed the door behind her. Adam felt a pang as the lock clicked. They were friends once, became lovers and now, only Julie bridged a chasm growing daily.

Adam pulled away from a house purchased over a decade ago, when as newlyweds life began. They happily struggled with each payment in the early days, loving how they put themselves on their own map. Now, he still made the mortgage each month but Katherine didn't care. The house was a simple convenience, in a good neighborhood, and close to Julie's private school. It was Adam's duty to make the payments, his penance for the bumbling that brought unwanted national attention. Katherine came from East Lake Shore

Drive, Chicago old money. Their family's fortune predated Adam's immigrant great-grandfather's, but instead of shipping was built from real estate and western territory land grabs. Adam didn't reject his wealth as much as he kept an eye open for his own place in the world. After a decade, Katherine remained the darling of her widowed father and her uncle, the former vice president of the United States.

He and Julie spent Saturday tramping around old town Annapolis. They met Julie's friend and hit music stores as well as a tiny recording studio with a band making an album. Adam hoped to never hear the small group again. The girls, of course, fell in love. The day led to a chilly afternoon party for next spring's J-24 Seven Seas regatta. Neither girl cared about boats but sailors meant boys, if only in their dreams.

Adam could not relax. Every doorway, every man, every group of men were a threat. The kidnapping attempt ate at his insides. He didn't have a permit to carry a gun, yet on this weekend, wished for one. Julie and her friend were never out of his sight and never more than a few feet away.

After dropping off the other girl, Adam and Julie finished the day in Delaware's Rehoboth Beach for dinner and checked into the Boardwalk Plaza Hotel. He changed rooms twice, frustrating the staff, but assuring himself their rooms adjoined and if the worst happened, he could react quickly.

Sunday morning's walk on the beach became a memory for Adam on nights away. They were alone with gray surf and a salt breeze from his youth. On the ride home, he watched the rearview mirror until Julie finally asked him if they were being followed.

"Too many movies for you, sweetheart. I'm just being cool. Forget about me."

She returned her attention to the iPad, and he became more circumspect.

Homework ended the weekend in his apartment, with dinner at Filomena Ristorante. Julie waved skipping up the sidewalk to Katherine, still unsmiling, still with arms crossed.

He walked up the steps, waiting until Julie went inside. "I need to tell you something. Maybe it's nothing, but you should know."

She stared at him without answering, glancing at the tiny cut in

31

his eyebrow.

"I was mugged on Friday in DC, near the NASA building. I think you need to keep an eye on Julie."

"I always keep an eye on Julie." The retort was quick and barbed.

"Of course, I wasn't indicating otherwise." Adam took a moment and tried to explain. "This was a little odd, maybe more like … I don't know. Like a kidnapping attempt."

"Oh, for God's sake, Adam. What are you trying to pull?"

He tightened his jaw. "I'm not pulling anything. I didn't have time to change clothes because the car broke down—"

"You went to DC in your uniform?" Her voice rose, accusing him.

"Yes. And what's so wrong with that?"

She shook her head. "Well, you just answered your own question, didn't you? And now you'd like my sympathy. Is that it?"

He fought back angry recriminations. Instead, his voice was calm, deadly. "I don't care how much you hate me, Katherine. Don't let my daughter suffer because you stopped loving me."

He turned and left before she could answer.

* * *

The cell phone rang as he unlocked the apartment's door.

"Adam?"

"Miranda, hi. How are you?" he said.

"I'm not being a bother, am I?"

"Not at all. I've been thinking about you."

"Oh sure. After you barely escape a gang of bad guys, get bonked on the head saving a lady in distress, you're thinking about me? You'd better work on your lines."

"Okay, okay. What I meant was, I wanted yesterday to continue. With you."

"I felt the same way, Adam."

"I wish you'd accepted the invitation, although we did end up spending the night at the shore." He kicked off his shoes and fell into an overstuffed chair.

She giggled. "Had I known that was to be included, I might have decided differently."

"That's a relief. I had the feeling you thought I was a dud."

This brought a bigger laugh. "Dud? Do all soldier boys have such a way with words?"

"Just me, thank you very much." He enjoyed their banter, picturing her lovely face and recalling the tiny freckles. The contrast from his conversation with Katherine gave him a start.

The lightness left her voice. "I have to catch a flight this evening, so I didn't want Saturday to end weird."

"Wait. I thought you were working all week in New York."

"Ah, ha! You don't remember, do you?" He said nothing. "I'm meeting some people who are putting together a project."

He struggled, then recalled a snippet Lynn and Miranda shared. "You're an actress. Television, right?"

Her sigh cut through the connection. "No, silly. You never even heard me tooting my horn?"

"I'm sorry. I wasn't a very good date."

"And I thought you were just playing hard to get. I'm going to read with Dick Roberts tomorrow morning."

"Dick Roberts. Okay, but does that mean you won't be home tomorrow night?"

"I'm really not going to impress you, am I, Adam?"

"I'm plenty impressed. I just hoped you were going to be around. I'll be in Fort Dix, New Jersey in the morning, and I thought if I got held over, we could have dinner."

"Real disappointment," she said. "I can always tell when someone's acting. You're very sweet. I was afraid this thing was going to be a little lopsided."

He reached over and clicked the table lamp, wondering what she meant by *thing* when it struck him. "Wait. Dick Roberts, the movie star? You're going to be in a movie?"

"Oh, you are *so* killing me here. Lynn and I were talking about the new film. She's coming with me, and maybe get a part or something. She's very photogenic. Do you remember she and I were together off–Broadway when she first arrived in New York?"

"I missed all that, I'm afraid."

She giggled again. "You're telling me."

"Will you be coming back soon?"

"The movie's not for a while," she said. "They're filming on location in New Orleans … if Dick Roberts likes me. And, yes, in a week or so."

Adam felt on firmer ground now. "He'd be crazy not to like you. And you'll call me, so I'll know. Right?"

"And, you're going to be on the first plane or train when I get back, or I have entirely underestimated myself for the better part of my adult life."

He tapped a pencil on the tabletop. "As I recall, that won't encompass very many years."

"You're hung up on age, aren't you? Years are someone else's measure of time. Don't disappointment me, Adam Michaels."

* * *

Adam and Sergeant First Class Patrick Goodell sat in the chilly, glass-enclosed operations room. The *whop-whop* of a helicopter approached in the dark. Lights behind the pair reflected off the glass, leaving the world a dark landscape beyond. Adam carried the cancelled shipping documents that would have sent the missiles aboard a government-leased oceangoing ship, the *Oka Tadashi*. Someone must have protested that their container would be removed to make room. Now, the answer was to send replacements aboard a C5A Galaxy transport aircraft. Highly unusual, but allies were squawking and this was the fix. Besides, this might have been Brad's compromise to placate an angered Israel by getting replacements quickly.

"You must be coming up in the world, Major. A clean-green-flying machine and all for you."

Adam looked around at his young sergeant and laughed. "If I were coming up in the world, Patrick, I'd be getting a 170-mile-an-hour Blackhawk and not a ninety-knot granddaddy."

Goodell laughed. "Better than twenty miles an hour at rush hour, sir."

The UH-1H Huey settled outside on the pad. High and low, red and green position lights turned from steady to flash as the powerful beam of the landing light extinguished. The aircraft's high-gloss green paint contrasted with its former olive drab from the war years in Vietnam.

Ubiquitous to the DC area, in recent years the small helicopters

34

had become private taxis to high-ranking military and other VIPs. The true mission provided emergency evacuation to the Congress and other government officials, something that had never happened. And yet, the helicopters remained at the ready.

Adam smiled. "I'm in awe how you always see the sunny side." He liked the six-foot-three sergeant, a friendly double amputee from Iraq. Unless someone looked closely, they didn't notice the two lower legs taken by a car bomb and replaced with prosthetics. The persistent, good-humored young man talked the Army into a desk job. Or maybe they just wanted to be rid of his incessant cajoling. Goodell loved having the Army surgeons make him an inch-and-a-half taller.

"It's an insurance policy, sir," Goodell said once. "I can always claim it wasn't me jumping out of the boudoir's back window. The descriptions won't match." Goodell would never be called a lady's man, and devoted his energies to making his wife Janice happy. He never stopped talking about her promotions in the Treasury Department.

Goodell quieted for a moment. "I don't mean to get personal, sir. And you can just tell me if I am. I heard rumor control, hallway gossip, you know? Was your dad a Syrian jet pilot?"

Adam glanced over at him. "Someone said that?"

"Ah, geez." Goodell's face dissolved with a cringe. "Sorry, sir. I don't like people talking about me, either. It's just you've got a Top Secret with a special clearance and all. I told them to pound sand. Nobody can get all that when we're technically at war with Syria."

"You might have to apologize to your friend, Patrick. My biological dad was a Syrian pilot and he managed to shoot up the Raghadan Palace before he got shot down in the 1970 war with Jordan." Adam glanced over. "That was a long time ago, and at least twenty years before I was even born. I don't think even the DIA would yank my clearance before I was a twinkle in someone's eye." He smiled. "At least they didn't in my case."

"For sure, sir. Sorry."

"And I'd appreciate it if you don't discuss with anyone what I just told you. We're friends, and I trust you."

"Yes, sir. Of course." Goodell's eyes found somewhere else to be.

The crew chief stepped into the glass-enclosed lounge and gave them a wave.

Adam hadn't known about his biological father until the day before the FBI visited their Bingham estate. Even then, he still had only half the story. He recalled holding his mother's hand and her tiny birdlike bones so prominent, so fragile as she told him of her impetuous love affair with an older man. Adam smiled with the recollection of her as a young, rich, and impressionable woman. She'd left college and loosed her sights on the Mideast's cauldron of politics and romance. She fell in love with a Syrian war hero, someone highly placed in a foreign regime, a dashing pilot twice her age. When his mother told him, Adam didn't have to work hard replacing William Michaels, fictitious philanthropist. He understood then why no one before explained his mocha skin in a blue-eyed Irish family.

He roused himself as the pitch of the UH-1H's blades changed, surprised he'd napped. They touched down on the Fort Dix helipad moments after reveille. A cream-colored van waited at the concrete pad's corner.

Goodell pointed at the ride, and gave Adam a thumbs-up. "Hero," he mouthed over the racket of the blades.

"Bullshit," Adam replied in like silence.

Goodell laughed as he grabbed up their overnight bags. The van wound between the drab wooden buildings of the supply complex before stopping in front of a squat, brick office building. Adam's thoughts drifted over the Verrazano Bridge to Miranda Cinclaire. He'd Googled the highest-paid Hollywood actor of the decade after they hung up, and felt pretty dumb. Dick Roberts. Everyone knew this guy. Adam put Miranda's name in the search engine and kicked himself one more time.

The officer in charge, Lt. Colonel Webb, bore a gut and a wide face ribboned with small red and blue veins around his nose and cheeks. He sat behind a desk piled with folders and two computer screens. "What's the big deal, Major? Why does the Pentagon send a whiz kid to this lonely outpost?"

"Pressure from above is my best guess, sir." Adam ignored the whiz kid remark. He stood in front of the man's desk and wasn't invited to sit down. Webb could help or hurt their efforts, and Adam needed cooperation. And, of course, he could confide none of the secrets from Room 422. "You know how touchy things get now and then."

"Actually, I don't," said Webb as he leaned back to take stock of the man standing at attention before him. "Relax, Major. We've had things pulled out of the field before, and I can't remember them ever sending me a field grade officer to check out the replacement paperwork." The man's unsmiling eyes watched Adam. "Did you piss someone off, or isn't there enough to do in that cushy job of yours? You can always come on up here and I'll put you to work."

Rancor among superiors was not uncommon and Adam smiled. "If General Miller or Colonel Benchley won't mind, you will certainly get no argument out of me, sir. I'm ready to leave the puzzle palace." Of course, he was not.

Webb leaned his head back, not amused to have his bluff called. "Brad, huh? Does he still have a belly full of fire?"

"Sir?" asked Adam.

"Benchley, your soon-to-be the youngest brigadier general in the Air Force. I've heard rumblings there's big stuff in his future."

Adam recognized the animosity of someone shunted and living an undesirable assignment. He hadn't known about Brad getting a star, but did not like the ground both men tread.

Webb waved a hand when Adam didn't reply. "Never mind. Brad and I go way back, to the National War College at Fort McNair. Back then, if you didn't agree with his political science or his patriotism, you were the enemy. You had to protect yourself at happy hour, especially when he was drinking. That's years ago, a different lifetime. Things change, people change, right, Major?"

"Yes, sir. I'm sure you're correct."

Goodell knocked and entered the small room. "Excuse me, sirs. Just need to let the driver know. What are we doing?"

Adam glanced around. "Give me a minute, Sergeant."

Webb looked at his watch. "If you're here to monitor the *Oka Tadashi*'s loading, you might as well head for the motel and be back at 0700 hours. Your secret squirrel stuff was moved from railcars into the Dix warehouse. And there it sits."

Adam shook his head. "The shipment is going C5A, sir. All

37

I'm doing is putting the Good Housekeeping Seal of Approval on the paper that proves nothing got lost between the manufacturer, Dix, and McGuire."

Webb stabbed his keyboard and read. "Not according to what I have." He peered more closely. "This comes from your office, Major. This cargo's set to go by ship, not by air. Left hand doesn't know what the right's doing?"

Goodell stepped back into the room. He'd listened from the hallway. "That's true, Colonel. The load is supposed to go to McGuire, a change from Port Elizabeth." He looked at Adam. "The Huey is waiting to take us to McGuire, sir."

From sergeant to any superior officer, the statement meddled at best. Adam turned and gave Goodell a small shake of the head. "Well, good point, Sergeant Goodell." He turned to Webb. "Any chance we can double-check the location of the cargo? We sent it to McGuire, not Dix. I'm here to check the paperwork and hand-carry to the C5A dispatcher."

"High priority shipment, huh?" The corners of Webb's mouth turned down as he pushed the computer screen around so Adam could see. "Have a look."

Adam did and sighed. "Okay. Thank you, sir." He turned to Goodell. "Is there something at home, Sergeant? Do you need to make a call?"

Webb eyed Goodell, and said, "Use my phone. I'll give you privacy."

After the room grew quiet, Adam said, "Careful around him, Patrick. What we say and do here will be in General Miller's office long before we get back."

"Yes, sir. But they knew those devices were moved into the warehouse for staging. We didn't have to be here until tomorrow, or maybe even the next day. That's a load of crap … sir."

Adam nodded. "Yes, it is, but come on. It's your Army, too, and we all work in strange ways."

The younger man pressed his lips into a straight line and watched the desk for a moment. "Yes, sir. I'll let the driver know, and release the Huey."

Adam couldn't recall a time when he'd seen Sergeant Goodell

38

impatient to the point of impertinence. He picked the receiver off the desk and waited as the STU III scrambler connected. "This is Major Michaels," he said to the voice answering the secure number. "Can you get word to Colonel Bradford Benchley the shipment's departure will be delayed at least eighteen hours? There's a SNAFU at point of departure."

"Yes sir," the voice on the other end of the phone answered. "But the colonel's already left NATO command. He's on his way back to the States."

"You must have misunderstood. I'm sure that's a mistake. He was heading for Tel Aviv on Sunday, and waiting for word from me. That's the word I'm giving now. The embarkation is delayed. The paper is, as I said, 'Situation Normal, All Fouled Up.'"

The other voice said, "I'm certain, sir. Confirmation is in my hand. Departure was Brussels, and after a stop in Lisbon, the C-17 is direct to Andrews Air Force Base. Touchdown tonight at 2330 hours. And sir? The colonel departed Andrews on Saturday, not Sunday."

The timing didn't make sense to Adam, especially after Friday night and the hooligans that failed to snatch him off the DC streets. Brad should have spent the day with DIA; he was after all, Adam's superior officer. Instead, he flew to Europe and now, was headed home. He didn't even go to Tel Aviv. Miller would be pissed, and with good cause. For a moment, Adam wondered who was pulling whose strings, but his day started early and he was probably just out of the loop. If Brad left on Saturday instead of Sunday, this was simply a change of orders. "Thank you, Corporal. Do you have any messages for me?"

"No, sir."

"How about Sergeant Goodell?"

"Just a personal one, sir. Sorry."

"That's all right, go ahead. This is already one very strange day."

"Yes, sir. Can you pass along that his aunt can't make dinner tonight?"

Adam shook his head with a sigh. "Sure, sure. I'll let him know."

"Thank you, sir."

That explained Patrick's angst. Adam didn't know his aunt was in the DC area. Goodell's family was from Ellabell, a little town near Savannah, Georgia. Brad's family originated from Georgia, too. The pair shared a silly affinity for the Atlanta Falcons.

Within a few minutes, Adam and Goodell sat in a government passenger van driving out the gate and into little New Hanover Township. The trip included a happy conversation between a new driver and the old Goodell, not the impatient one. The two had shared an assignment in Germany before Iraq, and they filled the drive with tall tales and gossip. Adam heard Patrick thump his titanium legs, heard them both laugh, yet his mind drifted to an actress living seventy miles north in New York City. Of course, three thousand miles separated them tonight.

At their destination, Goodell surprised Adam by barely acknowledging the message from his aunt. "Thank you, sir. Do you mind if I crash at Barney's tonight? I'll save the government some money, but I don't want to leave you alone."

Adam laughed. "I'll check with Mom, but I think it'll be okay."

Goodell flushed. "I didn't mean that."

"Hey, just kidding, Patrick. I wouldn't waste this trip on me, either. Go and enjoy yourself. I'll see you in the morning."

Goodell's face lit up. "Yes, sir. Thank you, sir."

Adam heard the high fives exchanged as he slid the van's door closed, and felt a hundred years old.

Chapter 6

"I can't take your call," said her mobile voice mail. "You already know what to do."

Adam waited until seven for a return call, gave up, and walked downstairs to the restaurant. An unseen refrigerator hummed in the sparse dining room. A group of four and a solitary old man ate from small blue-rimmed plates. Adam picked up a wrinkled newspaper and chose a table near the front glass. Away from the other occupants, he watched the cold outside and a sky gray beyond the streetlights. The foursome left as his pork chops arrived.

Before he could pick up a knife and fork, the old man from the corner stood before his table. He studied Adam's face for a moment, then said, "Major Michaels?"

Adam looked up, muscles tensing. "Do I know you?"

"No. May I sit?" The man's dark face bore lines of years and concern as he removed his coat. Adam scanned for weapons.

"I'd like to talk about your father."

"My ..." Adam exhaled and pushed the newspaper to the side. He watched the front door over the man's shoulders. Friday night was still on his mind as he readied to defend himself. Finally Adam said, "My father's dead and he's been that way for a long time."

"Of course." The man slowly folded his russet woven overcoat across his lap and looked up with a tiny smile. "Thank you for not sending me away. I am most happy to finally meet you. I have been anticipating this day for many, many years." An Oxford inflection produced clipped sentences.

"Who are you? Did you know my father?" Adam kept his attention split between the door and the man, yet felt himself relax.

"Alhasan Sharifi?" he said with a small laugh. "Yes, of course I knew him."

Adam's grandfather had steeled him against those who might take advantage of families with wealth. With the Internet, scams were the commonplace tools of grifters.

"My father was Dr. William Michaels, sir."

"Nonsense," the old man said. "Alhasan was your father. You

41

look very much like him. Dark, brooding, handsome."

Adam took a bite of his pork chop and wished he hadn't. "What can I do for you?" He set his knife and fork down and gave the plate a tiny push.

"I was with Alhasan the night we were told of your birth in Switzerland."

Adam watched as the counterman flipped off the orange neon open sign and clicked the lock. "Take your time," the man called out. "I got stuff in the back to do."

Adam placed his fork on the plate. "You have me mistaken for someone else. My father was a member of Doctors without Borders. He was killed before I was born." This was the only story the public was supposed to know. "What do you want from me?"

"Lillian? Is your mother well?"

Again with information available on the Internet, except this man wasn't up-to-date. "No, she isn't," Adam said. "Although that depends on your beliefs. She died on September 11th last year, so she might be in a better place."

The old man's breathing turned ragged for a moment and he looked down at the table. "I didn't know."

Adam regretted his flippancy. "Are you okay?"

The man nodded without looking up. "I'm sorry. And I've been rude." He looked at Adam, his eyes wet. "She was a lovely woman who loved your father, but headstrong, like so many Americans."

Adam said nothing.

The man smiled and wiped a handkerchief at his eyes. "Yours is a wondrous race, you know. Not too different from Syrians. My daughter was your mother's best friend in Damascus. Rana was like Lillian in so many ways." He smiled with a recollection. "A handful. Outspoken and opinionated, very strong, the new Muslim woman for the twenty first century. They were dear friends, but Rana has been dead for years now, killed in Hama by the government." If it were possible, his face grew even older. "I already know you are familiar with tragedy and death, and that you are fearless. Like your father and your mother."

Adam composed himself. "You seem to have some notion about me and my family. If I actually believed you knew my mother,

42

which I do not, you're talking about someone else's history. Not mine. I don't have anything to do with who or what my father was, except he was a doctor. For that matter, my mother was pretty much her own person, too. My birth was a decision between the two of them, or maybe I was just an accident in a fit of passion."

"Allah decides who is born," said the old man. "Birth is no accident."

"Well then, in my case, let's just say Allah wasn't paying attention." Adam stood. "I don't think you knew my mother. You certainly never met my father. Anyone with a computer can put together a story. If you tried to prove any different, I've got the wealth of a small nation behind me to put a stop to you. I've had my fill of Muslims. If you want to believe I was born to a Syrian, then so be it. We live in a free country. But, birth is an accident, sir and is not predestination."

The smile beneath the lined face faded as the man looked up. "I understand your frustration, but not your hatred. Why do you hate so?"

Adam almost blurted out that he fought and killed terrorists, and did not have dinner conversations with them. Instead, he said, "My father was not Alhasan … Sharifi, sir." The name sounded odd to his ears, otherworldly. This was not the first time he'd spoken his father's name, his own true name, of course. He couldn't recall hearing it on the lips of anyone else however, other than his mother. "The name is Adam Michaels. Check my Swiss birth certificate."

"Stay and eat. I shall leave." The man stood and unfolded his long coat. "By the way, I never said your father was a Syrian. You did. He was, of course, as are you. You were committed to Syria and her rulers before you were born, and will be forever. *Allah Akbar* is not a dirty word. Only misused by others to incite animus, much like yours."

Adam resumed his seat, angry with himself for being duped into an admission.

"When your father was a young man, a very young man, he could be provoked like you. He learned to listen and prepare himself." Deep-set eyes watched Adam. "Our comfortable little worlds have many dangers if you are not ready."

Adam's fork clattered from the plate to the floor. The owner had emerged from the back and started toward them, but stopped.

"And how did dear old Dad do in life? Was he the inspiration to run up the flag when you needed a little money?"

The man looked away as he slipped an arm into his overcoat. "In your homeland, Alhasan … Adam, little reason or justice prevails. Your father was not Hamas, yet he died avenging them. We are killed by the Israelis, murdered by the Shi'ite and Sunni alike depending upon our beliefs. Arabs conspire against Arabs, and are hated by the Americans who can't tell the difference." He smiled. "You resemble your father in so many ways. When I talk with you, I feel the years wash away."

"I am not—" Adam almost said, *my father*.

"I know, I know," said the man. "Perhaps someday you'll understand without the pain so many others experience." He looked for a long moment at Adam. "You are my nephew. Your father was my younger brother. We have an interesting history, Adam. Perhaps someday, you will want to learn of your other family." The man turned, but stopped and looked back. "We were not the ones that attacked you and your young lady. You must be very vigilant of those that would steal lives in the name of God."

He walked out without looking back. The food congealed on Adam's plate. After another minute, he dropped bills on the counter and left.

A few patrons sat next door in the small lounge. He ordered and drank two bourbons in rapid succession, playing and replaying the peculiar meeting. On that very odd Christmas vacation when he was twenty-one, his mother told him about a highly placed uncle with the Syrian regime who was captured in Jerusalem. At the time, the Israelis identified his uncle as advisor to Hafez al-Assad, the former president. Adam researched the Internet after Lillian's story, discovering the man spent twelve years in a Tel Aviv prison before an exchange took place for a captured Israeli soldier. His uncle later became a British citizen and a college professor, and hadn't returned to Syria since Bashar al-Assad, the son, took power and the civil war began.

Adam knew spinning a lie around truth always makes for the best lie. The attempt to force him into a van only a few nights ago shook his world. He would email his grandfather in the morning and tell him of the meeting, but not the assault.

Chapter 7

When the cell phone alarm rang, he hit the button yet the beeper did not silence. He struggled for a moment with a cloudy mind, then rolled over and touched the phone. "Hello? Who is this?"

"Oh Major, how quickly you forget." Miranda laughed. "Can you talk, or have I been replaced already?"

"Miranda?" he said, trying to rid himself of a very deep, alcoholic sleep.

"Yes?" she said with a laugh.

"I have the feeling you're enjoying yourself." He propped up a pillow from the unused side of the bed. "I thought you were my wake-up call."

She laughed. "I wouldn't mind that job, but do you always get up at three in the morning?"

He grinned. "No. But then, I don't always get calls from ladies at this hour, either."

"Who says I'm a lady?"

"Me."

Her mirth evaporated. "Thank you. That's very sweet. I keep forgetting you come from different stock than the people I'm used to."

"That I come from a different time is more accurate."

"Do you ever accept compliments, or do I just forget that part of our relationship?"

He chuckled. "Sorry. Still sleepy."

"Never mind. I didn't get your message until just now. My phone is somewhere in California and the new one came uncharged. You're not all that far away, and I'm due in rehearsal at eight. I'm really disappointed."

"Where in the world have you been until three in the morning?" He laughed. "I'll be damned! Scratch that. What a thing to ask."

"That's kind of nice too, but please try not to sound too much like my big brother. I'd feel a little funny the next time I have to seduce you."

"Thank goodness. There's going to be a next time."

Her sigh whispered over the phone. "I wish it could have been now."

He looked at the dark motel room walls. "Me, too."

"Okay," she said. "How about tonight? I mean later today. Come have an early dinner with me."

"Barring something unforeseen, my sergeant and I will be back in DC by three this afternoon."

"In that case, I'll see you tonight."

He smiled. Julie used the same General Sherman tactics rolling over the opposition, or in this case, setting fire to reality. "That would be great, but the decision's not mine, Miranda. While I'm in the Army, others control my life."

"Please try. I'd like us to get to know one another. And besides, I signed my half of the contract for *Marsh Island* opposite Dick. We need to celebrate." They fell silent a moment. "I have to get my sleep, Adam. I'll need this job until next summer when we start shooting."

"Congratulations on landing the movie."

Her voice grew tired and sleepy. "We'll have a signing party in a couple of weeks, with the producers and a few stars. Here in New York. Will you come?"

"Yes, of course."

"You'll have to make it a date. Black tie. This is most important."

"I will," he said. Her silence wasn't encouraging. "I'll make it, Miranda. Just tell me when."

She yawned. "Okay, I believe you. Until then, I still expect to see you every spare minute the Army will give you. Including tonight. But, if you can't, leave me a message. I'll check my cell after I wake up."

The phone disconnected.

Adam rose in the dark room and settled into a chair near the window. He pulled the drape cord to a wintery view of swirling snowflakes against a reflected sky. His iPad booted up and identified the motel's Wi-Fi.

"Movie Marsh Island," he said aloud. The result was an article in *Variety*. Several photos appeared of Miranda in California, leaving a

46

disquieting feeling. His mother's image appeared in similar photos, often drawn from the tabloids, laughing gaily and lifting champagne, offering wide and adoring smiles to movie stars and Hollywood producers. She knew all of them, yet none visited after her accident.

He thought of his mother drifting away in her sleep not too many months ago, and the many diseases that take advantage of bodies damaged in life's mishaps. He missed her and the long talks on a frozen veranda, her beauty never far away in his mind's eye.

In the morning, the depot commander delighted in telling Adam the cargo remained in shipping's custody. With a signature, the commander canceled the soldiers' orders and informed Adam a helicopter would be on the pad in an hour. Miranda's cell phone went to voice mail as they waited.

Chapter 8

Adam glanced at the kitchen clock, swearing under his breath. He hated to be late, and was about to be. Separating a banana from the bunch, he hurried to the apartment door. Coffee was left to cool on the drain board. For a moment, he thought to call Julie and let her know. That, too, would become obvious by the time he pulled up. The old Corolla's starter ground for long seconds before the engine caught. He slipped the car into gear and lurched out of the apartment's small parking lot, thinking about buying a new car, and how delighted Julie had been to drive in the red BMW. With his family's money and the untouched trust, he could certainly afford a car, and many other possessions that might win Julie's heart. After all, he probably owned the last standard-shift Toyota in North America. But for him, the car would just have to do. The depleted paycheck wouldn't allow the purchase, or maybe it was a point of honor after the disastrous divorce settlement. Besides, he wanted to see those eyes shine, delighted to see him and not a red BMW.

He patted for his wallet as he coasted downhill for the red light. "Oh, damn it all to hell!" He pictured the billfold with four concert tickets and his money on the dresser.

He shifted into second with a quick look behind and spun the wheel. At the same moment, a car rounded the corner behind him, accelerating hard and filling the rearview mirror with headlights and chrome. He twisted the wheel to avoid the collision and careened over the curb and onto the grass.

By the time he skidded to a stop the other car climbed the next incline, showing no signs of slowing. At a minimum, he expected a tongue-lashing from the angry motorist. Instead, the other car only showed its taillights. He took a deep breath and shifted into first as a porch light came on behind him, an angry homeowner, no doubt, wondering what just happened.

The rest of the drive in heavy traffic went fine even if his fingers still shook a little. The car coming on so fast, the van with three men trying to kidnap him less than two weeks ago. He looked at his young passengers wondering if he was being silly, or if he needed to engage survival instincts learned the hard way. Then, he recalled the DIA's blasé attitude during the debriefings. They decided it was a mugging gone bad. Nothing more. The DC police agreed and filed the incident as such. He relaxed. *Next thing, there'll be monsters in the closet.* Except that the van and gun were real, even if the men were bumblers.

Traffic at The Wolf Trap Center for the Performing Arts soon took his attention. The open theater was filled to capacity with people bumping one another, shouting to others, and many listening to a warm-up band instead of concentrating on finding their seats.

Sixx:AM opened the show with electric-guitar players jumping in flashing lights and generated smoke rolling across the high stage. Adam's three young charges screamed along with seven thousand others while he stuffed in earplugs and felt lucky most of the words remained unintelligible. The few he could hear didn't sound like an opener for Taylor Swift. When she appeared at last, Adam had a headache and a smile. He liked Swift, too. She seemed nice in an insane world. He thought of Miranda and what a hit movie with Dick Roberts might mean to her career, and to their relationship.

Three hoarse girls squeezed together in the backseat and never stopped talking on the return trip. Traffic snarled along the Capitol's beltline, so by the time her friends were dropped off, Julie was asleep. As Adam walked her up the steps to the house, he noticed a lighted-cigarette glow several cars down from his Corolla.

An unsmiling Katherine held the door while Julie hugged her father and headed up the stairs. He watched her go and was aware a visitor relaxed in the front room.

Katherine stepped onto the porch and closed the door. "Were you hurt in the mugging?"

Surprised, Adam said, "Not really, but thanks for asking." That would be as close as Katherine ever came to an apology.

She nodded, looking down at the porch boards. "Next weekend I'm going to the Poconos. Eric's family has a cabin. I'd like Julie to come with us."

He was silent for a moment. The next weekend was his. "What does Julie want to do, Katherine?" He and Julie already planned their next weekend, a long three days walking the beaches, fishing, and visiting Kill Devil Hills. He rented a house from a friend with property on the barrier island.

She took a breath. "This isn't easy, Adam. She's torn. Eric's a sweetheart, and they get along well."

Eric. Katherine's friend for over a year now. "I'm glad," he said, holding the words that threatened to leap out of his mouth. "I'm her dad. This is the weekend that she and I planned." Adam's fists balled inside his jacket pocket.

"This weekend is also a tradition for Eric's family," she said. "Everyone meets at the cabin. You know Eric has a son and daughter. There'll be nieces and nephews her age and she'll have a good time."

"She likes my family, too, Katherine." The words hurt his ears. "Sorry. That sounded stupid."

She pressed her lips together, and tightened her folded arms. "Can we let Julie decide?"

He nodded. "Okay. You ask tomorrow, but I need to know right away." He handed her an envelope. She looked up with a question. "The dance lessons," he said. "I'd like to pay for them."

"Thank you. Julie will appreciate it." Katherine didn't open the sealed envelope. Both knew that cash exchanged beyond child support dented Adam's small bank account. The sum was a personal sacrifice. "This is nice, Adam. Thank you."

"Tell her …" He stopped and looked over the bare trees with low gray clouds beyond. He liked this neighborhood. He had liked living here. He wanted to love Katherine again, and be with Julie here. He also knew that would never be. "Tell Julie, it's okay with me if she goes to Eric's place. We can plan for a different weekend. But, it's still her decision."

Katherine watched him, nodding her head. "Thank you, Adam. I'll call to let you know what she says."

The door closed behind her.

He turned and walked down the steps. Sometimes he felt they made progress, but not tonight. Not with Eric replacing him, the thought tearing at his guts. He was scared to lose Julie. He was scared to fight back and drive everyone away.

Before Adam traveled a block, the front fender dipped low. He pulled to the corner knowing a tire was flat. He looked around, but at this hour the street was quiet and empty. The spare went on in a few minutes. As he stood to lower the jack, a car pulled behind his. The lights blinded him as the driver closed the door and approached.

"Evening." Adam straightened and held up a hand to shade the bright silhouette.

"Good evening, Major." The man stopped before crossing the car's beams.

"Have we met?"

"No," the man said. "But, I know of you." Foreign accents meant little in Washington, DC, the most ethnically diverse city on Earth.

"Really?" he said, and knelt to finish the job. He pulled the two-foot tire iron from the jack.

"You don't need that. I only want to talk. To ask your help."

"I'd prefer you get back into your car and leave."

"This is a most important matter."

Adam gave no ground. "You've been watching too many movies, and I already told your friend in New Jersey I'm not buying."

The silhouette chuckled. "Yes, I know, he told me. But I only want to talk."

"And I don't." Adam glanced at the dimpled tire that lay between them. "You have anything to do with this?"

The man shook his head. "No, of course not. This is an unfortunate circumstance and I decided to take the opportunity. I'd planned to approach you at your apartment."

The thought sent a cold chill down his spine. "Okay. I'm listening, but please be short. I'm tired." The man knew where he lived, as well as where he used to live. He wondered if this were the car that he'd nearly hit in his parking lot.

"Do you think we could go somewhere?"

Exasperated, Adam said, "Oh, for Christ's sake."

"Perhaps for coffee?" the man said. "As I recall, an all-night restaurant is only a few blocks away."

"Why all the mystery? Your friend, my supposed uncle, didn't waste time with all this clandestine nonsense."

The man gave a heartfelt laugh. "Your uncle is an old man. A fine person, but emotional. He lives in the past and doesn't trust many

51

people." The cold Virginia mist grew into drops plinking off the car's metal. "Please," said the man. "I am not one of the men that failed to grab you. I promise. Coffee would be more pleasant than this night air."

Adam stopped breathing. How did he know about the kidnap attempt? Now he really wanted to see the man's face. A good description enhanced any security report and he didn't need to go beyond the restaurant's front door. "Okay. You go ahead, I'll meet you at Denny's."

"Thank you. You will not regret this." The man returned to his idling sedan, then hesitated. "Is there anything I can do to help you?"

The breeze loosened more drips from the bared branches. "No, I'm fine. I'll meet you there."

As the man drove by, Adam stepped into the street and wrote out the Pennsylvania license number on the palm of his hand. "Got you."

The stranger knew about Julie and his former home, so leaving him to sit at Denny's wasn't an option. The man had to be identified. He thought about calling the Alexandria police but if his reception was anything like the DIA and the DC cops, the effort would be wasted.

And then there was Katherine. Eric was there. He thought about warning her, but dismissed the idea, knowing this would be yet another incident held against him in the future. The house was a fortress when the alarms and security bars were set in place. Katherine's uncle had seen to that during Adam's first Iraq deployment.

He dialed the DIA phone number anyway, and got voice mail. He left a message just in case.

The large yellow and red sign marked the twenty-four hour diner's parking lot. Wind blew cold and wet. A handful of late-night patrons ignored one another as he pushed through the glass doors. The space smelled of pancakes and maple syrup. A man waved from a rear corner and slid out of the booth. Adam held the door ready to make his escape, but watched the wide, happy face. The man didn't exactly look harmless, and in fact was formidable. For a reason unknown to him, Adam found himself removing his topcoat and slipping into the rounded vinyl booth at the man's beckoning.

"I'm very glad you decided to come." The dark coals of the man's eyes glistened.

"I didn't see much choice," Adam said, surprised at the evident emotion. "You know where my family lives and I wanted to get a look at you."

"Wise, but unnecessary. I will gladly tell you all about me, but I am not the threat. All I want to do is talk, to acquaint you with some realities."

He spoke with a British accent and a cadence that sounded Middle Eastern, much like the old man. Like Adam, the man was tall but with heavier shoulders and big hands.

"You referred to the man in New Jersey," Adam said. "I assume you're going to talk about Syria?"

"You are correct, of course. Syria is my heritage, as it is yours."

Adam shook his head. "Here we go again. I'm an American, born in Switzerland. That's a far cry from Syria."

The man did not acquiesce. "And, I was born in London of Syrian ancestry. We are very much the same except that as the eldest son, you are heir to a great heritage and an even greater responsibility."

"I'm an only child," Adam said as the waitress placed coffee between them. They both waited until she walked to the next patron. "Technically, I suppose that makes me the eldest, but not necessarily the heir. Who are you?"

"Alhasan Halim Khaddam. Our first names are the same as I was named to honor your heroic father. My father is Professor Abdul Khaddam. You have met him."

Adam sipped at the top of his coffee and said nothing, wondering at the intricate lie.

"You're thinking we have different last names." Halim leaned into the table. "My father, your uncle, escaped from Syria and the al-Assad regime after a long imprisonment in Israel. He was a wanted man and made his way to England. He changed his name and started a new life. Our fathers were brothers."

"So he said. That makes you and I first cousins. Family, right?"

Even as a Brit, the man didn't understand the nuance of

53

American sarcasm. "Yes, we are family." A delighted laugh caught in his throat. "Call me Halim. I'm so happy to meet you. Finally."

Adam did not return the smile. "I explained to the old man, he is mistaken. I'm not who he thinks I am. And, I'm not Syrian."

Halim nodded dismissing the denial, and sipped his coffee, the smile refusing to leave his face. "I understand. But if you were Syrian, you should be proud," he said with a laugh. "The name Alhasan Sharifi is legend. He would be like Patrick Henry or Francis Marion in American history. Why would I lie about such a thing?"

"That is of course, the question, isn't it?" Adam leaned back in the booth, deciding one charlatan was a setup, two, however, probably knew the truth about his background. The DC mugging was never far from his mind. "Where do you teach?"

Halim smiled and nodded. "My father thought you were very astute. I am, or was at the American University on exchange from London, my home. I taught Islamic studies."

"Khaddam," said Adam, drawing on a memory. "Halim Khaddam. You wrote *Challenging Modern Islam*."

"*The Challenges of Modern Islam*," he said, correcting Adam. "My father co-wrote with me. I'm impressed."

"So was I. It's a good book. Insightful, but you missed the mark when it came to America's understanding of Sharia and why we will resist to the end." Halim offered scrunched eyebrows. Adam took up the spoon and glanced at the empty restaurant. "You see, we're a nation of Jews, atheists, Christians, Muslims, and so many more. People here can make up their own religion, and politics if they don't find something they like. Inside our borders, freedom is our strength: not our weakness. The Muslim Brotherhood will have a difficult time cracking this culture."

Halim considered Adam's opinion for a moment. "That's interesting, but my book celebrated the vagaries of America culture, as a strength to be admired, not a weakness for exploitation. I did not suggest the Muslim culture as an American replacement. Hardly. I admire America's lack of theocracy."

Adam wasn't buying. "What did the ... your father want? What do you want?"

Halim rotated the cup in the porcelain saucer. Rain and sleet

54

rapped on the dark glass. "This is not about America or its silly war for oil. Your country doesn't understand about true enemies. Those of mankind. Those who would prostitute your Bible and my Qur'an for their own purposes."

The waitress topped Adam's coffee at the silent table. "Get'cha anything else?" Before they could answer, she said in a country drawl, "You guys are brothers, right? I can always tell, you know?"

Halim smiled.

Adam did not. "Could we have the check, please?"

She rolled her shoulders and walked to the next table.

Halim continued. "Are you familiar with the Ahmadiyya Caliphate?"

Adam nodded. "Yes. The fifth caliphate."

"Very few Americans know of the Ahmadiyya. Not many outside the Washington Beltway study groups and think tanks have bothered to consider those who choose peace over the Kalashnikov."

"I attended the War College and we had these discussions. That's where I read your book."

Halim nodded. "The world of Islam knows of the fifth caliphate, world theocracy based on Islam. The Ahmadiyya believe they are the last Caliphate, the final world as prophesied by Mohammed in 622. Years before he died."

Adam thought for a moment and said, "The Ahmadiyya talked about the period of his life when he preached peace and coexistence with other believers in the 'book.' Jews and Christians." Adam recalled the swings in the prophet's life from poor to rich, peaceful to violent. The two followed hand-in-hand. As the prophet grew in fame and influence, so did the violence that overtook continents.

"Yes," said Halim, his eyes bright. "Thank you for understanding the difference. Ahmadiyya was a British Indian movement to return to the old ways, before Mohammed became …"

"Radicalized," said Adam.

"Yes."

Adam shook his head. "This is all wonderful and has absolutely nothing to do with me."

"You are wrong. Muslim and non-Muslim alike are affected by his prediction. After Mohammed became 'radicalized,' as you call it, he taught a single prophet would emerge after the Jews returned to Palestine. The prophet came, Alhasan. No one recognized him until now."

"If you want me to hear you out, at least call me Adam."

"Of course," Halim said, a smile working around his mouth. "Early in his life, Mohammad prophesized the strongest and wisest of all the previous caliphates would be peaceful, but would turn against one another in violence because the world would not understand. He warned a pretender would stir fanatical hatred when he was killed at the hands of Satan. His death would confirm the violence, much as Jesus' death confirmed peace and salvation. Osama bin Laden was the false prophet, Adam, and now his followers will seek revenge for a thousand years. Against you, as well as other Muslims."

"You mean ISIS?"

"Yes, of course, the Islamic State of Iraq and Syria, or Levant, if you prefer, among others. Bin Laden did more than knock down the Twin Towers and blow holes in the sides of American ships. He stole Mohammad's first prophecy—the true prophecy. The fifth was to be the last. Paradise on Earth would follow. Bin Laden," Halim searched for the right word, "hijacked the Qur'an. He is more evil now that he is dead. He established Al-Qaeda and ISIS to bring the evil caliphate to power in Levant."

Adam sighed and rubbed his face. "America virtually eliminated Al-Qaeda in Afghanistan. They're in shambles, reduced to fighting as tribes. The world will crush ISIS ... eventually. If they've stolen something from you, now is the time for the Islamic world to rise up and stand with us against the evil."

Halim shook his head. "Stolen from us? No, Adam. They stole from you. Do you see how treacherous they are? How insidious? Your Navy sniper might have pulled the trigger, but how did you come by the information?"

Adam knew the story of Pakistan's conviction of the informant doctor over the protests of the United States government and the CIA.

"Please, Adam. Don't be naïve. Where is this doctor now? Is he an American hero? A Pakistani hero? No. America is so easily duped. Put a story on a television and half your country believes it to be true. Put the same story in the *New York Times* and the next stop is a history book. The Muslim world is the same. They believe a radical imam even when they have facts that dispute him."

"You believe Bin Laden planned his own death to prove a point?" Adam held up a hand. "Don't answer that. America is defeating Al-Qaeda."

Halim searched Adam's face. "I wish you were right, but you are already too late. I'm afraid for your world, Adam. I'm afraid for mine. Peaceful Muslims will not live through the coming holocaust."

"I think the reports saying America is dead are premature, Halim. We have resources." Adam considered his words. "Maybe our resolve isn't as strong as it should be, but that's temporary. We always seem to find the right leader and strength when we need to."

Halim sighed and placed his coffee cup down. "All my life, I have wanted to talk with you, Alhasan. My father confided in me when I was young that you were living in America. I followed you, your mother, and your life." His smile weakened. "I've always known about you and now I bring you terrible news."

"I've disappointed you?"

He shook his head. "No, no. Of course not, but you are an American. You think wrongs can be righted and justice wins at the end of the day. You believe in superheroes." Halim laughed at himself. "And why not? You are naïve because you are a collective nation without a history and too arrogant to learn from the rest of the world's mistakes."

Adam felt himself bristle.

"I'm sorry to offend you, my cousin. There isn't enough time to give us the luxury of polite conversation. Al-Qaeda and ISIS are a decade ahead of you, and have already begun a final jihad. From the moment Bin Laden died, the last of days began."

The waitress dropped the check on the table, then eyed both men with a knowing smile and a wag of her finger as she walked away.

Halim's lower jaw worked as he made a decision. "Many of my compatriots have tried to explain to your government. They listen politely but do nothing. The British ambassador spoke directly with your Secretary of State. He could not have warned her any more clearly."

"Are you a foreign agent?"

Halim nodded. "Yes, if it means you'll report me and what I'm trying to tell you, then yes. A courier was compromised in a London whorehouse. We learned one of your cargo ships headed for Israel was attacked years ago. They took a command module from one of your missiles and then sank the ship to hide their theft. At first, they were only trying to keep the missiles out of the Israelis' hands. But then they learned what they had stolen."

Adam's face gave away nothing.

Halim continued. "When the Iranians shot down your drone during the First Iraq War, they came into possession of your research and, as you say, they put two and two together. Your government hurried to develop a new module thinking the missile was important. But do you not understand? The new one doesn't matter anymore, because Al-Qaeda already used your old one. They are only concerned now that you, Alhasan Sharifi, Adam Michaels, my cousin, might possess the secret to stopping them. They want your new module, or they want you."

Adam said, "I don't know what you're talking about. Stop what?"

Halim watched the black glass for a moment. "I don't know. I don't know what they plan. I do know if the Israelis discover what Al-Qaeda and the Pakistani radicals have done, they will attack. They are high-strung and political. We would then lose the cooperation of the peaceful Muslim world. They must be stopped from reacting with their fists."

"Cooperation for what? Is this the final caliphate nonsense again?"

"I told you this to explain how deeply rooted the culture is in our world, not to offer a solution." He stopped and watched the restaurant's door close behind a man wearing a blue watch cap. The man glanced around then took a booth near them.

Adam watched as Halim locked eyes with the strange man.

"I must use the bathroom," Halim said, and slid out of the booth.

Adam went on alert as his hand covered his table knife. Two men, even if they were in a public place, could take him. Somehow, he

58

wanted to trust this Halim, this author, this intellectual. He scanned the parking lot for a van, feeling a chill find its way up his backbone. He must stop them here. He must prevent this from leading back to Julie and his neighborhood.

Five minutes passed, then ten. The watch cap man smiled at the waitress as his cup was refilled and avoided Adam's gaze.

His anger grew. He'd listened to Halim, even began to like him. But this story was convenient. Too convenient. He shifted around the circular booth to face the door and the watch cap man. He would not make this easy for them.

Halim. Fury and disappointment bubbled inside. As for the end of the world, he'd seen plenty of Christians tout their fear tactics, too. Mongering panic used the same basic message of final days, and why not? Wasn't everyone fascinated with death, especially their own?

Five more minutes passed. Where was Halim?

When he could sit no longer, he scooted out and stood. He eyed the watch cap man and was ignored. The knife slipped up into his sleeve. An old black man swabbed the men's room floor. "Done in a minute, sir."

The closed women's door invited someone without the same cultural fear as Americans. He pushed on the door. "Hello?" he said into an empty room. The mopping man stopped and looked at Adam.

The hall ended in an alarmed exit door that stood several inches open. Adam pushed on the bar. No alarm sounded.

"Did you see the guy sitting with me? Did he come through here?"

"What guy was that?" said the man rinsing his mop.

Adam walked back to the table and grabbed the check. The watch cap man was gone. He added a five-dollar bill at the register. "Did you see the man I was with leave here?"

The woman made change. "Your brother? He ain't back yet, if that's what you mean."

"Back? Where'd he go?"

"I don't know. Into the back lot, I guess. I wish they'd lock up after ten. You get the crazies in here at night. I was just catching a cigarette...."

Adam grabbed the cell phone out of his pocket and dialed 911.

59

He didn't hit the send button, but held a finger near. He opened the door and stepped into the pelting sleet. The parking lot was empty.

"Damn it," he muttered. If the man planned to just run off, why all the drama? And who the hell was the watch cap man? He unlocked the Corolla with a final look around the abandoned blacktop. No van, no strange man, and no Halim.

Chapter 9

Adam spent the day with the DIA at the Aberdeen Proving Grounds in Maryland. Worn-out buildings intermingled with a new gym around a little-used parade field. He repeated the story to the two agents. They looked bored and he was turned over to a young female agent. He signed a statement for her. She, at least, seemed interested.

He ate a grilled cheese sandwich at the base exchange food court, and spent the rest of the day at the Army Research Laboratory. The scientists and engineers offered their data and conversation because of his early work with the original command module, hoping he could shed some light on their problems.

At three in the afternoon, he was called to the director's office for a phone call patched through the Pentagon's switchboards.

"Brad Benchley, returning your call."

"Hey, Colonel," Adam said. "I understand they turned you around and you're back in Israel. How is it going?"

"Long days, Adam. I'm working my butt off. Never piss off an Army general."

"I'll remember that, sir. Can you go secure? I need to pass on a report."

"Roger that." Both entered a code and the phones sounded *be-bonk, be-bonk*. "All set, Major. I need something too, but you first. What's the big secret?"

"Did you get the report on my meeting with the Syrian in New Jersey?"

"Yep. Passed down from General Miller. That's got to be quite a story."

"Yes, sir, it is. But the real news is Aberdeen failed the JSAM system. The new command module is partially inoperative."

"You mean just this batch, right?"

"No, sir. The whole line of JSAMs. Aberdeen Test Center ran two dry runs this morning from the shipment sitting in McGuire. That's why they were held. They're still in test and they're failing."

"I told you to join the DIA. That's some good, damn detective work. NATO and Israel are going to be pissed, of course."

Adam took a breath. "Here's the deal, though, Colonel. None of the modules from this tracking lot work. Every one fails when the artificial intelligence is engaged. I haven't a clue why we never got complaints before, but the Army Labs here are shutting down all JSAM shipments. We've got to take down the systems ASAP, and replace navigation modules with operational models from other vendors. Or, we just use the new ones without the fire-and-forget feature."

"That you invented."

"Yes, sir."

Brad's voice sounded scratchy despite the satellite connection. "Well, I suppose that's what all the Joint Chiefs hoopla is about." Adam didn't confirm he already knew about the recall. "I appreciate you staying up to speed with this."

"Yes, sir. I'll cancel the shipment now."

"No, no," said Brad. "Don't cancel the order."

"They don't work, Colonel. Aberdeen knows this. The only reason they fly at all is their backup system."

"Aberdeen will keep their mouths shut. We need some time. Give me the rest of the story so I can brief NATO Command and the Israelis first."

For a while longer, Adam remained a soldier. His instinct to balk gave way, and he swallowed the question. He repeated the story learned that morning at the research labs.

"Okay," said Brad. "I need you to slow roll the shipment in New Jersey. Don't let those useless new modules get shipped, of course. But, don't let anyone else know why. Cancel the aircrew. Once they spend a couple of nights in the warehouse, reschedule the flight to Gravesend, England. Don't send them to Tel Aviv, for God's sake. Got that?"

"Yes, sir. What's the cover story for the tactical airlift squadron?"

"None needed," Brad said. "We're the military. We're always screwing up shipments. Say nothing. You're in the right place, Major. I'll look for the SNAFU confirmation on Monday. The Israelis will be jumping up and down, but they're probably already reverse engineering the damn things and getting them to work where we can't." Brad barely took a breath. "Seen Miranda Cinclaire lately?"

Adam laughed. His commanding officer changed conversational directions as quickly as a hungry shark in a school of anchovy. "Yes, sir. We talked but missed one another last week. She flew to LA to sign for a movie."

"Oh, yeah. The one with Dick Roberts. Sounds like a great movie."

Adam sighed. "Was I the only one who missed the entire conversation?"

Brad's voice ebbed as it bounced off the satellites. "You're quite the piece of work, Michaels. Get your nose out of the office once in a while. She's a hell of an actress and will probably get an Academy Award nomination someday. New York's too little for her."

"Yes, sir. You said I could do something for you?"

"Oh, right, almost forgot. Can you plan my retirement party? I'm going to pull the pin on the thirty-first."

"Holy shit! Sorry, sir. Really?"

"That's affirmative. Made the decision this weekend. I talked with my dad. You remember the senator?"

"Yes, sir, of course."

"I'm going to run for Congress in the First District in Georgia. My kid brother Jack will step aside just in time to run for governor. He's got a hell of a good chance. I'll be the interim and get the nomination next summer. Dad's already got the political machine running at fever pitch. Better be nice to me, Adam. I'll be your boss one day."

"You're already my boss, Mr. Congressman. That's really great."

Brad laughed over the wires. "Nah, that's just politics, but I'll tell you what is great. You'll be picking up lieutenant colonel this cycle. The zone opened, and I've already got the word from the board. In the meanwhile, you'll sit at my job until they can find a replacement."

Adam sat stunned. He was being promoted? That seemed impossible. The Army never admitted mistakes, and they'd sealed his fate when they tossed him to the media wolves after the Afghanistan debacle.

"Speechless, right?" Brad laughed again. "I've got to run, buddy. Quit walking on the ceiling and take care of screwing up the shipment. I'm counting on you."

"Yes, sir."

The connection broke. Good news, albeit late. And bad news. How could Brad believe delaying the shipment wouldn't provoke the Israelis? A problem he couldn't solve, at least today, because right now he had a higher priority. Julie's slumber party tonight needed him to hurry the preparations.

Lieutenant Colonel Michaels? He'd have to think about that later, too.

Later turned out to be when I-895 traffic stopped him mid-freeway. The board's delayed decision made him the last promoted in his class still on active duty. He ought to tell someone. Not Katherine, even though she'd be the one most likely to appreciate the silver oak leaves, with the raise in child support. Maybe Julie, but at thirteen, she wouldn't understand why his glass ceiling was more like a steel one. To tell Miranda meant an explanation of the tragedy in Helmed Province, the most notorious twenty hours of a fourteen-year war. He could no more explain the personal loss to her than could he make sense of the promotion today.

Someone else would care. He opened his cell phone and called Marty Callaway, his family's Irish lawyer and childhood protector. They talked and laughed for ten minutes before he finally punched the off button. Adam mused that the length of the call with the taciturn Marty probably set their mutual all-time record for chitchat. The traffic began to move five minutes later.

Chapter 10

"Morning, Sergeant," called Adam as he hung up his overcoat. The snowstorm reached DC late Sunday night while a deep low over Kentucky gathered strength. Many agencies announced closure before the morning commute. The rest planned to shut doors by noon. The Pentagon notified Gravesend, England to expect a delayed arrival into the RAF Brize Norton Airbase near London, yet offered no explanation.

"You're early, Patrick," said Adam. "Gonna beat the weather out of here?"

"Yes, sir," answered Goodell, looking up from his computer screen. "I'll leave around noon."

"Those wouldn't be bloodshot eyes I see. Late night?"

"Uh, yes, sir. Pretty late." The sergeant's pink eyes contrasted with dark rings beneath.

The phone interrupted. "Major Michaels," Adam answered.

"Adam, it's Tom Connecelli."

"Hey, Commander. Good to hear from you. If you're looking to revenge the trouncing the colonel and I handed out, he's not around. You'll have to wait."

Goodell grabbed a file and left. Adam wondered why his chipper sergeant could barely keep his eyes open. Even his amputee shuffle looked painful that morning.

"Very funny," Tom said. "We can do that sometime soon, but as I recall, we handed you guys your asses last time out."

Adam pictured the lanky man's hard right forehand smash, theatrical grunt, and quirky spin. He also remembered Tom's freewheeling, happy-go-lucky attitude as PhD students together at MIT. Much had changed in the intervening years.

"We need to talk," Tom said. "Have you got a spare half hour this morning?"

"Sorry, Commander." Tom made rank well ahead of Adam, all but killing their friendship. "I'm committed to answering the CO's at Red River Depot and Reutilization in Mechanicsburg until eleven."

"I've got a meeting then."

"Would one o'clock work? Coffee, third floor, Corridor 10 between A and B? I know where they keep the pot."

"Okay. Thirteen hundred, it is."

The phone went dead. Adam wondered at the abruptness. The doctorial work at MIT should forgo at least a bit of military protocol. Apparently not. He glanced up, and decided to give the Pennsylvania depot ten minutes and then call.

An email from the Washington headquarters for the Library of Military Records needed a password. He opened the document and read the title page of his own decade-old "Treatise on Graphene Biometrics." As author, he needed to approve a Freedom of Information Act inquiry from the State Department's Directorate of Trade Controls.

Tom and Sheila Perez were named as coauthors and PhD recipients, even if the theory and structure were Adam's idea. Tom already signed off, likely making this the topic of this afternoon's conversation. NASA had funded a study for a deep space probe with a navigation system immune to outside influences. The Defense Department wanted a fire-and-forget weapon impervious to an enemy's countermeasures. Hence, the DARPA funding, independent of both agencies. Adam believed a single-cell living creature could be bonded in carbon graphite structure with yeast DNA. The theory was simple even if replication was not. That changed with 3-D copier technology. Microscopic plastic strands spliced onto live bacilli carried microelectric charges with a billion bits of information. When the yeast went the way of all living creatures by dying, a skeletal graphene framework remained. The downside and upside of the concept left a hardened molecular structure not easily altered with anything short of a catastrophic kinetic or electronic blast.

On their first day, MIT professor Sheila Perez, with pageboy haircut and happy smile, had written in the corner of their huge whiteboard, "Once it's laid, it's played." The theme remained un-erased for the year and a half they worked. She soon became the calm arbiter for the two young officers as the hours grew longer and tempers shorter. Only she could calm Tom's arguments over the little details, so when late-night work no longer included him, Adam understood. After the breakthrough, Sheila and Tom shared the credit as well as the marital bed. On the weekend before he deployed with an infantry platoon to Iraq, Adam served as best man at their wedding.

Tom Connecelli sat in the coffee area chair rubbing finger circles along the top of his cup. Adam grabbed the last of the pot and slid into the chair opposite. "Hey, Commander. You're looking good, but I think the colonel and I can take you this time."

Tom looked up and offered a short grin. "You had us beat last time, Adam. It's that notorious lack of Air Force-Army cooperation that sank your ship."

They both smiled at the tired joke. Adam said, "Everything okay? You look like they're working you hard."

"Sure, sure. Why should there be something wrong?" Tom cast eyes around the empty lounge area.

"No reason." Adam waited a couple of beats. "How's Sheila doing? I haven't seen her in a month of Sundays." The answer was a stare that stopped Adam. "Sorry, not getting personal, Commander. I just haven't seen you guys in a while."

Adam didn't add that Tom and Sheila rarely came around after the promotion board passed him over, and never since the public screaming match that became the centerpiece for the divorce.

"Forget it. She's been back in Jerusalem with her mother for the last few months."

Adam knew the recent Hamas bus bombing killed six tourists, including two Americans. "That's not a good place right now. Especially for one of us."

Tom nodded. "She's a civilian, of course. I did my best to talk her out of it, but, well ... you might recall she's a little headstrong."

"I remember both you Connecellis were difficult. Especially when you were right." Adam watched for some sign the mood might lighten. He saw none.

Tom said, "She's asked me to help her work out an issue with our old command module project. You might have seen the request from Mark's Center. It's reclassified now."

"Yeah. 'Sensitive But Unclassified,' SBU. Quite a change from the old Top Secret, 'I'd tell you, but then I'd have to kill you' days." Adam took a sip and grimaced at the hours-old coffee.

"You know all that stuff was given back to NASA, right?"

"I've been out of the loop," Adam said. "But yeah, NASA funded us, so I guess they can do what they want with our work. They only got the sanitized version. The DOD secret stuff stayed with the military."

Tom nodded again. "Right. Do you also know NASA was going to use the unclassified theory to capture and bring back a three-meter asteroid?" Adam shook his head, and Tom continued. "NASA dropped the capture project and gave it to the European Space Agency."

"Really? I suppose giving it away for free is one way of making friends. The technology is still the basis for the fire-and-forget. You'd think—"

"If it only went to the allies, I'd be okay with it," Tom said. "But it's not. Forty months ago, NASA gave their graphene module to the Europeans for a Russian Angara rocket installed with a Pakistani lasso-and-basket. They sent it to the main asteroid belt."

Adam looked off. "I didn't know that."

"Old news." Tom sipped at the dank coffee without noticing. "This is not for distribution, Adam, but the NASA version never made it aboard the rocket. The guidance system we gave them is in a thousand pieces and in a hundred locations in the steppe desert of Kazakhstan."

"Well, good," Adam said. "We shouldn't be giving our stuff away, right?"

"Wrong. What do you think is sitting in its place on the fucking Russian rocket?"

Adam's gut clenched. "Does this have to do with our little meeting?" Tom nodded. "It won't work," Adam said. "The technology is the same, but not the mechanics and the software. Why would they screw up their mission from the very start? The DOD version won't do what they want. It's fire-and-forget. Remember 'once it's laid, it's played'?"

"They've had a decade, Adam. What could the three of us have done with that much time and money?"

Adam blew out a lungful of air. "I don't want to know how you got this information. Have they put together a team, a think tank?"

"Not for this. Jet Propulsion Labs and Aberdeen—"

Adam held up a hand. "I know about it, and that's another whole and classified issue. We shouldn't talk about it in the open."

Tom nodded. "Okay, you're right. Do you like conspiracy theories, because not everyone agrees?"

"Well, not exactly," Adam said. "But what's the big deal? The Europeans get a jump on the United States with asteroid research, if they can even make the old DOD stuff work. NASA gets some data to keep a half-dozen of their engineers working." He paused. "Wait a minute. Are you talking about Sheila and the stuff headed overseas in the same breath?"

Tom nodded. "She's working on a grant."

"For the command module?" Adam asked. "That was just a lot of theory."

"Good theory that will work well in the civilian world. NASA bought into it before the old president made them give it away. He didn't like the *Constellation* and didn't want to go to the moon again. Already been done by us and the Japanese. Hell, even the Pakistanis. He wanted a legacy that said Mars or an asteroid."

Adam gave the coffee another try. "Don't get me wrong. I'm glad someone's interested in our work. We stayed up a lot of nights thinking up things our little graphene critters could do."

Tom stared at him for a long moment. "We did more than a couple of nights. The research is the lynchpin for one hell of a lot of technology coming down the pike."

Adam forgot Tom's seriousness and sometimes missing sense of humor. "They don't talk to me about applications. It's the government's property. Always has been up to now." Adam smiled at his friend who looked away with his lips pressed together in anger. "She's got a grant, you said? Good news, right?"

"Yeah, great news." Tom watched the far wall.

Adam knew Tom's personal signs of "don't go there," but he needed to understand this. "I must really be out of the loop, then. I hadn't heard. Congratulations. Just getting through the arms-trafficking regulation process is a hell of an accomplishment. That's got to be good for the Connecelli family's bank account." The International Traffic in Arms kept a stranglehold on everything domestic including intellectual technology and rockets.

Tom didn't look around. "Her part isn't anything not already in the industry white papers. Did you see them?"

Adam's cup paused halfway to the tabletop. He recognized that Tom was deflecting. "I did this morning in my email, but you said she's been there for months."

Tom ignored the comment. "The command module's been cleared for commercial sales. That'll save a hundred million dollars in research for anybody using our technology."

Adam's smile wavered. "No matter if it is or not. It's the government's technology."

Tom pushed away his cup. "Sheila has a promise from the Israeli company. The money's pretty good and like you said, we can use it. They want to form a consortium over there to use the microbial concept to machine precision parts for medical devices. Strictly nonmilitary use, of course."

Adam wondered how Sheila could negotiate their technology, if he'd just signed the papers this morning. "I guess clearing bureaucratic hurdles won't be an issue then. And, they'll have the arms trafficking clearance pretty quick."

"If a year is considered quick. And, a year is the process minimum. Nobody gets this done in less than five. You know the bureaucrats. Dot every 'i' or you start all over again. We developed the whole thing in twenty months. She could invent it again, improve on it, and save years."

Adam felt a squirm working through his haunches. "What does this Israeli company want Sheila to do?"

He stared at Adam. "Hand over her research, our research."

Adam shook his head and gave a short laugh. "No way that'll ever be approved, Tom. To do it any other way is a violation of the Federal Secrets Act. She'll be in deep kimchi fast. Our boys will yank her security clearance and have her transported back to the US in a heartbeat."

"She can always reinvent it," Tom said, his voice just above an angry whisper.

Adam fought his own annoyance at Tom's obstinacy. "People are getting time in prison for that kind of stuff. Jesus, Tom. It doesn't matter if this is for a friend like Israel, or even if the stuff is unclassified. It's still sensitive. Violation of the security policy, not to mention arms trafficking, is a big deal. They might just take pity, fine you a hundred grand, and send her to a nicer prison because she helped invent it. She signed her rights away, just like you and me. Don't let her do it."

Tom eyes closed to harsh pinpoints. "I never said she was going to do it, goddamn it. I said it's what the Israelis wanted her to do."

Adam didn't back down. "And, I'm saying the Israelis know better. It violates our oath. Pure and simple. Plus, you know nobody sells a goddamn orange in Israel unless the state's involved. I'm not faulting them. They survive by having their fingers everywhere."

Tom dropped his stare after a moment. "We talked about it. She just got mad. You know she's a dual citizen." The resignation in his voice irked Adam.

"Even if someone just proposes to compromise sensitive data, it's got to be reported," Adam said. "She doesn't have a choice. And, that includes you and me, Tom. Phone it in, or tell her to go to the US Consulate and let them know."

"You can see the catch-22, though, right?" Tom watched across the table.

"What do you mean?"

"Second-gen command module was the answer to releasing the first," Tom said. "Someone jumped the gun on the Freedom of Information, and the documents are already in the military library. It's only a matter of time before it's public knowledge. It probably already is."

"So what?" Adam said.

"So, there's no putting the genie back in the bottle. You even signed a release from the Mark Library. I saw the email notification."

"That's a formality." Adam's voice grew an octave. "The information is in an unclassified sensitive status. No one is authorized to put it out or on the web ... or give it to someone. Come on, man. We all take annual classes on this stuff."

Tom shook his head, his voice matching Adam's. "Now, you're being naive. In a matter of weeks or days, anybody who wants it will have it."

"That might be true, but they'll only have first-gen theory, Tom. Our theory. Nobody has the practical interface or most importantly, the computer code. It might have taken me a few Saturday afternoons to come up with the idea, but it took the three of us nearly two years of fourteen-hour days to figure out how to program the microbes."

Adam stopped and looked at Tom. The other man did not drop his stare. "Oh wait a goddamn second here. Is she working for the Israeli government? Brad Benchley was over there making sure they knew ..." The enormity of the implication hit him. "How in the hell did they know the new module didn't work before we knew?" Adam set his jaw. "This is bullshit, Tom. What's going on?"

"This is why it's good Sheila's working on it for a friend like Israel, before the other terrorists gets their hands on it."

"What do you mean *other terrorists*? Are you calling the Israelis terrorists?"

Panic rose in Tom's eyes. "No, no. For Christ's sake, I didn't say that."

Adam calmed himself, knowing their conversation involved far more than two old friends speculating. He placed both hands on the table and leaned in. "Our original theory was declassified under the ten-year rule. That's done. Technically, you might be able to argue the rules don't apply, but not just because the US and Israel are friends. Do you remember Jonathan Pollard? He went to prison because he didn't play by the rules. You and Sheila are walking a fine line—"

"I never said I was helping her."

"Bullshit. If you or she utter anything protected, our government will come down hard. Friend or terrorist."

"I told you it was a slip of the tongue. Drop it, will you?"

"Okay. A slip," Adam said, his stare remaining. "All you have to do is wait. You two will get rich building little medical machines, if that's really what it is, and you'll still have time to sail off into the sunset."

Tom's hand shook and the coffee cup toppled. Adam grabbed a napkin but Tom grabbed his wrist. "You don't have a fucking clue." His words were vehement and angry. "You've got a grandfather with all the money in the world, and some heroic father that ..." He stopped, as if knowing his anger drove him too far.

"A father that what, Tom?" Adam replied with more calm than he felt, wrenching his hand away. "Is this where the terrorist remark came from?"

"No, no," Tom answered and sat back, mouth breathing. "Look. This is about doing the right thing. There's always two sides to a story. We need to right a lot of wrongs here. There's a thousand years of murder, of blood running in the streets. You understand all this, right?"

Adam finished mopping up the coffee and said, "The Israelis can take care of themselves. This country is the one that needs help. Let's just be clear on a few things. Sheila needs to cease and desist. She can't work for a foreign government, and don't give me the shit about dual citizenship. She signed those rights away the day she joined us in the lab. You can't help her. You're a naval officer working as assistant to the Director of Naval Operations. That's damn close to crossing the line. Commander or no commander, Tom, you've gone too far."

The other man's stare dropped to the floor, but not in contrition. "Now I suppose you'll play little goody two-shoes and run to Defense Intelligence."

Adam fought his temper. "I will unless you promise me nothing goes forward from here. I think you're confused. The radical Islamists are the enemy, but that doesn't mean you can give anything to Israel on your own."

"Okay," Tom said in a near whisper. "It was a mistake to ever approach you."

"You've got that one right, sir."

Adam rose and spent the next ten minutes walking the halls until he could draw a calm breath.

Goodell hung up the phone when Adam returned to his office. "We've got a Huey lined up for tomorrow morning, Major. The snow should be over by then. They'll drop us in time for the 0900 meeting and then head north on another mission. We'll be on our own after that."

Adam smiled, covering his angst from the meeting with Tom. "Great. Sounds like we're spending the night."

"Yes, sir. I'm planning for a couple. Just in case." Patrick looked at a yellow message slip.

"Mine?"

"Yes, sir. I … ah …"

Strange day, today. "Come on, Sergeant. Give." Adam tried to smile but couldn't completely overcome the disturbing meeting with Tom.

"All right, sir." The young man looked up and said, "But, keep in mind I'm only a messenger."

Adam relaxed and laughed. He fell into the chair opposite Goodell's desk. "We stopped shooting those guys this morning. New Pentagon policy."

Goodell offered a half smile. "Colonel Benchley called and wanted me to pass on that Ms. Cinclaire was free tomorrow evening and expected your call." Goodell grimaced. "Sorry, sir."

Now Adam understood the hesitation. Goodell knew he'd entered into the forbidden territory of military protocol, once again. "Wow," said Adam. "That guy can be a … never mind, thanks. Anything else?"

"The phone number, sir."

"I've got it."

"Yes, sir."

"Go home, Sergeant, and take care of the wife. See you in the oh-thirty."

"Roger that."

Goodell left, and Adam sat alone in the office, thinking the kids would be out of school. Julie would not be alone. Katherine's office never opened for snow days. He had checked early in the morning but didn't call her, just the office. He didn't keep track of Eric, but he would if Katherine's relationship grew more serious. For right now, at least, Adam remained the preeminent male in Julie's life. That wouldn't last long for either Eric or him.

The snow stopped during the night and the storm blew out to sea. The ride launched from the Pentagon pad without a sliver of the coming dawn and over the reflected lights of a frozen and breathtaking Washington snowscape. The helicopter flew at a hundred feet across the Potomac and up the light-studded Anacostia River with its small

74

stone bridges and the bright Navy Yard. Fresh snow reflected from the Jefferson Memorial and off the rooftops. Adam sat on the left side of the aircraft and watched the Washington Monument, Capitol Building, and White House illuminated in the distance. He couldn't see the hidden military snipers waiting with shoulder-fired missile launchers, likely watching them as well, alert to any change in their flight pattern. At the Kenilworth Gardens as the repainted Pepsi Tower came into view, they departed the river's path and rose to five hundred feet for Baltimore's airport. The control tower worked very early jet airliner departures. The pilots began their chatter to overfly the field and Adam turned off his intercom. He leaned back and enjoyed the rhythmic vibration of a helicopter probably older than him. The sun would rise on the other side of the fuselage, and Patrick Goodell already slept. They would meet Lieutenant Colonel Webb again and hope for his cooperation. Adam couldn't explain about the slowdown that Brad ordered, and hoped the Army's inefficiency won out over political pressure. He settled into the dark corner of the noisy cabin, and in minutes found sleep, thinking about Miranda Cinclaire.

* * *

The JSAM paperwork waited for Adam at the depot. The one time he expected and counted on military inefficiency, he'd been thwarted. The documents were so precisely completed, he couldn't help but think the gods must be angry, or someone with influence had stepped in. Now, he must find another way to delay until Brad Benchley gave him the go-ahead.

Lt. Colonel Webb entered the office and flopped into a nearby chair, double chin and heavy belly prominent. Adam stood, but the depot commander waved him down. "You're taking over Benchley's place at the Puzzle Palace. Congratulations. Brad called to let me know, so don't try to keep the secret. And, you're on the lieutenant colonel's list, too." He grinned, looking over the tops of half-glasses. "Congratulations again."

Adam nodded and set his new iPhone scanner down. "I hope it's true. Thanks. I would welcome it, of course. I wasn't on the last two lists for obvious reasons. I can hardly believe they're making an exception to the twice-passed-over rule. Never embarrass the generals, you know."

The round-faced depot commander watched Adam for an uncomfortable moment, then said, "You're right, Michaels. But even a giant pain in the ass like the Army can sometimes get it right."

"Well … thank you, sir." The taciturn colonel's compliment surprised him.

"My nephew is PFC Hollingsworth. You might not remember him—"

Adam interrupted. "I know him very well, sir. His counter-fire saved the day. He did a hell of a job. He was badly wounded and in a lot of pain, and never quit on me."

Webb nodded and set his fleshy jaw. "He told me you were the best platoon commander he ever had and didn't deserve the pasting Uncle Sam gave you. You were shafted by bad orders, and those pricks were just covering their asses. You pulled Vernon out of the frying pan, and I appreciate it."

Adam recalled PFC Hollingsworth as the driver of the lead Humvee first hit in the ambush by the Taliban. Adam pulled him from the burning wreckage but couldn't do anything for the dead driver. He'd carried the bleeding private twenty yards in the open as the enemy overran the first three burning vehicles. Vernon Hollingsworth was one of four saved by Adam's actions that night, but heroics are never individual. Adam rallied the remainder of his platoon to drive the enemy back into the shadows. Men in the third vehicle called for help. Adam ran into the open but not before Hollingsworth and another set up covering fire, making four more trips possible for Adam. On the next to last, his luck ran out and he was wounded by a fragment from a rocket-propelled grenade. Even while bleeding, Adam managed to emerge from cover to rescue a last soldier from a burning truck. He had no way of knowing the man was already dead. The rescues were only possible because Webb's nephew and others set up counter-fire that kept the enemy's head down. Vern Hollingsworth was written up for a Silver Star, but downgraded to a Bronze Star with "V" for Valor. Adam received a Silver Star for heroics, that under any other circumstances would have been a Medal of Honor. The follow-up investigation of the eighteen-hour firefight made national news.

"The kid was scared and wounded but never quit firing his M4, Colonel," Adam said. "His actions saved men, including me."

76

The company admin stepped in. "They're here, Major," said the clerk from the doorway. "Looks like McGuire expedited and did something on time for once."

Webb stood and looked at Adam. "Our good friends in blue. Please conduct your pre-shipping inspection and let me know." He glanced at the clock. "Looks like you need to arrange an RON for at least one night anyway. Probably a good idea to make sure everything is squared away on this one. No mistakes."

Adam stood breathing relief. "Agreed, sir. This wouldn't be a good time to drop the ball."

Goodell arrived two minutes behind the company clerk. "Got us rooms at the Coachman tonight, Major. Okay with you?"

"Sounds good. I'll be down to the warehouse in a minute. I need to make a phone call."

Goodell grinned and gave a thumbs-up. Adam laughed. The colonel shook his head, still not liking the familiarity.

Chapter 11

He parked the Enterprise rental car in the Marina Café parking lot a half-hour early. One of the captains in the depot knew the Staten Island restaurant, and called it "out-of-the-way." He recommended crossing the Verrazano into New York City. But Miranda had made the reservation and Adam wondered why they avoided the nightlife.

A halyard clinked against an aluminum mast as he leaned on the rail, the sound and the sea smell reminding him of his grandfather's house in the Hamptons. Adam spent summers on the family's boat but attended only a single party as an adult. Julius insisted after the British Prime Minister, a former army officer, accepted the invitation. Adam showed in his dress uniform that day. The old man rarely visited the house, preferring beers with the workmen in his gritty shipyards. Adam agreed and didn't like lawn parties and local drama, either. Tonight, this marina's slips could only remember the bustle of the forgotten season.

He wore a dark sport jacket over slacks and his military overcoat with the gold major's leafs removed. The unexpected maritime chill chided him for not bringing something heavier. A Lincoln Town Car Limo pulled into the valet area. Adam watched as the driver tried to get to the back door. Miranda stepped out, pulling a shimmering coat against the breeze, and spotted him. She smiled, waved, and hurried down the wide wood steps. He walked to meet her.

"You weren't supposed to be early," she said. Her evening dress and elegant dark hair said "night on the town."

"Wow, Miranda. You look terrific. I might not be up to snuff here."

"'Snuff'?" She laughed. "You're so funny, and thank you. You look good to me. And, it's about time you called, Michaels. You were beginning to hurt my ego."

"Sorry," he said, holding back a tumble of words.

"Darn right," she said, taking his arm and pulling close. "I have to be careful when I throw myself at someone. Don't want to get tossed back. Hurts a girl's reputation."

"Any guy who'd throw you back should be shot at sunrise. I'll

78

do the honors."

"That's what I wanted to hear. Hungry?"

He shrugged. "I could eat." They hurried up the steps to the glass doors. A man waited and pushed them open. Miranda pulled close and whispered, "We need to talk. I have some *explaining* to do." She drew out Ricky Ricardo's famous line.

Adam nodded, his smile more subdued. "I have a question, maybe two."

"Ms. Cinclaire," said the maître d'. "Wonderful to see you again."

"Henry," replied Miranda. "You too." She hugged him.

The man grabbed menus and maneuvered through crowded tables toward dark glass with the harbor and ocean beyond. Miranda greeted an older couple nearby, as others turned to stare. "Will this be satisfactory?" asked Henry.

Adam nodded. "Yes. Thanks." He extended his hand. "Everyone seems to know everyone. I'm Adam Michaels."

The man smiled and returned the gesture. "Yes, of course, Major. Henry Cranford. My pleasure, sir."

"The pleasure is mine."

Adam was not in uniform and more questions bubbled as he took her coat. "You really do look beautiful, Miranda."

"I'd better. I've got another date tonight and it might be the big deal." She held her breath with a bit of theatrics.

His face revealed much more than he'd intended. "Really?" He sat and leaned back in the chair.

She covered his hand with her own. "I wanted to see you. It's why we're not in the City. I didn't want to be unfair and leave you with a three-hour drive back and nothing to show for it."

"I don't have those expectations, Miranda. We don't know each other well enough. But you have to admit it's strange having dinner in Staten Island when the most exciting city in the world is only an hour away."

She smiled. "I'll explain. Could we have a drink first?"

He motioned a waiter and ordered them martinis. "*Okay, Lucy.* Spill the beans."

She smiled at his humor, and turned to answer a question from a nearby table. She turned back and said, "First things first. I'm not in a relationship. I told you last time."

The waiter placed the martinis in front of them and asked if they were ready to order.

"Make it an appetizer to start. Ms. Cinclaire's favorite. Henry will know." He glanced over and Miranda nodded. "We'll decide after that."

"Thank you, Adam. I'm sort of playing tonight by ear."

Adam nodded at the waiter and the young man left with his eyes lingering. "You were saying."

She took a breath. "Tonight is the follow-up with Dick Roberts and the producers. Remember I told you about the black-tie thing." She cringed. "I couldn't get you an invitation. I'm sorry."

"No worries. Do you have the part in the movie?"

"Dick owns a big piece, but not the whole thing. He needs to get a couple other investors to buy off, too. I'm window dressing tonight. I've done some other movies but never with someone like Dick. My part is supporting, I get to sing the theme and maybe a little more, but I'm really going to give it my all. It's a breakout chance."

"What's it about?"

She looked stricken, as if she'd just realized.

"Miranda?"

"Oh, no. It's a story about an injured Gulf War vet and the search for a mafia hit man. The bad guys are the real thing and Dick Roberts, the hero, isn't up to the task. He loses his family … everything. A good ending, though. I'm the pretty face who turns out to be the reason he wins."

"What's wrong with that? It sounds great. Exciting."

She let out a breath. "Brad said I shouldn't talk with you about the war."

"Nonsense. Dick Roberts is the kind of action hero I like. Kind of the tough, lovable lug."

She laughed and sighed in relief. "Now, you're having fun with me. He's a major pain in the ass, but if all goes well, I'll have the right ink on a contract for my agent to look over."

He leaned back in the chair. "Wow. That's pretty big. A star? Why didn't you just cancel tonight?"

"A part, Adam, not a star. And, if you think I wanted to miss impressing you with a thousand-dollar hair and makeup job, forget it. I love Broadway, but movies are the brass ring. We only have an hour, and I hope you're as disappointed as I am."

"I just wanted to see you again, under any circumstances."

She watched him a moment, as if seeing him for the first time. "You're a nice guy. I'll need to remember that and be disappointed for the two of us. And, hopeful. Will you be here tomorrow night?"

The first of several well-wishers stepped up. For the next thirty minutes, she offered autographs and short notes to absent nieces, said kind words and thanks, and greeted every person with warmth.

When Henry formed a defensive line against other encroachments, Adam said, "You're nice to everyone. That can't be easy, the public part I mean."

She grimaced, but only a tiny bit. "It's just part of the job. Every person knows ten, and they know ten others. If one in a thousand buys a ticket, I can keep my day job even if the movie is a bust. I'm the ham sandwich, and the salesman, too."

"And, quite a lovely ham sandwich, I might add." He leaned back with a smile. "Oh brother," he said, shaking his head. "You know I've been away from all this for so long, my patter sounds like my granddad's."

She laughed. "I've got enough wannabe actors jabbering in my ear and using lingo-of-the-moment to appreciate the way you talk. Like proper English royalty with an American accent."

"Don't stick me in the bowler too quickly. You're hearing prep school coming out, and you never trust a preppy. You've seen the movies. How about if I come to your side of the river sometime and hang out."

She took his hand and dropped it when a flash went off. "You are welcome anytime," she said and smiled at the teenager who took the picture. The girl was embarrassed, yet Miranda waved her over after a quick word with Henry. She spoke in near whispers as they put their heads together. When the girl looked wide-eyed at Adam and Miranda nodded, they both laughed.

"What was all that about?" he asked as the teenager left.

"Girl talk, and none of your business."

81

"You seem to know your fans." The grilled oysters remained untouched. "I've got to ask one thing. You spell your name with a C instead of the S. Theater?"

She shook her head. "Oh, no. Old family from Louisiana. Iberville Parish. We're of the sugar plantation variety. Remember I mentioned Napoleon chasing off Great-Great-Grandpa? We were the Acadians—Cajuns—the locals who stole the land from the Indians before it was stolen from us. My family is Canadian, homesteaded on the Mississippi, lost their shirts a hundred years later in the sugar wars of the twenties and thirties, but didn't give up the land. It's still there. A dilapidated factory and a tourist plantation. My dad's people broke up the household and moved back to Quebec. I heard all the stories and watched all the old movies—*Suddenly Last Summer*, *The Pelican Brief*, *Déjà Vu*, so, I went to LSU. I moved my one-woman family back north, but only as far as New York." She looked as the driver entered the large glass doors, hurrying her words. "We're émigrés from America. Oh Adam, we have so much to talk about. I can't believe the hour slipped away."

He followed her glance toward the door. "Me, either. I still don't know the really important stuff about you, like your favorite song."

"'Moon River,' but I'll deny it if you tell *Variety*. I'll lose my Madonna status."

They both laughed. "Your secret is safe, Ms. Cinclaire. Old-fashioned, but safe."

"Will you walk me out and then will you tell me you're staying another night?"

"Of course I'll walk out with you, and the Army will decide about tomorrow. You know the drill." He called for the check and trailed as she walked through the well-wishers to the main door. Just outside, she turned as another camera flashed. "The paparazzi will make something of the goodnight kiss I'd planned for you. I guess we'll miss that, too."

"I'll be the one missing it." He smiled at her and was taken by surprise when she kissed his cheek too fast for the camera. "You'd better call."

She disappeared inside the car as the camera flashed one last time. He didn't notice the lens on him, because he was plotting how to spend an extra night.

He need not have worried. Anything the Air Force could do, including losing the paperwork and finding a replacement aircrew, held up the transshipment. The next day, he declared victory at noon and rebooked their rooms for another night. Patrick Goodell seemed pleased, too.

Chapter 12

"Miranda?"

She turned, grocery bag in hand. "Oh! There you are. Didn't know if you got lost. I made a quick trip to the store. No way I could wait in the apartment." She stopped the babble and dropped tense shoulders. A clip held back her long dark hair. She saw him looking at her with no makeup. "Oh, God, don't say it. I look like hell. I thought I had enough time to change."

"Quite the opposite. You look ... cute." He almost said 'seventeen, not twenty three,' but demurred as a man walked past.

She squinted lovely eyes. "Careful, dude. If you'd said 'perky,' I'd have to call this whole thing off. I don't do perky, and cute is getting mighty close."

"I stand corrected," he said with a laugh.

She smiled and moved to him. His lips touched hers. "Hmm. More," she whispered as a passing car honked a voice yelled. She pulled away and handed him the groceries. "Come on, let's go in. My neighbors will think I've taken up streetwalking." "

"Do you know those people?" He looked after the car.

She laughed. "No. That's just New Yorkers." They started up the steps to the brownstone. "You're about all I can think about lately."

"That's a relief."

She paused as he caught up. "Why?"

"Minds change." He touched her hand. "Circumstances, too. I'm guessing your date went well last night."

She fished a key from a sweater pocket. "Yes, it did. My agent signed everything and we're done."

"He was there?" asked Adam.

"There were about fifty people there ... including me." She stopped at the door. "I have a feeling you think last night was something it wasn't."

"I ... well. You called it a date. I really didn't know what you meant, I suppose."

She smiled and touched his arm. "Sex and the producer's

84

couch is a myth. Today, movies are all about the dollars, foreign rights, and residuals. Investors and producers won't last long if they don't pay attention to things like theater openings, disc distributions, declining revenue versus days on market, and critic reviews. I suppose the sex is still out there, but the dollar dictates. Actors, writers, and directors are just tools to reach goals. And, I'm not the star ... yet." She smiled.

A glass wall dominated the expansive living room. Original oils hung with small ceiling lights. A Native American breastplate with bone and turquoise beads hung over grain baskets in one corner with a faded print of a hovel and two fur-wrapped women.

"These look like real artifacts," he said.

"They are. Native North American anthropology was my college major before I switched to acting. When I could afford it, I bought something. I'm still interested, of course, just not as a career." She looked over at him. "You're looking at a Canadian plains Indian battledress over there. This is an elk hide medicine bag dating from the early 1800s." She held up a sealed glass display. "Came from near Cody, Wyoming. It was actually stolen from the tribes in the Northwest Territories, and can't be opened to the air." She gently placed the exhibit back on the shelf. So I suppose that puts me in league with thieves and grave robbers."

"I'm impressed," said Adam as he set grocery bags onto the kitchen counter. Copper-bottom pots hung on chrome hooks from a soffit over the black granite. "I'm going to say this, but don't misunderstand. You don't look like a starving actress to me."

She stared at him with her forehead wrinkling. "Adam Michaels. We've had two dates and shared a bed on one of them. You're going to tell me you haven't even Googled me yet?"

"Googled?" He was nonplused. "Well, sure. I read one of your reviews and I did accept your invitation on Twitter. I've never followed anyone with so many people following them. Impressive. I like you and no, I didn't research you, although I did Dick Roberts." She covered her mouth and giggled. "Should I have been more ... inquisitive? *Variety* thinks you're tops, and I agree."

"Well, I did Google you. You should be more careful. I could be after your fortune. 'Last of America's Royalty. Son of the landed gentry and grandson and heir to McCaffrey Shipping. New York's Most Eligible Bachelor.'" She laughed. "Not anymore. I'm taking you out of circulation."

"That bachelor stuff is fluff for lonely girls and it's old, old news. I'm a soldier and I don't have anything to do with the family business. Hey, someday you might get to meet my ten-year-old Toyota."

"By choice," she said. "*Celebrity* magazine wrote an article. Said, you were the millennium generation's new Jack Dorsey...."

"*Celebrity* doesn't know what they're talking about." He knew about the article comparing him to an eligible billionaire, because he'd refused the interview. The piece was already written so the reporter wasn't upset. "They're no different than any of the other magazines. They make up the news if there isn't any. I haven't touched the family business since the years I interned."

"Still ..." She allowed her sentence to trail away.

He did not talk about family. If the media ever looked into his background, they would find William Michaels, deceased physician and Lillian McCaffrey, also deceased of the McCaffrey shipping empire. He wondered how well the old story held up these days.

He touched the soft hair at the back of her neck. "I hope Hollywood works out for you. My niece is out west and I haven't seen her in a while. She's staying at the Coronado family house, and going to San Diego State." Now, he was being coy. "We could have dinner, walk on the beach, watch the sunset turn the world pink and green."

"Sounds lovely." She took his hand for a moment and looked into his face. With a quick squeeze, she withdrew and pulled a pot from under the stovetop. The overhead copper bottoms displayed for show only. "You're sweet, but too good to be true. I'm sure you hunt poor forest creatures and have rooms full of dead animal heads."

He laughed. "I'm lots of things, but I don't think 'sweet' is among them. But, thanks for the vote. No animal heads in the apartment you saw."

"Oh, you have a hunting cabin somewhere." She waved her hand dismissing his protests and filled a pot with water. He wondered if she knew about Marston Lodge, the family's skiing and hunting estate in British Columbia. He'd save that for later.

She grabbed the grocery bag from the counter. "We've got a couple of hours before I have to go. Hope you're hungry."

He touched her cheek. "I was thinking of something else, actually."

She came to him with food quite forgotten. Their lips explored one another. Then, their hands. They struggled with buttons and zippers. He lifted her to the cold granite in a single motion. She did not protest.

His fingers stroked and teased. She struggled and he said, "Stay still. Let me."

She relaxed as his lips became a feather, cajoling. "Oh my God, Adam. I …" Her voice disappeared with a catch.

When he felt a final shudder, he pressed and held her to him. As she regained her breath, he asked, "Where?"

"Upstairs."

He lifted her down. "Come," he said, and took her hand.

"Again?"

They both smiled and took the stairs two at a time. Ice cream melted on the countertop.

He watched her sleep, breathing deep and perfectly still in the soft bed. Dark hair spilled over the pillow and she breathed in a whisper. He pulled the thin blanket to cover breasts exposed in chilly air.

He had clung to the silly hope he and Katherine would reconcile until Eric became a steady presence. She made the transition to a new man within weeks of the decree. Too quick, he knew, and hoped Julie would not take a life's lesson from her mother's propensity to have what she wanted, when she wanted it. Eric should hold tight, too, because despite his connections at the State Department, Katherine had cheated before. Thinking she would stop now didn't make sense. He reflected for the hundredth time why she had quit believing in him, and if he had driven her to be unfaithful.

Now, he concentrated on Julie. He smiled recalling his grandfather's horrified expression when they'd told him the child would bear his name. "Julius? What kind of a bloody name is that for a girl?"

"Julie," Katherine had said.

"Ah, *Julie*," repeated the older man, savoring the soft sound with moist eyes.

There were other grandchildren in the family, but Julie was special to the old man from the beginning. The smile on Grandfather's face remained one of Adam's best memories. When the divorce became imminent, Adam was unsure who hurt more, him or his grandfather. He didn't know why the thought came to him now, unbidden in the chilled, dark room. He wondered if a man could commit so fully, so completely, twice in a lifetime. Miranda's soft breathing seemed to say … it was possible, yes.

He rolled from the apartment's loft bed and planted bare feet on the cold floor. Miranda stirred but didn't wake. The alarm clock wouldn't ring for another half hour. A few minutes more sleep would probably be good for her, so he found his pants, skipped the shirt, and headed downstairs. The cool air felt good on his warm skin.

A twenty-minute cab ride would take him to the theater, but he didn't plan to go. This brief visit would have to do, he decided as hot coffee dripped. He wasn't ready for the face paint and crowds. He recalled New York from earlier, wilder days, and had no wish to remake the acquaintance just now.

Reflected light through the shuttered downstairs windows reminded him that Miranda's profession stirred in the evening, worked until two in the morning, and then slept till noon. A new experience he anticipated with interest, even pleasure, but not tonight.

He drank water from her tap. His shoulders and chest flexed the muscles made on the football field and leading soldiers in combat, and nowadays kept strong with long runs and weights. Considering the hours wasted managing a desk and drinking endless cups of coffee, he was pleased enough, although he could stand to lose a few pounds.

Life might change soon enough. The letter from the promotion board waited in his briefcase. He must sign and return, a confirmation he would take the lieutenant colonel's silver oak leaves, and serve an additional three years. The obligation would mean another tour in Afghanistan or some other faraway place, and separation from Julie. Until a few days ago, he wanted the promotion and to use the skills he'd earned. As a lieutenant colonel and former centerpiece to a key American defeat, this might be a chance to exonerate himself in the eyes of the unbelievers.

Marty's second text message of the evening vibrated his phone. Adam read it, and knew he must speak with his grandfather soon. If Julius had his way, Adam would be on the superstructure of some great ship or in the bowels of a foreign dock office learning the family business. He would not be standing half-dressed in the apartment of a beautiful actress.

"That was a later interest," said her whispered voice from behind him. She pressed against his back, naked except for his open shirt.

Adam stood looking down at a glass case, and hadn't noticed her come downstairs. "It's a beautiful *hanbok*. Very traditional."

"I'm impressed," she murmured into his cool skin. "Most people think it's a kimono, but you're right. It's a very old, eighteenth-century *hanbok*, and took my last two royalty checks. Probably a silly purchase and has nothing to do with Indians, but I'm impulsive that way." She knuckled her eyes as he turned to embrace her.

"You are full of surprises," he said, as his chest touched her bare breasts.

"I haven't much time," she said, pulling him toward the living room couch. "Hurry." Urgency arched her back, demanding, not willing to wait. Hands found one another, the needs of the moment driving both.

In a few minutes, the room grew quiet once more as breaths calmed.

Miranda spoke first. "I'm supposed to be there by seven. There won't be any time to cook." She shifted to stand.

"I can make something," he said. An odd hollow in his chest regretted the moment's loss. "The show was the furthest thing from my mind."

"Thank God," she said with a smile, and pulled his wrinkled shirt from the floor.

He acknowledged they knew little of one another, and that a harmony of emotion would come with time and commitment. Yet, the abrupt physical severance of their two bodies cut a visceral swath deep inside him.

He pushed the thought away and swung his feet to the floor.

"Are you going to tell me what happened at the signing?"

"Another time. It's a long story about empty people."

He stood and kissed her lips, knowing the moment slipped away. "I'll cook while you get ready."

He didn't watch as she ascended the staircase. Instead, he found his pants and busied himself with pans, butter, and eggs.

He flipped the omelet as she hurried in. "I called a cab. Fifteen minutes." She looked in the pan, brushing back strands of silken, dark hair. "You're very accomplished."

"Self preservation. I make them for Julie when she stays over and we're running late for school." He didn't mention the money saved by avoiding the restaurants around his apartment.

She accepted a plate, taking a healthy bite. "Wow. This is really good. I bought this stuff?"

"Yes." She liked the food, and Adam would build on that. The plate was clean in three more bites. He laughed. "You either have a good appetite, or I starved you."

She dropped the dish in the sink. "Couldn't be shy in my house. Four brothers, and all hungry from farm work. A girl could starve if she demurred at our dinner table." She drained a glass of milk. "Are you going to tell me about growing up in America's richest family?"

Adam shrugged. "We weren't the richest and not even the most dysfunctional. No reality shows, although maybe more notoriety than our neighbors. I was an only child and got into as much trouble as I could handle. That's about it."

"One day, you'll tell me the real story. I need to know, and I need to get dressed." She stood on her toes to kiss his chin. "Thanks for dinner."

She ran upstairs and he wondered how much she knew about him or his family. The Internet and tabloids sold advertising with one-sided, jaded stories. They should have talked first, letting him tell the truth instead of having to unwind a poor impression of dilettantes and conceit.

As one of the elite children of the wealthy, legitimate press and scandal sheets pursued him. Once, he gave the latter headlines, just as his mother, a Grace Kelley admirer and bad girl of the seventies and eighties jet set did before him. He didn't like the results, or facing a disappointed grandfather, and never repeated the experiment. When he announced his choice of the Army, more than just the heads of reporters turned. He recalled the family argument.

The house was a hubbub of opinion. His grandfather put a stop to the dramatic flow of phone calls, texts, and emails by asking, "What in the world did you think was going to happen after twelve years in a military boarding school? Besides, a stint in the Navy will be good background for the family business."

When Adam said he was joining the Army, his grandfather roared with laughter.

A fun memory, Adam thought.

A few years later, the same New York magazine who named him a "Top Twenty Eligible Bachelor" called him an incompetent bungler after the fight in Kandahar. They likened him to Custer's similar bullheadedness. The wires and blogs picked up the storyline and of course, called for his head. Three of the four major networks used retired generals, most of whom had never seen combat. They analyzed the poor decisions and the chancy rescue, never getting the story quite right. One even used a computer model based on a video game to tell a fictitious tale of Adam's cowardice. The station received great ratings, yet no one ate their words because no one remembered when the Pentagon recanted.

"Earth to Adam." Miranda stood at the top of the stairs.

He smiled up at her. "Sorry. Lost in a moment."

"I wish you'd come and watch the play tonight," she said. "The crew will grab a late dinner at Sardi's after. Sort of a tradition. The theater's fun. Not like the movies. Every night is different, and there's always some crisis or gossip. Like a family, relating badly and loving every minute of it. I'll even introduce you to my leading man. He's unbelievably handsome and will drool all over you, so you'd better not like him."

Adam walked to the bottom step. "No worries there. I'm committed to you."

The glib remark stopped them both. They blinked at one another. She recovered first. "I'm going to keep an eye on you anyway. Girls on Broadway are going to eat you up. They're not used to a real man."

"Can I take a rain check? Tomorrow starts at six for me, and I've still got a little work to do tonight. I'm sorry if that spoils plans."

She watched him for a moment. "I wanted you to meet … actually, I wanted to show you off. It's not important. I'll just miss you and all."

"If it's something you want, I'll stay."

"No, I'm sorry, Adam. That is so typically selfish of me. You have a big day tomorrow, I'm sure. I'd call in sick, if this were any other night. Would you excuse me a moment?" She turned and was gone, leaving him baffled. The bathroom door slammed and he heard the water run as she coughed, and the toilet flushed. A horn honked at the street. She hurried down, no smile on her pale face.

"My cab. Lock up for me? I can't be late."

A peck on the cheek and she was out the door. The odor of mouthwash lingered, bothering the back of his mind. Something else he would need to learn.

He straightened the apartment, made the bed, and washed dishes for an hour before he left. An accident on the Verrazano delayed him with the traffic stopped high over the famous Narrows. He thought this might have been his great-great-grandfather's first view of his new home as Ellis Island greeted him and The Lady listened to his dreams.

Chapter 13

Adam dropped the car keys into the hotel's return box, noticing the early cleanup schedule. "You missed 211. We'll be out by five."

The young man looked up from his iPhone. "Thanks. I'll add it right away." He wrote the room number at the bottom of the list and checked the master copy. "The room is rented until the twenty-eighth, sir. You must be mistaken."

Adam shook his head. "That's Patrick Goodell's room. We're both leaving tomorrow. I'm going to grab a few hours' sleep, and then we need the van to take us to Dix." The clock behind the clerk read twelve-fifteen. He considered for a moment. "Maybe you'd better check. I'd hate to wake up someone I'm not supposed to."

The clerk sighed and ran his fingers over the keyboard. "That's not Goodell in 211. And there's no Goodell registered. Could he be under a different name? Yours?" Before Adam answered, the man held up a finger. "I think there was a checkout …" He turned to another clipboard. "Here it is. Patrick Goodell. Army. Checked out early. Said it was an emergency. There's a note he wanted a refund for half the room. I don't come on till midnight. We only refund if it's before five o'clock and nobody slept in the bed."

"I need someone to take me to the base."

"Sorry. No one's here but me."

Adam said, "Okay. Call me a cab, will you? I'm going to be checking out."

"I can't refund …"

Adam wasn't listening. He returned to his room and tossed a few possessions into the overnight bag while he pulled on his ACUs. The Army Combat Uniform served as the ubiquitous substitute for most informal military functions. As he walked for the door, the message light caught his attention. The cab. He didn't bother to call the front desk and went out the side door.

The cold air left his breath in vapor puffs in the parking lot lights. The forecasted weather front arrived early but no cab waited at the front doors. He walked back inside. "Do you have a message for 213?"

The clerk handed a folded paper to Adam. "*Depot Commander advised loading delayed until noon. Enjoy the late sleep.*" The bottom of the slip date-stamped at 5:15 p.m.

Goodell must have decided to see his friend. Adam could have gone to the theater and stayed in Miranda's bed until late.

A cab honked from the street. "He's here, sir," said the clerk, pushing the receipt across the counter. "See you next time."

Adam snapped up the paper, not trusting himself to answer.

The military security guard would not allow the taxi into the compound. Adam hefted his overnight bag and briefcase prepared to walk the half-mile. The wet night air seeped cold deep inside him. Strings of lights mounted on idled crane booms reflected the misting breeze, and reminded him of childhood phantoms waiting for prey.

As he passed the warehouse holding the JSAM, a light showed in the dispatch office. He dropped his bags and pushed at the steel-and-glass door, bending to pick up a soda can used as a stopper. Glass fragments crunched under his boots while his nose recalled a familiar, cloying odor.

"Patrick?" Goodell sat at the desk with his back to the door. "What are you doing here at this hour?"

The figure didn't move. As the door closed, the lock clicked in the still room. Adam looked around, then set the bent can on a desk. "Patrick?"

Bright red spots scattered across the floor. A Desert Eagle One .45-caliber pistol sat in a pool of blood at Goodell's fingertips. Adam turned the chair around. Two drying red stains centered on the young sergeant's chest.

The door rattled hard as a shadow pulled the locked handle, startling him. The figure pounded, and Adam took a single step then saw the figure raise a gun. Silent rounds exploded through the wired glass, as Adam fell behind the desk.

The intruder shook and pounded in frustration. Round after round smacked the outside metal plate. Adam chanced a peek. The machine pistol turned toward him and blew a jar of pencils into shards near his shoulder. Adam looked for an escape. The door behind him showed a sliver of black. He kicked Goodell's rolling chair to draw attention. As rounds followed the dead man, Adam scuttled through the back door and into the cavernous warehouse. A late round ricocheted through the opening and off the concrete floor.

Adam ran into the dark expanse and yelled, "Help! Anybody here?" An echo answered. A fire pull-handle under a large red arrow was only a few feet away. He started, then hesitated. Any emergency responders now would walk into a killing field with the maniac outside.

He ran to several doors, but all were locked. A dozen low pallets of drums and cartons centered on the huge floor. Hiding wasn't possible. He needed to join the fight, or escape to warn security. Huge, single lamps, high in the overhead, buzzed at their low-power setting, giving only a tentative light. Even higher overhead, dark glass reflected the night sky.

He spotted a dispatcher's desk on the farthest wall. With a suddenness he didn't expect, the lights of the huge building's overhead extinguished. His vision dropped to zero. The power had been cut.

Using his mind's memory as his eyes adjusted, he ran across the open space and tripped over the desk. He found the phone by following a cord. No dial tone. If the doors were alarmed and the electricity shut down, he reasoned security would come. Whoever did this had screwed up.

Nowhere to hide. For the moment, the "exit" sign batteries took over and a red glow illuminated at the far end of the building. His eyes adjusted slowly as he ran to the heavy outside doors. A thick chain wound through both bars. "Damn it."

A steel ladder disappeared into the high darkness. He didn't want to make it easy for the killers. Like the hundreds of other Army storage buildings in his recollection, open beams led to skylights of rectangular glass. He could climb out. With his hands outstretched he hurried around the perimeter until his fingers touched the ladder.

He grabbed iron rungs with wet palms and pulled himself off the floor. The climb was quick but not noiseless as his heavy-plodding boots reverberated every step. Before he reached the top, a *ka-oomph* froze him. He knew the sound. The M67 fragmentation grenade. A second, white hot blast blew an office door open and two dark-clad figures ran inside. They swung powerful flashlights. Adam remained motionless. It didn't help.

"There," a voice yelled from the office doors.

One figure broke away and ran to the bottom of the ladder. Adam scrambled for the top of the rungs.

"Kill him." The same voice from across the floor.

The figure below raised his submachine gun. Two quick shots from the shadows slammed the shape into the ladder, sprawling him motionless on the floor.

The other man, thinking Adam was armed, opened up, spraying wide shots into the roof. Rounds impacted the steel beams and flat sheet metal. Rapid fire returned from the dark across the warehouse. Adam watched the second assailant's flashlight fall on the concrete and roll in an arc. The beam stopped on an unmoving black-clad body.

Adam strained his ears to listen as a siren sounded in the distance. With the grace of a dancer or a demon, a shape flowed around an upright twenty feet away. "Come with me, quickly," a voice called across the wide expanse. "Hurry." A female's voice.

He panted breaths. "Who are you?"

"What does it matter? We need to leave quickly."

A kidnapping attempt, people claiming to be his uncle and cousin, and now a dead sergeant. Adam strained to see in the dark and settled his sweating body low on the beam. "I don't think so. First identify yourself."

A small flashlight switched on and found Adam, exposing him. He could do nothing now, and waited for the fatal shot. Instead, the shaft of light rotated to her face as she took off the night vision goggles and balaclava to reveal tightly cut blond hair.

His world rocked. She was familiar, so familiar. "Hurry," she said. "I can explain, but you must hurry. We don't have any time. Security's on the way."

At the same moment, the far double steel doors banged against the wall as men poured into the warehouse below. Adam looked back, but the space was empty. The overhead light clanked and began to power up.

"Spread out! Spread out, goddamn it!" a man's voice ordered.

Sweat ran down into Adam's eyes. He remained still, confused, trying to sort conflicting images.

"Two down, sir," a soldier yelled. "They're dead."

Men called at one another, boots clomped around the floor.

Adam made a decision, took several gulps of air and swung himself out, holding the lower edge of the support. "Up here!" he yelled.

The glass window above him screamed with a rusted hinge. The killer was escaping.

"In the rafters. Overhead!" Adam said to the men below. "Help me. The killer's up here."

"I see him, Lieutenant!" a voice shouted. A shot impacted high above Adam's head. Dust motes fell into the light as Adam scurried back atop the steel beam.

"Hold your fire, goddamn it. No shooting until I say so. You up there, show yourself."

Adam remained still as a flashlight beam traced the dark. The warehouse lights would take a minute to become full strength.

"Show yourself or we start shooting. That was your last warning."

"Wait," said Adam, pushing himself up and sitting with his legs crossed under the beam. "I'm here."

"I see him, sir!"

"No shooting, goddamn it."

Adam yelled, "Don't let her escape. She's on the roof."

"Come on down here," said the man.

"I'm a major, and I'm giving you a direct order to get people on the outside. Now."

"Sir? This is the military police, and I don't give a shit who you say you are. Come down or I tell this private to shoot you."

Adam knew the soldier shouldn't trust him. In quick moments, he worked backward and down the rungs, knowing all weapons were centered on his back.

The sweat-streaked lieutenant looked at Adam's embroidered gold oak leaves and offered a salute. "Sir. We've been in a firefight with I don't know who. These two are dead. Are you sure you saw someone up there?"

"Affirmative," said Adam. "Get people outside. Make a perimeter at least one block around. It was a woman with blond hair."

"A woman?" The lieutenant scrunched his face. "Could I see

97

your ID? This has been a hell of a night. I already lost a man, and I'm not losing anyone else. And, there's some dead GI in there."

"Who are you?" asked Adam while he pulled his wallet from a pocket and offered the chip-encoded plastic.

"Second Lieutenant Jared Graham, sir. I'm security OIC for the compound, but I only got here last week. Jesus, I just got out of OCS."

"Sir?" A breathless private ran up to the group. "Hanson and Kowalski climbed the outside fire escape. Zilch."

"Okay," said Adam. Both young soldiers saw blood smeared on Adam's tunic. "Yeah, I found him. Sergeant Patrick Goodell. He's a Bronze Star recipient and a hell of a guy. He's also married ...." The sudden realization chilled him, stealing his breath. He might not have recognized Janice on the street, and even now, he wasn't completely sure. But the resemblance ...

"Are you okay, Major?" asked the lieutenant.

Adam shook the image away. "Let's get our people in place, Graham."

Janice Goodell. A look-alike maybe. Patrick and Janice wanted kids. They attended a party together before Adam's divorce. His mind jumbled facts and fantasy.

"Sir?" Adam looked over at the lieutenant, wide-eyed and young. "I'd like to call Fort Dix and have reinforcements sent. I'm pretty sure CID needs to process this whole thing. And, maybe you too."

Adam considered Graham's position for a moment. "You're right, Lieutenant. You need to hold me for CID. You also need to get your butt in gear, and do what I've just told you."

"Yes, sir." He turned to a sergeant. "Call the MP shack...."

As the pickup drove to the security office, Adam wondered if mentioning such a thing would mean even more misery for the widow. The blond woman shot and killed the two men who likely killed Goodell. Janice supplemented a sergeant's salary as a low-ranking manager at Treasury. No way she would dress like a ninja and be an expert marksman. Nothing made sense. He settled on giving a description and keeping speculation to himself.

Several persons from alphabet agencies, and the local police chief, interrogated him. Most questions repeated earlier ones. When

Adam recognized a criminal investigation man from an interview that morning, he stood. "I don't want to be impolite, Agent, but I'm done for now. I need to grab some sleep."

"Just a couple more questions, Major." The agent scratched at a pad poised on a lanky knee.

"Nope, we're done. Really. You can't possibly ask anything not already asked and answered." Adam stretched out his arms taking in a giant lungful of air. The evidence team already seized his blood-spattered uniform shirt and pants. Now he wore a brown pullover sweater and a sweat-suit bottom. They also took his boots, and left him with a pair of incongruous dress shoes. Adam pointed at the man's tablet recorder. "You guys put your notes together while I catch a snooze. After that, we can have another go. What'd you think?"

"I'm not sure I can authorize you to end this interview."

"I'm not asking for permission and I don't want to be a jerk, but I'm telling you what's going to happen for the next couple of hours." The man didn't move. "Look. You don't see a lawyer in the room because I haven't exercised my rights. I'm trying to give you everything I know so you can catch these bastards, but I haven't slept and I'm beat. I need to close my eyes."

The agent snapped his notebook closed and clicked off the iPad. He stood as well. "Okay. You have a visitor before you head off to bed. By the way, you forfeited your rights to a lawyer when you accepted your security clearance. So don't try and pull your civilian crap on me."

Adam accepted the rebuke. "Yes, sir. Who is it?"

"Lawyer," said the agent with a smile.

"Military lawyer?"

The man shook his head as he grabbed the doorknob. "Not military, family. You have the right to a visitor, Major. Don't forget the security agreement you signed." The agent pulled the door, but stopped again. "I'm sorry about Sergeant Goodell. You've lost a man and that's tough. But, this is the way we do things, tried and true even though I've never figured out who this is harder on, you or me."

"I appreciate it. It's not my first rodeo, either."

The man nodded and left.

Wearing dark pinstripes, Martino Callaway looked up from a

plastic chair. Opposite him sat an armed soldier.

"Thanks for coming," Adam said, extending his hand. "How did you know?"

Marty gripped Adam's shoulder and closed the door behind him. The family lawyer withdrew his iPhone in silence. As always, he dressed with sharp creases and a perfect tie. After a moment, the app turned from amber to green. Marty switched off the phone and placed it back into his briefcase. "We're good."

Adam shook his head. "This is the US Army, Marty. Not the gulag."

"How are you holding up?" Marty asked, ignoring the remark. "Your grandfather called me when he heard a rumor. Why didn't you call me directly? You know better."

Adam knew he'd disappointed an important person in his life, possibly two. "I'm not a suspect, just a witness. I didn't want to hold things up. These guys need to be caught."

"Witness today, suspect tomorrow, Adam. You should've called me. That's why your grandfather keeps me employed."

"You're family, for Christ's sake."

"All the more reason," Marty said, standing and pulling a curtain aside from the steel-reinforced glass. He let the cloth drop as a diesel truck rumbled down the street outside. "I read a report you filed a few weeks ago about an assault in DC. You didn't think to let me know about that, either?"

"Sorry. It's been hectic."

Marty glanced at him. "Uh-huh. You might want to keep it to yourself and let me brief Julius. He'll be disappointed, but of course that's up to you. You being all grown up and everything. Making all your own decisions. Doing a fine job of running your life." The sarcasm confirmed his disapproval.

"Geezus, Marty. You're right, I'm wrong. Things seem to be moving a little faster than I'm handling."

The lawyer nodded and took his seat. "I agree things are moving fast. The problem is the Army just confirmed this as a thwarted terrorist attack. For some reason, your sergeant is at the center."

Adam considered the woman in the warehouse, her

resemblance to Janice Goodell, and his near acquiescence. Was she saving him or luring him?

"Okay," Marty said, opening his suit jacket and leaning back. "I think it's time you tell me what you told them, and, what you didn't tell them. You're going to be out of the Army soon, and if you haven't figured this out yet, they will use you like an old dishrag and throw you away. Time to start getting smart about protecting yourself. Start from when you left DC. Every word, every detail. Don't leave anything out. And that includes Miranda Cinclaire."

Adam smiled for the first time that morning. "Why am I not surprised?"

Marty didn't return the gesture and took a magazine from his briefcase. "'*Hollywood Glitz* names Top 10 Most Beautiful Women.'" Miranda's picture displayed prominently among them. He flipped to a dog-eared page where a paparazzi's photo showed Adam receiving a kiss from the lovely Miranda. The title read, "New Bad Boy Beau?" The article dredged up Adam's failures as a teenager and a soldier. "You've pissed off a lot of people in the last fifteen years, Adam. They're still out there gunning for you and your grandfather. You need some backup."

"Okay," said Adam, dropping into the chair and beginning another recitation. This time, he left nothing out.

Chapter 14

A dream-ridden sleep overtook a tired body. He was back in Afghanistan, except now Patrick Goodell replaced PFC Hollingsworth, first man wounded in the attack. In the dream, Goodell stood atop the burning Humvee, being torn apart with machine gun fire. His legs were the first to go. No matter what Adam did, Goodell's body ripped into parts that Adam ran around trying to gather up.

When he rolled over, the sun topped the houses and trees to the east. He drank from the motel room's sink, stripped and dressed in the sweats and his dress shoes. A gray sky and falling mist were perfect, and he needed a run. Pounding morning commuter traffic and the hiss of wet tires disappeared as he found peace along the busy roadway, plodding in the uncomfortable shoes. An hour later he stood in a shower with steam filling the bathroom. For many minutes his body remained, letting the images of a life spent in a single night sluice down the drain. Goodell's death mask joined the others he stored from those lost over the years of his short life.

The hotel's mini bar offered canned orange juice. He drank both and filled an empty with water, and drained that one, too. Calling Katherine was out of the question and Julie didn't need adult drama. He thought about dialing Miranda's apartment just as a knock at the door stopped him.

"You awake?" was the call from outside. "It's Brad Benchley." Adam was still barefoot in his shorts as he pulled open the door, grinning and happy to see his superior officer. "Casual dress today, Major?" Brad held out the overnight bag the MP's seized yesterday with a fresh shirt, blazer, and slacks from his apartment in Virginia. This was not a good sign. "Tell me what happened."

Fifteen minutes later, Brad shook his head. "That's a hell of a tale."

"Yes, sir." Adam adjusted the knot in his tie. "The entire episode is like a dream, except Sergeant Goodell is dead."

Brad leaned back on the small settee, his face grim. "I need you to undergo a clearance evaluation with the National Security

Commission. Upgrade the one you've already got. It won't take too long." Adam started to protest, but Brad held up a hand. "After you're cleared, you have orders to proceed to the Indron laboratory in Denver, special assignment."

Adam blinked his confusion. "I'm not sure the NSC will give me a pass. The grilling over the last two days …"

"Cleared you. They were hard on you, because I told them to be hard."

"What for?" Adam held back an irritation that threatened.

"You needed to be clear of any suspicion. Captain Rodriguez will handle my … your office."

Adam sat on the bed across from him. "I'm not sure I understand, Colonel. What's going on?"

"Others will brief you. I'm just the messenger." Brad dug for a candy lemon drop in his coat. Adam accepted one. "The base commander told me these guys were terrorists. Do you think they were the same creeps from DC?"

"Somehow, I don't think so. DC made me feel like we were dealing with the Keystone Cops. These guys were, well, vicious, and they wanted to kill me. They killed Patrick."

"Yeah. DC was like something was thrown together at the last minute."

"I agree with you there." Adam pulled over a wood desk chair and sat facing Brad. "I've worked this through my mind a hundred ways. There were two groups in the warehouse. One chased me in and ended up dead. The other was a gal trying to save me." He paused. The warning from the agent about his security clearance came back to him.

Brad watched him for a moment, then looked away. "I'm going to miss you, Adam."

The non sequitur was typical when his friend didn't want to talk or hear about something. Brad always played the consummate politician.

"What am I doing in Colorado?" Adam asked, and leaned back.

The other man brightened. "You're going as a new hire. Recently released from the Army, you play yourself. Rhodes Scholar, PhD, inventor of the command module protocol, all of it. General Miller gave me an overview of the plan. You'll be hired at Indron short term. Miller will build you a cover at NATO. On paper, you're just doing my old job. By the time the cyber highway figures this out, you'll be done. He thinks maybe two months. Are you up for it?"

"I don't understand the NATO part."

"General Miller has several months of reports on a portable drive he'll claim are from you. They're logistics, schedules, shipping and receiving. All the things I did when you went to Dix and I fawned at the feet of our allies over the screwed command module."

"Sorry about that, sir."

"Forget it," Brad said with a laugh. "You'll be working your ass off. You need to keep your eyes and ears open. Find out why the delays and the excuses on the upgraded JSAM guidance system. You invented it, Adam. This should be a walk in the park."

"Why isn't the plant's liaison doing this? He's in a better position than me."

"Come on, you're missing the point. You're out of the Army as soon as you get back to Dix, today. You knew, right?" Adam didn't, and remained quiet, his face a mask. "You check out and turn in your ID. This blazer is your uniform now. You're a new hire, and only a limited number of people know your true identity."

"You're talking undercover? Like in the movies?"

Brad shrugged. "I suppose, but you don't change your name or anything. Only the company CEO will know what you're really doing there. Do we have a problem?"

Adam took a deep breath. "No, I guess not. When you say out of the Army ... I'm really out of the Army?" Sometimes decisions made by others resolved unsolvable conflicts.

"The bureaucracy won't let it work any other way. And oh, by the way. You haven't signed and returned your promotion agreement, have you?"

"No, sir."

"Something you want to explain?" asked Brad. "A lot of my personal capital went into making those lieutenant colonel leaves happen."

"I know, sir. Thank you." Adam didn't want to talk about his doubts and the family pressures. "Just procrastination, I guess. This makes it easier though, doesn't it?"

Brad pulled the agreement from his own briefcase. "Not really. Here's a copy. Sign it, date it last week, and I'll take care of it."

Events moved quickly, but if Adam was out of the Army in a few hours, what would it matter? He scribbled two signatures and handed back the sheets. "How's this going to work?"

"The documents will be walked through the records in St. Louis. We have our person there who'll make certain the right paper ends up in the right folder. If you still want, after Indron, you can have your rank and a new duty station. Although I have no flipping idea why. Ten more years of this crap?" He shrugged. "But to each his own. We've got you covered."

Adam thought about his orders. "Who's 'we'?"

"I don't have the answers. I'll be working for Keith Miller for a couple more days. Then, I'll be the junior congressman from Georgia on the Armed Services Committee."

"Congratulations. That's great."

"Right, thanks. It's good to have friends in high places, Adam. Get this job done right, and you and I will stay in touch."

Adam knew what Brad meant. "I understand, sir."

"Good." Congressman-select Brad Benchley stood and walked to the door. "Make certain you get a pass from the NSC. You're out of the Army today. Don't screw it up with loose talk. Stick to the facts. Nothing new in your story." Brad's eyes locked with Adam's.

"Yes, sir."

"One last thing. There's a rental SUV in the parking lot. We already bought an airline ticket in your name to London out of JFK. Captain Rodriguez gets a promotion to gold major's leaves and will use the ticket. No use having the country's supercomputer going crazy with you being you in the States and in England at the same time. He's dark like you … sort of, maybe," Brad hurried on. "You drive to Colorado. You've got new credit cards in the glove box. Your name is the same of course, but different financial history, social security number, backup, etcetera. Someone tracing the accounts will take some time catching on. That's what the US Marshalls tell me anyway. They're the ones covering your cyber identity. Oh, yeah, there's cash, too." Adam nodded. "Let Katherine know you're off to NATO. No one else gets a phone call, including Miranda."

Brad tightened the strap on his overcoat while sleet ticked off the window glass. "If you don't like the weather in New Jersey, give it a minute, and it'll change." He turned to Adam. "There're a lot of people counting on you. I've convinced some very influential ones you're up to the task. Don't let me down."

* * *

Adam found the Ford Edge at the curb with keys in the headliner. He decided Brad needed a quick course in the real world. Two hours later, he left Fort Dix with separation orders in his hand. A pang of abandonment confused him as he unlocked the motel room door and hung up his sport coat.

When his NSC contact failed to show, he drove to McDonald's. With a cheeseburger and Coke he sat at a plastic table, comfortable with strangers, and watched kids, recalling Julie at that age. Katherine still found him interesting then, and she hadn't yet begun the interminable campaigns for her father's reelection. The Hatch Act gave Adam enough excuse to stay away, although he would have anyway. He disliked politics and preening for votes. Once, he posed for pictures in uniform with her family and the vice president.

Near the end of the last campaign, she admitted to having an affair with a White House staffer. Probably not her first, as he later came to find out. He was blood angry and moved to a hotel for two weeks. Deployment was less than a month away and for a time, he raged until depression slowed him. He called Marty who offered evidence her infidelity was most likely opportunity and alcohol. One of the few mistakes his friend ever made, but such was the power of office to hide proof until the change of administration. He and Katherine reconciled. Afghanistan was a convenient excuse to let wounds heal, except his world crashed first.

When he unlocked the door to his motel suite, a slight man sat at the room's desk. "Who the hell are you?" said Adam, gripping the door and poised to make a quick retreat.

"Leonard Simmons," answered the man in a pleasant, nasal voice. "National Security Commission. May I ask where you have been?"

"You may ask anything you like." Adam stepped in and removed his jacket.

106

The man held out credentials. "Now, I'd like to see your ID."

Adam reached for his wallet. "Will a driver's license work? It's all I've got until the paperwork catches up."

A short man, Simmons's physical presence suffered from ill-chosen clothes. But this didn't matter, because Adam had seen him before and knew the power he wielded with just a nod of the head.

"Why didn't you introduce yourself at the *Morning Dawn*'s briefing, Agent Simmons?"

The man looked up and reset small round glasses on his nose. "What would it have mattered, Colonel? I was only there to observe."

Both knew that was a lie. They exchanged identity cards.

Adam handed Simmons's back. "It's Major, Agent Simmons. So, what happens now?"

In response, the agent repeated the original question.

"McDonald's. I got hungry."

"Did you meet anyone there?" The agent's eyes didn't blink.

"Thirty of my closest friends. We all had Big Macs." Sarcasm was lost on the man, so after a moment, Adam said, "I met no one."

"I've been asked to complete the interview confirming your security clearance." Simmons withdrew a small stack of papers. "You've been through this before."

"Yes, but isn't this a comedown? I mean you were in the war room and privy to all sorts of secrets. This is just a clearance investigation."

Simmons watched Adam take the top off a cardboard container of coffee. "There's another cup in the bathroom," he said. "Would you like to share?"

The man eyed the coffee and started to shake his head.

"I'll get the cup." In a moment, both blew across the top of Styrofoam.

Simmons took the extra creamer. "I like their coffee, and it's been a long day. Thanks."

"Sure. No big deal."

For the next hour, Adam handled the agent's questions until the issue of liaisons surfaced. "Look, Agent Simmons. I've seen this woman a few times now. We're certainly friendly, but that's a long way away from a relationship."

The NSC agent took off his rimless glasses, extracted a cloth, and polished the lens. "I sympathize, Major Michaels. You must realize for a civilian Top Secret clearance with special access, I need to ask specific questions about her."

"Okay. Her name is Miranda Cinclaire."

"The actress?"

"That's her."

"Really?" said Simmons. "I'm having a bit of trouble believing an ex-jock like you knows someone like her."

"Miranda Cinclaire," Adam said again, a smile working at the corners of his mouth.

Simmons sighed. "Please, Major. It's late and I'd like to get out of here and see my first grader before I have to pay his college tuition."

"Call the colonel, Agent. I'll step out for a breath of air."

He walked into the parking lot and tossed the dregs of his coffee. "Spooks," he said with a grin.

The reflected city lights dulled any chance to appreciate the night. The air chilled him but in a minute, the door opened.

"I'm sorry to doubt your truthfulness. I thought you were just pulling my leg."

Adam walked back into the room and sat down. "That's not the way I follow orders. Do you?"

Simmons sat opposite. "No sir, it isn't." He took out his iPad and started recording again.

Chapter 15

The morning's frantic interstate festivities skewered any hopes of a quick transit as he approached Baltimore. He'd left early in the morning after sitting for three more days in the motel. As the sun rose in deep, gray overcast, he pulled into the Alexandria parking lot. The Corolla sat, encrusted with melting snow grayed and piled against its fenders. He made coffee and ate toast and the last eggs in the refrigerator. The rest disappeared into garbage bags he tossed into the Dumpster. He scrubbed the refrigerator, the sinks, and bathrooms. The dishwasher churned to life as he inspected the work and turned to the bedroom to pack suitcases. A knock sounded at the door, stopping him.

He smiled when saw his visitor through the curtain, until he saw Brad's grim face. "Hi, Colonel. What's going on?"

"Geezus, Adam. What are you doing here? I specifically told you to head for Denver after the NSC briefed you. I was under the impression you understood."

Surprised, Adam stepped back and let him enter. "I am on my way to Denver. Agent Simmons came and left. I waited for a call but didn't think re-buying my wardrobe was part of the deal."

"You need to get the hell out of here. You're supposed to be sleeping off an Atlantic crossing in a London hotel. Do you know what strings I had to pull in the last two days?" Brad didn't wait for an answer and held out two manila envelopes. A Veterans Department return address appeared on one. "These were going to be couriered to you in Denver. As long as you're here, read the top one first." He stepped in and tossed his overcoat on the chair, saw the coffeepot and found a cup.

Adam shook out the papers. He finished the second paragraph *… medically unfit for duty*. "This is a sham, right? Like an undercover story."

Brad's anger, always a quick thing, already calmed. "It's more of a change of plans."

"Change of plans?" Adam didn't believe for a minute the US Army could change plans and paperwork in a couple of days.

Brad moved the hang-up bag and sat. "You would've known if you had followed orders and stayed in Jersey. The NSC are the ones who called me."

"Come on, Brad. I own a mobile phone and I waited for nearly three days. You didn't answer my calls and didn't return messages."

"I'm on terminal leave, buddy. The Army took back their iPhone and I haven't bought another. Your pink ID is in the envelope."

"I resigned, not retired, right? Pink is for retired. Maybe I don't understand."

"Read on."

Adam noticed the Congressional lapel pin on Brad's suit coat. "Whoa, look at that. I guess congratulations are in order." He walked over and extended his hand.

Brad brought up an easy politician's smile. "Yeah, thanks. It's been a wild week for you *and* me." He paused. "Look, I didn't mean to get all over you. I was supposed to head for Atlanta this morning when I heard you'd left the New Jersey motel."

"I was being watched?"

"And followed, yeah. Security. Did you forget about the terrorists that have fallen in love with you? I had to cancel some pretty important meetings to get here this morning. Goodell's death really screwed everything up."

Brad's churlish tone irritated Adam. "I'm sure he didn't mean to."

Brad looked up, stunned, not realizing the impact of his words. "Ah Christ. Sorry. I'm going to have to learn not to stick my foot in my mouth. He was a good guy and I didn't mean anything."

Adam sat down. "Me, too. How's this going to work?"

"Thanksgiving's going to screw up this week...."

"I forgot about Rodriguez," Adam said. "He's married with kids." He watched his former boss. "What can we do?"

Brad's impatience strummed through his tapping fingers. "I'll get him on the embassy flight out of Lisbon." He eyed Adam. "But only for the weekend, okay? He's got to be there for Thursday and Friday. The Frenchies don't give a shit about our holidays."

Adam didn't think he could push it further. "That's great, Brad. I know he'll appreciate it."

"Miller's going to have my ass."

"Ah, he's a pussycat, right?"

Brad rolled his eyes and laughed. "Okay. You got me. Here's the deal, Rodriguez will remote in the reports and keep the processes moving for the next month or so. Three weeks after is Christmas and the western world shuts down. You see why you need to get to Colorado?"

"Wait. I'd like to have my Thanksgiving, too."

Brad shook his head. "That's gone, I'm afraid. National security. You're supposed to be in Europe, remember?"

"Yeah, but I still don't see just what the hell we're doing. This is a lot of hubbub about just a little rocket system. There's something else going on. What is it?"

Brad stared at the floor. "There *is* something going on, buddy, but I don't know what it is. I'd be willing to bet there's not ten people in Washington who do, and they're keeping it quiet." He looked up. "I only know your part is one hell of a lot more important than mine. There's a reason why my nomination was pushed through without a fight. There's a reason why suddenly everyone suspended all the rules and got you and me the hell out of the service. I just don't know why, and it's scaring the crap out of me. I don't know what they want from us."

Adam rose and poured him the last of the coffee. He splashed water into the pot and set it upside-down in the sink. "Okay, I believe you. I'd like to call Julie. How can we do it?"

"That I can do. We'll have your cell routed through the Pentagon and Gravesend, England. It's the only way to prove to anyone listening you're in Europe. For now though, you got to get on the road and a few hours under your belt." Brad indicated the big envelope. "My personal contact information is in there including the number to my dad's farm. I'll be using that as a base of operations for the campaign … and for anything else that might come up." Both men's eyes met. "There's also a travel advance in there. A little cash but a much bigger cashier's check. Be careful with it."

"Okay, but you don't need to give me money."

"It's not mine, Adam. That comes from … well, it comes from a pot with no strings."

Adam thought he was joking. "No one gives anyone in DC anything without strings."

Brad gave him an odd look. "Everybody's also got an opinion in DC, and you might want to keep that one to yourself."

"Didn't mean to offend. Our family's been around politics for a long time. I'm jaded." Adam tossed the big envelope onto the countertop.

Brad rose and rinsed out his cup. "Use cash, don't write checks. Don't use your personal credit cards. Only the ones in the glove box are backstopped. Don't make contact with anyone not cleared by Simmons."

Adam nodded. "Okay."

Brad pointed at the second, smaller envelope from the VA. "Read and then give it back to me. Reseal it. They've already spoken with Katherine."

"Someone talked with my ex-wife about this?" Adam felt his pique rising again.

"Only to make it easier for you, buddy. In case of an emergency, they wanted her to know why you're in England."

"Okay, but Julie is with me over Christmas."

"Not this year. You're under orders."

"Bullshit. I'm a civilian now, Brad. She can come with me to Denver. We'll have a ball."

Brad shook his head. "You'll be a civilian in Fort Leavenworth if you screw around."

Adam sighed, exasperated.

"Your country needs you to get to Indron. Take some time to read your orders— I mean, instructions."

Adam said, "I got that, but you should know this is half-assed. Something else is going on. Why can't you just tell me?"

Brad flushed with anger. "Because I don't fucking know. I'm out of the Air Force without my star, and I'm following orders just like you. I don't like being a pawn, so neither one of us are very happy, are we? I mean, I like being fast-tracked into Congress and all, but I'd like to know why." He paused and calmed himself. "You got your promotion, and I didn't get mine. So that's life, right? Just do what you're told, Adam. If this gets out, I'm screwed in the fall election

112

anyway. But frankly, I think the stakes are bigger than me."

"Well, that's mighty American of you, but if you don't know what's going on, who the hell does?" Adam felt himself digging in. "I want to know who's running this screwed-up deal."

Brad dropped his shoulders, and smiled. He'd witnessed Adam's stubborn determination, the same drive that made the younger man such a fighter. The same tenacity that allowed twenty to hold off a hundred and fifty in a forgotten gully on a lonely road in Afghanistan. Brad wanted no part of the argument.

"Okay, you're right. I told him this wasn't gonna work. You can talk to the man himself." He opened the door and nodded toward the parking lot and two black Chevrolet Suburbans. "You want a better explanation? I think you're going to get one."

Keith Miller filled the doorway. The general turned to Brad. "I've got this, Congressman. Head to Georgia and win in the fall. Have a nice life."

Brad sucked in a ragged breath. "That's all I wanted in the first place."

Miller's grin didn't engender friendliness. "Sure thing. I'll be looking forward to working with you."

Brad stuck his hand out to Adam. "See you around. I'd say, stay in touch, but ... well, anyway." He walked into the misting day.

Adam stared at the closed door.

"All right, Michaels, let's get this done. I'm pretty busy. You're not the only game in town." Miller sat on the couch and began. "What you need to know is in the second envelope. What you'd like to know is in my head. Grab a chair."

Adam picked up the small envelope and a pen, and sat.

"No notes. I'm going to mix facts with speculation here," Miller said. "We believe Sergeant Goodell was killed by a terrorist organization called Rahim Tajalli, named after the leader of the group. We don't have much intelligence except they probably stole the brains out of one of our early JSAMs. You heard their name in the war room briefing."

"Yes, sir, but you mean lost at sea."

"No. The ISIS commander said, stolen. As in, fool the shit out of the Yankee devils. All this time, we were thinking the secret was

113

safe at the bottom of the ocean. Hell, we even have the GOES satellite sitting there watching the graveyard for us so no one steals the body."

"After all this time, graphene is mush, sir. This is a wasted effort."

"But it looks good on paper, and to anyone watching, right?" said Miller.

Adam understood. "I see. Whoever did this won't know we're on to them."

"And they said you weren't a quick study."

Miller's sarcasm stung many, but Adam took no offense. "The replacement doesn't work, General. Why are we sending it to Israel? It's a boat anchor, no pun intended. It's gotta be fixed."

"Right, and that's your job. Go and figure this out."

"I think the Israelis already know second generation doesn't work." Adam didn't want to expose Tom Connecelli. "They're tear-ass. They're already conducting research without our government's consent."

Miller raised his eyebrows. "Where are you getting your information, Colonel?"

"Just putting two and two together, sir."

Miller searched Adam's face for a moment, then continued. "We've got bigger problems than pissing off Israel. Thirty years ago, Professor Rahim Tajalli disappeared from the Al Ahlia University in Palestine. He was the teenaged physicist genius having visions, who then murdered a half-dozen of his colleagues and disappeared. He showed up in Iran a week after the Shah got kicked out. A few days later, students took over the embassy, and he drops off the grid again...."

"Only to pop up in Pakistan," said Adam.

"Very good, Michaels. Suddenly, this guy is in the Pakistani university system—"

"Doing crystalline copper-to-graphene grafting research. I've read Tajalli's papers. Studied them. He's brilliant but makes giant leaps of logic that's all over the map. Commander Connecelli used to talk about his work all the time. The temperatures he claimed to reach would destroy the atom-thick graphene sheets. He was ham-handed and used medieval mysticism when scientific logic failed him."

114

Miller settled back, impressed. "You overcame the problem."

"Yes, sir, but we approached the issue a different way using bioorganic compounds, not chemical ones."

Miller screwed his eyebrows together and opened both palms. Adam said, "What I mean sir, is our calculations were based on carbon organic materials. Rahim Tajalli used isotopic compounds. He was hardheaded because I'm sure he's read our PhD thesis. We proved it could be done and higher temperatures weren't required. Sheila ... Dr. Perez built the little creatures and Commander Connecelli filled in the blanks. Engineers, not scientists, solved the production problems."

"Like Indron," said Miller.

"Yes, sir. If my job is to find out why the second generation is screwed up, you don't need all this cloak-and-dagger. They're on a defense contract. Pull the reports. I'll review them from here. I was an engineer first, so maybe then we can all get on with our lives."

Miller reddened. "God, I wish I had your view of the frickin world. It's not that simple. Don't underestimate what we've got going here, Michaels. I'm not your stuffed suit. All you know is the background, so now, are you ready to hear what our overpaid think tank believes?"

No one could put someone in their place like Miller. "Yes, sir. Sorry."

Miller waved with impatience. "Benchley isn't cleared for this information. Very few people are, and most only know a piece. Like me. Understand?" Adam nodded. "You're aware several years ago, the European Space Agency, the French, sent a robot to capture an asteroid."

"I was in Afghanistan, but it made the rounds with some of the Frenchies at Bagram. They talked about NASA's mission getting hosed up with budget cuts."

Miller nodded. "You're probably aware at the same time, the administration was pumping a trillion dollars into bailouts—autos, steel, even green goddamn solar cells."

"I only remember we were low on critical supplies and spares. Companies that screw up shouldn't be bailed out. That's not how this country works."

Miller shrugged. "Whatever. The point is the French tossed

115

together a shot using US, European, and God forbid, NATO pieces and parts. The administration jumped at it. Swords into plowshares, that sort of bullshit. In a couple of months, we had an entirely new space policy, cancelled the Constellation program, and cheered the Europeans and Russians. The Russian Baikonur Cosmodrome launch facility sent the robot up. The world hailed the mission as the first true international deep space adventure coming together. We couldn't stop slapping each other's back. Then, we all promptly forgot about it and got back to screwing each other."

"I'm not sorry I missed it," Adam said. "But what does that have to do with me going to Denver?"

Miller rocked back and stood. "That was then, this is now. A couple of years after the launch, the robotic probe fired a rocket and veered off course."

"Really?" Adam said. "Who commanded the firing?"

"Good question, Michaels. The primary navigation system was taken offline. The secondary guidance system's brain is your command module."

"You're joking."

Miller rubbed his bristled head in the quiet room. "Wish I was." He walked to the glass and watched the world dormant for the season. "The Russians said it wasn't them. The French and Germans blamed one another. NASA even went to the command center in Russia and analyzed all the communications. No one gave the order from there. The NSA reported no radio signals went to the spacecraft from Russia, or anywhere else on the planet. Leo Simmons's NSC and the FBI investigated and came up with nothing. Almost."

"Almost?" Adam asked.

"One of the original launch engineers is from Kazakhstan. He was on the team that orbited the Pakistani satellite around the moon."

Adam shrugged. "Not every Muslim wants to see us dead, sir."

Miller harrumphed. "That might be true, but hold onto the thought. This Muslim went missing. A week after the launch, he's gone. Smoky tennis shoes. The Russians never saw fit to let us know someone left town. Didn't show up for work at the height of the world's accolades. They wouldn't give us anything until the FBI got involved and the administration threatened their oil sales."

"Money talks," Adam said. "This guy wouldn't bear a resemblance to Rahim Tajalli, would he? He'd be in his sixties now."

"Very good," said Miller. "I knew you were bright. A lot of documents walked when he left."

Adam nodded. "That's why you think an answer might be at Indron, the only mass-production facility in the world for graphene."

"Right."

"That's great, but why me? I'm not a spy or a spook."

"Because you invented it, Michaels. And I'm one of the few people around here who knows your background. And your ethnicity."

Adam's face darkened, and his voice vibrated. "I'm a soldier, or, I was."

"Control yourself, goddamn it. If I thought for a minute you were anything but a patriot, I would've ordered that ass-kissing Benchley to kick your butt out of the military a long time before this. I want you to think about a NATO missile guidance system we just couldn't wait to give to our wonderful allies, so they could send a Russian Proton rocket to catch a baby asteroid." He paused and looked around. "Starting to make sense to you?"

"A little."

"Now the goddamn thing is off course and the US is pissed at the Europeans, who are accusing Russia's Putin of shenanigans. They say, 'Nyet,' of course. The robot is supposed to be on a collision course with Eros, some great big goddamn asteroid that's a couple of miles in diameter. This is not the mini rock NASA wanted to put around our moon. The CIA has a dozen opinions." He laughed without humor. "My favorite is that the Europeans secretly wanted to land boosters on that big-ass comet and put it into orbit around the earth. This comes from the same group who fifty years ago gave Castro exploding cigars."

Adam's brain didn't hear the last remark and instead, kicked into research engineer mode, trying to figure how such a thing might be possible.

Miller slammed his fist into a hand and Adam looked up. "Two moons? Jesus Christ, who thinks this shit up? Just because we can do it or think we can, doesn't mean we should." He took a deep breath. "If something went haywire ... Now Michaels, I want you to think like the dickheads who are doing this. Can you figure out why all of a sudden everybody's scared shitless and trying to get to you?"

Adam already knew. Things were making sense. "Because they're afraid that ... that the someone who built it, might also be able to figure out how to stop it, and their mission fails."

"Bingo."

Adam shook his head. "Someone in our government that's thinking I can figure out an answer is just about as crazy as the idiot sending me to Indron because of a ten-year-old PhD dissertation."

Miller's impatience seeped through. "Don't spoil my good thoughts about you, son. I've got to have somebody who knows this system and can tell me what the hell's going on. The bozos in Homeland Defense don't want to talk to me, and *they* won't talk to the FBI. I want some goddamn answers, because I don't need any more goddamn questions."

Chapter 16

The icon on his mobile showed four messages. Because of security at Indron, the phone didn't accompany him inside the plant. His second week of orientation classes discussed safety and worker benefits, and factory protocol of little use to him. Because the rules wouldn't allow use of the phone while driving, he waited for a bourbon at home with the daylight gone.

He listened to his messages and swirled the ice cubes. "Daddy? Mom said on Friday night, I have to go with her and Eric to the Kennedy Center for a concert. On Saturday Lorrie Peters is going to have a slumber party and it starts at four. We can still go to the Smithsonian if you want, but can Lorrie and Jessica come, too? Call me." Julie's recorded voice paused and then she recited the home phone number.

He sighed, troubled that a number as familiar as his own name should be read as if he would not remember. She was asleep now. He drank, angry at the silly Denver posting. What could he do? He didn't even know how to report back if he found anything.

Julie could go to the slumber party, of course. He would accept the invitation for Saturday night, and called McCaffrey Dispatch to cancel the company jet.

As he sat in the darkened room, two men tossed a football on the frozen lawn across the street. A couple of inches of old snow had them slipping and laughing as they ran looping, uninspired patterns. Sometimes they kicked the ball, or tossed using two hands over their heads. Adam gave them points for enthusiasm while new snow swirled under the amber streetlights. For a fleeting moment he considered joining them, thinking he could use the exercise after sitting all week in a classroom.

When the ball was thrown long and bounced over the stone pathway, the young men disappeared. Adam topped his drink with a final inch of Wild Turkey and headed to the small shower off his bedroom. He stripped and stepped into hot water, not bothering with the wall switches. The reflected light of the apartment grounds gave him enough.

Dressed in sweatpants and a T-shirt, he retrieved the bourbon as the furnace clicked on. The Denver nights certainly grew colder faster than Virginia. He left the television off and settled onto the stiff rental couch. He was still two hours lagged from so many years on the East Coast. Maybe get up early and go for a run if the snow wasn't too deep?

Time drifted with fanciful plans intermingled with sips of the liquor. Maybe he could take a midlevel manager's job someplace like Pascagoula or Bridgeport. China was a thought. He'd spent time in Shanghai, a city of over twenty-five million people and home to one of McCaffrey's biggest shipyards. He thought about his old friend, Kim Jaegwon in Busan, Korea and the wild internship during his junior year at college. He couldn't forget about the broken arm aboard a coastal cargo vessel when the ship's woman doctor made them put into port at Gunsan and take Adam off. The embarrassment of having to answer to his grandfather for the screw-up would have put a damper on the rest of the summer, except for Kim. They became fast companions on the dockyards and the nightlife. Now Kim was the senior regional vice president for eastern operations, and Adam didn't want to impose on their friendship. Besides, Korean cold winters and hot summers reminded him of a war in another far-off land. He needed to quit avoiding the inevitable conversation and talk with Julius, without violating one of the government's silly rules.

With a suddenness that rippled the liquor, Adam sat upright. When invited by the soldiers, men and boys in Afghanistan played the same uncoordinated football. The world learned soccer, round balls, not football with pointed pigskin. Round balls bounced with predictability. These men floundered when they should have pounced.

Adam moved to the bedroom. The dark room had one small window. He could see nothing but empty grounds, shrubs, and new snow falling to cover the sidewalks. People from all parts of the world converged for hundreds of reasons on the high mountain city, and especially on the technology centers. The paranoia of the failed kidnapping and the warehouse shoot-out returned.

He tried to set the feeling aside, and washed out the glass. The Wild Turkey bottle went back into the cupboard. The tranquility and grace of the gentle snow drew his attention outside.

He froze.

Across the adjacent short expanse of lawn, two sets of tracks traced their way to the side of his building. They were not there before his shower. Wind and light snow filled in the footprints. A stand of bared aspens and evergreens twenty feet away blocked his view. His breathing stopped as a man moved in the shadows.

Adam snatched his phone and stepped out of sight from the outside. He dialed the Pentagon and whispered, "Code twelve, triple one." The line buzzed as a patch completed over long seconds.

Adam panted, but not from fear. He wanted the fight. He welcomed the fight. He thought of Patrick Goodell who didn't deserve what he had gotten.

"Miller."

"Adam Michaels. Two men are hiding beside my apartment. Do we have people out here?"

The general covered the mouthpiece for a moment and then said, "Describe them."

"Impossible, it's too dark, but earlier I saw two males, young, twenties. Probably not American born. Tell me straight, General, because I'm not in the mood."

Miller exhaled. "Why do you think they have anything to do with you?"

Anger welled. "Well, I don't know, let me think. Maybe the last couple of weeks has me not trusting my fellow man, what the fuck?"

Miller paused, then said, "All right, Michaels, settle down. Don't confront them, and don't leave the apartment."

Adam slipped the phone into the pocket of his sweat pants. The general never asked for his address. From the top shelf of the closet, he pulled a Walther PPK .380 still in its box. When just married, a nervous Katherine, spending nights alone in DC after a lifetime of security on Chicago's North Shore, wanted home protection. They made it to the range once, but she didn't like to shoot. After Julie was born, Katherine insisted the pistol be unloaded and stored in a different spot from the ammunition. When Adam left on his last deployment, he put the pistol in their storage locker, and she asked the vice president to arrange for security.

Adam loaded the two magazines with seven small bullets each, then pulled back the slide to put a round in the chamber. He popped out the magazine, replaced the bullet with one from the box and clicked the magazine back in place. He flicked the safety to fire, armed now with as much power as the little pistol could possess.

The breeze coming off the high mountains and the falling snow left only an etching of the footprints. Just as on combat patrols, he began to doubt himself and his interpretation of shadows. He remained motionless in the corner.

The phone buzzed in his pocket. "Yes?" he said in a whisper, expecting Miller. "Hello?"

The line disconnected. Adam clenched his teeth. He should have been ready, but now he would be. His hands were steady. He felt and paced his breathing. Trouble just called him.

"Come and get me," he said into the empty room.

They caught him not thinking once, but not again. And they made the mistake of affirming their presence and their intent. They would try to kill him or take him tonight. Red blood filled his brain and muscles, readying the body for a fight to the death.

The cheap clock from Wal-Mart hummed in the silence of the room. Red digital images glowed. Adam chose the kitchen nook to ambush anyone coming through the front door or the sliding glass. The small apartment could be covered from one position. The bedroom behind him was a problem. He pulled the door closed and wrapped the lamp cord around the knob. An intruder could get inside the bedroom through the cheap window, but not open the door without pulling the lamp off the table. The crude alarm should be a warning if the enemy flanked him.

One hour, then two.

From outside, the sound of snow crunching under a foot. His hearing, honed razor sharp, told him they were coming. A mirror in the dining nook showed a dark form approach the locked sliding glass. The figure glanced inside the darkened room. Adam cocked the small hammer and watched the image tug the handle with the touch of a lover.

Locked.

The shadow gently slipped a thin, metal shim between jamb

122

and door. The quiet space scraped as the shim missed. Adam could see the thin silver blade glint in the reflected light. He tried again and missed. It was only a matter of time before he caught the hook and the door opened.

Adam held the pistol at the ready, and planned to take the figure's head off as soon as the door slid back.

Just then, a set of headlights drove around the corner and stopped in the middle of the street. Adam watched the reflection in the mirror as a man threw open his car door, only to slip and fall to the frozen street. He wore a hoody and stood back up, weaving and shaking his fist. "You bastard! You goddamn bastard. Come out here and fight like a man. I know my wife is in there. Come out here."

The tall, lanky driver grabbed for a handhold and fell a second time. When he managed to stand again, he reached inside and laid on the horn, yelling and giving Adam's apartment the middle finger. Porch lights came on. A man in a T-shirt two doors down stepped out and watched.

The dark shadow at Adam's glass inched the shim free and backed into the night. The drunk brushed at his ski jacket and yelled something Adam could not make out. Two shadows disappeared around the corner.

The drunk fell into the car door, righted himself, and sat gunning the engine. Then he wheeled in a crazy circle, spinning his tires, only to disappear around the corner. The street turned quiet once again. People walked back into their homes and switched off the lights. Adam waited without moving. Several minutes later a police car drove slowly down the street, turned and was gone.

Adam watched as two dark figures crossed the field a hundred yards away. A van without lights slowed and stopped, and for a moment, he thought they might try for him again. He hoped they would try. The two figures climbed inside and the van started away. At the last moment, the headlights came on and they were gone.

He dialed with quick, staccato fingers. "Who the hell was in that car? What an act."

"What car? What act? Are you drunk, Michaels?"

Chapter 17

Adam drove the SUV through the upscale neighborhood. The big tires crunched in refrozen tracks as he approached a large house with high peaks and dominating windows. An imposing Christmas tree glowed from inside reaching high in the tall room's glass. Many cars parked bumper to bumper alongside the plowed curbs. A black Cadillac Escalade angled catawampus across the sidewalk. A couple held one another's hand, high-stepping over ruts of frozen slush and laughing. Adam drove by, turned at a cul-de-sac and parked a half-block away on a downslope.

Invitations to the holiday party identified employees with high company positions or those with a bright future. Some people who failed to receive the invitation were known to begin circulating their resumes. CEO Judy Walsh handpicked the guest list, carefully crafting the right people, mix, and message. The RSVP on any other Indron document could have read "mandatory."

Adam had not known this fact until later, and was glad circumstances chose for him to attend.

Music came from inside and out, and for a moment he didn't think the ringer would be answered. A smiling man in a tweed sport coat pulled the door open.

For a moment, the greeter searched the visitor's face. "Ah, you're Adam Michaels."

"Yes, I am." Adam extended his hand.

"I'm Mr. Judy Walsh," he said and laughed at his joke. "Please come in."

The warmth of humanity welcomed him after even a short walk in the twenty-degree night. "Thanks." He shucked his heavy overcoat and tossed it on a stack of others. "That accent would be Brisbane, if I'm not mistaken."

"What makes you say that?" The man raised eyebrows and peered askance.

"The way you rounded off your vowel. And, because my college roommate was from Queensland and spent hours educating me on the differences between Adelaide, Sydney, and Perth. Usually, beer by beer." Adam wasn't fooled by the graying hair or the stooped shoulders. The strong handshake sent the message.

"Ah, you were wise to choose an Aussie as a roomy, Adam. We're by far the most fun. Smartest, too." He smiled. "Where'd you go to school?"

"Dartmouth."

"Ivy Leaguer, very good. Columbia for me. I was supposed to go back home after school, but got a nice job offer from a law firm in DC, and then Chicago. Spent a couple of years there, met and married this exciting redhead who convinced me to join a law firm in Colorado."

"I hope that redhead is your wife, Mr. Walsh."

"One and the same," he said. "And, I'm Peter Heath of the convict Heath clan. Darwin. Quite notorious. But as you point out, transplanted to Brisbane by my parents early on. Call me Pete. I'm only Peter when Judy's mad."

"Pleasure to meet you, Pete. And sorry for the last name mix-up."

"No worries, mate. Judy had an upwardly moving career when she tired of my pleading, and finally agreed to marry me. We never exchanged last names, but that's another story. For right now, we need to get you a drink. Let me walk you to the bar. Judy assigned me door duty, so mustn't be a sluggard. She's terrifying, you know. Everybody says so."

"I'd heard she was charming and driven." Adam found Pete likeable.

"Ah, you're late of the State Department, I see. Very good."

Pete saw Adam's smile at a few of the familiar faces. "Here's the bar. Order what you like. Want me to introduce you around? Otherwise, I've got to return to my station."

Adam shook his head. "I'll be fine, Pete. Thanks so much."

"Ta," he said, and weaved for the front door.

"Wild Turkey, please. With ice."

"Old Forrester, okay?"

"You bet, even better." Adam was impressed. Judy or Peter must know their whiskey.

The bartender nodded and drew out a glass, took a bottle from

125

the rack while dropping a napkin in a practiced, quick motion. "Multitasker," said Adam.

"I try," replied the young man. "I'm interning this year in 'plans and products.' Ms. Walsh offered me this gig so I could meet people, and make a little money."

Adam reached a hand over the bar. "I'm Adam Michaels and happy to meet you."

"Louis Ing and I've heard about you. You joined our research department from the East Coast, right? You're the guy that came up with—"

"Very good," said Adam, slowing the conversation about to venture into classified or at the very least, company proprietary information. "Good hands, and a quick mind."

"Thanks," Louis said, and flushed crimson across his wide Asian face. "Sorry."

"No problem."

"Keeping my mouth from running away has always been hard."

"Forget about it," said Adam. "Really, it's all past tense."

Louis popped the top on a Coors and poured for a man who toasted his thanks and walked away.

"Mentoring my best and brightest, Adam?"

"Ms. Walsh," he said and extended a hand. She set a full cocktail on the bar. Louis was quick to make the first glass disappear and mix another drink. She was a slight woman wearing an open white silk blouse and black slacks. Two gold oriental clasps held generous, swept-back red hair. Adam's research said she always wore black, in business suits or evening dresses. Like a trademark. The magazine said her colleagues called her the Black Dragon, but only behind her back. Known as a ferocious and intimidating competitor, Indron resulted from her winning a long fight with a Silicon Valley venture capitalist group.

"Let's save the Ms. Walsh for the office," she said. "Tonight, Judy, and I'm happy to finally meet you." She wore high heels and looked at him with wide and intense eyes. She glanced at the bartender. "I'm glad you've met Louis. If he can get the wanderlust out, he'll be one of our directors, and soon be after my job. I think he's

126

interned in two other companies since getting his PhD from Cal Poly."

Louis blushed. "No way, Ms. Walsh."

"Way, Louis. And, I welcome you into the fray. It's the challenges that keep us strong, so stick with Indron. Quit shopping around for a better deal."

The young man dropped his eyes and Judy smiled. George Strait finished as Dean Martin picked up with "Silver Bells." The wide fireplace burned an iron log.

Judy took Adam by the arm and propelled him toward the dining room. "I'm glad you could make it."

"Thank you for inviting me."

She waved this away. "In an hour, meet me in the pool house. Go through here." He glanced at the French doors leading to the outside patio. "The walk is cleared, but slippery. Be careful, and be discreet."

The warning had little to do with the ice. He nodded. "I'll be there."

She smiled. "Have fun, one hour." She turned, but stopped. "By the way. Drop by the office tomorrow morning … Sunday, I know but my secretary's working. Pick up a folder. I'm told there's a plane ticket and some documents inside. You're going to Pasadena on Monday morning early, and I'm sending Louis with you. He knows boatloads of people at JPL." She eyed him for a moment. "We like Louis, Adam, but he's not read in to any of this. He's only going to make introductions. Got it?"

"Yes, I do."

The smile didn't reach her eyes. "Have a nice trip."

Adam pondered that not following this woman's orders likely led many to a quick dismissal. He watched her walk away then joined a little group bemoaning the latest loss for the Denver Nuggets.

After a while, he spotted his new research team near the fireplace and walked over. Two laughed at a phone's screen, while the third member smiled at Adam's approach.

"Adam Michaels, right?"

In high heels, the woman was nearly eye-to-eye with Adam. She wore blond hair in a ponytail, and showed off a slim figure with a red sweater with tan slacks.

"Andrea," he said.

"Very good. I never remember people's names the first time."

"You got mine right."

"Mnemonic trick. Andrea Montgomery, Adam Michaels," she said. "Same initials and close enough so even I won't forget." She turned to the others still laughing at their phone. "Tune in, geekdom, please. Meet Adam."

He greeted each and repeated their names. William and Sara. "I was under the impression this was a party," he said. "Are we working on email?"

Andrea sighed and cocked a head toward her colleagues. "No. They're YouTubing last year's Christmas party for Pete's dance. I shouldn't have mentioned it. Pete is Judy's husband."

"Yes, we've met."

Andrea shook her head. "I was here last year and someone took a video and put it on the Internet. Pete was doing *Havana Nights* to a little techno with one of the secretaries." She laughed. "It was hilarious, and he was pretty good. When the video made office rounds, Ms. Walsh was a little ticked off."

"Peter was really getting into it," William said looking up. "Some of us were hoping for a repeat." His young cheeks, stubbled by a fashionable two-day Hollywood growth, fell short. He tried too hard as he cast a glance at Sara, a pretty and young Asian girl, who smiled back and then, looked elsewhere.

"Seems sort of unkind," Adam said. "Invited into someone's home and sneaking a camera shot that puts down the host."

"You'd think so," Peter Heath said walking up. His big smile never faltered as the group's cell phones disappeared. "Actually, the video made it to my Denver office, too. One of my more Internet-savvy partners had it taken down. But not before it went viral. At least, viral locally. Obviously, there's still a copy out there."

"We're sorry, Mr. Heath," said Andrea. "We got to talking and it was me who brought up last year. I apologize."

The tall man held up a hand and laughed. "No worries, Andrea. I'm Australian and we have our fun. You need to consider my wife, however. She's not like me, and sometimes has other ideas of fun." He raised his eyebrows. "She does enjoy public floggings, so she's not all bad. No pictures this time. Agreed?"

When the little group ducked for cover, Andrea stepped in. In military parlance, she was the small unit leader, and she did her job well. Adam liked that.

"Agreed," said Andrea. "And, thank you." She turned to Adam as Heath stepped away. "Escaping death by Judy makes me thirsty. Walk me to the bar?"

He smiled. "My pleasure."

Pete patted Adam's shoulder as they walked by. Louis Ing saw them coming. "White wine spritzer and Old Forrester rocks," he said.

"Wow, Louis." Andrea clapped her hands. "You're very good."

"Ah, shucks. Twernt' nothing, ma'am."

Andrea smiled. "Cowboy, Louis? I thought you were from the Bay area. Are there many cowboys in San Francisco?"

"TV, Miss Kitty," he answered, remaining in character.

"Old TV, too."

Adam glanced at his watch. "Would you mind too much if I took a rain check on the drink?" William approached the bar with an empty beer glass. "I need to talk with someone who's leaving early."

"Certainly." Andrea smiled and turned to William. "Running low?"

* * *

The French doors led to steps scraped clear of ice. A blue plastic bubble sheet covered a pool with escaping steam wisps cavorting beside shoveled snow. The pool cabana's glass reflected the house lights as Adam pulled on the front door. "Ms. Walsh?" The dark room revealed a tall and lanky silhouette.

A familiar voice spoke. "Jesus, Adam, close the door. You're letting what little heat is in here, out."

"Tom?"

"Yeah, yeah. Come on in."

Adam saw the tall Navy commander's silhouette against the window. "What in the world are you doing here?" The room was nearly as cold as the open air. "I thought you were in England at Gravesend."

"I caught a ride with the Guard into Buckley a couple of days ago."

"Wouldn't a phone call have been easier? Does this have to do with going to Pasadena on Monday?"

General Miller shifted in the chair. "Yes and no. We needed a face-to-face. A lot has changed."

Adam looked to the shadowed corner. "Evening, General. In two weeks?"

"In less time than that," said Miller. "Anymore evening visitors?"

"No, sir. But what's happened?"

Tom spoke up. "You're going to hear about this from the NSC but it's better to hear from us first."

"Okay," Adam said. "Let's hear it."

Tom cleared his throat. "You remember Sheila was working in Israel, right?"

Adam said nothing. He never reported the breach of security.

Tom said, "That's okay. General Miller is aware of what's going on. I called Sheila after you and I talked. She was tired, kept losing the thread of the conversation. Said her mother was sick, so I flew over to help. Had some leave on the books, wanted to surprise her, you know. But, she wasn't in Ashdod. In fact, the medical device factory said they never heard of her. I called but she got mad. She wouldn't answer the phone after that. I must've made a hundred calls, but she dropped off the grid."

"I don't understand, Tom. What'd you mean? She's a guest, and nobody can drop off the grid in Israel."

Tom paced his words, devoid of the emotion. "Yeah, right. I got slow rolled by Israeli bureaucrats, then got a phone call to get on the next plane back to the States."

"I don't understand. Who called you?"

Miller stood and turned his back to look out the black glass.

"It doesn't matter who," Tom said. "She called me two days ago and told me to leave her alone, she's okay, but I needed to just get on with my life."

"What the hell is that supposed to mean?" Adam said.

Tom sighed. "My words exactly. She's not all there sometimes."

Miller stepped back in, bulldog and forceful. "Before we state the obvious, there's some background you need to know, Adam. Some things might not set right with you."

"Hey, General. Sheila's a friend of mine. Seems there's a lot going on that isn't setting right."

Tom fell onto a chair.

"Okay," Adam said. "I'm listening."

"Well, first of all, Goodell was Mossad...."

Adam reacted quick and harsh. "Ah, bullshit. Patrick wasn't—"

Miller interrupted with a hand raised. "It's no bullshit, Michaels. He was recruited by Mossad in Germany after the amputations. We knew about it. He was an easy mark. Did you ever consider why the Army would let a double amputee remain on active duty?"

Adam didn't back down. "Because he was the best goddamn man I ever knew, that's why."

Miller's voice rose to match Adam's. "That might be, but Goodell started working for them in Europe. He stayed behind for nearly six months...."

"Requalifying," said Adam.

"Being trained by Israeli agents," Tom said from the chair. "He was turned. That was the deal, Adam. He got turned and we knew."

Adam looked from man to man. "How did you know?" Silence floated between both men. "Okay. Then tell me how an American like Goodell gets turned by an ally."

Tom said, "It's pretty easy. Happens all the time, to both sides. They give a little, we give a little." He looked at Adam. "I'm CIA. Sheila is too, or was. She is working for someone else, now."

Adam's world spun. "What the hell are you talking about? You're a damn naval officer, for Christ's sakes. And my fucking friend."

"We were recruited at MIT when the three of us were working together. And, before you go all high and mighty on me, I'm an American, too. There's no split in loyalties here, Adam. We all work for the same Uncle Sam."

Tom's curt rejoinder cut at Adam. He turned on Miller. "I guess that makes you a spook, too. Right, General?" His words

131

accused and indicted.

Miller kept his temper. "In a manner of speaking, Colonel, you could say something like that. But no, I'm an Army officer."

Adam's self-control threatened. "You kept tabs on Patrick? Gave others reports?"

"Off and on," said the general. "When he was assigned to Benchley and you, it was convenient and safe. But then, when your divorce got … well, messy, and Benchley decided to become your champion, we had to pull back. Too much attention, too big a chance to be exposed. We found other ways."

Adam's angry, disbelieving breath rasped in the room's silence. "So that would include feeding me crap so Goodell could report it. Did that make him a target? Am I the reason he was killed?

Miller faced Adam, much the shorter of the two men. "For Christ's sake, Michaels. What I'm saying is, the world is out of control, and we can't use the old ways of doing things."

Tom spoke up. "Look Adam. We need to get beyond this. Israel spies on us, we spy on them. It's not condoned, but everyone knows what's happening. Remember you asked me if I'd learned from Jonathan Pollard's arrest? Well, that's what happens when someone doesn't play by the rules. When they do play nice, the politicians get what they want, and everyone is happy." He stopped and sighed. "The problem now is that someone flipped over the apple cart. This isn't anything like the Pollard screw-up. Goodell was murdered by the Rahim Tajalli. A cell was activated. We didn't know about it, because it was too deep. Think, the Denmark massacres. They're running free in the US right now."

Miller said, "We have to dance around the freedom we give to these terrorists. Listening posts and NSA monitoring is so restricted, we get nothing useful anymore. Israel doesn't bother with this bullshit. It's kill or be killed, worldwide, including here. Sometimes, we need them because we can't do the job ourselves."

Tom cleared his throat and raised a hand toward Miller, who stopped and stepped back. "Goodell was more than just Mossad." Adam watched as Miller returned to his chair without another word. "Have you ever heard of the right-wing Israeli group called Yigal Amir?"

Adam shook his head. "No."

"They're radical Israelis who assassinated Yitzhak Rabin, the former prime minister. Killed him for winning the Nobel Peace Prize and signing the Oslo Accords. Goodell didn't just turn. A year later, he went radical. He joined a group of Yigal Amir admirers. Very secret and very tough. We confronted Mossad about it. They denied turning Goodell, of course. We told them about Yigal Amir and convinced them to let it run. Patrick doubled for years, to the benefit of both us and the Israelis." Tom took a breath. "Then, the radical jihadists figured it out, and they killed him."

"The Desert Eagle," Adam said, recalling the bloody .45-caliber pistol. "Patrick's?"

"Yeah," Tom said. "I had to get to it before the MP labs did. Too many questions."

Adam joined his former general on the couch. "Patrick was a good man with a nice wife, General."

Miller snorted from the other end. "Yeah, right. His nice wife was also Yigal Amir. She worked for Treasury and stole as many secrets as we could feed her. She was also Goodell's handler."

Adam looked at the man and wondered if he knew Adam recognized the woman trying to coax him into following her. Now was not the time to reveal that fact. "I'm sure this isn't the end to the story. Where's Sheila in all this?"

Tom swallowed a lungful of air. "Gone to Yigal Amir. We've protested to get her back, but Jerusalem doesn't recognize a radical Jewish group in its midst. Look, Adam. Sheila's my wife and I love her. We're putting some heavy pressure on the Israelis right now, but so far, we've got nothing."

"What can I do, Tom? Can we trade her for the graphene model? Maybe it's all they want. Mossad can jump in at the last minute, Entebbe style, and squash this Yigal Amir like a bug. If they're not lying to us."

"We've evolved far beyond that," Miller said. "This is not about stealing a secret or giving one away, or saving a CIA agent that's flipped sides. That's old news. We've got bigger problems."

Tom spoke up. "Let me, General. This is the reason I insisted Adam be reassigned to Indron."

"You insisted?" Adam looked from face to face. "Who the hell is running this show, anyway?"

Tom watched Adam for a moment. "That would be me. Sorry. I know you must feel a little …"

"Used? Manipulated? I don't know. What the fuck would you call it, Tom? Commander? Spook?"

"Look," Tom said with a sigh. "You can punch me in the nose later. Right now we've got bigger problems than your lousy choice of friends. The graphene module must be modified. Sheila's trying to find out how."

"Graphene can't be modified. It's physically impossible. You know as well as I do, once the bio-atoms are aligned, any attempt to change them makes chaos. Chaos can't be controlled, hence its definition."

"Ten years ago, you're right. But not with the new technology. It doesn't matter much now, but the Israelis were marginalized by our old weapons because apparently the Muslim world figured out how to modify the module's orders. The bad guys have had over ten years to work on this. Ever since they stole one from the *Morning Dawn.*"

"This was the big fluff-up over the new JSAM, then?"

Miller shifted and spoke. "Again with the old news, Michaels. None of this matters anymore."

"This might matter to the Israelis, General." Adam's words were harsh and angry.

Miller shook his head. "They don't give a shit because …"

Tom interrupted. "General? Let's not confuse the chain of command here, please." Miller didn't answer and instead, struck a match for a cigarette. Tom turned to Adam. "The general's right. We're beyond turf wars, or even right and wrong."

"I understand," said Adam, forcing himself to think. "We've got to get her back."

Tom shook his head, resigned. "No, not even that. We've got bigger problems than my wife and a ten-year-old design flaw."

Adam tried to search his friend's face. "What's more important than finding Sheila?"

Tom sighed. "I don't know." He glanced at Miller, who smoked and watched out the window. "Neither of us knows. Leonard

Simmons will get around to you after a while. When they decide to read you in, I think you'll find out before we do, if we ever do. He told me to have you ready for a brief. This is it, and now you're ready. The general and I have orders to get the hell out of the way."

"I still don't like this," said Miller from the darkness.

Tom buttoned the top snap on his ski jacket. "Yeah, tell me about it. Sheila's knee-deep in something and they won't let me in. Since when does our government … ah shit, never mind."

Adam watched the two men walk for the door.

Miller turned. "This is bad, Michaels, and it all comes down to your fucking guidance system. God save us from scientists and engineers." He slammed his way out of the cabana.

Tom hesitated before pulling the door closed. "Don't take it personally. He's been kicking me for the last six months."

Adam sat alone in the dark room. Six months, and only now they came to him? Adam thought to add generals and Navy commanders to Miller's list of scientists and engineers.

Chapter 18

Impersonating a new Indron employee turned out to be easier than he imagined. Only his title, "Dr. Michaels," took some getting used to.

"Found your way to the new lab yet?" Judy Walsh asked, leaning over the blotter of her organized desktop to accept his hand.

"No, today's my first day in the lab. Someone's going to walk me back there in a few minutes."

Judy's secretary closed the office door behind her. "I apologize for not showing you around weeks ago, but DC is a zoo. One week bled into the next. I barely made it back for the party." Short by today's standards of power, Judy still oozed strength and confidence.

"Thank you for inviting me, Ms Walsh and there's no need to hold my hand. Louis Ing is everything you promised. Thanks for sending him with me to the Jet Propulsion Lab."

"Louis is a keeper," Judy said. "I'm glad we were able to break him away for the trip. They didn't give me much time to put it together. So, how did it go?"

"Good, but I'm afraid all Louis got to do was sit in the waiting room while I was briefed. He never complained, even though everyone else in the company had Christmas week off."

The two had spent four days at the NASA lab in Flintridge, California. Adam spent ten hours a day briefing and being briefed on the European asteroid capture mission, and the possible role of the American command module. A panel of scientists barraged him with questions about the biotech graphene role in the JSAM guidance system. The PhD dissertation and presentation was a walk in the park compared to the grilling by NASA. At the end of each session, including Christmas day, the men and women of the panel returned to their labs and desks for more hours of work. He returned to his hotel, and fell into bed.

"Louis went because he's a climber, Dr. Michaels. He would've been angry if anyone else got the task. He's also a PhD like you, smart as hell, and knows everyone in Pasadena. He was a personal acquisition from NASA by me."

"Everyone has been very helpful," Adam said. "I'm looking forward to getting to work, real work."

She nodded with a glance toward the door. "Our mutual friend explained to me we've experienced a new urgency. I'm required to bring you up to speed as quickly as possible, and then to let you have free rein." She did not look happy.

Adam slipped the new-employee routine. "I'd like to understand why you're doing this. I'm not questioning loyalties, but I am asking what's in this for you and Indron."

Her lips formed a straight line, and he saw the famous cross-table intensity. "I was forced to take you on and let you run amok in a two hundred million-dollar lab playing your little spy games. That doesn't make me very happy."

Adam never blinked. "How? This is a free country. What did they tell you to get me in here?"

"They threatened to cancel my contracts. Your General Miller can be very persuasive when it comes to closing his checkbook." She leaned toward him. "Look, you seem like a nice enough guy. I know your PhD is real, and you're the one who brought graphene to the table … a decade ago. Your information is old as hell. Every day you're away from research, that's a year you've got to spend to get back. Your thesis is declassified and useless. Miller told me you went into the infantry like any other Tom, Dick, or Harry. Jesus, Adam, you're a goddamn dinosaur. My youngsters will have you figured out in a heartbeat. And then, you're done here. I won't be able to keep you without blowing your cover. I told Miller, but he's too stupid or ornery to listen. If you don't get what you need in a month, get the hell out."

Adam refused to be intimidated, even by this renowned woman. "If I don't get what I need in a month, Ms. Walsh, I'll take two, maybe three. Blood's already been spilled. I don't know all the parts of this mission, but lives are at stake."

"That's fine for you. I got it. You're a hero. Whoopee-do. I'm a CEO in a business that needs government contracts. The day we slip below Wall Street projections is the day I get canned by the board of directors. Pure and simple. It's dollars and cents, so don't screw around with me. Get what you need and get the *hell* out of my company."

Louis waited for him as they walked out. "Hey, Dr. Michaels. You ready?"

Judy Walsh held her wide smile. "He most certainly is. You'll hand him off, right?"

"Yes, ma'am. My badge won't get me past the gate anyway. Maybe someday?"

Judy ignored Louis's plea. "All right then, Dr. Michaels." She held out her hand. "Best of luck in the new position."

"Thanks, Ms. Walsh. I won't let you down." Both sets of eyes leveled at one another. At that moment, Adam decided she could kick the hell out of any cross-table competitor, and he felt sorry for them.

Adam and Louis traveled the complicated crisscross of hallways and checkpoints to the lab section. "You'll learn your way soon enough," Louis said. "It only seems confusing now." Adam studied the floor plan to the plant the evening before, and wasn't at all confused. He said nothing.

Andrea waited behind an open chain link fence with wide, bright-blue eyes and a smile. She pulled her thick down jacket closer. Her blond hair tucked under the collar to thwart the wind. "And, we meet again."

"What a great surprise," he said, and accepted her strong handshake. "I thought you were in production, with Louis."

She slipped her card into the reader and touched several numbers. "Subterfuge. I spend a week each quarter on the production line, but the lab is my real home. We trade positions so everyone is familiar with everyone else's job. You'll get used to it. Like walking in someone else's moccasins."

"Interesting concept," he said, and stepped through the gate.

"And of course, I was spying on you. Making sure you'd fit into our little group."

"I passed?"

"You're on probation," she said with a smile. "But then we're all on probation. Every day, every hour."

She let the lock click behind him. "See you later, Louis."

The young man stood outside the chain link fence grinning. "Hey, sure thing, Andrea. Someday, I'll be on the other side."

She laughed. "I'll be looking for you."

Louis hurried back toward the warmth of the other building.

"Well, come on in," she said. "It's freezing out here. I like San Diego better."

"The whole world likes San Diego better. That's why it's wall-to-wall people."

She smiled at him. "You're right and I'll remember that. These cold days really get to me, though. Someday, I'll be a CEO in the tropics." They crunched rock salt under their shoes. "Did you bring your wife back with you after the holidays?"

"No, Louis and I were in California. I didn't go home to Virginia for Christmas." Adam thought she would have been aware of the Pasadena trip.

Her eyebrows crunched. "I didn't get the email. That's not usual, though. Judy is very hands-on, but speaking as your new supervisor, employees deserve time with family. Judy doesn't necessarily see things my way."

They stopped at a thick steel door with a palm reader, card reader, and dial pad. Andrea misunderstood his silence. "I didn't mean to get personal about your family."

"It's not that. I missed Christmas with my daughter, but it's not the first time."

"No explanation needed. Sorry."

"No problem, really. My daughter lives with her mother in the DC area. Julie, that's my daughter, was skiing with my family in New Hampshire. My first cousin and his brood make for fun companions. I don't think she missed me."

"Daughters need dads." Andrea patted, swiped, and tapped. "A few of us are grabbing drinks after work on Friday. You interested?" She pulled on the steel handle.

"Sure, thanks."

Warmth flooded out. "Good," she said. "Put it on your calendar. We meet at Bender's after five. Try to make it. Louis will be there. He's an honorary member."

They stepped into the break room.

"What is this?" Andrea called to the break table. "A Starbucks?"

Two others sat with Sara and William drinking coffee with a

pastry box between them. Only William looked up with his face reddening. Andrea smiled at him and took a small roll heading for her office.

Chapter 19

He pulled the SUV into a space next to plowed snow. Flakes drifted from a low sky, but not enough to cover the exposed blacktop. He left the engine on and the heater running. Julie answered on the first ring. "Daddy?"

Caller ID. "Hiya, sweet pea. How you doing?"

"I'm okay. Mom's being a pill."

"That's her job. She's the pill and I'm the nice guy."

"Uh-huh. That isn't what she says."

Adam pictured his daughter standing in the kitchen and casting glances toward Katherine. "Be nice to your mother, or I'll make you come live with me."

"Okay," she said.

"And, you'll do all your homework, and no cell phone, no TV, no dates, and no boyfriends until you're twenty-one."

"Oh, Daddy."

"Tell me about Bingham and my lousy cousin Todd, and all those delinquents he calls kids."

For the next ten minutes, Adam heard about their skiing trip to Attitash Mountain and Grandpa Julius's airplane. Apparently, the Gulfstream wasn't big enough for all the invited friends, so they took the Boeing. Adam listened, disappointed and knowing he'd let an opportunity pass to watch his daughter grow up. She'd turned fourteen in the fall.

He touched the phone's off button after he and Katherine talked. Their conversation was brief and not uncordial. She mentioned Eric, that they were "taking it to a different level." He kept the clever jibes to himself, and in doing so, felt part of his life slipping away without a fight. Memory was a convenient, if ineffective tool.

For a while, he sat in the Ford with the windows down, letting the cold air beat the self-pity from him. After several minutes, he dialed Miranda's phone.

"Hi, Adam." She sounded out of breath.

"Hey, you. Busy? Is this a bad time?"

"I'm okay. We're taking a break. Lonely?"

"In a word, yes. Also a little angry at being stuck here, with you there."

"Oh, that happens I suppose with you soldier boys." Her voice rung a glib note that sounded odd, constrained. He didn't tell her about his mission or that the Army was quickly becoming a memory in his life. "Are you coming back anytime soon? I mean to New York."

"Next weekend. As promised."

"I'm talking about going back to the Pentagon, Adam. You know, the East Coast."

"I've been committed to be in Brussels a while longer." He squirmed, uncomfortable about continuing the lie. "After that, I'm free."

"Interesting choice of words."

His discomfort grew. "How'd the Philly shoot go?" The new movie required a scene on a college campus in the rain. Philadelphia fit the bill. Miranda didn't have lines or even a scene, but wanted to be a part of the cast early.

"You're changing the subject," she said, her voice clipped.

"This is a bad time, isn't it?"

"If you were really interested, Adam, the *Variety* website would be on your favorites list. You would know the anticipation is off the charts, and we're working out a few kinks for next year's Academy Award Best Picture speech."

"When do you head for Hollywood?"

"New Orleans, actually." She sounded distant to him, and he wondered if his luster was growing thin with only the occasional weekend hiatus. "There's some big production company renting a bazillion square feet to film almost the entire movie indoors. They want to use me for a month of live shots, computer graphics, and my voiceover of course."

"New Orleans sounds like fun."

She sighed. "Oh , for god's sake Adam, stop. Is there something you need to tell me?" He said nothing. "Did you have some trouble when you were here in October?"

He paused several beats. "Well, maybe a little."

"Damn it, Adam." Her voice rose. "Were you in a shooting on your base? Was a man killed and were you the one who survived?"

Miranda had a temper he realized, and a lie now might cause irreparable damage.

"Yes. Patrick Goodell was killed." He heard her moan. "Miranda, please. I wasn't hurt. I just found him is all. The MPs were there pretty fast."

"You're really telling me the truth?"

"Absolutely. Understand this is hush-hush, and I'm not supposed to talk about it."

"Well, someone better tell the *New York Times* because they busted the story wide open this morning. They're calling it a terrorist attack on a top-secret military shipping terminal and named you—"

"Me?"

"By name, Major and newly promoted Lieutenant Colonel Adam Michaels, who didn't think the dream you talked about was important enough to tell his girlfriend ..."

Girlfriend? Adam grinned. *I've got a girlfriend?*

"... as the man who foiled the terrorists by fighting them off singlehandedly, at great risk to himself, and kept them from stealing one of America's secret weapons." She took a breath. "Is all that true?"

He laughed, deep and heartfelt. "Hyperbole, Miranda. I promise, although maybe the Captain America-hero part's true."

"Adam!"

He chuckled. "Sorry. Hardly any is true. Someone's just selling newspapers. I told you that's what they do when they don't know anything."

"Adam? Are you telling me the truth?"

"Sweetheart, I didn't do anything except call 911 and hide." That was true enough, he decided. "Hold on." The phone vibrated with a missed call from the Pentagon.

She didn't hold, and kept talking. "Adam? I don't like it when you keep things from me."

"And, I won't, Miranda. I promise. Just let me finish up with the Army—" He'd slipped.

"What do you mean? You're quitting the Army?"

"Well ... yes." He wondered if past and present tense when shading the truth equaled a lie. "When I'm done here, I'm done with

143

the Army."

"Oh, God." She became the old Miranda, the warm and caring Miranda. "Adam, that is so wonderful. You could come with me when we make the film. After that, we can live together in a little cottage in California."

He laughed, feeling on firmer footing. "Interesting. I was thinking about asking my grandpa for a job in Pascagoula. That isn't very far from New Orleans."

"As long as you're with me every night, you're talking my language."

And they did talk each other's language until she was called away. He killed the engine, clicked off the phone, and stepped into the chilling air that flowed from the high Front Range peaks. At least it wasn't snowing, like last week's meeting at Benders, his first happy hour with the lab geeks.

"Over here," called a familiar voice. Louis Ing waved from a round corner booth packed with several bodies. Andrea was one of them and she smiled. He grabbed up a chair and faced the little crew from the aisle side of the table.

Louis was already wide-eyed with an alcoholic buzz. Just like last week. He laughed with Sara, the short Asian girl with pretty features who seemed very taken. The attraction was mutual, leaving William Lee with dark-rimmed glasses and long stares.

Andrea grabbed up a near-empty pitcher. "We thought you were going to stand us up. Where've you been?" Her tone was pleasant enough, but exacting, as if this were a meeting instead of a get-together.

Adam shrugged out of his coat. "I was talking with my daughter."

Andrea was taken aback. "Oh, God, I'm sorry. That was kind of bitchy of me."

"Just kind of?" asked Louis, jumping into the conversation.

"Be nice, Louis," said Andrea, tipping the last of the pitcher into Adam's glass. "Don't tell all my secrets, or you'll never see the inside of the lab."

"Don't worry about it." Adam signaled the waitress. "Everyone okay with another?" An agreeable chorus answered. He laughed and circled his fingers over the table.

"Don't start buying rounds," Andrea said. "These kids will start expecting it, and you'll never know if you're a colleague or a sugar daddy."

"Interesting concept," he said with a laugh. "Anyone looking for a sugar daddy?"

Only William scowled. Adam needed to make this young and brilliant man his friend. He leaned toward William. "I was pretty impressed today. I know we don't talk shop outside of shop, but I believe you've really got this stuff down. We sure could of used you ten years ago."

The young man blinked as he processed Adam's compliment. "Oh, well. Thanks. Yeah. Appreciate that, Dr. Michaels."

"Well shit, you should, homeboy." Louis again, chortling. The beer appeared to be the young company hopper's nemesis. "This is the guy that invented that shit and actually made it work."

"No more, Louis." Andrea was stern. Louis was grinning.

"My fault," said Adam. "Bad subject. William and I can talk on Monday. He's got some great ideas."

"Okay, sure." William returned to his beer and turned off the antagonism toward Adam. "Cool stuff," he said under his breath. "Very cool."

Adam answered in a murmur. "Oh, yeah. So cool." They shared a nod. He turned to Andrea and asked about the other two from the lab.

"They never show up," said Andrea. "It's a new generation. A drink-after-work ritual was mandatory at AT&T my first few years. When the boss invited, you went. A lot of business went on at happy hour." She looked around the table with a sigh. "Today, unless they're prowling, it's off to the gym and fitness for all. Have you seen those clubs around Broomfield?"

Adam returned her smile. "I have and they're crowded. I can't blame them though. They've inherited a much rougher world, and my generation hasn't helped. They'd better be fit. They'll need it."

Louis glanced at Adam. "You talk like an old guy. You aren't that much older than us."

He wondered to himself, feeling like a generation apart. Yet,

145

Louis was right. Barely ten years separated them. Two wars and a lot of dead friends trumped the decade of time, however. He felt older and knew more than he wanted.

The waiter placed a pitcher and fresh glasses on the table. As Adam handed over cash, he said, "Chronology isn't always the right measure of time. I'm as old as the hills. Our boss, on the other hand, is not that much older than you."

"Well thank you, kind sir," Andrea said inclining her head. "But unfortunately, not true. I was with Judy Walsh for the AT&T days in Dallas, before she broke out on her own. That was seven … eight years ago, now. She's the one who headhunted me to Indron. A year here, a year there, another two years learning the ropes. She's pushing me through the wickets as fast as I can figure out what I'm doing." She sipped at the top of the fresh beer. "The years add up after a while. Especially when you figure out what you've given up to biology and your social life." She glanced at Adam with a grimace and returned to the mug. "Louis isn't the only one with a low tolerance for alcohol at high elevations."

"Who's got a low tolerance? I can drink you all under the table." Louis turned back to Sara.

Adam laughed. "How does he do that? I'm mean he's talking Sara's ear off *and* listening to you."

"He's trying to talk something off," said Andrea. "But I don't think it's her ears."

"Multifaceted approach," Louis said, this time without breaking from Sara.

The younger girl gave William a shove to slide out of the booth. Louis watched her alluring figure heading to the bathrooms. "Damn, William. You let'r go. That leaves me and you and Andrea. Adam doesn't count."

"Spare me, Louis," Andrea said. "The only reason I haven't shaken you by the scruff of your neck is because Sara's in a different section. Company rules, you know."

Adam knew many young lieutenants over the years who danced on the line never to be crossed. He decided to change the subject to something safer. "Where in San Francisco, Louis? Where'd you grow up?"

146

"Went to Berkeley. Grew up in Oakland."

"Tell me why you called it Frisco the other day? I always thought the phrase was forbidden by San Franciscans."

"After six years in the 'City and County of San Francisco,' I gotta right to call it as I see it." Louis's tone hardened as he addressed Adam. Very unlike their week in Pasadena with NASA and last Friday, right here in this bar.

Adam only smiled his reply, recalling what Judy Walsh had said: *"My youngsters will have you figured out in a heartbeat and then, you're done."* He wondered if Louis had done just that.

"Excuse me," said Andrea, rising and trailing after her young charge. William also left the booth, punching numbers into his phone.

Louis waved a hand at the bartender.

Adam noticed and said, "Maybe you ought to back off a bit."

The young man's mouth turned down. "Maybe you ought to back off on the advice, Granddad. You're the new guy around here." The waiter approached the table. "How about two shots to go with my beer?"

After the waiter left, Louis's smile dropped altogether. "I looked you up this week, dude. There's a lot of press there about Kandahar. Sixteen soldiers died while you hid in a ditch? That is *so* lame."

Many knew Louis's *Washington Post* version of the ambush. Most people were too embarrassed to bring it up, and only a few persons bothered to read the follow-up story printed six months later.

"The entire affair was a pretty dim chapter in a very long war, Louis. But just for the record, an investigation exonerated—"

"Yeah, yeah. I read that, too. The royal heir to an American fortune can apparently buy his way out of any jam, even mass murder."

Adam's gut gripped as Sara and Andrea approached the table. William trailed. Louis grinned and said, "Look at all the loveliness. You're not included in that, William."

The young researcher picked up his parka. "Didn't think so."

"We're going to take off," Andrea said. "I'm giving Sara a ride to her car."

"I'll walk you out," Adam said, rising and grabbing his coat as

147

the waiter returned with two shots of amber. "Call a cab, Louis. Listen to your old granddad, here. Don't drink and drive." He dropped two tens on the wet tabletop and walked after the little group, feeling the hate but not knowing the why.

The walk was slippery in spite of the sand and rock salt. William waved and grabbed the door handle of his pickup truck. Andrea and Sara aimed toward a little Miata with bright silver paint and a black cloth top.

She noticed his admiration. "Perks of the new job and salary, with no one to spend it on but me."

"Well, look no further, Ms. Montgomery. I was a soldier once, and I kind of liked being taken care of."

His joke sounded flat and he regretted the flip remark. She offered him a vapid smile. "If you were a soldier, Adam, you'd know never to volunteer for a suicide mission."

He accepted her gloved hand. "Great advice. Thank you for the last couple of weeks."

"You're welcome." She dropped his hand and unlocked both doors. "I'm afraid Louis was getting out of control. Thanks for not taking him down a notch."

Adam didn't realize she'd heard the last of their conversation. When the powerful little engine started, vapor encapsulated him from the rumbling tailpipe. He waved and stepped back as they pulled away.

For a moment, he thought about returning to the table and mending the strain with Louis. In the end, he decided the alcohol intake prevented any real communication. He'd seek out Louis on Monday and clear the air.

He walked to the leased Ford Edge, thinking that after standing next to the tiny Miata, the SUV was a monstrous Detroit aberration. He pointed his fob and the door lock clicked open just as a hooded man stepped from behind him.

"We need to talk."

Adam pivoted and lowered a shoulder, his body tensed for the charge.

Backlighted by floods, the man held up a hand. "Please, no. I didn't mean to startle you."

Adam's foot slipped on an ice patch, and he fell to one knee.

148

The man pulled a pistol from inside his jacket. "Please stop, Adam. I have no wish to hurt you."

"Halim?" Adam got to his feet. "How'd you … What the hell are you doing here?"

"We must speak, as you are in great danger."

Adam zipped up his coat. "Listen, cuz. You either shoot me, or leave me be. But get the hell out of my way because I'm tired, and don't want to listen to any more bullshit." He put his hand on the door handle.

"Do not be so anxious to die, my cousin," Halim said. "Death comes to all of us eventually."

Adam turned back. "You know, I don't swallow this whole family thing for a second."

Halim stepped closer. "Please indulge me. This will not take long."

Adam dropped his hand from the door handle and took a deep breath. "Okay, Halim. No coffee at Denney's. It might be Friday, but I'm beat and need to sleep."

"Of course." Halim worked the small gun back into his overcoat pocket. "Sorry about that, Adam. I reacted before I thought."

"Me too. So what's up? You know I'm going to report this meeting, and I don't care if we do look alike."

Halim chuckled. "Did you know that Abdul and your father were only a year apart? They were like twins. People always mixed them up. The same people now say there is a resemblance between you and me, despite our different mothers." He smiled and shook his head. "Personally, I don't see it."

"You don't …" Adam laughed; too much beer. He liked this guy, even if he did have a gun in his pocket. "Okay, Halim. I'll bite. How do people know what we look like together?"

The handsome man's dark eyes twinkled in the dim light, as if Adam were the fish taking the bait. "Because we watch you. Take pictures of you. They took pictures of you and me at the Alexandria restaurant." Adam didn't return his smile. "I'm sorry. I'm aware photos are considered an invasion of your privacy."

"Why did your people kill my sergeant, Halim? He was a good man."

"The Rahim Tajalli killed your Sergeant Goodell. You were saved because we informed Mossad. We were too late for your friend, I'm sorry."

"You're trying to tell me Mossad and you, a Muslim, work together?" The skepticism in Adam's face showed.

"Yes, although maybe not all the time. As Syrian rebels, we recognize the right for Israel to exist among many other important differences. That is a change, and welcomed in Tel Aviv. The US prefers not to take notice, however. They will not help us in our struggle."

"Go figure. Look at some of the people you're in bed with, like the Muslim Brotherhood. They say different than you, and they speak for the rebellion."

Halim shook his head. "The rebellion is made up of many people, many groups. Just as your American Revolution had many ideas: theocracy, democracy, monarchy. One would eventually win out over the others. We will win out, Adam. America was lucky to have strong men to resist temptation. Mossad cooperates with us. We are a small group, even smaller than the exiled National Coalition, and on the verge of dying out if support from the outside is denied. We are also strong, Adam. My father is strong, even though he is old. I am not a terrorist, but a revolutionary. Your government must learn the difference."

"So what happens now? You kidnap me?"

"No." Halim looked aghast. "You need to listen. The Rahim Tajalli will kill you when they discover where you've gone. They are rigid fundamentalists and mystics, but you should not underestimate them. They will wait a thousand years to get their revenge. This is the same Ottoman group defeated at the Great Siege of Malta in 1565. They waited a long time for their revenge against the Christians."

"You're losing me, Halim. I'm not a scholar like you."

"You know the Rahim Tajalli has your guidance system. Yes?" Halim looked for acknowledgement, and saw none. "Okay. You must ask yourself why they are no longer concerned the Great Satan gave this to Israel. This no longer matters to them, Adam, and the question is, why? The Rahim Tajalli is trying to stop you, not because you are the enemy, but because you are the threat that might stop them."

150

Adam fingered his keys. "They don't know me, except I'm a soldier, and we're enemies. I kill them, they kill me. Simple. I'm going home."

Halim touched his arm. "The nature of the Rahim Tajalli is to kill you, yes, though they venerate the brilliance of your work. They are the scorpion that kills the frog even as the frog swims the rising river to keep the scorpion from drowning."

"But not you, Halim?"

"Every Muslim is not a murderer or a radical jihadist, Alhasan. I am speaking of politics, not religion, and the wisdom to separate the two. Rahim Tajalli is allied with Bashar Hafez al-Assad and his Ba'ath Party. For those of us who oppose him, we must find strength in allies. We are crumbling because the United States should be our hope, but failed us. Russia exposed your empty threats and your disappearing red line. Doesn't anyone remember Russian treachery? They will step into the void America left behind."

"You're saying Israel is your ally?"

"God alone will judge me if I am wrong, Adam." Halim glanced at the sky, as if gathering a moment to remember later. "The Qur'an tells us about a man who saw a raven become friends with a stork. The birds perched together and flew together in contentment for years. The wise man couldn't understand how two birds so different could be companions all through their lives. One day as the man was dying, he wanted to solve the mystery. He left his deathbed and went to where the birds hunted for their food, only to discover that both had only one leg."

"Jesus, Halim. You're turning my world upside down and giving me fables from the Qur'an." Adam brushed snow from his sleeve. "Okay, so you didn't kill Goodell. It was the Rahim Tajalli."

"I swear none of us had anything to do with the death of your sergeant. The Rahim Tajalli want Syria and Iraq for themselves. They believe this is the first step in reforming Levant, the ancient heritage of Islam and the last caliphate. This is a mirage. After they vanquish the enemy, they will turn on their allies to subjugate the world in their image. Just as the scorpion stung the frog, everyone will drown."

Adam dropped the car keys back into his coat pocket. "Okay. What else?"

Halim stamped his feet against the frozen asphalt. "Sheila Perez is with the Yigal Amir. The Rahim Tajalli tried to kill her and failed. She was injured, quite badly, but is now in a safe house agreed to by your government. You and Ms. Perez, not Commander Connecelli, put together your state secret. She is safe, while you are not. For now, my cousin, believe me when I say, fighting a war against jihad is the least of our world's problems."

Chapter 20

NSC Agent Leonard Simmons idled in a compact Chevrolet as the Ford Edge took a nearby parking spot. He switched off the engine when Adam approached.

"I thought if I parked in your space, you'd know I was okay." The frozen snow crunched under Adam's feet as the other man stood up and stretched.

"What's up, Agent?"

"That was Halim Khaddam, right?"

"You saw?"

"Of course. You were being monitored."

"You're aware he had a gun? That he pointed it at me?"

Simmons rocked his hand back and forth. "Not at you, as much as in the area. We weren't concerned."

"You weren't …" Adam stopped and shook his head. "Unbelievable."

"Inside, please," said Simmons. "It's too cold out here. I'm from Florida and I'll never get used to this weather."

Adam unlocked the sliding glass door. "You might've told me you were around. I'm not a 'secret agent man' like you. I don't meet a lot of guys with guns in parking lots." Adam didn't like the petulance he heard in his own voice.

"How would we have done that, exactly, Colonel? You were pretty tight with the group of youngsters in there tonight."

"Wait a minute," Adam said, stopping under the stoop. "You're the James Bond here. I'm sure you guys have some sort of gizmo you can use, like a bat signal, maybe?"

"Of course. I just wasn't sure if you wanted the vibrating suppository, that's all."

Adam watched the man for a moment and then laughed aloud. He slid open the door the rest of the way, shaking his head. Simmons shucked his parka, even smaller now without the heavy coat.

Adam turned the thermostat up and took off his own jacket.

Simmons said, "The CIA confirmed the Sharifi-Khaddam family connection. The old man, Abdul Khaddam, is the former Abdul

153

Sharifi, late of the Tadmor Prison in Syria. You do have an uncle, but frankly, short of a positive ID by a witness or DNA, there's no way to confirm the old guy is Abdul. Halim is definitely his son, though. That part is true. But he's always showing up at night and rarely under the lights. For now, we think it's him, but maybe it's not all that important."

"Maybe for you, *Leo*." Adam sighed and stepped into the kitchen. "Can I get you something? You want a drink?"

The man glanced at the full bottle of bourbon. "No, you go ahead."

Adam did not and instead, fell into the chair opposite the agent. "You had my coat wired, as always. Did you hear everything?"

This brought a nod. "Yes, but that isn't why I'm here. I need to brief you on something." He slipped a manila folder from an inside breast pocket of his parka. "I'll give you some time," he said, and looked around. "And oh, you forgot to ask, but yes, Leo is fine. And I'll take that drink. What the heck."

"Sorry. Glad to hear it." Adam took the papers entitled "Adam Michaels aka Alhasan Sharifi." In surprise, he said, "Me? Why are you doing a background check on me?"

"This is about your Arab family, a history. I thought you might not know much about them. Your cousin Halim is in there. So are several others. Most notably is Abdulkaader al-Saleh. If you're not familiar …"

"I know him." Leo looked up. "I know *of* him. Syrian rebel leader from Aleppo. Killed in a government airstrike."

"Yeah, very good. He's related to you, kind of distant. Did you know he was America's great hope for a stable Syria? His death created a leadership vacuum and they're still scrambling over there." Leo sipped at the top of the glass and smiled as he settled into the chair opposite Adam. "This is good," he said. "You might be interested to know Halim is next up to bat."

Adam looked up with raised eyebrows.

"He's kind of the best of choices, a synthesizer," Leo continued. "Doesn't really have a following, just a couple thousand true believers. But, he's acceptable to a lot of members of different movements. Kind of like the old days with your father, always right

154

next to the power and in the middle of the political mix." Leo took another sip. "This is really good stuff, you know."

"Help yourself, Leo. I'd like to take some time to read."

"Go for it." Leo poured another while Adam began to thumb through his family's dossier.

After nearly two hours and several rereads, he closed the folder and looked up.

Leo held up a hand. "I got orders, Adam. I'm not supposed to talk about it." He glanced at the folder and drained his glass. "They wouldn't let me read it. Your eyes only."

Chapter 21

During the day, Adam kept up with the younger geniuses at Indron. During the morning breaks, he watched sweet coffees and fried pastries consumed by the handfuls. Adam sipped his coffee black and listened while some questions and problems devolved into arguments. A few might be ego boosted, but others interested him with solid scientific speculation and facts. He was having fun.

The first couple of times he stepped in and solved an issue, they considered him an aberration. When a technical question grew out of his reach, he guided with advice and deduction. He didn't have the ego, so soon became a mentor and arbitrator.

On this morning, Andrea shared the last of her coffeepot with him after the others broke up the meeting. William talked, bright-eyed by the possibility of shifting magnetic polarization as an outside energy source to realign dead graphene molecules. The others at the table ganged up, mob style, and derided a phenomenon occurring only once in every one hundred million years. William maintained if a small Laschamp event reversal in the earth's crust could account for the phenomenon, then it might be duplicated on a micro-scale. They headed for their workstations continuing the argument into the corridor. Adam knew nothing of geomagnetic reversal, but liked William's ability to think up the wild and crazy. He returned to Andrea's desk taking up his cup.

"I've got to say, I'm pretty impressed," she said. "I told Judy you'd be gone in a week, two weeks tops. I told her these guys would eat you alive. I'm glad to be wrong."

He smiled and sat. "Thanks. They're pretty good people. Smart, driven, unhealthy. We need to do something about that. I'll bring carrots tomorrow."

"I hope you like them. Unless they're dripping in sugar, these guys won't bite. Sugar is their brain food. It's what fuels their tanks."

"What do you like, Andrea? What gives you the inspiration to supervise six, soon to be eight young minds?" Last month, Judy Walsh brought in three new researchers from a firm in Seattle. Indron grew in quick strides as the government awarded contract after contract.

"That's a lot of responsibility."

She licked the ends of her fingers and laughed. "Sugar helps, but I'll pile on the pounds if I eat like them." He smiled and waited. "I'm happy to be at this job for more than just a couple of months. Makes me feel more stable and productive."

"Hmm. I'm happy you're happy, but you're avoiding the question. Let me rephrase: What would Andrea Montgomery like from her upwardly rocketing Indron career?"

"Are these questions you normally ask of your superior?"

He realized with a start his temporary nature let him relax and dig. Her desk phone beeped, and she smiled.

"You're right," he said, climbing to his feet. "That was out of line." She scrunched her eyebrows in disappointment and at the interruption. "I'll let you get to work."

He was nearly out the door when she stopped him. "Adam? Judy Walsh's office passed a message. You're to call a Marty?" She raised a questioning eyebrow but didn't ask.

"Okay with you if I head up to the front offices to return the call?" There were no cell phones in working spaces, and security prevented any outside dialing.

"Of course," she said. Cornflower blue eyes watched him. The concern was real. "Is everything okay?"

"I'm sure it is," he said, grabbing up his heavy coat from a break area chair.

She handed over a packet of drives containing a confidential research report. The company trusted paper, and heavily controlled and restricted electronic devices over their own secured internal network after a hacker broke their defenses the previous year.

"Let me know if I can do anything," she said, her hand rested on his forearm. "And, I'm sorry for being a bitch and trying to pull rank. I hide it from my friends, but my true nature got away from me this morning."

He took the package and dropped his arm. "You're nothing of the kind, and thanks for the offer. Can we talk later?"

"Yes, yes," she said and stepped back. His gesture to break physical contact was not lost on her.

Marty never called unless he needed to say something

157

important. Adam accepted the slip from Judy's secretary and grabbed up his cell phone from the small locker.

He stepped outside. The houseman answered on the first ring. In a moment, Marty said, "Adam?"

"Yeah, what's up? Everything okay with Julie?"

"Yes, as far as I know. I spoke with Katherine yesterday. The visit last weekend must've been good. She didn't bite my head off."

Adam took his first full breath and relaxed. "She's in love, Marty. Julie tells me the Under Secretary of State and her mom are getting quite serious. There might be wedding bells in DC. I guess he's an old college chum."

"Does Julie like him?" asked Marty, his daughter's Dutch uncle.

"Do teenagers like any adults?"

His family's consigliore offered a brief chuckle. Adam never heard the man give more than that. "Good point," Marty said. "The reason for interrupting your day is to let you know, Julius will be landing about five-thirty tonight at Broomfield. He asks that you meet him for dinner on the plane."

"I can do that."

"Good. I'll confirm with the pilot. He's flying out of Pascagoula this morning and on to Seattle for the night. Then, he's headed to Seoul for a conference with Kim Jaegwon. The board is really putting the pressure on Julius. This week is his sixty-ninth birthday, you know."

"I've had Amazon trying to deliver a present to him for over a week now. They can't catch up."

"Well, good luck with that. Hold on. I'm walking outside." In a moment, he was back. "I assume you already know about the pressure on your grandfather."

"I do."

"And, you're already aware he's been told of your resignation from the Army."

"I didn't think it would be a secret too long." Marty never offered unsolicited advice, making this a momentous occasion.

"You owe Julius an explanation, Adam, and a plan. He's been holding up his end of the family until the wild hair you called the

Army played out. The day came and went. You never talked to him. You're out of time, and I won't ask your decision. That's between you and Julius. But you need to understand he's invested a great deal into you."

"What did my cousins Todd and Marianne tell him?" Marty fell silent. Adam's uncle, Don, died a year almost to the day after Lillian. The question was the second of the morning out of line. "Sorry, Marty."

"That's okay. You've been away for a long time. You probably have PTSD or something seriously wrong with your head to ask me such a bullshit question."

"Geez, I'm sorry. What can I say?"

"Say you'll talk to your grandfather and tell him the plans for the rest of your life. Tonight. Todd and Marianne could care less about the business except how it affects your grandfather's health. Marianne loves Wisconsin and she loves her life partner. She'll never come back. Todd's paintings are works of art. He's successful and happy, and that's what he wants. Your cousins also talk with Julius all the time, and have been a real part of the family. You might wish to consider something similar. Those two made connections some time ago and you haven't even made peace with yourself." Marty paused as if taking a breath from a long flight of stairs. "Sorry for the PTSD crack. Anything I can do for you, Adam?"

Marty and his curtness were justified. And, he was right. Adam needed to discuss his plans with his grandfather. "No, but thanks for asking. I'll square my stuff away."

The phone clicked off. The rebuke sang in his ears. Adam hit the off button and leaned back against a post. The sun's brilliance reflected off the snow. A blue sky against the Rockies' Front Range left a contrast no other place on Earth could claim. The decision he must reach subsumed the beauty of the moment.

Chapter 22

Adam stood in the small fixed-base operator's office as the Boeing 767 taxied to the far ramp. The man signaling with lighted orange wands looked tiny against the behemoth and the powerful beams coming from wing lights in the night. The engine's tremendous noise vibrated the steel walls and glass windows of nearby buildings. A golf cart waited outside to take Adam, but he declined, wanting the walk in the cold air. A sliver of moon illuminated clouds forming along the slopes. By the time he stood with the lineman, a ladder truck arrived and the passenger door opened.

"Thanks," he called to the men as they drove off in the little cart. They looked up at the huge airplane and shook their heads muttering about rich people.

Julius waited at the top of the stairs without a coat.

"Christ, Gramps. You'll freeze."

"Nah, too mean. And, don't call me Gramps." The two enveloped one another in a bear hug. "It's about time you surfaced, Adam. I've been wondering."

"Yeah. I know. Marty kicked my ass this afternoon telling me what a shit I was."

"That wasn't news though, right?"

"I pretty much knew what he meant."

"Good," said Julius, pulling him inside so the crewman could shut the door. "That'll save us some time. Steak okay for you? Not a vegan or anything, right?"

"That's Todd. I'm the soldier. I usually just rip the faces off and hardly bother with cooking."

"Shocking me was a long time ago, usually left for your mother."

Thoughts of Lillian and her absence from their lives entered the cabin with the two men who loved her like no others. They smiled, acknowledging their mutual loss.

"A drink before dinner, sir?" A voice from behind.

Adam turned and stuck out his hand. "Hey, James. How're you doing?"

"I'm great, Adam, and you?" Squat, square with a balding head and a bone-breaking grip, James doubled as Julius's bodyguard and advisor. A Grambling University judo and boxing champion, the loyalty was mutual and long-lived.

"Same. Still globetrotting with my demented grandfather?"

"And thankful for every minute of it."

"Does he actually listen to your advice, or just blunder off doing his own thing?"

James laughed. "He's a smart old coot. He listens." James might have saved Julius's life, but he was also the corporation's expert and often ambassador when it came to African culture and trade.

"Can you two guys knock off the lovefest?" Julius said. "I'm starving."

James and Adam smiled at one another. "How can you continue to hang around this guy?" asked Adam.

"Just blessed, I guess, Adam. Just blessed."

Julius moaned. "Will someone get me a sick sack?"

"Okay, okay," said Adam, clasping the iron shoulder of an old friend from his childhood. "We'll catch up later."

"James?" Julius said. "We're going to take dinner in the rear lounge. Can you get the crew fed and then rustle up filets with the works? Do you want to eat with Marty and us?"

"No, sir. I'll eat with the crew. You guys catch up."

"Oh shit," said Adam. "I'm going to get yelled at, right?"

James just smiled. "Sometimes we all need to examine ourselves."

"Okay," said Julius. "Dinner for three in the back." He stopped and looked at his grandson. "His hair is longer, but he probably still eats like a soldier."

James smiled. "Yes, sir. I'll let the captain and the cook know."

Adam greeted many of the office staff by name on the trip rearward; the rest were introduced by Julius. The Boeing 767 400 was hardly an extravagance. The corporation didn't have a home office, corporate buildings, or a fleet of limousines. The twelve worldwide offices were dockside metal buildings meant for working men and women. Everyone was expected to produce, including the CEO. The Boeing 767's ability to fly over three hundred and fifty passengers in excess of five hundred miles per hour was reduced to modern office spaces and living quarters for thirty-five persons conducting a fifty-billion-dollar annual business in twenty nations around the globe. Complete dedication and compact Hertz rental cars were requirements not lost on Todd and Marianne McCaffrey, or on Adam.

Marty stood up as Julius closed the door. The older man turned to his grandson. "We need to talk, Adam. You'll be getting a visit from the NSC in a couple of days. I don't think our government is telling you everything."

Adam looked from one to the other. "They never do, Grandpa." He glanced at Marty. "But, I think it's time for me to tell you everything I know and what's been happening. This is not an excuse, maybe more of an explanation."

"I can eat with the crew," Marty said.

"No, please," Adam said quickly. "I'd rather you hear it, too, if that's okay with Grandpa. I need both of you."

Julius settled into a chair. "Fine with me. This is long overdue."

Adam sat across from his grandfather and Marty, and thought of the Denny's, the warehouse, a dead sergeant, and a near death escape. He also considered the terrorists, and the Israelis—both friends, and with a different agenda. His part in all this was small, and yet, events swirled in his head like a whirlwind inside a room, picking up papers and books and lamps and slamming them against the walls of his mind. He knew a misstep had huge consequences, and that he needed unadorned advice with solid experience behind it. And, these two men were his most trusted.

He took a deep breath and started from the beginning, leaving nothing out.

Chapter 23

Adam squared the folder in his hands and glanced at Leo. They sat on the apartment's stiff couch as wind buffeted the trees against the glass door. The agent swirled ice cubes in an empty glass and watched the night.

Adam looked down and read.

Executive Summary
Eyes Only

Background: In 2008, the Japanese Aerospace Exploration Agency (JAXA) successfully brought the Hayabusa probe back to Earth with asteroid samples. The mission was to be followed by a US program to capture a minor Near Earth Asteroid (NEA) using Lasso and Basket Technology (LBT). The mission was canceled at 98% complete due to a change in US space priorities and thereafter transferred to the European Space Agency (ESA). A successful launch in March of the following year from the Russian Cosmodrome was monitored by permanent personnel of the Japanese moon base facility. Pakistan subsequently launched and established a remote lunar operation two months later. Pakistan Space and Upper Atmosphere Research Commission (SUPARCO) established a moon facility in the Taurus-Littrow Valley, twenty km from the Japanese. The stated mission was to monitor communications between commercial resupply vehicles. The Pakistani outpost was manned by a crew of sixteen—twelve men and four women.

Situation: A guidance signal sent to the ESA robot explorer caused an unanticipated trajectory resulting in a rendezvousing and docking with the unmanned Pakistan supply vehicle in elliptical lunar orbit. A subsequent course correction placed the ESA and the Pakistan supply ship on course for Asteroid 433 Eros (second largest NEA estimated at 21 x 7 x 7 miles in diameter). European authorities from four countries lodged a formal protest with the UN. Pakistan denied involvement, advising their moon facility personnel were not responding to government orders. Radio traffic monitored by the NSA confirmed the survival of three personnel from a moon-based mutiny. NASA modeling indicated SUPARCO employed command module guidance with graphene technology. In a secret executive session, the UN sanctioned Pakistan who continues to deny the allegations.

"Jesus," said Adam, looking up.
"Keep reading," answered Leo. "That isn't the half of it."

Twenty-four months ago, NASA reported the NEA Eros emitted a debris field indicative of multiple explosive strikes in the megaton category. Natural causes are not suspected. The original ESA robot is incapable of an explosive charge. The total explosive power is estimated at 20 megatons each in at least four strikes. Intelligence confirmed the supply vessel's potential ability to transport and detonate explosives of nuclear strength. NASA theorized a simultaneous nuclear detonation in the near vacuum of space would be strengthened to many times that of one conducted in an Earth-like atmosphere. A debris field of several hundreds of thousand objects left the original orbit of Eros. NASA Jet Propulsion Laboratory in Pasadena estimates at least 40% of the debris field contains objects in excess of .2 to .5 kilometers. The Earth will pass through a retrograde debris field in late

March Year + 2. The original orbit of the remaining Eros asteroid appears unchanged.

Adam looked up. "What's a 'plus 2' mean?"

Leo swirled his drink. "NASA-speak. *Event plus two*, means two years after the Eros explosion. You know, like two years ago. Like this March." He swallowed the remainder of his drink. "A bunch of space rocks in like in how many goddamn days ..." He rose and refilled his glass.

Adam watched the man for a moment, then continued to read. In addition to the multiple debris, a single fragment estimated at a 6 km diameter will ellipse the sun on a possible collision path for Earth. Course divergent angle planes appear guided to take advantage of the Sun's gravitational field and significantly increase velocity. The remaining asteroid fragment is considered suitable to cause a near "Dino Extinction" event and may be held in place and guided by the Lasso and Basket technology developed by the US. NASA estimates probability of second strike at 15.025%. Note: Previously, the earth's probability of an near Earth Extinction Protocol (EEP) was less than a one hundred millionth of a percent.

Summary Conclusion:
First Strike

Initial strike probability 100% from retrograde orbit & will result in damage similar to multiple low-yield, nuclear detonation in 50 to 80 Kilotons range. (1945 Hiroshima yield was 14 Kilotons).

Second Strike

Scenario 1 (worst case): Less than 10% probability that strike will result in extinction protocol with worldwide loss of all animals, 97% of vegetation, and global conditions unfavorable for life beyond

165

simple insects for foreseeable future.

Scenario 2 (best case): Maximum non-extinction protocol damage is NOT a given. A glancing blow, favorable angle of impact, or non-populated impact, will result in minimum disruption.

Other *Possible* Scenarios in varying degrees

Multiple Scenarios: Strike could result in reduction of 1.5B world population within 744 hours (one month); 3.0B of the present world population (of 7.134B) within 4320 hours (six months). Likely causes of death: starvation and malnutrition, societal and economic disruption, disease, lack of transportation, fuel, medical shortfall, and loss or reduction of law enforcement resources.

Within 1 year of impact, debris clouds and fuel fires will warm world climate and reduce sunlight resulting in extended winters adversely impacting growing seasons. World GDP (gross domestic product) will drop at a continuous, downward rate of $3.5 quadrillion per year for six years. World trade will reduce by 70%. World GDP will stabilize in year 7 at less than 20% of previous period and remain for approximately 120 years.

Near zero survival rate of urban-based population/economies will occur. A 40% loss of agrarian resources worldwide is estimated within ten years. The USA and Canada's loss will exceed agrarian-based economy losses, leveling at 80% due to extensive use of chemicals that will be no longer available. A pest incursion will represent the largest challenge to North American, European, South American, and other industrialized-nation survivors. Hunter Gatherer Population (HGP) based economies and survival rates in remote locations estimated at 50% of present. With

166

reestablishment of barter/cooperative trading between nearby settlements, HGP will account for remaining world economy.

An expected change of climate due to impact and consequent shift of Earth tilt, wobble, or orbit is unknown.

Document Ends

Adam turned the two pages over. Large black swatches covered the third sheet's paragraphs. He looked up, his mouth dry and breathing shallow.

"Redacted," Leo said with a laugh. "The government actually believes if they keep a secret, somehow they'll survive." He laughed and swirled a lone ice cube. "Idiots."

Adam's thoughts went to Julie. "This sounds like bad science fiction."

"If it's fiction, buddy, we're paying a lot of NASA and Department of Commerce people way too damn much money. Not that it matters much anymore." He tippled the watery remains into his mouth, and stood to pour another. "Fifteen of the world's biggest intelligence agencies sent all their stuff to Ottawa. They put this together over the last six months. This is an updated report, a couple of weeks old."

"This is pretty grim, Leo. What's not being said?" Adam thought about his conversation with Julius and Marty, that the government withheld information that was important to him. Julius knew of the movements of resources, the subliminal buzz of clandestine meetings, and heavily guarded computer systems.

"Keep in mind that all those dire predictions are based on a fifteen-percent impact chance." Leo added another ice cube before he sat. "I think you're a cynic, but, because you asked, I can tell you the supply ship was guided to Eros. That's true. Probably with signals from the Pakistani moon base. Once a chunk was broken off, the lasso-and-basket captured it and is now bringing it back to Earth by slinging it around the sun. We're not running into a second debris field like we are the first. We're getting smacked by a big-ass rock aimed right at our goddamn heads. Nobody can figure out how to guide it away. That's you, buddy. You're our Hail Mary pass."

"Good Lord."

"We can only hope He's good. Ever wonder why our government declassified your stuff while we were still flying it?"

"Of course," Adam said. "But maybe now, I see why. You let people have the technology, and then have the NSA monitor the hell out of them. Patriot Act be damned."

"More than that," Leo said with a laugh, as bourbon splashed unnoticed over the rim of his glass. "But that's very good. You should'a been an agent. The NSA geeks embedded a screwworm into your little technology, so anyone fooling with the module or using the computer links in the military library is going to leave a trail we can follow. Clever folks. I think the real miracle is how this was kept secret. Maybe someone out there can figure out how to beat your system. Maybe you should figure out how to beat your system."

"Is Indron involved?"

"I don't know. I'm an intel guy. I send intel to Washington. They send it to the NSA, JPL, DHS, FBI, CIA, and other alphabets I can't name. Everything is analyzed. I get zero feedback. Somebody knows something, but it sure as hell isn't me."

Adam leaned back and watched the ceiling for a moment. "Okay, but I trust you and I know you've thought about this. So tell me what you hear *and* what you think."

Leo's short legs angled on the chair's cushion, his feet not touching the rug. "You're the first guy who's asked my opinion, so I'll give it to you. In some respects, I think we're toast. When people find out, all hell's going to bust loose. Global confidence will collapse like a house of cards. People will start doing what people do, like panic, shoot their friends, go on bucket list trips. Generally, I think a lot of people will give up before we even start to fight." Leo's eyes shone and his face flushed. "We won't need an asteroid to hit us, 'cause we'll take each other out. Hell, you'll probably get a target on your back when some bright reporter runs this story."

"That's comforting," Adam said.

"Oh, sorry. Didn't know you wanted comforting."

Adam held up a hand. "Okay, I deserve that."

"One note here, Adam. You and I can talk, but nobody else. Miller hasn't a clue. He thinks we're tracking a domestic terrorist cell trying to steal missiles, for Christ's sake. Brad Benchley might be a great guy, but he's clueless, too. I think even Mossad's out of the loop and they're royally pissed."

"Okay," said Adam. "Let's put some information together."

"You're just a glutton, aren't you? Okay. The big boys are afraid Al-Qaeda ... the Rahim Tajalli is going to win. Even if the Arabs blow all of us to hell, they're going to heaven anyway so what's the worry? Rahim Tajalli plans a welcome for the first debris field. They're making an hour-long video production, Hollywood style, to whip the world into a frenzy. Cells will begin posting to social media in a hundred or so countries twenty-four hours before the first debris field hits. When the big one comes around the sun, I'm sure they hope the chaos from the first hit will leave nothing salvageable in the non-Muslim world." He laughed without humor. "The Rahim Tajalli will claim credit for sending us all to hell without the virgins. The shit's going to hit the fan, Adam. Society as we know it could cease to exist, and that's not just a tired old cliché. You don't want to read the memo speculating on that if you want to sleep tonight."

Adam watched as Leo drained the glass and rose to pour himself more. "My handler at the NSA told me that Rahim Tajalli sent a message to all the heads of non-Muslim countries. Nobody's saying what was in the message, but I can guess. This just might be a hell of a good time to start negotiating with terrorists. Maybe they've already figured out how to stop this thing, and all we have to do is figure out how to make our women wear burkas." He sat and leaned forward, pointing his glass at Adam. "What can your little group of geeks do? Can you get to Sheila and put your heads together without getting killed in the process?"

"Do you know where she is?"

"Nope. But if I did, could you guys pull a rabbit out of a hat?"

Adam thought for a minute. "If I said yes, are you the guy to get me there, wherever *there* is?"

Leo looked down and brushed at his chest. "Hmm. No 'S,' huh. Guess that means I'm not superman." Leo's words slurred but grew steel. "But I am the guy who carries water, Adam. I can't do shit

169

except to whisper in someone's ear. But you gotta tell me if I'd just be blowing smoke if I did."

Leo stood and made a wavering aim for the half-full bottle. Adam beat him there with the cap. "We need to think tomorrow. I've got an extra bedroom. Crash here tonight. Too dangerous to drive."

The small man accepted the rebuff with a laugh. "Danger is my middle name, but why don't you answer the goddamn question?"

Four days ago, Adam conceptualized a problem for William to solve. The military module, the same one stolen and flying in space, contained a destruct circuit, while NASA had no need for such a contingency. Adam thought the self-destruct circuit could be reprogrammed to deliver a code and fire a steering rocket. William thought he could figure a way to remotely put that off. They would still need a delivery system and of course, the right code.

He steered Leo toward the spare bedroom. "I don't know if I can or not, Leo. One of the kids in the lab has some ideas, and Sheila's smarter than the two of us put together. She's the one to write the code. We have some big hurdles to overcome, but in answer to your question, we have the right people, but we need at least eighteen months."

Leo swallowed a burp and looked at him. "Nobody's got eighteen months. Weren't you listening?" He wavered on his feet. "Bathroom."

"First door on the right."

In a moment, he heard the man throwing up behind the closed door. Adam didn't blame him one little bit as he picked up his cell phone and dialed dispatch.

At five the next morning, McCaffrey Shipping's Gulfstream V sat under the lights at the Broomfield Airport. By five-thirty, Adam and Leo moved at five hundred miles an hour to a five-hour stopover in Manassas. Leo would go home, and Adam would see Julie. At two in the afternoon, Adam scheduled the Gulfstream to Teterboro Airport near New York City.

***

Adam lifted his hand to knock a second time when the door opened. "I'm sorry if this is a bad time. I should have called."

Miranda said, "Oh, Adam." She went to him in a fierce hug, as tears streamed down her cheeks. The thought nudged at him she was crying before he'd arrived.

Chapter 24

Miranda had left fifteen minutes before, for the evening show. Adam would be gone when she finished and he already missed her. The better part of a day wasn't enough time. He called William at home and posed another question. The young engineer-scientist was so excited, he hung up without saying good-bye.

He wiped at the kitchen's drain board, wondering what else he could do, waiting for the cab to honk. A McCaffrey Citation Jet refueled at Teterboro and would fly him the short hop back to DC. He'd sleep in the Dulles crew quarters for a couple of hours, call William first thing in the morning for an update, and then drive Julie to school. The next couple of hours would be spent with Katherine and the lawyer. She insisted on a meeting now that he'd left the Army and the DC area. Of course Adam could tell them little, but he wasn't unhappy about the meeting. In fact, he looked forward to seeing her again without Eric at her side, even under these circumstances. For several years they were good, and she would forever be the mother of the most important person in his life. The angst over the divorce found its way into the past, and Katherine was in love with someone more closely allied with her dreams. Adam's difficulty lay in realizing that not fighting wasn't necessarily giving in or up. The confusion would take him more years than they all might have, so he contented himself with wishing her happiness.

A knock at the front door. The stove clock read nine-twenty. Why hadn't the cabby honked? He flipped off the kitchen light and grabbed up his small valise.

He looked through the peephole at the back of a man's head. "Who is it?" he said, hesitating with his hand on the knob.

The man turned. "Keith Miller." The general's mouth was a single hard line.

Adam pulled the door open.

"You're goddamn lucky you're not in the Army, Michaels." No greeting. Right to the point. "I'd bust you so fast your head would spin."

Adam stepped back and held his own temper in check. "That

172

was your choice, General. We all live with our choices."

The man's jaw locked as he stepped in. "Interesting words, Michaels." He wore a gray wool overcoat over a sports jacket and tie. Dark rain clouds threatened. "You left your cover in Denver and compromised an NSC agent. If we could catch up with you, why not the Rahim Tajalli? You're goddamn lucky you're not on your way to Islamabad in a steamer trunk or dead in a ditch. I can't punish you because you're a civilian, but at least Leo Simmons is headed for Leavenworth."

Adam maintained his equanimity, and paced his breathing. "Rahim Tajalli apparently isn't interested in me anymore, General, and if Leo's under arrest, you'd better get your best lawyers together before tomorrow afternoon is out. I'll have an injunction in the District Court of DC and New York with a writ of habeas corpus, and have it so goddamn fast, I'll spin even your hard head. Oh, and give your boss, Tom Connecelli, a quick call. Tell him to sublet my apartment because I'm not going back."

Miller's face darkened.

Adam pulled out his cell phone. "I've got Judy's number here. Excuse me, General. I need to resign from your foreign service."

"All right, all right. You've made your point."

Adam watched the other man. "No way, General. You don't quit that easy."

Miller sighed and snapped his own phone out of its holder. "Put him on United and send him back to Denver." He listened. "It's a no-go, goddamn it. He got a weekend at home and probably got laid to boot. So what? Just put him on the goddamn airplane." He closed the phone and looked at Adam. "Anything else? Mint on your pillow?"

"That's a chocolate, sir, and no, thank you." A honk sounded outside. "Well, as long as you asked, how about a ride to Teterboro? We can talk in the car."

They drove the Battery Tunnel through lower Manhattan as the rain started. By the time they crossed the bridge into New Jersey, the sky opened and the traffic slowed to a crawl. When the rental car pulled up to the airplane, both men understood the other a little better. Adam told the general some facts and wondered if he might have violated part of the Secrets Act. He no longer cared. The general needed to speak for Adam, and he couldn't do it if he wasn't convinced. The rain came down hard in the dismal night, and Adam waved the steward back up the airplane's stairs.

"I'll get going, General, and I'll do my best. But if they haven't made contact in a week, Tom and I will need to put our heads together. We've got some big problems to solve and one of them is getting to Sheila. She's the brains, and Yigal Amir probably has her. Mossad is ticked off, but those are the facts, so let's work with them."

The Citation sat on high struts on the puddled ramp looking sleek and beautiful.

Miller turned in the seat. "Commander Connecelli still works for the US Government and as you know, he's running this operation. But, I don't work for him. I'm free to report up my chain of command. I'll take what you told me and do my best. But you pull another bullshit stunt like this without letting me know something, and I'll have you arrested for a violation of national security and let the lawyers figure it out."

"And Sheila will be lost to us forever, General Miller. There's more at stake here than getting her home. I can't talk about everything, but Leo can. I suggest you talk to him. There's a fight coming, and I want you on my side."

"What do you know, Michaels? What did Leo tell you I don't know?"

"Sir. I am not being the asshole here. I don't really know who knows what. I obviously don't have the whole story. Maybe no one does, but like you say, we do what we're told, and do it the best we can."

Miller chewed at his lower lip until he nodded his head with a sigh. "Okay, Adam. I'll talk with my White House contact." Miller had never called him by his first name before, and the world rocked. "I understand. Tom's military and he's got me. You're civilian and you've got Simmons. Just keep in mind if we get too many moving parts, we're just as likely to explode as to come together and fix this thing … whatever this thing is."

"Good advice, General. I'll keep it in mind."

Adam cracked the door as Miller said, "Satisfy my curiosity. Why did you join the Army when you've got all this going for you?

174

Airplanes, ships, rich family. What in the hell made you want to be soldier?"

Adam thought for a moment. "Pretty much the same reason as you, sir. We all just want to be a part of something that's bigger and more important than us. We all want to do something we'll be glad we did for the rest of our days."

Miller sighed and said, "Well, I hope you chose right."

Chapter 25

Adam unlocked the door to the cold apartment at thirty minutes after midnight. His hand stopped mid-reach for the thermostat when his cell phone rang. "It's William, Dr. Michaels. I think I've finally got something."

"That's great," said Adam. "Think we can talk about in the morning over powdered doughnuts?"

"I'm in the lab right now. Been here since you called the other night. Can you come over? I can get you in."

Adam looked at caller ID on his cell phone and laughed. "Are you calling through the switchboard? How are you doing that?"

The young man chuckled. "Easy. I'll show you when you get here. It's really simple."

Three hours later while much of the world slept, Adam reached into Andrea's tiny refrigerator and extracted two Cokes. "Here, you deserve this. That's one hell of a good piece of research and a damn interesting theory."

William blushed. "Thanks. That means a lot coming from you."

"You overrate me. Let's take these back and run the same thing through one more time."

"Awesome," said William. "My mom says three's the charm."

Five industrial-sized magnets surrounded the heavy plastic of the chamber. Ten-gauge extension cords, each thicker than Adam's index finger, ran to separate circuits in different parts of the lab. They needed power, lots of power. Adam wondered how he'd explain the requisition to Andrea. Inside, the ultrathin sheet of programmed graphene prepared itself to accept commands, break the action into thirty-two terabytes on a five-hundred-thousand-dollar, three-dimensional, reproducing copier. The machine would make a new object from raw materials. In this case, a simple coffee cup was replicated after thirty-two million molecular commands in less than an hour.

William theorized when the graphene rejected the signal, just as when the JSAM received its unchangeable command, the die was cast. For the military, this meant no changing course, except for the destruct command, the sole circuit left un-commanded in the military version.

Adam watched the 3-D copier replicate a sixteen-thousand-dollar coffee cup in the output port. "We're running up the charges here, William."

"Okay," the young man said, his eyes and face aglow with excitement. "Now the real test."

William replaced the used graphene sheet, walked to the command inputs, reproduced the exact sequence, and turned on the magnets. As power built, Adam felt the hairs stand up on the back of his hands. The young man focused a laser on the input circuit of the graphene interchange module. He tapped in a sequence of codes via the destruct-command circuit. He glanced at Adam, his eyes glassy. "What'd you call it? 'Once laid, it's played'?" He grinned.

Both men slipped on protective goggles as William activated the laser beam. Fifty-five minutes later, the 3-D additive manufacturing copier produced an obelisk twisted into the symbol of infinity. Not a coffee cup. The Infinity symbol joined two other objects, Pi and Beta.

"Three for three." William's eyes glistened and his voice rose in a near-squeal of delight. "This is so totally awesome, Dr. Michaels. We've done it."

"You've done it, William. Doesn't matter what we design the graphene to do, your code, magnet, and laser makes the graphene command do your program and not mine." Adam grasped the young man's shoulder. "I'm truly impressed, William. America's enemies could only wish they had you."

"William?" The voice, sweet and familiar, turned the young man's head.

"Sara? Wow. Did you see this? Did you see what we …"

Her lovely Asian face smiled as she raised the heavy-caliber pistol and shot William twice in the heart. His shirt erupted blood as he slammed backward and flipped over the metal table. Adam grabbed out for him, missed, and then reached for Sara. She turned her weapon and aimed between his eyes. "Meddling old man."

The next shot exploded her head, spraying blood and brains

177

over the stainless steel laboratory. Before he could turn, a dart pricked his neck. He hit the floor as rubber legs gave way.

Strong hands rolled Adam over and lifted. William's lifeless eyes gazed toward him.

"Hurry," a voice whispered.

"The guy's a horse." Several grunts.

Adam flung an arm and hit meat.

"Ouch, goddamn it."

"Give him another shot if he won't stop fighting."

"What the hell's wrong with him?"

"Quit being such a baby. Give the drug a minute."

"I'm going to tape him."

"Not his feet. He's got to walk."

Adam watched as doubled silver tape wound around his wrists.

The voice grunted. "Stand up. Geezus, he's heavy. Take my gun. This drug is shit."

The slap to the face hurt. A second slap. "Stop that," Adam said, in a voice not his.

"Help us, Adam." The other voice. "Come on, please, you must walk. This was the only way. You wouldn't come voluntarily, now would you? You've got to help us."

Adam couldn't answer.

"Oh, God. Did you see the kid?"

"Yeah, yeah. I thought we had more time."

"Well, guess what? I had to kill her."

Adam's knees buckled, and he was propped up.

"No more drugs," the voice said.

"Let me get the door. Hold him."

"We should've said something before. Christ! Who knew about Sara?"

"Just do what the hell you're told." The voice was a near scream. "Otherwise, all this is shit. Just shit."

The familiar sound of the hand analyzer beeped, followed by a tap of the combination. The frozen air braced his face.

Adam's vision wouldn't focus. William's chest. Blood. "These assholes shot him. Gotta help William." Adam pulled away from the iron grip on his arm.

"Hey!"

He brought up a knee and caught his captor in the groin. The man went down with a cry. "Help me," he gasped.

Adam saw the hypodermic needle in a hand and kicked out. Missed, and the point pushed through his sweater and shirt, deep into his chest muscles. He twisted, but too late, and the half-empty tube fell to the ground. The cold spread. He fought the flutter of his eyes. "I've given him enough dope to drop a cow."

"So sue me. I asked and that's what they gave me. He was supposed to—"

"Just grab him, and for God's sake shut up. What are we going to do about the cameras?"

"Forget the cameras. Hurry. The drug isn't strong enough. I've given him two doses."

Adam felt himself pushed into a wall.

"What're you doing?"

"We can't do this alone." A hand slapped his face with snow, stinging as if it was fire. The chain link door shook and opened. "Hurry." Affable Peter, the accent was unmistakable. Another slap with stinging, hot snow. "The bitch's probably got others with her."

Hands shook him. "Adam, listen to me." The voice near his face. Judy. "This was supposed to be William. Do you understand? It was going to be easy, no one was supposed to get hurt. But now, it's you. William's dead and you've got to help us. What the hell were you doing in the lab, anyway? Jesus Christ, Adam. We're all dead if you resist. You've got to get away from here."

Adam watched the frozen sidewalk and put one foot in front of the other.

"Good. Good."

Fire. Heat on his neck, the crackle grew loud. An explosion.

"Get the gate, hurry, Peter. We gotta get out of here."

"He's cooperating. Finally."

"God, you're such an idiot."

"Who's the bloody idiot? You didn't give us enough time."

"*He* didn't give us enough time. Get the fucking door. Hurry."

Adam understood he was being taken … or saved, but Tom's people should be watching. The Rahim Tajalli must have killed

179

William. The last door closed behind him. The fire was loud now, with explosions and heat and buckling metal walls.

"Get the door. Shit, oh shit, the bastards have burned my lab."

"Fuck your lab. Hurry!"

Another explosion, then a pistol popped. Adam felt himself pushed into a snow bank. Several slugs hit the metal walls. Harsh whispers. "Kill him," ordered Peter. "He can't fall into their hands. You know our orders."

"No," Judy said. "They're bozos. If you do that, all this is for nothing. We can make it. Come on, Adam, please. *Help*."

Adam shuffled as an engine started. A screech of tires from the far end of the parking lot. Another shot popped, followed by replies from a different direction.

"Go, go!" A familiar voice. Not Peter or Judy.

Adam heard the racking of a shotgun. *Pop, pop,* then a loud and deafening shotgun blast. A hard shove, and he hit a cold metal floor. The side door slammed followed by rapid shots, one after another.

His mouth tasted of copper and he felt acceleration. The back window burst spraying glass over his face. His head crowded the floor. Sleep, finally sleep.

***

He groaned as his weight shifted. His mouth was dry. Every movement sent white pain to his eyes. He could see nothing. A blindfold over his head, and binding around his wrists.

"He's coming awake," a man's voice said in the dark.

"We won't be much longer." A voice in control.

"Water," Adam said, his words a bare croak. He rolled and pain exploded white. "Please, water. Thirsty."

"Another IV bag." The man's words spoke with authority. "No water. He'll vomit and drown."

"Okay. He needs to recover, though. What the hell did they give him, anyway?"

"It doesn't matter. Make sure the blind is secure."

The noise of rushing air. Adam grew up with the sound, as familiar as almost no other in his life. A jet aircraft, in flight, far above the earth's surface. Yigal Amir kidnapped him, and the Rahim Tajalli tried to kill him. *William. They killed William.* The hope, made possible, died with the young man, and might end any chance to avoid the end of life on Earth.

Adam wondered at the uselessness of struggle as cold spread from his hand. His mind drifted. He knew Tom's voice, of course.

Chapter 26

Adam opened his crusty eyes a crack, peering into a painful room.

"Still thirsty?" asked Tom.

He nodded a wobbling head. "Yeah. Really thirsty." His voice was gravel. A cup was held to his lips and taken away after his first sip.

"Take your time. I'll get the curtains. I heard about the aftereffects of a pregabalin-and-pentobarbital cocktail. You'll have a headache for a while but it'll go away just about the time the photophobia goes. Give it a couple of hours."

Adam heard the drapes slide closed and chanced another look. He recognized Tom Connecelli's back. "What are you doing here? Wherever here is."

"Hey Adam, how're you doing?"

"Fine. Can you let me in on the secret, now?"

The Navy commander gave him a quizzical look. "You really didn't know, did you?"

"Know what?" He touched and rubbed sore temples.

Tom motioned with his hands. "Keep it down. Let me explain before they get back in here."

"Okay. Who are we talking about? What's going on?"

Tom took a deep breath and sat in front of Adam. "You know all this has been going on for almost two years, right? I was going crazy out of my mind."

"Okay."

"So I had to do it, I didn't have a choice."

"A choice to do what? Quit talking in code." Adam smelled cedar and cooking chicken and his stomach rumbled. "Man, headache or no headache, I'm starved."

"I think Sheila's making supper."

"What? You found her?"

Tom hunched his shoulders. "Not so much found as was given permission to see her. Let me explain this, okay?"

Adam rubbed at the intravenous bruising on the top of his

182

hand. "Okay, go."

"Sheila was kidnapped, that's all true. What I didn't tell you is I spent months with the FBI and the Shin Bet looking for her. The kidnapping wasn't just recent. I lied to you about that. This was over a year ago. The Israelis closed the borders, the military searched everything in and out. We went on raids, arrested suspected terrorists. Oh hell, we even tortured a few." His eyes reddened and watered. "But no dice. We came up empty-handed."

Adam said, "And, then?" He took another small sip.

Tom breathed deeply. "And then, about a year ago, a guy calls me on my mobile. Tells me if I inform the FBI or Israeli security, Sheila would probably be killed. He sounded, well, reasonable is probably the best description."

"He's going to kill your wife and he sounds reasonable? What the hell, Tom?" Adam's anger, always quick, bubbled below the surface.

"He didn't have Sheila, but he knew who did. He knew a lot about you, but I wasn't supposed to talk to you about it. I was really pissed that day in the Pentagon. I thought you knew something about Sheila all along, and didn't tell anyone."

"Think, Tom. I didn't even know she was gone. How could I, especially after you guys dropped me like a hot potato. You told me, remember?"

"Yeah, well, maybe. I told him to give the information to the FBI and collect a million dollars. He told me money didn't matter. It was scary, Adam."

"What was his name?"

"Alhasan Halim Khaddam, your cousin."

"I've never told you about my name or my heritage."

Tom stared for a moment, eyes hesitant. "I've had two years searching and researching, diving into every CIA database in existence. I was desperate to find her, Adam. I flipped over every rock, including yours. This was personal, and I joined her."

"What does that mean, you joined her? Like a Stockholm syndrome thing?"

"More like a Benedict Arnold thing, at least that's how the agency sees it. The Rahim Tajalli had her at first. She was held for

183

almost three months with them getting everything they could about the code from her. Then we found her, or maybe Halim found her. The CIA said to leave her there. I said bullshit and … traded with the Yigal Amir to pull a raid. We got her back and hid her. For the last year, she's been working her butt off trying to duplicate what the crazy Kazakh did with our command module system. She hasn't been able. And because she failed, we're all going to die, aren't we Adam?"

"What did you give the Yigal Amir?"

Tom stared. "Me."

"You defected?"

"Don't give me that crap. What the fuck would you do if it were Julie?"

"I'm not judging you. Just trying to understand."

Tom breathed hard, then sighed and relaxed his shoulders. "All right, then, thanks. I was moving back and forth pretty good, but they caught me just after I saw you in Denver. I got the chance after a debrief and I ran." He wiped his face with a hand. "I gave secrets, and even helped Sheila recreate what the three of us did in the lab." He clenched his teeth together. "You know what really frosts me? Those bastards in Washington are calling me a traitor. They've pulled some shit with the Israeli government, but so far they're not going overboard. If I tried going back now, I'd be in the Portsmouth lockup until I die. The only reason that's not going to happen is because there won't be a prison, or a country to hold a trial."

"You need to tell me how you know all this. There's probably not a dozen other people in the world who know."

His long face turned from Adam. "Yeah, well, you know more. I know you got the president's briefing from Leo Simmons. That's why the Rahim Tajalli tried to kill you a week ago. And, they'll try again."

Adam shook his head. "A week ago?"

"Eight days actually."

"The mole was Sara." Adam's memory of the pretty Asian face kaleidoscoped with the twisted mouth and hate-filled eyes.

"Yeah. The Agency's been following a lot of people, including Sara Lin Chen. Obviously, they thought it was me and I had to run." His mouth worked. "That nearly cost you your life. Yigal Amir hid me

184

in Denver, but in order to keep Sheila safe, I was in on your snatch."

"She killed William," said Adam, his words sounding useless and hollow. "He was a nice kid."

"Yeah, and she was a professional assassin, trained by Al-Qaeda in the Philippines. A sleeper. We took out Sara, but it was close. Took a firefight to get you out, not that you made it easy."

Adam looked up and stared hard. "You could have told me, Tom. Trusted me."

"You're a boy scout. You would've turned us down, and me in to naval intelligence. No way you would've come willingly to join the Yigal Amir."

"So that's what I've done?"

Tom grew angry again. "What the hell do you think?" He shook his head in disgust. "I told them you were going to be useless."

Adam sighed and leaned back in the cot. "Okay. Give me a clue. Where are we, 'cause I'm betting this isn't Kansas, Toto."

"Rmaich, Lebanon."

"You've got to be kidding me."

"Yeah. We moved the Tel Aviv lab here. Halim has some contacts so no one's been suspicious. So far. Mossad was working us hard, but a few high-level guys squashed that, too."

"You're talking Yigal Amir?"

"Yeah, who else?" Tom said. "They made a deal to cooperate with the Arabs. The Israeli government can't approve openly. You can imagine the uproar if the Israeli population found out. A few years ago, they started cooperating with moderate Arabs to fight ISIS and Bashar al-Assad." Tom looked over at Adam. "You might want to remember these guys are on our side."

"How do you know this?"

"A couple of reasons. I know because the Israeli government needs to keep tabs on everyone, and especially the Syrians' second civil war with ISIS. And, I know because your cousin is fighting Bashar al-Assad. Halim is the one who forced the Syrian National Council to recognize Israel's right to exist." Tom dropped his eyes. "Not that any of this matters anymore. I tried and can't do it. I decided to spend the earth's last days with the person I love." He looked at Adam. "That's what's really happening, isn't it? World coming to an

185

end?" Adam didn't answer and Tom shrugged. "I'm getting right with … everything." His face hardened. "If you want to know the truth, I wasn't in favor of bringing you in on this. I thought William was a better bet all along. We just waited too long."

A light knock at the door and both men turned as Sheila entered with a plate of chicken and greens. She dressed in a long muslin caftan with, a snood and shawl covering most of her face. She smiled at Adam, set the plate down, and touched Tom's cheek.

After she left, Adam turned. "Tom? What was that?"

He released a breath. "I know. Sheila was … shot … in the head during the rescue."

Adam moaned. "Ah, God."

"The Arabs tried to take her out when we raided the lab in Palestine." Both men quieted for a moment, until Tom continued. "She knows me. Most of me. Some gaps in her memories. She adopted Orthodoxy and joined Yigal Amir. We've spent the last year getting to know each other again, building a bridge from our past. She's committed to them. I'm not so sure, but I'm committed to her. We either defeat the Tajallis or we figure out a new way to make it in the afterlife …." He trailed off into silence.

Adam recalled Tom's haughty ego and Sheila's sweetness. "What are you saying, Tom?"

"I'm saying everything is fubar. Half the time, I don't know who my friends are. Right and wrong is all mixed up."

"No way, Tom. Everything might be 'fucked up beyond all recognition,' but there's a bunch of radical bastards out there who want to kill everyone who doesn't agree with their vision of the world. That's the enemy. We stop them. Simple Simon."

Tom Connecelli huffed himself into silence, saying nothing.

Adam relented. "Look, Tom. I'm glad Sheila's alive, so don't get me wrong, but we need to work together, all of us. That includes your friends at the CIA and the Knesset."

"Maybe, maybe not. As you can see, Sheila doesn't remember you. Maybe she would if we had more time. When you consider she was shot at pointblank range by those bastards, we're lucky she's even alive."

Silence settled between the two men until Adam spoke.

186

"Where does my cousin stand, Tom?"

Adam shocked himself by referring to Halim as his cousin.

Tom didn't notice. "He's balancing a lot of people who have no idea what's coming. One screw-up, everything collapses and the world will do the Rahim Tajalli's work for them."

"You're pretty dramatic. As I recall from what I read, there was less than a fifteen percent chance of the asteroid managing even a glancing hit. And even then, there's all sorts of milder scenarios. Besides, I'm sure the rocket boys will have something up their sleeves."

Tom considered the ceiling for a moment. Food cooled on the table. "Did you know NASA is stymied? I don't have the NSC briefing papers like you, but the Israelis are feeding Halim, so I'm getting some things secondhand. Twenty-kiloton bombs from the gods. If a little piece gets near a city and explodes in the air, millions will die. You already got this, right?"

Adam gave no sign.

"Yeah, yeah. Boy scout to the end." Tom took a breath. "And, that's just the debris field. The main event's still on the other side of the sun, the only one we can do anything about. It's not going to matter much because people will be going crazy by then. Time to get your affairs in order, buddy. Panic and chaos. People with big pantries get offed by people with bigger guns. We're not prepared for this, and there isn't any Hollywood crew waiting to take a space shuttle to save us. Hell, there isn't even a shuttle anymore. We're the hope."

"So what do you think we're doing here?"

Tom considered his companion. "What indeed. We're hedging a bet. The first rocks are going to hit. No doubt about it. Our guys think the command module is guiding the big rock for a second hit with the solar sails the US invented. They also think it can hit a target. Geezus." He blew out a lungful of air and leaned back. "That goddamn Rahim Tajalli figured out what all the others couldn't. Including us. He reprogrammed the asteroid capture robot and the giant solar sail 'to rain fire from the heavens.'" Tom laughed. "Genesis 19:24, or al-Qur'an 3:191. You choose." He paused. "We need to find the bastard's grave and dig him up. Maybe he'll tell us something if we can pry him away from the virgins."

Adam stood and paced. "And what do they expect us to do, Tom? Maybe your CIA shouldn't have killed him."

"I never said that."

"Someone believes we can reverse his program. Do you know any reason why we can't use our own code?"

Tom leaned forward. "What do you know? Can we?"

"Answer the question."

Tom fingered his lips for a moment. "This is their final jihad. They can aim the damn thing, and no, we can't countermand once the module accepts the signal." He paused. "Or can we? Come on, Adam. What were you and the dead kid working on?"

Adam didn't want to believe this was an elaborate setup, and Tom wasn't that good an actor. Not yet, he decided. "We were thinking up theories and shooting them down."

Tom watched him, and after a moment said, "Yeah, then okay. So it's like in the briefings, we can't stop it. Whoever survives goes back to goat herding in Levant. The ones who don't, get the virgins."

Adam picked up a fork from the cooling chicken then set it down. He shoved the plate toward Tom, who shook his head.

"Am I a prisoner?"

"After what I've told you, and assuming you believe at least a little, how can you ask that?"

"Because unlike you, my world does not begin and end in Lebanon. I have family and a special friend in the States. I also have a country I'm not going to abandon."

The old, competitive, take-no-prisoners Tom returned. "Well rah-rah for you, Yankee Doodle Dandy. This is all pretty hopeless, if you haven't figured it out yet."

"There's no quitting, Tom. You don't get to back out of the human race just because it suddenly got tough."

"Who the hell says I'm quitting?" Tom's voice rose and his face reddened. "You supercilious son of a bitch! I'm working hard to save the world."

Adam leaned across the table, his voice growing soft. "You're working, Tom, but we've got to work smart, not just hard. There's too much at stake here to depend on just us."

Tom wasn't calmed. "So who else is there to depend on?" He

was shaking with rage. "You?"

"Yes. You, me, Sheila, and a lot of others. We need smart people to try other things. We can't hole ourselves up and work like monks. Too much is at stake."

"You think I don't know?" His voice rose to a near scream. "That's why the hell you're here. You're the last goddamn person I want to work with."

Adam stood and grasped both Tom's arms, and spoke even more softly. "I know it, Tom, and I'm sorry you hate me. I can't undo the past, but I can help you and Sheila. Others can help you, too. Someone has to be in charge to keep everyone straight. Someone's got to take what we know and explain it to scientists in other places. That's you. Halim can help you make contacts. Maybe you being free of the CIA is the best thing that could happen right now. You're free to talk to anybody and I know you've got clandestine contacts all over the world. No one can tell you to stop. We just have to be smart."

Tom stared at him, his breaths raspy and sour. At the same moment, the door opened and a man with a kaffiyeh on his head stepped in. Behind him, two more men followed with machine pistols.

Alhasan Halim Khaddam unwrapped the face cloth. "Hello, my cousin. I am happy to see you again." He embraced a surprised Adam as the others left the room. For the next hour, they spoke. Adam laid out ideas for a plan.

Chapter 27

Adam felt a hand on his shoulder. He was still weary from the travel but also from reviewing Tom and Sheila's work nonstop for the last thirty hours. The darkest part of the night eased between the rough curtains.

Halim spoke in a whisper. "Get dressed, Alhasan. We have a car and only a short window of time. The Lebanese Internal Security is sleeping. Wear this kaffiyeh but please hurry."

Adam stood, pulling on pants and a shirt. He took the headcloth with no idea how to wear such garb.

Halim watched for a moment, and then offered a small laugh while he folded the white-and-black pattern around Adam's head. "Ah, my American cousin. You make a fine Bedouin, and have so much to learn."

He followed Halim from the tiny room, through a quiet kitchen and into a dirt alley between brown-clay brick buildings. The odors of evening meals remained in the still air.

Tom watched the hard-dirt ground as they approached. "I'm staying here," he said to Adam, "because I'd never pass for anything except what I am. You on the other hand, fit right in." His voice was not kind.

"I'll take that as a compliment."

"Take it any way you like, but I think we're wasting a hell of a lot of time. All you've done is go over our work. Where's yours? We're putting in twenty hours a day trying to rewrite this code. We don't have these kinds of luxuries for a spoiled, rich brat."

Adam held his anger in check. This was the Connecelli he knew, terse, demanding, and unpleasant. Tom's eyes challenged, but in the end, said nothing else and walked back inside. The door closed behind him. They would soon need Tom's single-minded, dogged purpose, Adam told himself.

A dented black Mercedes idled in the alley. Halim sat in the backseat. "Sit in the front, Adam, and don't worry about your Navy commander. He is under great pressure." The car shifted into gear. "If we are stopped, either Daoud or I will talk. Hebrew or Arabic.

Understand?"

"Yes," said Adam, glancing at the Israeli giant behind the wheel.

"How is your Arabic, by the way?" asked Halim. "I've never heard you speak."

"Probably not as good as yours." Adam only spoke Pashtu and a little Kurdish, neither of which were Arabic. Being arrested as an Iranian or an Afghani might be preferable to American.

"I'm still working on the phone call you asked for. If you will tell me what message you wish to relay, I might be able to do that."

"One step at a time, Halim. Give me some geography."

The car bumped up and onto the rough stone street accelerating between squat buildings. "This is Markaba in southern Lebanon, a no-man's-land between Israel and the sea, and site of many Shi'ite conflicts. We are five miles from Kiryat Shmona, a former Arab settlement and now a small Israeli city. It is a tiny place in the middle of a beautiful valley of trees and vineyards, sharing a dispute between Lebanon, Syria, and Israel. The Golan Heights sit above us. Fifty years ago, twenty Israeli children were murdered by the PLO. A scar remains never completely healed for either Jew or Arab."

Adam listened, knowing the distinction between Lebanon and Israel could often amount to a dirt road or a rise in the terrain. Given the opportunity, Adam intended to run for the border.

Daoud maneuvered the Mercedes between small hovels with lights hidden behind thick curtains. A dishelmed mosque sat at crossed streets.

Halim leaned forward. "Why did you want me to see this, Adam?" Rough timbers and debris sat where the distinctive roof and minaret should have been. The windows were broken, too, but a wall free of fallen bits and pieces stood near the courtyard.

"Stop, here," Adam said.

Daoud glanced in the mirror to the backseat. Halim nodded.

Adam walked to the masonry wall and knelt. Small fountains trickled water through curved stones still wet from the washing of feet.

"Why is this important?" Halim asked as Adam returned to the walkway.

He held his cousin's eyes a moment. "Because I could be

191

anywhere, Halim. But finding a destroyed mosque with the fountains still working is more difficult. Once a mosque is so designated, the land can never be used for anything else. This may very well be Lebanon."

Halim smiled. "Very clever, Adam. You are right of course, and not washing one's feet before prayers is unthinkable. I must learn never to underestimate you. And yes, this is Lebanon. I am a stranger here, much as you."

The car began its slow trip into another alley of scrub trees and bushes when the phone rang from the rear seat. Adam couldn't hear the low words. The phone tone sounded and Halim spoke. "You've got what you wanted, Adam."

When they regained the pavement, Daoud accelerated into the night. The road turned to potholed dirt with finger-size rocks rattling in the wheel wells. Daoud drove with speed until in the distance, Adam saw a dilapidated silhouette against the night skyline.

They pulled off the rocky path onto matted brown grass and stopped a hundred feet away. The engine shut off and silence surrounded them. Chirps of insects began again as if they'd held their breath, too.

"What is this?" said Adam.

"Wait," said Halim in a whisper. "Be ready, Daoud."

Long minutes passed in silence. Then, a single flash from a high floor. "Wait," said Halim, again. Again a minute passed. Adam said nothing. A second flash of pinpoint amber light.

"Now," said Halim.

Daoud turned his parking light on and then off. The ghosts of men left the structure and disappeared into the blackness.

"Say nothing, Adam," said Halim. "Do not fight. You will be safe."

Adam's door opened, and before he could react, a sack pulled down over his head. A hand gripped his upper arm propelling him from the car and into the house.

Another pair of hands pressed him into a chair. "Take off this bag," Adam said. His hands weren't bound, but he remembered his cousin's admonition.

"Blindness is for your own protection and for ours. If you are

192

captured and cannot identify us, we might live."

"You obviously know who I am," said Adam.

"Of course, Colonel Michaels. We know you well. Most importantly, we know you are the designer and the architect behind the guidance device. And, you are likely the only person who could defeat the system given the time we have left."

"So unless you are Rahim Tajalli, I'm safe and shouldn't be wearing a hood."

"You are in no position to demand, but you are right about some things. You are safe with us."

"The Yigal Amir?" said Adam. "Why would I consider you safe after killing your own prime minister?"

Someone whispered a protest. "Silence, please," the voice said.

Adam spoke. "You're an American, Midwest or North Central."

The man laughed. "And you're a linguist as well as an engineer? Very funny, but also, very close. I left Utah many years ago when my parents immigrated to Israel. I still return to ski and see old friends. I've never given up my dual citizenship."

"So you are an American?"

"In a manner of speaking, Colonel. And, fighting every day for survival."

"Call me Adam or Major, please. That was a mistake in bureaucratic paperwork."

"As you wish. I am a major general in the Israeli Army and also leader of the Yigal Amir. I cooperate with the Syrians who fight Al-Assad for their freedom and their survival. Your cousin Alhasan Halim Khaddam is the sole general who is not Muslim Brotherhood. Some might consider me a traitor and I acknowledge Yigal Amir has made mistakes. I do not expect you to be a traitor, but defeating an unclassified system is hardly treason."

Adam snorted. "Cooperating with a foreign nation without the knowledge or consent of my own government is questionable at best, General. If I were in your army, would you agree with that logic? And, don't forget you kidnapped me. Now, I'm supposed to willingly cooperate? You're an American, so you tell me, how that would sit with you?"

"Unabashed liberty is overrated," said the general.

"Hardly," said Adam. "And, if that's your answer, you left America just in time. Tell me something. Why is Israel leading this effort? Why isn't the US just as deeply involved and committed?"

"You answer your own question. Didn't your Commander Connecelli send you to Colorado to find answers?"

"That's not proof, and I won't work for you, General. I just spent thirty hours reviewing all the work to date, and frankly there's no reason for me to go back."

The man sat in front of Adam. "Because the answer is found?" Adam said nothing. "Because we are hopelessly behind?"

"Listen, General. I will work for America, and I'll not answer your questions. That's my offer to you."

"You have something in mind."

"Yes, sir. I do. What's your nearest airport with an eight-thousand-foot runway?"

"Kiryat Shmona," he said without hesitation. "Israel. Why?"

"With a call, I can arrange to have people I trust flown into Kiryat Shmona. They will have an escort I also trust. I'll speak with them, but no interference from you. Once I do and if I get the right answers, I'll work to defeat the command module. But you've got to trust me. No matter what."

Adam heard a muffled protest from another part of the room. He resisted the temptation to take the bag from his head.

The general stood. "One moment, Colonel." Several pairs of feet shuffled out of the room. From inside the black bag, he heard men's voices. One sounded angry, as another gave an order. Only a single pair of footsteps returned. "We must make arrangements, first."

"No," said Adam. "You only need to give me access to a mobile phone and rights to enter Israeli airspace. I'll consider anything else to be deceptive."

The other man's silence gave Adam hope. Light unexpectedly bathed the room, attacking Adam's eyes inside the cloth. "Remove the bag, Colonel."

Adam pulled the rough material from his head with a half-dozen bright lamps surrounding his chair. Opposite him sat a mobile phone.

From behind the wall of light, the Israeli general said, "Make your phone call. Be circumspect with the information you give. Your life, as well as those of many others, might depend upon your words."

Chapter 28

Adam spent the next twenty-eight hours alone in the same small room. He slept through the first breakfast and ate like a man starving when Tom shared their noon meal. Only a few words exchanged between the men. Tom granted Adam's requests for a more powerful laptop computer, access to the Internet, paper tablets, and a supply of pencils. He'd slept only in snatches since the tools arrived and worked nearly around the clock.

When night fell and the village was called to prayers, Adam dropped back in the chair to listen. The sound was not unpleasing and he wondered that some believed their god required them to kill the world, while others, following the same god, believed love and acceptance was the true path. If the world survived, Adam wondered, would historians forget this simple truth and make the coming conflagration into some intellectual, geopolitical battle of economies, have and have-nots, or some other intellectual claptrap? Nothing would be further from the truth, or do survivors a bigger disservice.

The last of his encrypted emails arrived when he stretched out on the small cot. He tried to imagine the reception his request would receive in Washington, Bingham, and Atlanta. Getting the government to move quickly doomed a plan to failure. The family owned several Gulfstream jets able to make the flight nonstop, but they would not come. Only one aircraft could do what he proposed.

When the door opened, his eyes opened. "Adam?" said Halim in a whisper. "It is time."

Adam swung his feet to the floor and grabbed up his shirt.

"No, my cousin. You must wear a thwab this time. This will be very dangerous crossing into Israel." Adam looked at the long-sleeved cotton robe Halim held. "In this garb and with your skin, you will stand a better chance. But remember even though nearly half the population is under twenty-five years old, they know and feel the pain of fifty years ago. Any one of them would shoot you without hesitation. We must be careful."

Halim helped with the change of clothing. Sheila met them by the back door and hugged Adam around the waist. An ugly purple scar

196

at her temple marred the smooth skin and still pretty face.

She saw his glance and pulled her hijab to cover it. "I'm sorry I don't remember you, Adam. Tom has told me so much, but they are all new memories. I can only remember the code and then, maybe not so well."

Adam glanced at Tom who kept his eyes on the floor. "We were good friends, Sheila," Adam said. "We still are, the three of us. The Three Amigos. Even if the memory is gone, that fact will never change."

She smiled up at him, and sighed. "I'm against a stone wall. Tom, too. He does wonderful with NASA and so many other scientists, but we need help. And of course," she added in a near whisper, "we need some way to send and have our signal read by the module. Halim explained your young colleague might have discovered something on the night he was killed. I believe Tom and I have a single line of code acceptable to the graphene, but ..." She stopped and looked at Adam, and then Tom, her eyebrows scrunching. "What was I saying?"

Tom spoke. "She's trying to tell you we are slowly unraveling the code. At our rate, in a thousand years when our planet is dead, Sheila and I will have the answer."

She put her hand on her husband's forearm and gently squeezed. "It is a start, Tom. A trip of a thousand miles, and so on." She turned to Adam again. "I remember some things, yes. And others?" She rolled her shoulders. "What you and your unfortunate friend discovered is vital. Now and today. I'm sorry to put this all on you, but really, weren't you the one who conceived this in the first place?"

The dark worm of guilt twisted his gut. "Yes, and I'll do what I can, Sheila." He looked at Tom. "You and I have got to bury the hatchet. If this goes well tonight, we'll have more work than we can handle. We need to recruit the brightest minds."

Tom bit a lower lip and nodded. "One step at a time, like Sheila says."

"I agree," said Adam, and stuck out a hand. "Here's my first step."

Tom looked and then accepted. Neither man smiled.

Halim cleared his throat. "The schedule is critical. We must go."

Daoud again sat behind the wheel. The big Jew handed a silk bag to Halim.

"No," said Adam. "If you put that on my head, this deal is off. I'm either in or out."

Halim considered his cousin for a moment, and said, "Okay, Adam, no bag. But I warn you, no other changes. Too many lives are at stake."

An invisible dog barked as they passed an olive grove with old and twisted trees reaching into the night. Adam saw a rocky road that wound down the hill and between scrub, and wondered if it led to the old house. At an alley between two war-damaged buildings, Daoud braked and turned. A small truck idled with a single red taillight.

"We will switch vehicles, Adam. Show no one your face. Wrap your kaffiyeh tightly. Do not make eye contact and get into the bed under the tarp. Be very quiet."

Adam nodded and did as he was told. He felt someone tuck the corners of the heavy oiled canvas around the boxes. The sickly odor under the heavy cloth spoke of petroleum, earth, and vegetables. A hand slapped the metal and the truck lurched away without a door opening or closing.

Tires whirred with the pavement as an occasional rock struck the under-fenders. After a half hour, brakes squeaked to a stop. A voice spoke and another answered with a laugh. The weight on the truck's springs shifted. Another voice, but no laughter this time. The canvas pulled from above and a crate shifted a few inches. Insects chirped in the night. Adam watched the dark cloth above him without breathing. Another voice in Arabic. Adam breathed again when hands tucked and tied the cloth.

They soon bounced over rough pavement as the bed came alive with rattles. Adam jostled and slammed. When at last the truck came to a stop, an accented voice whispered in English, "Come out, sir. You are here."

Adam struggled from under the cover into a stark, star-filled darkness. He looked around at the rocky hillside. "Where is here?"

"The blue line. You cross at the Yir'on Cemetery, but we must

198

wait."

Adam faced the driver. A boy, maybe sixteen though probably younger watched the shadows, wary and listening for any sound. He never moved more than a few feet from the cab. Adam saw a Kalashnikov rifle wedged in the front seat.

One moment, they waited in a rock-strewn field, the next, six black-clad men surrounded and seized their arms throwing them spread eagle to the ground. "What is your name?" whispered a short, powerful man wearing a black balaclava and holding a small machine pistol to Adam's temple. A wrong answer would end in his death.

"Adam Michaels."

"What is your title?"

"Colonel, major, or doctor. You pick."

"What is your home state?

"New York. Of late, Colorado. But, let's not confuse things. New York is my residence."

"What is your mother's first name?"

"Lillian and that's enough. The answers I've given you are all correct. Either we go or send us back. You pick."

The man wasn't done. "What are your three highest commendations?"

Adam breathed through his teeth. The man had memorized a script. "Silver Star, Bronze Star, Purple Heart, and that's enough. We're wasting time we don't have."

"Strip the rifle," ordered the man. The AK-47 dropped to the ground in pieces. "You were to come unarmed."

"I am. Don't blame the boy. He was probably never told."

"Come quickly."

The small group of men surrounded Adam as they moved down the slope of boulders and squat trees. He heard the truck start and drive off behind him. A sign in several languages warned trespassers of the frontier crossing. Adam saw movement-detection boxes on high stands and heard the low swish of the rotor blades, a familiar and gut-clenching sound. Just beyond a stand of small trees and stone monuments, a Sikorsky S-65 idled with its position lights extinguished. A distinctive camouflage pattern, refueling probe, and bulbous infrared night-vision pod protruded from the nose. The

199

Sayeret, a secretive and elite Israeli commando force feared by their enemies, often used the American helicopter as their workhorse.

"Come," said the leader, taking Adam's shoulder and propelling him toward the lowered ramp. The team boarded as the helicopter lifted into the dark sky and sped bare inches above the tops of trees toward the black hills of the Golan Heights.

The ramp stayed open as Adam watched the night landscape fall behind them in a surrealistic swirl of heat exhaust and dark trees. The leader leaned into his ear. "Your contacts landed thirty minutes . ago. You are late."

Adam nodded.

The twinkling lights of the sleeping countryside passed under and trailed behind the open ramp of the huge helicopter. In scant minutes, the nose pitched and they arched into a tight buttonhook. Adam gripped the aluminum seat frame as the rear wheels planted on the taxiway and the nose lowered.

"Go out the back," said the leader, yelling and gesturing with his hand. "Turn left and walk toward the airplane. You go alone."

Adam grabbed the loose folds of his thwab and ducked under the swinging rotors. A hundred feet away he saw the Boeing 767's bright aluminum skin reflecting the building's security lamps. A diesel ground-power cart chuffed dark exhaust and rumbled in the cool night. Airstairs waited on one side while gunman fanned the perimeter. Two Israeli Humvee jeeps with men at the machine guns bracketed the big airplane.

A powerfully built man stepped from one vehicle and stopped Adam. "We are drawing unwanted attention, Colonel. Make your decisions quickly."

"I'll do my best, General." He glanced up at his grandfather's grim countenance framed in the lighted doorway above, and didn't wait for a reply. He took two steps at a time.

"Never quite out of the fire, are you, son?" said Julius as they embraced.

"Sorry, Grandpa. This was just too important and I couldn't think of anyone else to ask."

Age made their final inroads on Adam's first and most-loved mentor. "About time you gave an old man his due." They stepped out of the framed doorway. "Not that I'm complaining, but why isn't the government supporting you?"

"They're too slow, bureaucratic, and ask too many questions. I'll bring them in, but for now we've got to be quick."

The old man glanced at the soldier on the ramp and nodded. "Whatever I've got, you've got, too. It's always been that way."

"Thanks, Grandpa."

"Of course, you've never asked me for anything before, so this does mark a first."

Adam looked at the empty main cabin of individual chairs, desks, and couches. Julius McCaffrey's business staff was gone. In their place sat Leo Simmons reading a sheaf of papers.

Julius said, "We made a stop in Malta. Joseph Muscat's father and I worked together many years ago. His son, the new prime minister granted a visa for my staff to take a quick vacation." He shrugged his big workman's shoulders. "I left them with a pile to do, so they won't have much fun. They're also scared shitless, just like me, so keeping busy is best. Everybody knows something is up."

Adam walked to the NSC agent and took his outstretched hand. "Thanks for coming, Leo."

"Happy to help, but I'm afraid the news isn't good." Leo's mouth set in a grim line.

Adam nodded. "Were you able to fill in my grandfather?"

Leo shook his head. "No. My information is a game changer, but it's not the latest. You need to make that decision."

"Okay, you two," Julius said. "Code talking went out of style seventy five years ago. I know more than you think." Julius poured some cranberry juice. "I work all over the globe, so I've got an idea what's going on. A terrorist somehow hijacks a rocket and blasts an asteroid. Now, we've got trouble on Earth. Adam's got a piece of this and probably has something to do with the doctorate at MIT. Sound close?"

Leo looked at Adam, who held up both hands. "Not me. I never said a word about that. I only explained the shootout, the attempted kidnapping, and the introduction of my new family."

"Give me some credit here," interrupted Julius. "I wanted to know why my grandson would get in a big dustup in New Jersey, quit a career in the Army when he just made lieutenant colonel, and join a government contractor out west. Don't forget, he has the keys to one of the world's biggest corporations. It doesn't take a rocket scientist to figure he's on some kind of mission." Julius turned to Adam. "Then, two weeks ago, you're involved in a murder in Colorado, and you disappear. You sort of left out the stuff that led up to that, didn't you?" Adam couldn't say anything. "Right. Why all of a sudden is the media on your side? Hero of Kandahar disappears. Somebody's pulling some strings."

"Wait. Media?" said Adam, turning to Leo. "Sounds like that's not the abduction you were talking about."

The agent accepted a glass of the cranberry juice, as Julius scowled. "You took a hell of a chance, Adam. And not very smart, if you ask me." He scowled at Leo, who held up his hands.

"I can't disagree with you, Mr. McCaffrey."

"I know it wasn't your decision, Leo. Forget it." Julius turned to Adam. "Then, a woman is blogging, gets on TV for every national and local outlet and demands action." He drained the juice. "And, lo and behold, she gets it. She's lovely of course, so they have her on the morning shows and nightly news. She makes some pretty strong pleas and shakes up some politicians. They start calling for action, too. Brad Benchley's leading the parade. That's not providence my grandson. That's a plan."

Adam smiled at the thought of Miranda Cinclaire calling Brad on the carpet. "I'm guessing you don't watch many movies, Gramps."

"Movies? Of course not," said Julius. "The entire world is hunting for you and don't call me Gramps."

"This is all gratifying, of course. But what does it really mean? It's like Dick Roberts demanding world peace. He only gets attention because he's a movie star."

Leo walked over and cocked an eyebrow toward Adam. "I don't know what you're talking about. She's been a major pain in the ass at the Commission, raising holy hell with me and everyone else. My boss called me to explain why MSNBC and FOX were calling him … personally. Keep in mind the NSC boss talks to the president daily, not little shits like me."

Adam thought of the strong-willed Miranda using her lovely

face and success as a bully pulpit, and smiled. "She is really something."

"You could say that," said Julius, offering more juice. "She is a pain in the ass. I kind of like her."

Leo voiced their concern. "I'm sorry about William. We should've known better. Bad decision to let them get too close. We tried to keep eyes on Rahim Tajalli but never saw Sara Lin Chen coming. That was a royal screw-up." The small man fell into the chair. "A month I'd never want to repeat." Then he thought about what he said. "Maybe I would, if we can stop this."

Adam said, "It is what it is, Leo, but now we need our secrecy for just a little while longer. How'd you get Miranda to back off?" He poured water from a decanter.

Leo looked confused. "You mean Miranda Cinclaire?"

Julius said, "The movie star?"

"Right," said Adam, looking at both men. "If she hadn't stopped raising Cain, as you guys put it, Rahim Tajalli might get back on point. How'd you get her to back off?"

Julius stood. "As far I know, she never said a word. It's Andrea Montgomery raising holy hell."

A surprised Adam sipped his water. "Really? Not Miranda? Okay, I'll have to think about that later." He turned to Leo. "We need to bring Julius up to speed. Were you able to get the documents?"

The three sat forming a small triangle in the quiet hum of the big airplane's cabin.

"No, sorry. Yesterday, I got a visit from Homeland Security. They went through my desk, and even served a warrant at my house. The agents took everything. I don't know why they didn't arrest me." He drew out two handwritten sheets. "I sort of wrote down everything I could remember on the trip out here." He handed the paper to Julius. "Sorry, but this is all I've got." He looked over at Adam. "You might not be privy to the new security level in DC, but we're at 'Severe.' That's red on the silly color chart. Homeland Security is blacked out …" He paused to consider for a moment. "Maybe the color should be black. Most of the alphabets agencies are unplugged and networking inside their own firewalls. The NSA cut all outside connections inside their hardened facility. After last Monday's briefing, all I've got is my memory."

Adam watched his grandfather read the paper and turned to Leo. "How does isolating everyone help? If no one's talking, we learn nothing."

Leo shrugged. "I know and you know, but everybody's got regulations they follow. It's the DC way. Individual thinkers are swallowed. This is what happens when the government's just too damn big, which is why we wasted time serving a search warrant on me." He shook his head. "I don't want to end my days in jail."

Julius handed the pages back. "Sorry, guys, but my people wrote a much more updated briefing paper on this weeks ago after I met Adam in Boulder."

Adam smiled in wonder. "You're something else, Grandpa."

"That's probably old now, too," Julius said. "I'll get an update."

Adam watched his grandfather walk to a bank of phones. He turned to Leo. "Don't worry. I'll do everything I can for you." The other man nodded and said nothing. "Tom thinks the Rahim Tajalli researchers are working the same angles we did at Indron. That's not good, but they don't have our resources."

"You've got a theory?" Leo asked, taking a deep breath and tuning back into the conversation.

Adam nodded. "William developed the concept and they killed him for it. It's why my grandfather and the shipping company are important." They both looked at Julius who'd hung up the phone. "You'll be way out on a limb here, Grandpa. We're going to need the military, too. We're got bigger problems than holding off the Rahim Tajalli."

Leo nodded. "I'm tracking, Adam, but this will get touchy fast."

"We're already way behind," Adam said.

"We need Madison Avenue," Leo said. "Somebody's gotta sell this to the leadership."

"You're right, and I know just the guy." Adam smiled. "A new congressman with a winning way about him."

Julius waved his hand between the two men. "Knock it off. I feel like I'm at a tennis match. What are we talking about here, Adam?

I assume you want to bring company resources to bear."

"Yes, sir, I do. We'll need a lot more than just McCaffrey Shipping. Were you able to bring Marty with you?"

The old man jabbed an intercom button on the couch arm. Marty Callaway stepped in from the front cabin. His black hair showed the first hints of silver. Adam stood up and embraced the man.

"Oh, boy," said Marty with his best Boston accent. "We must be in real trouble for a greeting like that."

"I ... the world really needs you and your talents, Marty. We're already too late to stop the first move, so we're in damage-control mode." Adam turned to Leo. "How long to first strike?"

Leo didn't need to think about the answer. "Less than twenty days."

"We need some time to talk this out and lay out a plan." He turned to Julius. "Is there a way we can disappear for a day and come back tomorrow night? I know your schedule's probably full but—"

"Nonsense." Julius turned to a computer screen and with quick and adept fingers, typed out orders.

"I'll clear the tarmac," said Leo. "Give me a minute." He left out of the main cabin door for the stairs.

Julius lifted the intercom phone and spoke a moment. He listened and then laughed. "What're they going to do? Shoot us down?"

The thought sounded like a possibility until Leo stepped back in with a grin. "Let's go."

Marty swung the big door closed. "I'm glad we're on the same side, Leo. What'd you say to that guy?"

The two big turbofan engines whined as they started up.

Leo shrugged. "The Israeli lieutenant wasn't too happy, but I told him my boss could beat up his boss."

"What?" said Adam with a laugh.

"Yeah," Leo said. "I told him to put me on the horn with his guy. We talked and agreed. Wasn't that much to it."

Adam laughed. "I recognized the guy out there running this security op. He was the badass from the other night. An American and former US Army, spec ops, now of the Yigal Amir."

Leo glanced up. "Very good, that would've been Ben Halevi.

You should've been one of us, Adam."

They smiled at one another, quite the contrast of men, and yet firm in solid friendship.

Adam buckled into a chair next to Julius, and said, "Is Kim Jaegwon still your choice for CEO?"

"The job is yours, Adam. It's always been yours."

Adam put a hand on the wrist of the only father he'd ever known. "You've got the right guy, Grandpa. He's terrific even if he's not a McCaffrey. The best in the world."

"That's ironic," said the old man, buckling his own seat belt. "Kim says the same thing about you. I assume you want to include him in this briefing?"

"Yes, I do unless someone objects."

Leo shook his head. "Not me. I don't know what you're thinking, but I'll cover for you."

"Good," said Adam. "Once we're up, can we get him on the Satlink?"

Julius said, "Sure. Kim is in Vancouver at our Canadian shipyard."

"Great." Adam calculated for a moment. "New York. Have him meet us at LaGuardia. We're seven hours away and he's five. It'll work. We can brief on the way. We need to bring him in as quickly as possible, and face-to-face is best."

James stepped. "Dinner anyone?"

Adam laughed, unbuckled and hugged his childhood friend. "No vacation in Malta for you?"

"Life's a vacation for me, Adam. Dinner's a half hour after we level off. I'll let the captain know." The man left the cabin heading for the cockpit.

The big plane moved off the ramp and taxied for the runway's end. "Adam?" said Julius. "Why don't you move to the forward conference room? I'll handle setting up the Satlink from here, and get Kim on the Gulfstream. We'll brief in twenty minutes."

"Why?" Adam unbuckled, confused.

"Just go. This will help both of us."

Adam snapped on the overhead light as he closed the door behind him. Andrea looked up. "Oh. Are you taking drink orders?"

Surprised, Adam said, "Hi. I didn't know you were here."

She shook her head and sighed. "Hi, yourself. You are one very tough guy to supervise."

The aircraft accelerated as the power demand from the two huge turbofan engines increased. "I guess my grandfather kidnapped you."

"Seems to be all the rage these days. Very cloak-and-daggerish. I'm assuming neither you nor I are prisoners, and that William is still dead." Andrea's voice had an icy edge.

He let out a breath and buckled into the seat next to her. "We had nothing to do with the grab, I promise. I'll explain everything, but others are pulling the strings." She eyed his robes as they bumped down the runway. "There's a lot going on you need to hear, Andrea. I'm glad you came along."

"I didn't have much of a choice after all the fuss."

"We'll have more options once we clear Israeli airspace." She arched an eyebrow but said nothing. "We have some things to talk about."

She patted his hand. "Yes, we do."

Adam told her the whole story. They would need someone articulate and aggressive to be with Brad, and she already had a national audience.

When the last Israeli F-15 fell behind the Boeing, he stopped talking and flipped off the overhead light. The dark Mediterranean below reflected stars as they flew toward North America.

A quiet knock at the main cabin door told both their few minutes were over.

"Thanks for joining our ragtag crew," Adam said. "I hope it was more voluntary than not."

"In a manner of speaking, volunteerism is over rated. You might remember that."

"I'm not sure how to do this, Andrea. Leo's a pretty straight guy about the rules and all. But I have this feeling you'll not tell anyone what I've told you tonight until you get the go-ahead signal."

"Smart boy," she said. Her bright blue eyes crinkled at their corners. "In for a penny, Adam. Let me help."

He breathed relief. "Great, join us in the main cabin. We need your mind and the loud voice I heard about."

"Big mouth, you mean." She grew serious. "How much time do we have?"

He watched her for a moment. "That really is the question, isn't it?"

Chapter 29

The F-22 Raptor pulled off as the McCaffreys' Boeing touched the concrete of New York's LaGuardia runway while the eastern sky edged against the night's retreat. Long streaks of rubber obliterated much of the numbering and white striping over the years.

The big airplane taxied in the closed airport, stopping at the Art Deco Marine Air building. Several airport vehicles waited with rotating yellow lights. Behind them an array of silent black Suburbans of somber men waited. Each was armed with H&K MP10 machine guns.

The pilot turned to Adam with a grin. "I just got a patched phone call from the mayor. He asked us to get the hell out of his airport so he can open up."

"I got it, Frank. We'll be fast as possible."

Adam watched from the pilot's vantage point, but wasn't interested in the mayor or the armed escort. She wasn't there. He'd pictured her dark hair ruffled by the morning wind and now, forced himself to dismiss the image.

The copilot ran the shutdown checklist while the engines quieted and the auxiliary power unit started. "Thanks, guys," said Adam, standing to return to the cabin. "And thanks for the change of clothes. You up for a five-hour return flight?"

"No sweat, sir," said the captain. "We're picking up Bernie and Theo. That'll give us 'round-the-world crew so we can go anywhere for as long as we need."

"Thanks," Adam said and backed out of the cramped spaces. Julius waited in the forward cabin, alone. Adam searched his face. "No good, huh?"

The older man shook his head. "I called an associate. He's trying to find her. You know it's barely five in the morning here."

"Yes. If she isn't at the apartment, maybe she's out of town."

Julius pressed his lips together.

Adam knew his grandfather's expressions. "Okay. But you're still looking, right?"

"This isn't a good idea, Adam. Maybe we should stick to

209

business."

"This might be my last chance, Grandpa. She could be in California or Louisiana. Before Tom decided to have me kidnapped, she talked about a studio in a New Orleans facility. She might've gone there."

Julius shook his head. "No. This is the last week of the play, Adam. I've checked. She's not in Louisiana or California—" Julius's phone buzzed.

Adam blew air from puffed checks as his grandfather took the call. A car without headlights pulled from beside the Marine Terminal and toward the stair truck.

Julius punched the phone off. "They found her, Adam. She'll be here in an hour." The man's face was drawn. Something he wasn't saying. "Sorry, son."

Adam's eyes dropped as he tried to shake off his grandfather's disappointment. Kim bounded up the stairs. He was shorter than Adam's six-one, but wide and powerful. The men didn't bother with handshakes but hugged, slapping one another's backs.

"Damn, it's good to see you," Kim said. "I was worried sick when I heard."

The man before him was fifteen years Adam's senior and a fierce businessman. He'd proved a great friend and mentor learning the shipyards and its people.

"I'm glad to see you, too, Kim. Let's get coffee and I'll tell you everything I know and think we need."

Kim slowed as he considered his friend. "Other than the world coming to an end, what's the matter?"

"Girl problems," Adam said with a laugh. "Sorry."

"Well, screw the world, let's talk girls."

That gave Adam a chance to let loose a belly laugh. Kim joined him and it felt good. "Okay. I get the message. I've got some ideas from Indron. In truth, they're a dead guy's ideas. Tell me what you think."

Kim grasped the basics of the science and planned the logistics of support before the second cup of coffee filled his cup. "The *American Farmer*'s re-provisioning and refitting was completed in Pascagoula last night after some deck repairs," he said. "Julius found me in the yards in Vancouver, BC, and said we needed an empty containership. The *Emma McKinley* just completed her offload in Yokohama and is getting ready for new cargo. I can stop that and wait for the equipment."

"Yes," said Adam. "We'll need both. One in the Atlantic and one Pacific. Both southern hemisphere, so they'll have to run fast after they're loaded." The cabin grew quiet in thought. Julius had joined them. "Did you have any luck with intel on the Japanese space agency, Grandpa?"

"Yes and no," Julius said. "The Japanese keep denying their moon base had anything to do with Pakistan's satellite shot. Toshi's on the PM's staff and he's my friend, but he's under pressure from the Diet. Some in the Japanese leadership are running for political cover, interested only in saving face. We might need to crack this nut a different way."

"Who's to blame can wait," said Adam, gesturing toward the couch as Leo came in to sit. "We need access to the airport at Haneda. Japanese cooperation might not be as big a problem as getting the right equipment to the right place. Time is our biggest enemy now."

Julius worked on that problem, too. "I've called in a favor from Weatherford Benchley."

"Jesus, Grandpa. Do you know everyone?"

"Not by a long shot. I'm afraid my contact is an old man who's already passed the baton." Julius scrunched bushy eyebrows. "Oh, yeah, sorry. Congressman Benchley got here ten minutes ago. Are you ready for him?"

Adam turned to Kim and Leo. "Are we?"

Kim nodded. "Sure. Whatever you need."

Andrea spoke for the first time. "If I'm working on public relations, Congressman Benchley will be key. I'll go introduce myself."

"Thanks, Andrea," Adam said.

The aircraft cabin fell silent for a moment. Leo was calculating on an iPad, and finally tapped his answer. "Okay. I think I've got most of this for now. I'll call my boss to make contact with the embassy in Japan. They'll have to give the okay for the C5As to land at Haneda. A lot of the equipment is at dozens of military bases and factories all over the country. That's a lot of flying. Getting stuff to Mississippi is easy compared to Japan. Permission to do this takes a month, and you're giving me what, a couple of days?" He leaned back and kicked out his short legs to stand. "Okay, no problem."

Everyone had a quick laugh. Brad stepped into the airplane's conference room. "Did I miss something, or were you telling another Brad Benchley joke?"

Andrea was a pace behind the tall, blond man.

Adam stood and shook his hand. "Hi, Congressman. We need to borrow a couple dozen Air Force cargo planes. And, the Boeing 747 Airborne Laser from Edwards."

Brad looked from face to face, realizing the seriousness of the request. "I can manage the cargo planes, but the YAL-1 was mothballed a year ago."

"Oh, shit," said Kim. "We need it to shoot down a comet."

Brad rotated his head to look at the man.

"Not really," Kim said. "But close to it."

Brad nodded. "I know you guys aren't kidding. Not when my father calls me at two in the morning and tells me to get my ass to LaGuardia pronto." He looked at Adam. "I'm just an old helicopter pilot with a day job now, and I'll get you the cargo airplanes, but I don't know about the rest."

"It's a start, Brad," Adam said. "Judy Walsh's second-in-command from Indron is in charge of locating the equipment. Judy and Peter are otherwise occupied with one of our alphabet agencies."

Leo said, "Don't forget government regulations. There's no time to reorient departments, so we all need to keep our crayons coloring inside the lines for a while longer. We get crosswise with one of the bureaucracies and they use rules to make decisions ... old rules that don't apply anymore."

Adam agreed. "Keeping things under wraps is good advice for all of us. Brad? Can you call the boneyard at Davis-Monthan and see if the YAL's still flyable? I think that's how it's stored. I also searched the missile shoot-down concept, a couple of solid-state lasers, and a megawatt-class, oxygen-iodine power generator. The equipment's probably in boxes at Edwards Air Force Base. Nobody tosses government equipment after only a year. We really need to hustle if

212

we're going to get all the pieces and parts in the same spot at the same time." He looked around the room. "Did you guys know, out of twenty-two tests against twenty-two incoming missiles, this thing never missed?"

Julius said, "And this is the program we dumped?"

Adam answered. "Yep. The base commanders need to turn their guys out of bed and start looking for our stuff. Now. Get the technicians who kept it working until a year ago."

He turned to Brad. "We're not shooting down an asteroid. We're going to send the guidance module new orders. A young friend of mine from Colorado had an idea that might work, but only with a laser powerful enough to leave the atmosphere and go into deep space. The systems to produce that kind of power are huge, far bigger by an order of magnitude than what a Boeing 747 Freightliner or a YAL can lift. My idea is to build them on two containerships. Unfortunately, the ship systems can't aim the signal as precisely as the YAL. Three lasers, two big ones, and one small but dead accurate aiming beam. Hit the damn guidance module when it comes out from behind the sun. What do you guys think?"

Brad calculated with the mind of an ex-aviator. "The closer in, the more deflection you'll need to make it miss. The farther out, the signal will disperse more. There is a sweet spot we'll need to find." He turned to Julius. "I've met the base commander at Davis-Monthan, sir. Can you get me there? Maybe I can motivate him to get the airplane en route to … where?"

Adam spoke up. "Point Mugu Naval Air Station, on the coast north of LA. Edwards isn't too far away. Tom Connecelli told me Mugu has the research and test facilities we'll need to make sure the thing is put together the right way."

Julius picked up the cockpit phone. "Frank? Will you get the Gulfstream crew to plan …" He looked at Brad. "Yuma?" He received a nod. "You'll need permission to land there. When you call, tell them to wake up the commander and expect a phone call from Congressman Benchley. They need to call Edwards and Point Mugu, too. Same deal. When you get that done, reverse course and get the Congressman and Ms. Montgomery to where they need to go. They need to do some PR planning."

213

Brad turned to go but stopped, putting his hand on Adam's arm. "Do you remember Lynn Kostunica from DC?"

Adam smiled. "Sure. Nice lady. Beautiful and very smart lady."

"Beautiful, yeah, but not so smart." His eyes twinkled and yet, a worry line creased his forehead. "I convinced her to marry me." He stopped. "Don't mean to gloat, Adam. You know me, Mr. Bigmouth. Sorry."

"No way," Adam said, grabbing the man's hand. "That's great. I'm really happy for you."

"Thanks." But he wanted to say more. "Adam? Do you think we can do this?"

"I ... I don't know."

Brad's eyes misted and dropped to the carpet. "I want time with Lynn. I want to make a life with her, but now ... crap."

Adam took him by the shoulders. "We'll all try. I'll try my damnedest, Brad. You know I'd do anything for you."

The cabin grew still and quiet. Brad pressed his lips together. "I'm sorry, man. I just—"

"No worries. We all have work to do, you more so than anyone. You've got to rally the public so the government will get in gear."

He nodded and took a breath. "Thanks, Adam. Miranda's waiting in the lobby." He shook his head. "She had a few words for me. Sorry, again."

Adam kept the smile. "Okay. Good luck out there to you and Andrea, and be persuasive."

Brad nodded to Andrea and the two left out the main hatch.

Two minutes later, Adam swung open the building's door. She stood there in a long coat and heels, looking tired and drawn. Instead of going to him, she withdrew into herself, pulling the coat close.

"Are you okay?" he said, reaching out his hands.

"Fine," she answered with a sharp edge, and sat down. "I'm fine. They told me you were kidnapped. Dead probably. It was all over the news." Her angry words clipped around phrases. "What is going on, Adam? Why didn't you call me?"

"I couldn't. Actually, I was kidnapped in a manner of speaking.

214

In all honesty, I remained there willingly enough."

She watched him, her eyes intent on his face. "Well, I was kidnapped, too, Adam. Right out of bed. By the NYPD. What kind of bullshit is that?"

"I know, and I'm sorry. I didn't have any time and just wanted to make sure you're safe. You weren't answering your phone."

She ignored his calming voice. "Before you start with me, Adam Michaels, you better realize you don't own me." She breathed hard. "Don't you *ever* send a bunch of thugs to knock down my door again. This is all part of the deal, you know. Stan Jacobs is my producer, and I do what I have to do for my career. I like you, Adam. Maybe I like you too much, but I don't appreciate being tracked down in the middle of the night like some criminal. What the hell is Stan going to think? They braced him, you know. In his own home."

Angry tears welled. For a few minutes, he forgot about the world. He considered the weekends flying back and forth, the late nights loving this woman, and then catching up under tiny reading lights in the Gulfstream or the Citation. The actor's world, tempest-tossed with deals and compromises, life and love, give and take. Miranda had found the harbor she needed. He knew what was coming, but she didn't. This lovely woman might need all the skills she possessed to survive. Could he blame her?

"Stan Jacobs," Adam said. "Are you and he together?" Miranda watched him, a tear tracing a path down her cheek was his answer. "Okay. How long?"

"Does it matter?"

Adam shook his head and watched the floor. "No. I suppose not."

"He made it clear to me that if I wanted a future in movies … well. You know the rest of that already, don't you? Didn't you already accuse me of this when you showed up on my doorstep an hour after he left?"

"It doesn't matter, Miranda." Adam wrapped her in his arms, kissed the soft sweetness of her cheek, and felt the trembling of her body. Now, he needed to get to Katherine and Julie. "Miranda? Will you go to Bingham and my family's farm, and wait there?"

She pressed her lips together. "No, of course not. I live here.

My career is here. I can't survive on another farm and I wouldn't want to."

"Bingham will be safe. New York will not. No big city will be safe. My home isn't really like a farm, farm. We have indoor plumbing." Flat joke. "Please go, Miranda. There will be others there."

"What's going on?" she demanded, holding his eyes. "Tell me."

"You'll have to trust me. It's better you go to Bingham and wait."

She shook her head. "No. Stan and I have a meeting with Dick Roberts in Manhattan a week from Tuesday. Call me after and we'll talk."

Adam doubted the conversation would ever take place. "Okay. My friend, Marty Callaway, will check on you in a couple of weeks."

"Don't bother. If the meeting goes right, I'll be in Los Angeles then back to New York with Stan. We're going to Miami for a game show appearance. And then maybe Jamaica to … relax."

Adam watched her face until she finally dropped her eyes and stared out the windows.

"This is just the way it is, Adam. Accept it. We can still be together, just not … together."

The breath escaped his lungs and suddenly all the hours, the days, the tension stole his energy, and he felt tired. And old.

"Okay," Adam said after a pause. "Marty Callaway, Miranda. Don't forget his name."

Chapter 30

Adam spent the next two weeks with Tom and Sheila, hidden in the village of Markaba. They struggled with ideas and calculations under the watchful protection of the Yigal Amir. Tom was as good as his word and organized a dozen think tanks around the world. The best minds of the twenty-first century got little sleep. Adam forgot day and night, and simply rolled off the cot after a few hours and set back to work at his computer. Others around the globe used the time differences to join in the effort to develop a code to stop the cataclysm to come.

At noon Tehran time as the third week began, Rahim Tajalli made an announcement via Iranian state television. Worldwide affiliates joined with thousands of Internet websites to carry the announcement. The YouTube video alone took nearly a million hits in a few hours, crashing the site and giving many countries time to take it down. The media release from Tehran ranked the follow-up announcement as the second most-watched program of the decade behind World Cup Soccer finals. POTUS, his advisors, and Adam shouldn't have been concerned with secrecy. Rahim Tajalli set an excellent stage.

Start News Feed

NBC News feed, AP wire, CNN Satlink.

Rebel conservative Iranian religious leader Mahmoud Mossadegh and outlaw Pakistan Taliban cleric Sami Aziz jointly announced today a declaration of war against the Americas, the European and Asian nations, and the Pacific nations opposed to Islamic conversion and submission to Sharia law. The United States in particular was called out to immediately lead a nationwide declaration of submission.

"The coming attack on infidel homelands and

the devil USA will destroy all those opposing the will of Allah," the leaders are quoted saying in a joint communiqué. The two fell short of laying out details. "Initial strikes will occur on April 14th from the heavens and against non-Muslim world enterprises and peoples. Immediate and heartfelt conversion to Islam and the Prophet Mohammed are a must to enter Paradise."

Most western nations raised their security alert levels.

Although specifics are scarce, an official of the Iranian space command and the rebellious offshoot of the Pakistan Taliban's high military commanders composed a backdrop for the public speech. The Pakistan president and government denounced the coup d'état as rebel soldiers and elite Iranian Revolutionary Guard attacked key Islamabad facilities, driving government forces out. Countries around the world, including the United States and other key nations, condemned the attack and announcement as incendiary and counter to world peace. The UN Security Council pledged its support to the legitimate and duly elected government of Pakistan. Warrants were issued for the arrests of Aziz and others. Fighting between dissidents and loyalists erupted throughout the country. India mobilized nearly five hundred thousand troops in the Kashmir region in response to the coup. Fears of a nuclear holocaust were expressed throughout the world as the United Nations called a special session.

The Israeli government went on high alert and national mobilization.

The Iranian government repeated its open call for jihad and terminated talks with the United

States and the European Union. Officials of Great Britain's Astronomical Association reacted to the announcement, speculating the communiqué may refer to the Eros Asteroid mission hijacked by the errant European Space Agency robot rocket. A mysterious pulse of energy from the area of the Japanese moon base was observed thirty months ago, and remains unexplained. At the time, a South African amateur astronomer observed debris from a mysterious explosion as a coming meteor shower. The Russian space agency that launched the joint European asteroid mission had no comment. Several world scientists speculated a global calamity would result from impact with the fragments of the Eros Asteroid. Markets plunged to decade lows shortly after the announcement. Fighting broke out between sectarian groups and radical ISIS cells in Paris, New York, Detroit, and Amsterdam. World leaders called for calm. The Rahim Tajalli called for jihad and death to infidels.

End of News Feed

Adam, Tom, and Sheila worked around the clock as before. Now, the only sleep they found was a head on a desktop or while standing to make more coffee. If it were possible, after the first strike, their urgency grew. Governments and corporations around the world hacked into the computer systems of others while allegations and counter-allegations tested friendships and formed new alliances. .

"Being on a computer connection to the Internet is dicey at best now," Marty said in the hovel's quiet little kitchen.

Adam's face was ashen from a lack of sleep and questionable nutrition. "I understand Julius had a narrow escape." Dark circle rimmed tired eyes.

Marty nodded. "He was on the horn speaking with French president Robert Surcouf, to arrange time on the Altix supercomputer, when the first chunks broke through the atmosphere."

"Thank God he made it." Adam unscrewed the top from the plastic water bottle and poured. "Without Julius …" He stopped and gave a pump, and lighted a match. The hiss adjusted with the twist of a knob and he settled into the chair to wait on the kettle. "I don't think I could have gone on."

Marty sat at the tiny kitchen table watching Adam. "The airspace was cleared only about fifteen minutes before the first fragments hit the atmosphere around Dallas. There were so many planes with so many passengers, your grandfather wouldn't pull rank. Everyone waited on the FAA to get their orders and evacuate the area. Two minutes lag time separating altitudes …" He shook his head. "They couldn't have people running into each other. My guess is Julius continued to horse trade with the French president while poor old Frank finally got his clearance and was fighting for altitude."

Adam smiled. "Of that, I don't doubt. I'm glad he got time on the supercomputer, though. A lot of countries pulled their scientists and researchers after the announcements. I think the Frenchies just wanted to make sure they could share in the data."

"You getting any sleep?" Marty asked. "You're looking a little drawn."

"Is that a nice way of saying I look like shit?"

Marty smiled. "Yes, but not a lot different than probably half the rest of the world."

Adam nodded. "There's lots of people working to unscrew this royal screw-up."

"I hope that's not self-blame or pity, I hear. Doesn't fit you."

Adam smiled. "Maybe a little of both, but it's gone."

"Better be," Marty said. "You getting the news? You know the South African astronomers confirmed the hit was the detritus in retrograde orbit."

"Yeah. I got an email from a couple of guys in the Netherlands this morning. They're saying Rahim Tajalli took credit. The bastards are chortling for everyone to hear." Adam looked over. "A lot of people died in the last twenty hours."

"Yeah. You guys need to pull this off, or no one's going to be around to mourn them."

They sat in their own thoughts for several minutes. The kettle hissed, then whistled. Adam stood and made tea. Marty pushed over the small packages of thumb drives. He'd made this trip twice a week for the last three.

Marty said, "Mullahs supporting this crappy terrorism are urging conversions as the first step to paradise. Fence sitters made their choice when the first of the meteors hit the upper atmosphere. A lot of people crossed over and it didn't matter if they were Christian, Hindu, or Buddhist. National governments were a little slower. Lots of fistfights in parliaments around the world. Easier for monarchies. They just made a decree like it's really going to matter." Marty accepted the cup of tea. "Thanks."

Only infrared imaging saw the first meteor to light the daytime sky. Entering on a northeasterly trajectory over Antarctica, the first space rocks to penetrate the earth's atmosphere struck an empty ocean, unfortunate for the Falkland Islands. At many times the power of the largest Tsar hydrogen bomb, a plume of ocean bottom and debris rose forty thousand feet into the air—slight compared to what was projected to come. A thousand square miles of sky darkened, then drifted on the southerly winds. Stanley, the capital of the tiny British protectorate, managed a six-second burst of panicked signal before communications severed. One hundred percent of the human and animal population died in the first thirty seconds. The International Space Station alerted the world with video made viral.

"I saw it, too," Adam said. "It took almost five hundred thousand square miles of ocean to dampen the tidal wave."

Marty nodded. "Three hundred kilometers farther north and the Falklands might have survived."

The United States and Mexico felt the next strikes as the meteors exploded along a line from Chihuahua, Carlsbad, Clovis, and Amarillo. A twenty-mile-wide swath of destruction streaked across the sky breaking windows and eardrums. Loose stands of equipment and pictures fell until the last piece exploded on impact. The blast mirrored a nuclear weapon with an epicenter destroying a power-production plant near Dalhart, Texas. Few survived the initial explosion in a twenty-mile radius. Only a few persons north along Highway 385 lived, as a second, third, and forth plume rose from the innards of

221

America. Survivors suffered third-degree burns in a ninety-mile radius of each fragment. Anemometers tore from their mounts as winds topped two hundred and fifty miles an hour. Hospitals and burn centers opened triage in the parking lots when the buildings could no long handle the burgeoning crowds. A cattle and coal train traveling seventy-five miles an hour near a junction at Stratford disappeared in ash and fragments.

Panic erupted in major American cities. The governors ordered the National Guard to duty but could do little to assuage the panic. Most survived the mayhem, although the bodies of the soldiers and rampaging civilians lay side by side for nearly a day as the cities burned.

Marty spoke again. "You know it wasn't only America and the Falklands, right? A hit in the Indian Ocean, sixteen hours after the Falklands, drowned nearly a million people in Cilacap on Indonesia's southern coast. Only a few survived, but they described three-hundred-foot-high walls of water sweeping away two hundred years of building a new nation. Rahim Tajalli and ISIS claimed the religious tolerance of Indonesia's Muslim majority cost them paradise." Marty smoothed the newspaper and quoted, "'The Islamic world must rise up and kill infidels of all races and creeds.'"

Adam poured more hot water. "The Islamic world needs to rise up and kill the radicals."

Marty continued, scanning the page and reading the occasional line between his summaries. "There's lots of cities fighting it out right now. Nine nuclear-armed nations changed their threat levels, readying for immediate attack. Bombers launched to secret loitering positions to wait, missile silo crews were doubled and locked down. Nuclear submarines of a half-dozen nations settled onto the oceans' bottoms and programmed their missiles. Two keys are already in American dual locks waiting orders, or a countdown. Most countries called for calm. Many did not. They called for war." He blew out a breath. "We just can't seem to kill ourselves fast enough for some people."

Adam brought stale cookies to the table. His eyes were reddened and watery even as the light outside dimmed through the pulled blinds. "All this from a PhD project?" he said and sat.

Sheila walked in and pulled a clean cup from the counter. Her clothing was disheveled and her hair in sleep tangles. "Got any to spare?"

The two men smiled at her. Adam set the package down and wrapped her in a hug. "How much did you hear?"

"I heard enough," she said, pushing him away with a gentle hand. "I can't help what's already happened. We need to fix our future."

Adam sat her in his chair. "I'm sorry you heard it, but you're right. I keep circling the same calculations. I'm positive the concept's sound. I just can't duplicate the power or the delivery that William calculated."

She exhaled and sipped at the cup. "If it were not for William Lee and his research, we would be following my false trail. Remember that. Tom and I were off in nowhere land, certain that electromagnetic pulses held the key. We at least have a chance now with the laser."

Adam pushed the package of flash drives from Marty across the table. "Share these with Tom when he wakes—"

"I'm up." Tom stood in the doorway. His face was lined and gray. He picked up a drive and the last cup. "We might not have the chance to understand because this would take years for testing, no less for production. In the meantime, those guys managed to figure out how to turn the earth into a cemetery." Sheila went to him, silent into his embrace. "How many more hits?"

"Three," Marty said. "The last one to fall was a glancing fireball across Perth. Broken glass and a lot of scared people. It bounced then hit in Changsha Hunan."

Sheila's tears welled. "Do you know more than two million people live in Changsha? Add them to the millions who died in the tidal wave, the Falkland Islands, and America." Her breaths came in starts and stops. "Oh, God. Did we do this?" she said, sliding to the floor. "This is all our fault."

Tom stared into nothingness as Adam knelt down. "Sheila, please. We can fix this. We've got to fix this. We share a guilt, yes, but with the rest of mankind. I know this doesn't mean much, but can you really say all this is our fault? God will question us one day, but until then, we are humanity's best hope. We're not starting from zero. You and Tom and I need to push through our own feelings. Maybe then ..."

223

He watched Marty as his voice trailed away.

She nodded and pulled herself up. "You're right," she said and stood, moving closer to Tom. "I was just having a pity party. I'm done."

Tom took a cookie and his cup. "I need to get back to work."

Marty watched their bedroom door close in the silent little house. "I'll be back in a couple of days. Want me to bring you anything?"

Sheila's lamentations aside, Adam already knew the true fate of their immediate future. Errant chunks of asteroid fooled no one with access to a library or a computer. The asteroid would have to be bigger than all but two or three of the known mini planets circling the sun to do the physical damage first predicted. The true danger lay with the modern world's economies and the population's reaction to stepping back five or more hundred years. Very few would survive such a cataclysmic change to the world's prosperity.

"Marty? I've got to ask you about Miranda."

"She didn't call. I'm sorry. My guys are keeping an eye on her, it's getting tougher all the time. She's been in a house in the LA hills since New Orleans burned. She's still got phone service in LA, and she's got bodyguards." He took a breath. "Look, Adam. I can call her personally, against my better judgment. If that's what you want."

Adam shook his head. "No. No, thanks, anyway."

Chapter 31

Foot-high, orange plastic wedges chocked the wheels on Julius's Boeing 767 at the Bingham airstrip. An umbilical from a shed ran to the belly to maintain power on the systems, while lights shone through the cabin areas and sixty five people worked without a break. Adam stood on the tarmac and watched as a second airplane, a Gulfstream G550, back-taxied on the farm's landing strip. Big lights swung, following a lone lineman waving the business jet to the fuel pumps. The twin engines whined down into silence as polished aluminum skin opened, and the hatch became an airstair. A new crew would take Adam to Pascagoula following the evening briefing. After that, Julius ordered all McCaffrey employees to return to their homes, or go into hiding at the company compounds around the world. The shipyards were locked and reduced to skeleton crews.

Adam reread the text message on his phone. He'd pleaded with Katherine to allow the Gulfstream to pick her up along with Julie and Eric, and his family. But she refused. In the early afternoon she married Eric, allowing the family, including Julie, to be hidden away from a collapsing society in a secret government facility. Soldiers would protect them. He talked with a tearful Julie for many minutes and then made a final appeal to Katherine. He offered them living quarters in the secured area for as long as they wanted, but Katherine said no.

He prepared himself for the second disappointment of the day. Even after weeks of global chaos, he was hopeful Miranda would come. He hired and sent a private team into the city and thought the Gulfstream waiting in Santa Monica would convince her.

Marty stepped onto the concrete, saw Adam, and shook his head. "She said no. I'm sorry."

He nodded. "Okay, thanks. What's it like? In the streets, I mean. Looting, murders, that sort of thing?"

Marty again shook his head. "No. Actually, it's quiet enough in the more stable parts of the city. Others … not so much. The military have the streets cordoned off, and there's a curfew in place. The ex-sergeant I hired says the place is an armed camp waiting to pop its top, though." He looked at Adam's drawn face. "Sorry, I could lie if you want."

Adam chewed his lip and watched the black horizon. "Okay, then," he said, sticking hands deeper into the coat's pockets. "Thanks, Marty. I don't think there's anything more to be done. I hope for her sake, she's careful."

Marty fell silent. A small boy and an only slightly larger girl emerged from inside the plane. Adam turned and said, "And, this must be the Simmons clan."

Leo closed in behind his two oldest children. "Evening, Adam." A small woman with a baby asleep in her arms followed. "This is Carly, my wife. Leo junior and Karen, our son and daughter." The boy nudged closer to his dad, who put a protective hand around both children's shoulders. "I wanted to tell you how much we appreciate—"

"Forgot it, Leo. You've been a great friend and an even greater American. Without you, the world wouldn't have stood much of a chance. This is the least anyone can do for a real hero."

Carly glanced between the two men. "What did you do, Leo?"

"Nothing, hon." She wasn't convinced. "Really, I didn't do a thing."

Adam laughed. "After this is all over, I'll give you all the dirt, Carly. This guy is the real deal. They're going to make a movie about him." Leo, Junior looked up at his dad with new eyes.

"Enough," said Leo. "You keep talking and I'll have to spend the night in your doghouse instead of your guest house."

A Ford van pulled up. A large, slouched man with a Yankees ball cap ambled to the sliding door. Adam introduced them. "Nelson is the property boss, and can get you anything you want. Do you think I could steal Leo for an hour, Carly?"

She touched his forearm. "Yes and thank you, Colonel Michaels. We won't be a burden."

"Of course you won't," Todd said, stepping out of the van. He grabbed up Carly in a hug. "I'm Adam's cousin Todd and my motley crew are here, and can't wait to see you guys."

"Sorry, Carly," Adam said. "He's got no class, although I do like his sixteen or seventeen kids. I don't quite remember how many."

226

"Five," said Todd. "They're all just like me, happy and irreverent. Don't believe a thing this guy says."

The two men looked at one another for a moment. The string in Adam's heart broke at the thought of Julie's absence. Todd saw, and grabbed his younger cousin in a bear hug. "She'll be okay, Adam," he whispered into his ear. "I talked with Katherine. She promised."

Adam nodded, not trusting his voice. He hugged back.

Nelson cleared his throat. "Mr. Michaels? The house car is on its way. I'll take the Simmons family." He turned to the woman. "Good evening, Missus. You'll like the guesthouse. You'll have separate, very private quarters." He looked at the children. "And the pool is heated. Do you kids swim? I can unlock the pool for you in the morning. Mr. McCaffrey's children will be swimming then, too. And, we've got horses you can ride, chickens, a few goats, and sheep. And ducks too, I think. After the long winter, they're back." He glanced over at Adam who nodded. "I can show you everything in the morning. But first, we must get you there."

The compound also had hidden living quarters and an interconnecting underground tunnel from the Cold War nuclear era. No one mentioned that.

The fresh Gulfstream crew arrived in the house car and grabbed their luggage and flight gear. "We'd better be going," Adam said to Leo. "The briefing should be starting soon." He turned to the crew's captain. "I'll be back soon. Everybody eat?"

They all nodded while Leo hustled his family into the van, then joined Adam. "You don't know how much I really appreciate this—"

"You know, Leo, I'm going to make you get drunk with me, again, if you keep this up." They both smiled. The crumbling world around them wouldn't allow for more.

The president personally approved the feed into the McCaffrey study. Others would receive viewings in government offices or the war rooms of selected heads of state. The decision to depart from protocol took no prompting when the president realized the shipping company owner had provided over a billion dollars in private assets as well as his civilian son and heir. Besides, the US Navy prepared for an inevitable war while evacuating thousands of US citizens and assets from hundreds of far places. An FBI agent stood among the small gathering to assure no recording devices or uninvited guests listened. The study's eighty-inch screen held the image of a vacant podium at Flintridge, California, NASA's Jet Propulsion Laboratory.

Adam sat between his grandfather and Bill Haverford, the man who would relieve the captain of the *American Farmer* in Mississippi. Adam grasped his grandfather's shoulder. "Thanks for doing this, Grandpa."

"It's important that as Americans, we all step up. Just like Ben Franklin said, 'When things get tough, we all must hang together'."

Adam smiled. "You're right, but he actually said, 'We must all hang together, or assuredly we shall all hang separately.' But I get your drift."

The older man's eyes twinkled, and Adam realized he'd been had. Again. "Excellent. I just wanted to make sure the high-priced education gave you something more than just beer and girls."

Adam laughed and turned to Bill, a tall and angular man with powerful arms and a thoughtful, intelligent face. Their friendship spanned the same time as Adam and Kim's. "Good to see you again, Bill."

"You too, mate. Good to know about that Ben fellow, too. I understand you'll be accompanying us?" Even as an American citizen, the man's British accent never lingered far from his words.

"Yes, if that's okay with you."

"Of course. The boat's present skipper wanted to be relieved anyway, so that'll give us an extra cabin. With your snoring, I need you elsewhere so I can get my beauty sleep."

Adam smiled. "I don't know if anyone will be getting much of that on this trip."

"We got a good crew, Adam. Small but all volunteer. The ship's mostly automated anyway but the seven of us should do just fine. Because of the number of passengers on board, Samantha Hardy volunteered to come along from our Riyadh operation. Sam's a physician's assistant, and she and I sailed together many times in the Mediterranean." He winked at Adam. "Not someone to be stuck with on a desert island, but competent and hardworking. You'll be the ninth. The other thirty or forty are the engineers and technicians that'll put that contraption together. Anybody else gets stuck aboard, does

228

manual labor."

The briefing would begin in Flintridge and then handed off to the Pentagon's war room. On the monitor, a man walked to the screen's podium and tapped the microphone. "Is this thing on?"

The man's abrupt words and unsmiling face chilled watchers. Off-camera, someone answered. He nodded and looked at the desktop. "Good, okay. I'll read from a prepared statement." His mouth worked for a moment, and then he looked up and began. "The Webb Telescope was repositioned approximately twelve hours ago to watch the upper left, or the second quadrant, where the Eros fragment will emerge. Most scientists estimated sixteen days before we see it for the first time. Of course, everyone knows now the guess was in error. The announcement yesterday reset all our watches. In about a hundred and twenty hours we should see the remaining fragment reappear after an elliptical orbit of the sun."

He glanced up, the monitor picking up the flush in his skin. "We detected an anomaly in the magnetic fields indicating that the Islamic broadcast was more correct than ours. Once the Webb confirms, the satellite will resume its monitoring status and will track Eros's progress. All other telescope activities will, of course, cease."

Adam watched as the man rattled a paper hidden by the podium.

He took a deep breath and began again. "A three-hundred-meter-diameter asteroid impact would be the equivalent to forty-five thousand tons of TNT, or forty-five megatons. If the asteroid strikes an ocean basin, the resulting tsunami will wipe out most flush-facing coastal communities."

"You might recall the theory that the Cretaceous-Tertiary dinosaur extinction was linked to a ten-*kilometer* impact. The terrorist asteroid would be roughly one-one-hundredth of its size yet will devastate whole regions and in some cases, entire countries. In 1908, the eighty-*meter* air explosion over Siberia caused human clothing to be ignited forty miles from impact. That meteor was estimated at one-hundredth the size of the present Eros fragment. Obviously, the earliest reports overstated the damage. With an airburst, exponential multiplier …"

The man continued for nearly five more minutes, until finally,

229

he said, "That ends my briefing, but I'm not done." He gripped and balled his prepared text. "I just want to say this whole thing is bullshit. You people knew this was coming and you didn't tell anybody? You've known for nearly two fucking years. What kind of monsters are you?"

A voice from offstage called to the man.

"Yeah, well I'll have my say." The man's eyes were wide and angry. "You bozos in Washington had plenty of time to negotiate with these terrorists. Don't fucking worry about being boxed into some diplomatic corner now. There won't be any more corners when they get done with us. They can aim this damn thing, and you knew it!" He nearly screamed his words. "A quarter degree one way or the other, three hundred million miles away, gives them the ability to hit anywhere on the earth or miss completely, for Christ's sake. You did nothing to—"

The feed blinked off, replaced by the Pentagon spokesman. Adam recognized Colonel Lowe and the basement's tiny, hardened amphitheater. "Madam President? I've been informed the feed from Flintridge was cut on their end."

An instantly recognizable voice answered from off-camera. In her distinctive Texas twang, the president said, "I understand. If they come back up, we'll let them finish after State and NSC. Let's take a moment and check in with our other listeners and make sure everyone is here."

A moment later sixteen countries including Japan, Great Britain, Canada, Australia, Mexico, and Germany confirmed. Brazil and Chile also confirmed. Ominous in its absence was France, as well as several key Islamic allies.

The president stepped behind a podium with the Seal on the wood face. "Before we start again, I want to apologize to the heads of state and government. The man should not be taken too seriously. He was obviously under tremendous pressure. We'll have a Webb Telescope update for you soon. Okay, Mr. Secretary."

The image of the Secretary of State with a different backdrop replaced the Pentagon's dais. Adam thought most critical government persons already monitored the broadcast at remote sites throughout the United States' eastern mountain ranges. Julie and Katherine would be

230

somewhere nearby, too. He prayed for their safety and security.

The lanky secretary cleared his throat. "Let me summarize the terrorist situation. ISIS and the Rahim Tajalli presented a cadre of announcements on hijacked television and radio feeds throughout southwestern and southeastern Asia, and of course the Internet, to announce the date and time of the asteroid's appearance. All other major communication outlets worldwide picked up the story. Such coordination would seem a feat of magic, except many communications facilities fell to attacks, including several in Europe.

"The announcement said only the faithful will be saved. ISIS read prepared statements saying Allah sent Eros in a final jihad to all who were not of the caliphate in Levant. Let me paraphrase: True believers would not martyr in final honor. Instead, the faithful would inherit the earth and be given paradise in due time. All others are to be denied and become slaves under the boot of ISIS."

The secretary looked into the camera lens. "They also said the asteroid strike would impact only the western hemisphere. I presume they mean the United States, Canada, and Mexico. After listening to NASA and the first speaker, and considering the debris hits of last month, this appears to be more of a possibility."

The secretary's index finger rubbed at the bridge of his nose, moving a reflection on his glasses up and down. He glanced back at his notes. "I have several reports of gangs roaming major world cities. Some have closed off highways and will let only food deliveries pass. Churches, as one would expect, have filled. Synagogues and mosques as well. France reported that full-scale fighting broke out between the authorities and fundamentalists groups until communications ceased three hours ago.

Dark shadows framed the man's tired eyes as he looked into the camera. "I hasten to note, France is a nuclear power along with several of its neighbors. American Embassies and some consulates have reverted to high-frequency radio or have been silenced. The inaction of friendly Islamic nations and groups remains troubling."

The man shrugged his slouched shoulders. Adam recalled this Secretary of State, a former college professor years ago, once ran for the presidency. He felt fortunate the Texas woman made decisions in the White House now.

"Across Europe and Asia, thousands are dying at the hands of their fellow citizens. Western civilization is quite literally crumbling before our eyes." His last words were mumbled to the closed circuit audience.

"Anything else, Mr. Secretary?" the president said. Her voice was strong and upbeat. Adam liked those qualities.

"No, ma'am. That is quite enough."

"Thank you for your efforts, Mr. Secretary. Please keep us posted." There was a stirring off-camera as the feeds switched to the Pentagon once more.

Leo, who sat in the second row of chairs, touched Adam's shoulder. "You know, I've been with the commission for fifteen years and this is only the second time I've heard the commissioner give a briefing."

Adam nodded, appreciating the challenges faced by an agency such as the NSC. Like the FBI, the commissioner was a presidential appointment, approved by Congress to serve a single ten-year term. The position sometimes found itself at odds with the White House and Congress, and rarely given to the vagaries of popular political winds. The present commissioner emulated these virtues as a no-nonsense, tireless straight arrow driving his agency and his agents hard. Standing erect and square behind the lectern, the retired Marine Corps general nodded and began.

"Madam President, Mr. Vice President, and heads of state. This evening the Congress and Executive Branches suspended the prohibition of *posse comitatus* and invoked martial law for a period of ninety days. The Supreme Court will review this decision in two hours. In the meantime, this is my first briefing of homeland military activities. This plan is in concert with US Code, Title 18, Part I as defined in a Joint Resolution, 19 United States Congress 141."

He cleared his throat and only barely relaxed the hard line of his mouth. "The US Army posted liaisons with the National Guards in all state capitals, and in most other major cities in the fifty United States, Puerto Rico, the Virgin Islands, and the South Pacific to include American Samoa in order to protect strategic food storage, power substations, communication, and transportation infrastructure. The airlines have parked most of their fleets under US Air Force

232

protection in military facilities around the country and the world. Except for a number of aircraft authorized under the War Powers Act, business and pleasure travel among the civilian population is suspended.

"Mexico, Germany, Great Britain, and Canada joined the US in opening their most secret intelligence files to one another." He took a deep breath and looked into the camera, his notes unneeded. "Cadres of military special operations forces from five nations secured over a thousand volunteer scientists and supporting personnel. Some were taken from hiding, none was taken by force. Military helicopters moved these personnel to rally points. Many of those selected who could be found are temporarily housed on a reactivated military base in Reykjavík, Iceland. Ten hours ago, airliners began to shuttle selected members of this group for embarkation. The rest will continue to work in Iceland."

He nodded to the camera. The feed switched again, to the Pentagon's war room. The spokesman for the Joint Chiefs, a Navy rear admiral, stood at the podium. "On Tuesday evening, twelve thousand members of the First Marine Expeditionary Force deployed from Camp Pendleton, California and conducted a successful incursion of Kabul, Pakistan. The invasion failed to provide the intelligence or the means to avert the asteroid."

Adam thought he could hear the sighs of disappointment through the feeds from around the world.

"An invasion of American soil by ISIS, Rahim Tajalli, and hired Mexican mercenaries of several drug cartels is underway along our southern border from San Diego to Tecate. Seized Mexican artillery and drones have neutralized police departments and the remaining noncombat military personnel left behind following massive worldwide deployments of combat troops. The drawdown of the US military forced the decision to revert all remaining assets to defensive positions only."

His jaw tightened in controlled fury. "Fighting pockets of resistance were largely ineffective in stopping the invasion. Intelligence provided to the Joint Chiefs indicated the ISIS forces are leapfrogging to Point Mugu near Los Angeles, in an attempt to compromise the Boeing YAL-1. Enemy drones are in extensive use as fighting continues at this hour in the Oxnard and Simi Valley area. Civilian and military casualties are high. Muslim leaders in communities near Los Angeles and in Detroit have been quiet."

The grim and angry spokesman paused a moment and added, "At the enemy's current rate of advance, Point Mugu is expected to fall in less than twelve hours. Reinforcements from the 82nd Airborne Division are en route, but are not expected to be on station in time to prevent capitulation." He folded his brief and stepped away from the podium.

The president's image centered on the screen with yet another backdrop. Her brown hair swept back from a strong face. "I won't make a speech," she began in her soft accent. "I will however call upon every one of us to stand together, firm in our belief that we will come through this stronger and wiser. No matter how the enemy is beaten, and they will be beaten, the United States remains your vigilant partner. As president, I promise the United States will stand with the seventeen of you who formed this coalition. We'll also stand with our absent neighbors who decided to wait and see, because they'll be back. You can count on that.

"What of our enemies, both domestic and foreign?" She paused. "Well, let me tell you this. They will pay with their treasure and their lives. We will crush them with all our will and strength. No quarter will be given. I promise you this." She offered a small smile. "After that, we'll see about reconciliation."

Leo leaned forward to Adam's ear. "Holy crap, man."

Adam nodded without taking his eyes from the president's image. "Holy crap is right. I wouldn't want to be on her bad side."

Chapter 32

A young manager for the McCaffrey lines in Yokohama emptied the warehouses of two laboratories and the Japanese space research center without getting arrested or shot as a looter. The last of Chinese, Taiwanese, Malaysian, and Russian scientists joined their Japanese colleagues as the final equipment craned into the below-deck holds. As the President of the United States issued her promise to revenge aggression, tugs pointed the *Emma McKinley* for an full speed dash to a midpoint in the South Pacific. The plan devised by a confluence of the brightest naval and aerospace minds positioned the *Emma* just south of the thirtieth parallel and north of New Zealand. The *American Farmer* would assume a complementary position in the South Atlantic. With the seasonal tilt of the earth and the direction of Eros's approach, both ships offered the greatest opportunity to guide the asteroid into a miss.

Adam took his place on the *American Farmer* in Pascagoula as time focused the world's future. Dockside cranes lifted the last of the equipment into the holds after the final technicians and scientists scurried to set up for the voyage. A bank of giant, two-thousand-horsepower diesels churned brown bottom mud when the huge, high-riding containership broke free of the Gulf Coast barrier islands. Already forty hours behind schedule, the *Farmer* prepared to dash into the open Atlantic Ocean not bothering with Coast Guard or international boundary restrictions.

For the next twenty hours as the big containership swept by Alabama and Florida, helicopters, sometimes two at a time, dropped equipment and supplies on the makeshift landing decks. A day after the *American Farmer* crossed the tip of Cuba, the last of three big Sikorsky helicopters paced beside the rolling ships.

Adam stood in the bridge listening to the give-and-take on the radio. The last hovering helicopter called, "*Farmer* this is 66 alpha, we've got the landing area in sight."

The reply's background noise caught the wind and the other helicopter blades as the big flying machine grew near. "66 alpha, roger. You've got a crowded deck. If you wait thirty minutes, we'll try to clear you an area."

"Negative," answered the pilot. "We're at bingo fuel. Tell them to keep their heads down and I'll squeeze in between the bridge and the other bird."

The radioman ran out yelling and pointing toward the big CH-53, one of the world's largest helicopters. The blades worked up and down as swirling air buffeted the big machine. Pacing alongside, the aircraft slid sideways slowly, mere feet from disaster.

Adam watched from high amidships on the bridge. He didn't see how enough room remained between the parked aircraft, equipment, and the ship's steel superstructure. Heavy cable lines fouled the area, even if the aircraft could shoehorn into the tight space.

The helicopter pilot's calm voice spoke over the radio. "I suppose it'd be too much to ask the captain to stick the ship's nose into the wind for ten minutes or so?"

Bill snatched the microphone from above Adam's head. "This is the captain speaking. Sorry, Marine. We're making up for lost time so every minute counts. Good luck."

"No sweat, skipper."

Bill hit the overhead public address. "This is the captain. Clear the landing immediately. Clear the landing area immediately. Post fire watch."

Adam watched as people dropped their loads and ran for the hatches.

Bill flipped the radio switch to the man controlling the landing deck. "We're going to bring the helicopter aboard, but I want no one on the deck. Clear the landing area immediately and get your fire crew ready." He turned to the helmsman. "Give me fifteen degrees to the port. Let's do what we can. God help those people."

He punched in another number. "Samantha? Can you prepare the sick bay? The last helicopter to come aboard isn't going to be pretty. We're probably going to get some injuries." He listened for a moment. "Thanks. Pre-staging triage on B-deck is a good idea, but there's no time. He's almost out of fuel. He'll be down in a minute."

Adam watched him hang up and felt the big ship begin a turn.

"That's Sam Hardy. I mentioned her before. Volunteered to be the doctor on this trip. She's a good one." Bill watched the helicopter

236

creep closer, then back off, only to adjust and try again. "He doesn't realize that we'd waste an hour trying to turn the ship. I just can't do it." Bill hit the intercom to fire control. "Ready a single life boat. Go only on my command."

Adam nodded and watched the disaster in the making.

The big helo worked closer, hovered, and was buffeted by the swirling air. The big blades worked up and down, then without warning, pitched left and slammed onto the deck. Sparks flashed from the tail rotor as the spinning blades scraped the steel of the ship. For a moment the collapsing struts and flattened tires threatened to bounce them back into the air or into the superstructure. Both would be disaster. But the maneuver held, and the full-powered rotors pressed the helicopter hard into the ship's deck. As if everyone held their breath, the pilot came on the air. "Now that's what I call a tight squeeze."

Bill laughed in relief and snatched the microphone. "Minimum authorized personnel to tie the helicopter down. Secure the lifeboat. We won't need it."

Two deckhands ran out and threw chains over struts as the blades wound down.

Adam breathed again. "He's pretty damn good. That couldn't have been fun."

Captain Bill Haverford hung up the instrument and called to the helmsman, "Back to course one-seven-five." He turned to Adam. "I know it's hard on the crews and the machines. These guys are up to the challenge, although the legitimacy of my parentage is likely being questioned at this moment."

Adam nodded with a smile as the helicopter's cargo ramp lowered. "I'm sure they're not happy about being stuck so far from shore, they can't get back." The distance, widening every minute, prevented the last crews from going home. Besides, they needed to save the ship's limited aviation fuel for the final operation. The last of the best minds of many countries disembarked from the green machines. Stranded pilots and crews would pitch in where needed.

Bill picked up his binoculars and watched the methodical unloading on the windswept and pitching deck. "I understand the last helo's pilot is a chef in Seattle as his day job. At least we'll eat good."

237

"I thought you called him a Marine?"

"Reservist," Bill said. "The active guys are fighting wars in a dozen places, so hardly anyone is left. Bloody stupid, reducing the world's biggest superpower to nil."

Adam watched several people grab cases from the cargo bay. A tall woman, a ponytail stuck through the strap of her baseball cap, stepped off the last helicopter and tucked two cases under each arm. Adam turned away. "I've gotta get my hands dirty. I don't want to just stand around and watch everyone else work."

Bill understood. "The techs are too busy to babysit a geeky guy like you. I recall you can peel a mean potato. You up for that?"

Adam grinned. "Oh hell, yeah. Where do I go?"

Bill picked up the intercom phone. "Robbi? Can you use a scullery man?" He listened, keeping an eye and a grin on Adam. "Nah. He doesn't know shit from shinola but he's willing. I'll send him down. But be nice to him, 'cause he owns this beautiful ship." He replaced the phone. "She can use help, but you don't have to. I can use you up here, too."

"I'll relieve your watch when you need rest. I just … need to pitch in with something physical. Besides, you'd never let me hear the last of it if I don't do this, and Julius will get a kick out of it."

Bill nodded. "Okay, but before you go, read the latest update on the airborne laser. Just came in. We're also keeping our eye on a storm down south. I'll keep you posted."

Adam picked up the email knowing two thousand miles away, men and women struggled inside the equipment bays of the big Boeing while radical Islamists fought at the gates. Reborn and surrounded by workers, the plane sat on the ramp of Point Mugu Naval Air Station. Mortars fell as stolen artillery pieces attacked the few remaining active military forces holding back the tide of radicals. Guards around the Boeing YAL had already shot up a sapper team that breached the wires in a stolen armored personnel carrier. Two enemy drones carrying deadly missiles died from a pair of ancient sidewinders salvaged from a Navy scrap heap. The ISIS attack was well-planned and coordinated, and counted heavily on lone-wolf recruiting of young, radicalized American men and women.

Adam checked the date stamp knowing the huge airplane's

critical departure time approached. The buffer was already gone, and the aircrew should have been en route to southern Argentina hours ago. Base shops and craftspeople worked to replace key parts and pieces, often in danger and under fire. Already, a man on a machine press died from a sniper shot, and several technicians were injured when fluids over-pressured and burst a line. The chance of rejuvenating the old machine lessened each hour the parts failed and the supply system collapsed outside the wire. Shortly before his own death on the barricades, the Navy Air Station commander reported they were holding, but riflemen were becoming scarce.

Adam dropped the emailed briefing on Bill's desktop and tried to smile. The captain only nodded and returned his gaze to the sea. Adam stepped into the passageway elevator, eyeing the chart panel, knowing the captain's confidential titanium safe lay hidden behind the fixture. He hoped the world's scientists, astronomers, and space engineers drew closer to an agreement on the code. Adam had no wish to have Bill retrieve the laptop's final instructions hidden inside.

Chapter 33

The *American Farmer* cut a wide wake in six-foot seas. The giant orange-and-gray ship plowed deep into wide swells then lifted high to reveal twenty feet below the waterline. Top speed dispersed a wake hundreds of feet around as the ship made its way past the equator. The mild gale-force six would soon grow to eight, and then nine before midnight. The ship must slow down and waste more time, or risk disaster from a sea growing more violent. A thousand miles south fierce winds churned, making for a beautiful, pink-layered sunset.

Adam visited E-deck during a break from kitchen duty. The heaviest activity slowed in the last six hours as chemical and mechanical specialists fed twenty-foot-wide banks of resource tanks. Other technicians monitored the charging process while everyone grabbed for hand supports. The deck, thick with technicians and forklifts, operated in spite of the rolling and shuddering ship. More than a few fell to seasickness and minor injuries. Adam stood back from the crowded floor and watched men roll fifty-five gallon drums of potassium peroxide, chlorine, and iodine into place. The pace never slowed, even as the most dangerous of all the chemicals arrived on forklift tines.

After he took a place on the food line to serve, he heard a tech's fingers were crushed when a barrel came loose. A research supervisor stepped in and blocked the drum of caustic liquid with spare dunnage before it rolled into a bulkhead and burst. When a second barrel came loose because of the hasty ties, she took over the loading by slowing the crew and having all the securing straps redone. She also picked up the phone and chewed out the captain, demanding the ship slow while the most critical of tasks wrapped up. Bill Haverford remembered how close the helicopter and crew came when he could have turned back north and into the wind. He could live with losing a brave crew and burning wreckage, but an inoperable laser would end the *Farmer's* usefulness. He slowed the big ship at a critical time.

Adam stood with a handhold on the bridge chair and read the

240

commissioner's email. The Boeing had finally departed California in darkness for the ten-hour flight to Tierra del Fuego.

Adam breathed again and continued to read.

At the last minute, when the ISIS forces mounted a final push that would overrun the base defenses, civilians armed with handguns and hunting rifles attacked the enemy's rear. Men and women armed with target guns acted as snipers, taking out many ISIS and cartel soldiers. Forced to fight on two flanks, the easy enemy victory turned into a bloody standoff. Two hundred armed schoolteachers, garage mechanics, retired police officers, and government workers harassed the jihadists. Many of the civilians drove from the Muslim community, taking up arms and joining with their neighbors to hold the line against the invaders as they waited on the 82nd Airborne's arrival.

The communication operator accepted the paper from Adam's hands. "Good news, yes?"

"Oh, yes," Adam said, showing his first smile in hours. "A little glimmer in a grim operation." He fell into a nearby chair. "We're like a country of lucky amateurs."

"Maybe," Bill said. "But we do have the bright spots."

"Give me another one." Adam's words sounded more sour than he'd meant.

"We've got one heck of a crew," Bill said with admiration. "Take the research supervisor. Except for her, my friend, E-deck would be closed for the day to vent fumes. We would've missed the window for sure." He glanced toward Adam who hadn't seemed to hear. "She read me the riot act, I'll tell you. Right here on my own damn ship." Bill laughed. "She's a handful."

Adam knew how close they'd come to scrubbing the *Farmer*'s mission and becoming bystanders with the rest of the world. Whitecaps ripped at the roiling gray surface and wind buffeted wings. He fought the malaise as the world conspired to thwart their chances, thankful that Bill Haverford captained their ship.

Adam also knew leadership was one-tenth brilliance and nine-tenths chutzpah, and Bill had plenty of both. Adam said, "The sea is going to do what the sea will do. Even with a big-ass storm in our way, we'll make schedule because you're on top of this. Just like the accident on E-deck. Thanks, Bill."

"Whoa, mate. That wasn't me. You got some pushy damn supervisor driving everyone crazy. My only contribution will be to get us to the church on time. You and your crew below will save the world."

Adam stood and placed a hand on Bill's shoulder. "Just get us close. I expect to see the calculations coming from Reykjavík any time now. We might not need to be precisely on our spot … although that will be ideal."

"Wonderful, Adam. Did something change?"

All communications went through the ship but Adam, as an owner, had a private channel. "We'll use the airborne laser to aim the ships' beams. But someone at Johnson Space Center came up with a way to get the Webb Telescope to predict the trajectory even more exactly."

"That's good, right? What are you so morose about?"

Adam breathed. "At the time, he was actually working on the last-ditch plan. The one that's locked in your safe."

Bill looked over at his friend's drawn face, and drew a breath. "All right, so tell me. What did the boys and girls back home decide?"

Adam pulled him out of earshot from the helmsman and opened a printed copy of the communication. "The Webb mirror. They'll control one of the ship's beams to deflect off the mirror, and use this changing algorithm to direct the asteroid to miss. If it doesn't miss, they'll do the same thing all the way to impact. It's pretty ingenious, actually."

"Impact with what?" Bill said, his face growing ashen while he eyed the cryptic email.

"The Arctic."

"Oh, bloody hell. Let's just stick with the original plan. We're going to fire up a laser from the *Farmer* and one from the *Emma McKinley*. Your Boeing YAL is going to aim those two lasers at a point where the Webb Telescope predicts the asteroid to be." He looked at Adam closely. "Far, far away. Right?"

Adam nodded. "Far away."

"Good, because that just works fine for me. Then you're going to send up a signal to make this big-assed rock go someplace else … like Mars. Don't give me a doomsday plan. I want my world back. I want my bloody ship back. I'm sure Kim wants his, too."

"Okay. No problem." Adam folded and tucked the faxed data into his shirt pocket. "It's just an idea."

"Well a pox on that idea. Throw it overboard your first chance." He eyed the pocket while Adam buttoned the small flap. He finally shook his head and looked away. "Plan B. Sweet Jesus, Mary and Joseph."

The two watched the rolling sea from the high perch of the bridge wings for several minutes. Spray broke over rails as they plunged into another swell. The ship's shuddering vibrated through the soles of their feet.

Adam spoke first. "What else can I do to help, Bill?" An idea occurred to him. "I don't want to be in the way, but maybe I can help in the sick bay. You know, offer encouragement."

"Most are tired or puking their guts out. If you can stand that, they'd probably like to personally thank you for this cruise by throwing up on your shoes. Check in with Sam Hardy. If you haven't met her, you should." He dipped his shoulders. "A little dour, but give her a chance. She'll grow on you."

Bill glanced toward his bleeping fax machine. He ripped off the sheet and muttered, "Not very common, this storm. Maybe there's something to climate change, after all." He read the fax. "Forty knots sustained with gusts to fifty-five in fourteen hours. Last satellite showed slight movement southeast. A cold front will accelerate the storm in twenty hours. Data buoy in the area showing sixteen-foot seas." He looked up. "Bloody bad luck, Adam. These storms aren't rare, just unusual. As soon as it blows into the colder water … well, anyway. The *Farmer* won't have a problem with the weather or the sea. I can't say the same thing about your folks, or that contraption on E-deck. In a few hours, we'll need to start tying things down. They'd better be finishing up soon."

"Is there a way to cut in behind the storm, or maybe go around?"

Bill shook his head. "Not really, considering the time constraint. Best option is to drive straight on."

"Will you have someone let the *Emma* and the Boeing YAL know, and get a status report? Tom and Sheila are with the operation

243

in Tierra del Fuego as of two hours ago. They need to know we might be the weak link in this plan. Maybe there's something we haven't thought of yet."

"I'm sorry it's the *Farmer* falling short."

Adam hesitated at the door, and said in his best accent, "No worries, mate."

"That's the Aussies. Come on, after all this time?"

Adam just smiled.

As he passed by the communication room, Adam heard the *Emma*'s captain on Satlink reporting their position and the movement of their technicians to shore. He knew Kim Jaegwon monitored in their Korean corporate command center as well. Except for the *American Farmer*, the plan remained on schedule. The Eros fragment was still many hours away from detection. Most in the world held their breath, while far too many others anticipated with an ugly glee.

The sick bay smelled of PineSol, antiseptic, and vomit. After multiple tours in Afghanistan, Adam ignored the odors. The man injured in the near disaster greeted him with apologies and a hand swaddled in a large bandage. Adam listened and reassured him. Others in the onboard hospital ward, he greeted with encouragement.

Samantha "Sam" Hardy was a large woman with a soft voice who trailed after him. She looked tired and overworked. As a McCaffrey regular on oil and containerships in the Indian Ocean and Mediterranean Sea, Sam had just returned from a thirty-day stint out of Jeddah, Saudi Arabia and volunteered when she heard of this mission.

"I'm very grateful," Adam said as he stood in the hatchway, about to leave.

"They had no idea." Dark skin ringed under her eyes. "Some never been on a ship."

"They'll be happier when we get them ashore. It won't be too much longer."

Her gaze held his. "How much longer, Mr. Michaels? Can you tell me what the time schedule is?"

He could, but would not. "If we can just keep them comfortable. That's what's important."

She watched him a minute, nodded. "You don't remember me, do you?"

244

Adam shook his head. "I'm sorry. Where did we meet?"

She pressed her lips together, and was about to speak.

"Oh, my God." Adam laughed. "You were ship's doctor when Kim and I were screwing around and had to put in at … Gunsan," he said. "Oh, geez. That was awful. So embarrassing."

Only the slightest smile came to her lips. "Yes, that's right. You broke your arm wrestling as I recall."

"Yeah. Taekwondo." Adam was rueful at the recollection. The captain, a no-nonsense man, had warned the two about horseplay. "The arm hurt less than my grandfather's stare."

She watched him, unamused, then turned and left to attend to her charges.

Adam thought Bill had been right to call her dour as he dropped several ladders down and into the assembly areas of the number-three container hold. Fifteen years later, and she still seemed as angry as the captain of the small steamer had been. They both had good cause, he supposed.

Rounded tubes stretched from bulkhead to far bulkhead looking like a gigantic, old-time radiator tipped onto its side. A digital clock mounted twenty feet high on the far bulkhead counted down thirty-seven hours until the ship arrived on station and the evacuation would begin. The asteroid would cover over a million miles in that time. *God made the world in seven days, mankind will take far less time destroying it.*

The moment his feet left the ladder, the swells sent Adam reaching for a handhold. Only super containerships such as the *Emma* and the *Farmer* could accommodate such a big structure. Overhead klieg lights remained on day and night across the expanse of E-deck.

A crew of several dozen worked the flexible piping into a basic layout on the steel plating. Others walked with care through a confluence of intricate tubes and wires, holding and snapping braces into place. Adam walked outside the activity and gazed at the huge machine. Rain or shine didn't matter as long as the hatch rolled back. The electrons were wide and harmless until synchronized into a single wavelength. Although good for only several hundred thousands of miles, when doubled by both huge ships, reflected by the Webb Mirror, and aimed by the Boeing YAL, enough focused laser energy

245

could be created to send the embedded code commands well outside the moon's orbit. Proper aim was vital. Only the slightest nudge would command the asteroid to miss earth. Despite all their calculations, a rollicking and uncaring sea threatened to doom their efforts and let Rahim Tajalli and ISIS fulfill their final jihad.

Adam stayed clear of the organized pandemonium. Some sat to aid their balance as they worked, while others picked their way with caution as the deck moved under them. Men and women labored in near silence, some with calculators and tablets, others with the strength of their hands. Men and women struggled with fine, stainless steel nuts and bolts while a selected few connected critical tubes and fine wires. More than one greened with seasickness, and yet they persevered.

Adam looked, but didn't find the crew supervisor. He managed a few encouraging words into the ears of some while he tried not to break anyone's concentration. Only one or two looked up. Most smiled, nodded, and continued to work.

He was about to leave when a slight, older engineer said, "I think she's in corridor seven. Over there."

"Thanks," said Adam, then noticed the man's dim pallor. "I can help you back to your quarters. You're not looking too good."

The man shook his head with a half smile. A yamaka topped his aging, bald head. "I get seasick drinking water. Always have, always will. Then?" He shrugged. "I toss my cookies and I'm okay."

Adam noticed the stain on the man's shirtfront, and said nothing. "I appreciate what you're doing. This takes a lot of guts. The world will appreciate it."

"Sure, sure. I only hope the world never finds out for your sake," he said, his New York accent heavy, his smile disappearing. "Not for mine. I've watched the news broadcasts and they never stop talking about you, debating you, lifting you to the heavens. *The man who'll save the world*," he said in a singsong. "Win or lose. That isn't good, my friend."

Adam ignored the news once he heard them use his name. He knew what the media did and how they did it. The story was made for coverage, especially with his privileged beginning, American aristocrat marriage, and Ivy League background. That he was also decorated in a war only made media producers salivate more.

The man took hold of Adam's arm. "If we manage to escape this thing, you'll never find peace. I'm sorry for you. You seem like a good boy. The radical Muslims will run to the ends of the earth to make good on their fatwa. You'll be a pariah to them all, and to the loved ones around you. I'm sorry Colonel Michaels, but your life is over no matter how good we do."

Adam felt his faith shaken to the core, and with a gentleness he didn't feel, took the man's hand off his arm. "I'll be fine, sir. We just need to worry about getting this thing working." Sometime in the coming nights, he would understand the man's words and see why Miranda ran away from him and not toward him.

"Sure, sure," said the engineer, returning to his task. "That's the ticket. Save the world, be home for dinner."

Instead of returning to the bridge deck, Adam walked through a hatch and into the open flyway above the sea. He breathed the wet, cool air into the depths of his lungs. Life took many strange twists, and the past was nothing more than callous indifference. He noticed another figure gripping the high rails and moving with the roll of the sea. A ball cap captured her blond ponytail.

"You're good with the ocean," called Adam above the wind's noise. "You must be the supervisor who saved the day."

She turned with a smile. "Hi, Adam."

He stared, incredulous. "Andrea. I don't believe it. How ... How'd you get here?"

She rolled her shoulders. "Just like everyone else, I suppose. And, I didn't save anyone's day." She laughed, the first Adam heard in days. "I got here by leaning on Indron. We made the aiming mechanism, you know. They needed someone from Denver to babysit."

"And you volunteered?"

"Of course," she said with a laugh.

"Seems I recall you didn't think much of volunteerism." He smiled, happy to see her.

"My crew made this thing and if you'd have stuck around, you could've helped. Besides, I needed to come and continue to work on my lagging supervisory skills. You're proof of that."

"What about the PR campaign?"

"Your buddy Benchley needs no handholding when it comes to the camera or looking good. You've got an ally there, Adam, and he's working his ass off. We put together some good stuff, but he didn't need me anymore."

Water shot out from the vibrating hull. "You shouldn't have come, Andrea. This is dangerous."

She cocked her head to one side. "Sir Galahad. Did you forget the whole planet's in danger? I don't think there's any place to hide at the moment." Her gaiety dropped. "Our world's become a very treacherous place. I feel safer here, to tell you the truth. Even with a hurricane out there."

"Cyclone," he said automatically, as his thoughts went to Miranda and the dangers of an America balancing on chaos.

"Are you okay, Adam?"

He'd drifted. "You bet. I would say your skills are wasted at Indron. I appreciate what you've done."

"I've done nothing, but we do need to get Indron's focusing parabolic guide mounted on the digital transceiver. Once they're completed fueling, we go to work. What happens from here, Adam? After the storm passes?"

He considered for a moment and had no secrets with her. "We test the system, everyone gets shuttled to the airport in Natal, Brazil. Less than sixteen hours now. Then, home. Except for a few essential crews who'll stay a while longer, each person will be back with their families in twenty-four hours. We've got scientists from every major space agency feeding data to Reykjavík to give us our best shot, no pun intended. Everyone waits at home with his or her loved ones, or in compounds courtesy of the US Government. Your choice."

"My choice, but not your choice?"

Wind whipped around them. "I've made my choice," he said after a moment.

Her blond ponytail rocketed off her shoulders as the wind turned. "How did you figure the southern hemisphere for the two ships? Was that a guess?"

Adam considered for a moment. "A worldwide group of observatories from hundreds of America and Canada's closest friends shared an encrypted Internet page. Everyone contributed. Tom

248

Connecelli coordinated their findings. Ever try to herd engineers?"

She smiled at him.

"Sure you have. So you can see why Tom is the hero for bringing this all together. The approach of the asteroid is angled from north to south, but none of that means anything to us on the surface if all goes right."

"And if it goes wrong?"

He looked at her for a moment then turned to the ocean. "Then it goes wrong. Tom Connecelli and Sheila Perez refined my plan, and roughed out the code's parameters. Before he found the camera with you, Brad Benchley and the Defense Logistics folks raided warehouses from Pasadena to Bombay. More heroes. We emptied storage facilities in Great Britain, Tel Aviv, and Mexico City, too. Even with all those resources, we could only gather enough material for two ships. A dozen would have been better. My grandfather and Kim Jaegwon had them available, but in the end, two was all we could outfit. The power of the signal, the angle of approach, the intercept of the asteroid … it's all pretty much a wag."

"Wild-ass guess."

They smiled at one another. Adam said, "Yes, it's pretty ironic the fate of the world rests on those never invited to the school dance, or always picked last in the baseball game. Do you think we'll ever learn to be better people?"

"Nah," she said. "Not with guys like you to rescue them."

He fell silent.

"Sorry, Adam. I know about your girlfriend. She'll be okay, I'm sure." He looked up, surprised. "Scientists and engineers talk. We're worse than a bunch of old men." She smiled and patted his arm. "I need to get back."

He didn't follow but stayed on the wing and in the wind. He thought of Miranda and the *Morning Dawn* resting hundreds of fathoms deep off the coast of Portugal, a plan spawned from the heart of evil with patience that might wait another five hundred years. He wondered what the crew must have thought in those last moments. Did they pray and ask for forgiveness? Did they curse their bad luck or wait until the last moment in a struggle, trying to control the uncontrollable? The hope of humankind didn't rest on the valiant

249

efforts of a few. Man's hope relied elsewhere, in his faith and in God, by whatever name He is called. *When will we ever learn?* Pete Seeger, twentieth-century philosopher.

A good question, thought Adam.

Instead of returning to the bridge, he joined the crew moving barrels and making connections. He offered a short wave to Andrea and found a pair of leather gloves, joining a tall Jamaican deckhand unaffected by the rolling deck. They toiled for hours into the night. When the storm grew wild, a horn sounded, securing activity. Andrea worked her way to each small group, ordering them to their bunks or the galley. Adam finished with the connections on the parabolic switching box by crossing both legs around the brace as he strained to start each nut, careful not to cross-thread. The tall black man beside him held a securing wrench in one hand and with the other, braced against the ship's roll. He tightened tiny, fine bolts into delicate electronics. A third man tested each colored wire with a multimeter, verifying the proper connections. When they'd finished, the big man patted Adam's back and retreated to quarters.

"Me, too?" said Adam as Andrea approached.

"You especially need to follow the rules, sir. The captain says the sea's too rough." In spite of determination and guts, her eyes widened as the ship smacked a vicious wave and twisted violently.

Adam said, "We'll be on the back side of the storm in ten hours. The sea will be calmer then. This is a good time to give everyone a break. I don't think we're too far behind schedule."

She nodded and grabbed a handhold. Breath came in gulps. "Are you coming?"

He could see, despite the bravado, the pounding concerned her. "Yes, give me just a minute. I want to check something."

She shook her head. "You never follow orders, do you? Don't be too long." Her words were not kind or playful.

He watched her trail the others into corridor seven, as a tiny light over the freight elevator came on. The empty car sat a moment, and he returned to the loose nut. The elevator *dinged* again but the nut slipped from Adam's tired grip and he didn't look around this time.

The klieg lamps clicked off. Only ambient and reflected floor light remained. He slapped a hand over the tiny chrome nut before it

250

rolled away. He tried again. The ship shuddered. The deck was quiet. He glanced at the red letters of the digital clock. Thirty-one hours. Fatigue and sore fingers worked the tiny bolt from the other side, but once again, the nut dropped. He needed the big Jamaican but couldn't leave this undone before heading to his quarters

He stretched once more as the iron rod caught the side of his head and knocked him to the deck just as the ship hit a swell. His limp body tumbled against the brace, then bounced down in a violent pitch-and-roll. The next swing of the attacker's metal bar glanced off the steel floor, the ship's movement saving Adam from another blow. His unconscious body rolled under the tubing, through the bracing, and into the deep scupper drainage that edged the deck. The figure climbed over the first ring of tubes to finish him off when the ship shook hard. The public address speaker sounded, "All hands, return to quarters. Clear E-deck. All hands immediately …"

Time was short. Nimble fingers cut wiring, snapped connections, and punctured a few critical tubes. A hatch opened from the far bulkhead, but too late. The saboteur stood and walked away with a wave. Shadows hid the completed work. The far man didn't see the mayhem and waved back, smacking the last of the light switches and throwing the wide chamber into darkness. Adam's body was lost as the figure escaped into corridor seven.

The storm grew through the night, much as Bill Haverford predicted. The *American Farmer* ignored the weather. The crews did not. The public address summoned Adam to the bridge without a response. A crewmember went to his empty bunk. The PA system called him again, but still he didn't show. A search began at the height of the storm. Andrea offered the captain an explanation of her last contact with him. The klaxon sounded for man overboard. The storm grew in violence. Several persons, including the old man from New York, appealed to the captain, but he wouldn't turn the ship around. A single man's life in trade, even that of a good friend, might haunt Bill to the end of his days, but would be a wonderful bargain to the world. All hands secured to their quarters as the worst of the storm crashed around them.

In the twelfth hour the seas calmed and a gray dawn broke. Bill Haverford ordered the searching to continue as crews prepared to disembark. One of the ship's mates found Adam four hours later, near death, his scalp split from crown to ear, the loss of blood significant. Without the right medical equipment the PA didn't know if his skull was fractured. The concussion was enough to kill him, although less important than the shock of so many hours in cold, unsanitary drainage, and with a fever already out of control. Throughout the next few hours Adam slept, taking IV after IV. Bill sat with him while the crew prepared to test-fire the laser. The Jamaican crewman who earlier worked with Adam sat with him, too. The PA's supply of antibiotics soon ran low as Adam's fever raged. A call was sent to the South African Navy, who dispatched a long-range C-130 from Cape Town. By late afternoon, an airdrop was made and recovered by the *Farmer*'s launch.

Adam slept the night around before he awoke. He rolled to one side and saw the back of the crewman. The man turned at the sound. "Hello there, Mr. Michaels. Welcome back."

He smiled but his head hurt. "What happened?"

"You don't remember?"

Adam thought for several moments. "You and I were working. I couldn't finish because I kept dropping a nut. Andrea sent me to my quarters, but I didn't leave. I was, thinking ... I guess. Then, here you are. What happened?"

The big Jamaican shook his head. "I don't know exactly. You took quite a blow to the head, sir. I believe you have a concussion. Let me call Sam and the skipper."

When he opened his eyes again, Bill Haverford sipped a cup of tea and watched him.

"Hey, Bill. What's up?"

"Good question. Dominic tells me you don't recall anything."

"All I know is my head really hurts." Adam touched the bandage.

"We've got a cutter headed this way to take you off. I think you're hurt worse than you think."

"I'm staying."

Samantha Hardy walked in. Bill turned to her and said, "You tell him, Sam. His hard head didn't save him this time."

The haggard expression on her face spoke more than words. "I don't have the means to help you, sir. I've got pills, but you need to be evacuated ashore for evaluation. You could have pressure building—"

"No," he said. He tried to sit up. She didn't move and he eased back to his pillow. "Evacuation isn't an option until this system is working. I'll leave when everyone else leaves." He rolled to look at her.

She glanced at the captain, and took a tiny light from her pocket to view each of his eyes. "This is not my decision. I'm okay as long as you don't convulse or vomit. The difference is only a few hours before we start evacuating." She turned to Bill. "I'm doing what I can. He's probably okay if he stays in bed."

Bill shrugged at his doc's diagnosis. "Okay, whatever you think."

Adam glanced at the medication. "No narcotics. If it gets bad, I'll let you know." He looked at Bill. "I just need a little sleep."

"Okay, but I'm telling you Congressman Benchley ordered the Navy to get their asses down here and take you away."

Adam smiled. *Brad.* "How much time?"

Bill chuckled. "A destroyer escort should arrive thirty hours after the asteroid." He shrugged with a smile. "Sort of a gesture of supreme confidence in you."

"I don't care how you do it, but turn those guys around. They have more important things to do, like being home with their families. We'll see after the Eros misses us."

Bill offered a quizzical look, but said, "Okay. I'll turn them around. But won't we all be drinking beer in Brazil?" Adam didn't answer. Bill nodded and picked up a folder. "Sleep now. Read this later. There's nothing you can do for the moment. We're preparing for the test and getting everyone else off the *Farmer*."

"Okay," Adam said and put the manila folder on the table beside him. "Get all the ships back to port...." His voice trailed away and he slept.

When the alarms sounded, he tried to pull himself up on the bed's rails. The PA hurried into the sick bay and began to dog down the hatches. He searched his memory and failed. "Is that the fire alarm?" he said over the horns and small, bulkhead-mounted strobe lights.

"Not fire," she said. "That's six short blasts and a long. This one means General Stations. We'll get the address in a minute." The horn blared.

Just then, the ship-wide sound system clicked to life. "All hands, all hands. Unknown gas leak detected on container deck three. National Ignition Facility crews report to your stations. All hands, all hands ..." The message repeated.

The sick bay phone rang. Sam grabbed the handset. "Yours," she said, handing Adam the phone, and hurried out.

"What's going on?" He glanced at the clock and saw only ninety minutes elapsed since he'd fallen asleep.

Bill Haverford spoke. "Sorry, Adam, but I thought you'd want to know. We have an unknown gas leaking. We're rigged to alarm for all sorts of refrigerants, preservatives, almost everything that's industrial, but the stuff you've got in your laser isn't common, so I don't know what it is. The mate believes the laser machine or one of the chemical blivets is leaking. I'll have the think tank at NIF on the line in ten minutes or so. You aren't going to follow Sam's orders anyway, so are you able to walk yet?"

He was, and waved Sam in from the next room to remove the IV. "I'm leaving on the next lift, Mr. Michaels," she said. "You're an idiot if you're not on that bird with me. Head injuries should not be downplayed."

When Adam grinned, she said nothing. One side of his mouth drooped at a corner. He felt the empty shirt pocket. The final Plan B codes were gone.

Chapter 34

Two hours later, the laser mounted in the *Emma McKinley* and the *American Farmer* aimed by the Boeing YAL and reflected by the James Webb Observatory's giant mirrors met at the predicted imaginary point far out in space. The command centers at dozens of observatories and nations' capitols broke into wild cheers, backslapping, and hugs. The shot was accurate to within a dozen millimeters, a million and a quarter miles from Earth. The cut wires and holed blivets were easily repaired aboard the *Farmer*. Bill Haverford watched the operation and decided the saboteur, while dangerous, was an amateur. His first officer and security crew never slowed their search. Now they were armed and Bill was mad.

The demonstration concluded and the cheering ceased. *Emma McKinley* and the *American Farmer*'s chemical laser refilled from the supply blivets. The Boeing YAL landed and did the same in Tierra del Fuego. The plan said for a microsecond, the sending computer and the space-borne, graphene command module on Eros's fragment could exchange query and response as the destruct circuit activated. The steering rockets aboard the European robot craft would then fire, thinking it followed a command to destroy itself, and instead deflect the guidance portion of the lasso-and-basket into an orbit that missed the Earth, calculated to eventually be pulled into the sun. Scientists and engineers across the globe settled on this test plan a hundred hours before. The problem remained to calculate and then codify the commands to alter the calculations with enough time to let the command module react.

The great minds continued to debate the sending code, and to resolve their differences as they had earlier. NASA's Johnson Space Center in Texas fired the tiny stabilization motors to move the James Webb's giant reflecting mirror back into place to search for the incoming asteroid. The wait began in earnest.

With work completed in the Pacific, the *Emma McKinley*'s last cache of personnel loaded and traveled to meet the rest of the fleeing population at the Fua'amotu Airport in Tonga. At four in the morning, a *Farmer*'s Sikorsky helicopter departed on the next to last trip to the shadowing Brazilian coast guard. As the smaller ship raced toward shore, a single flight remained to put the final crewmembers and captain aboard.

When the last of the crews evacuated, both ships would relinquish control to the command center in Colorado Springs. From there, a senior captain from McCaffrey Shipping would remotely stabilize their positions using GPS and satellite link. The final orders and the code to deflect the asteroid would come from Tom and Sheila in Tierra del Fuego.

* * *

Bill Haverford insisted he take the chair. Adam reduced the huge swaddling on his head to a single gauze-and-bandage wrap. One eye blackened where his unconscious head hit the steel. Adam watched as thrusters below the water level maintained the ship's position. Sometimes two of the mighty sideways engines started and the deck steel trembled. Most of the time, one of the main engines countered the current's flow with the auto steering, keeping the bow pointed and true.

"This is real bullshit. There's absolutely no need." The sea rose and fell with gentle, long swells.

Adam smiled. "Au contraire. My header into the scupper wasn't just my notorious lack of coordination, as my old football coach might claim. I happen to know you've got your boat cops looking for him." Bill said nothing. "Thanks for not denying it. You've taken the only sensible option to have the remaining crew search every nook of the boat, and catch this guy. When you do, let me punch him in the nose. Then, you're welcome to toss him overboard and leave." Adam grimaced as he tried to laugh. "I'd help you look, except he's already left."

"That's not the point, Adam. Everything is automated. The *Farmer* and the *Emma McKinley* don't need anyone aboard."

"What the heck do we need a captain for, then?" He smiled. "Nah, I'm here for the laser codes, Bill. Not the ship."

"Let someone else for Christ's sake."

"I invented this stuff. The *Emma*'s laser slaves to the *Farmer*. I'll be here to rewrite and make an adjustment as we get closer to the hour. That's the deal, Bill. I control both from here because little things can still go wrong." Adam looked at his friend. "When we're done, come back and take the ship. Bring a bottle of Jack or Turkey with you. Saving the world is thirsty work." Neither laughed. A sheen of sweat covered Adam's forehead. "There isn't anyone else, Bill."

"That's the bullshit. We don't need you *and* Tierra del Fuego to aim. You're injured. You just might make a cock-up of the whole thing."

"My part is Plan B. You know that. That's why I'm on the *Farmer* and the *Emma*'s slaved to us."

His friend swelled up with protest.

"Don't Bill, please. You've been great. The folks who put this all together in days instead of years should have streets and schools named after them. Kim ought to have a whole province named after him. You too, for Christ's sake. You're the only reason we'll even have a future for stuff like naming buildings." He took a deep breath. "Me, on the other hand? There are some things mankind should just not do. The most I'll ever be is an object lesson to the world." He held up a hand. "Not self-serving, just realistic. When you screw up, someone needs to pay. I'm just sorry it'll be so many others paying for me. Our best shot means the asteroid misses. If not … well then, everything becomes a degree of destruction. And for that, there will be a price tag."

"I know what the hell you're talking about. I know what's in that fucking envelope." Bill grew red-faced. "And, that's not going to happen."

"I think you're right. We've got the best and the brightest on this thing. We're going to be okay. Don't forget we have a less than a twenty percent chance this thing will even come close to Earth." Adam's drooping left eye joined the corner of his mouth. Both sagged when he smiled.

Bill wanted to say more. In all the years he'd known Adam, he'd yet to see him waver once his mind was settled.

"Okay, Adam. But you are one hardheaded son of a bitch." Bill's words were vehement and angry as he held out a folded email. "You might need these, but you better goddamn well not use them."

Adam looked down at the email and back up with a question.

"The big Jamaican kid that found you. Your shirt was wet and he thought he should, well you know. So, he gave them to me. He had no idea what they were, but I'm guessing this is fucking Plan B's codes." Bill's anger boiled over, and with good cause as he consigned his friend to the unknown.

Adam nodded. "Thanks. I know you don't agree—"

"We'll start the search again. Just in case." He reached to the communications bank and hit the master switch. The speakers overhead came alive. "You can hear the entire ship from the chair, Adam. Every passageway and every room is monitored by this station. CCTVs are on, too." He pointed to the bank of screens. "Use the joystick to switch from camera to camera, or to gimbal one around. The ship's intercom is up, so just yell if you see someone trying to avoid us."

"You're going to search, too?"

"No one knows the ship better than me." From under the navigation table, Bill brought out a Glock Model 24 semiautomatic pistol. "If this guy tried once and is still here, he'll try again. Listen and watch closely. Protect yourself, at least."

Adam racked the slide to put a round in the empty chamber. He checked the action. "Okay, thanks but, I'd like to search with you."

Bill sighed and dropped his shoulders. "Sweet Jesus, you're a knucklehead. Sit in the goddamn seat, will you? I need you to watch and pay attention. And I'm serious about your Plan B. No way, no how. Keep that thing away from the earth."

Adam grinned, wiping at a bit of spittle in the corners of his lips. "Sure, Bill. Sure."

Three teams of two armed men each spent six hours searching the ship. No space was too small to check, no cabinet or overhead storage too cramped for one of the searchers to climb into. Adam listened and watched for the glimpse of someone moving around to avoid the men. Except for the search team, the *American Farmer* was abandoned.

Bill unlocked the bridge and stepped in just as the big helicopter on the foredeck started up. "We're done, Adam. I want you to come with us. We just looked in every damn hidey-hole on this vessel. There's nothing you can do here by yourself. I'm the captain, and that's an order."

Adam smiled. "Yes and a hell of a captain you are, too. Take the crew and the helo. Catch up with the cutter. Get to dry land. Convince the South Americans and Africans if this thing does hit, the tidal wave could go as high as a hundred feet. Nothing within fifty miles of the coastal plains will be safe. We know the ISIS bastards are aiming for North America, but who knows if they can pull it off?"

Bill stared, his teeth clenched in anger. "All right, then. You're not going to come with us. But once I'm off the con, I can do what I want."

Adam grinned and wiped as the sweat ran from his forehead. Cool air flowed from the vents. "I'm counting on it."

"How far will the destruction go if your silly Plan B works and you hit the Arctic?"

"Shock wave? Everything above the equator will feel it. Think mother of all nuclear weapons. I don't know about the tsunami. Maybe as far southern England or Spain. The Pacific will be lucky and only feel the rumble. The Atlantic regions on both sides will get smacked. You gotta catch up with the Brazilian cutter, Bill. They'll make it okay but you gotta get going."

Bill turned to look at the helicopter crew chief far below on the steel deck, looking up at the bridge. "I'll stay with you."

"No." Adam was adamant. "You go and tell the damn story, quit trying to change my mind. You got a boat to catch." He held up two fingers with a drooping grin and offered his good friend a fifty-year-old peace gesture. "Make love, not war, and tell that to the idiots who started this."

Bill sighed. "Why don't you come back with me and run for office? Put your energies where your mouth is. You'd be a good politician."

Adam's laugh hurt his head. "There's no need to insult me. Now get off my boat, Haverford. Politician? Geez, talk about full of shit." Adam's words slurred. He wiped at his numb lips.

"Okay, okay. I want this ship back. Stick with the original decision, make it miss. I want you in hospital. That is a goddamn order."

Adam's crooked smile faded. "It'd give me great pleasure to give this ship back to you. Thanks for being here for me." He held out his right hand to hide trembling left-hand fingers.

The two shook. Bill never looked back as he locked the bridge door and slipped into the passageway to head for the elevator.

The huge helicopter below spun its blades to full speed as Haverford ran up to the crew chief. Bill lifted the other man's headphones off his ears and spoke. The man shook his head. Bill pointed to the steel deck under his feet. The man shook his head and stepped onto the large helicopter ramp. The clamshell closed and the helo lifted. Bill hurried back inside the ship.

The countdown clock on E-deck read less than ten hours, scant time until point zero. Fifty-two hours later, the world would know its fate.

Chapter 35

Adam sat in the unlighted bridge listening to the hum of the giant laser as the power kicked pressure back down. He wished William, the bright young engineer who loved to think up the wild and crazy, could see all this. At his elbow, a split-screen laptop displayed a copy of the beta codes from a hundred programmers and scientists in Reykjavík. Written in page after page of decimal columns, he used a comparison program with the water-sopped printout. A single column was changed. A footnote explanation corrected Adam's beta list to fine-tune the orders. A second Satlink email confirmed the data. Adam hit the enter button.

From where he sat, he would watch as the orders to activate Tierra del Fuego and the Boeing YAL took command, although he could still override if the system signaled a fault. The *Emma* and the *Farmer* postured in the two great oceans, about to pump out the most powerful laser ever shot from Earth, or for that matter, from anywhere. Embedded inside the light beam and reaching over a million miles into space, the beams would find the asteroid. The final command code using the technique discovered by William Lee could save hundreds of millions of lives. If the theory collapsed and a miss was not possible, Adam's laptop now contained the codes for the Arctic. The world had two chances to avoid destruction. The western hemisphere had only one.

The CCTV flickered behind him, but he didn't watch the sets. His head throbbed and wobbled on his neck. He was tired and laid his head back to rest a moment, but instead drifted into sleep.

The burst of radio chatter opened his eyelids to a swaying room. Stars touched the horizon on a calm sea, reflecting and disorienting him. The armchair satellite phone buzzed, yet his eyes wouldn't focus. Vision doubled, and the buzzing eventually stopped. The high-frequency radio came to life.

"Calling *American Farmer* this is Sealift Command, Cheyenne Mountain, over." The air cracked around the radio speaker as the call repeated. Adam slid off the chair as the bridge elevator in the corridor dinged and a key gentled into the outside lock.

The Satlink phone buzzed again. Adam watched the door behind him in reflection off the front glass. A figure pushed in.

"Adam?"

He knew that voice. A footstep.

"I know you're here. There's no need to hide. Why not just come out? We can end this."

Another footstep.

"You'll be dead soon, anyway. The hemorrhage is filling your brain with blood and killing you. You can save yourself and come to paradise with me."

The carpet pressed as a foot fell again. The hum of the ship's automated machinery quieted. Adam remained motionless as he held the Glock in his right hand. He listened to another soft step into the room.

"Your machine will not stop jihad. The will of Allah will be fulfilled. I will be in paradise with my brothers. Come with us, your pain will go away." The voice continued as the sound of the step flanked the room. "This would have been much simpler, if you'd listened to me. Slipping away in the night instead of a violent death, it's what we all wish for, yes? You escaped in New Jersey. I gladly take you and this evil ship to the bottom as penance."

Another footfall sounded against the soft nylon carpeting.

The voice drifted to him, hypnotic, reassuring. "Millions the world over have converted. Millions more in America and across the globe convert every day, and pledge to Islam. Anyone left after the jihad will be quickly fatwa. The mullah in each country will decide. Allah will deal most harshly with you, unless you come with me now. I will end your suffering."

"Stop right there." Another voice

The intruder spun and fired three quick shots sending the second figure backward into the radio bank. Reflexes cramped the trigger finger and a pistol round skittered across the table and into Adam's thigh. He crumpled but not before firing two quick shots, striking the first intruder in the hijab.

The pain hit Adam and he dropped to the floor. Blood pooled under his leg and dinner came up as he passed out.

When he awoke, he rolled to his back. The world outside

bathed in bright sunlight. A pounding in his head dwarfed the pain in his thigh. He rose only to stumble over a body with a bloody headcloth.

He reached the figure crumpled against the communication bank. His friend's eyes were open and watching as Adam approached.

"Bill, Jesus Christ."

"Hey, mate."

Adam fell next to him. "I thought you left."

"Ah, well," he answered, breathing in pants. "And miss all this fun? I'm glad you finally woke up. I thought I was goner there." He glanced at the overhead clock. "Ten hours. I slept, too. We must've been tired." He tried to smile but the joke failed in his pain.

Adam stumbled to the bulkhead and the first aid kit. He pressed a wad of gauze into the soppy, congealed mess around his friend's shoulder. "Hold this," he said.

Bill put his hand over the chest wound. "Barely nicked me."

"This isn't a cowboy movie, you British blockhead. I ordered you off this ship."

"Can't let you Yanks have all the glory." He took a deep breath as the lightheartedness left his eyes. "I ... I can't move, Adam."

Adam looked down. A thick bloody swatch lay under the man's backside. A small hole rimmed his stomach. "Oh, Jesus."

Bill laughed a little. "So much for your bedside manner." He turned his head and looked at the body between the two high stools. "Who's that?"

Adam took Bill's other hand and pushed into his stomach. "Press down. Do a Pinky Lee."

"Who?" He was breathless in the pain.

"Never mind, just press." Adam moved to the intruder, kicking away the gun. He moved the cloth. The hajib had caught brains, leaving a face distorted and anguished in death.

Bill groaned and looked away. "Ah, bloody hell. Sam?"

"Yeah," Adam said, pushing gauze into his own wound. Just then, he glanced at her hands. Chemical burns. "Oh, shit."

The laser.

The only place for her to avoid the crew's search must have been the laser's housing itself. The six men, who knew the ship so well, must have avoided the odd equipment with its warning signs, blinking lights, and shifting sounds. The PA couldn't escape fast enough when the device was tested and she'd been burned.

"I gotta check the laser, Bill. You'll be okay here for a while?"

"Piece of cake, mate."

Adam pulled the microphone off the radio bank and kneeled next to his friend. "I'll be back. Stick this in your hand. Call for help and press down on those wounds. Don't bleed to death on me."

Bill rolled his head to look at Adam. "I was thinking the same thing about you."

Adam grabbed his tablet and hurried to the elevator. As he pushed the call button, he heard the ship's sat-phone ring once, then twice. He should go back. Bill couldn't reach the Satlink but his mind told him he had no time to spare. He pushed the down-button.

The car jostled under him and he grabbed for the handhold, missing and crashing to the deck. His head rocketed with pain as the floor rose up to meet him. He closed his eyes at the surreal view inches off the work-scarred deck. *Tired, so tired.*

The elevator jolted to a stop and the doors opened. The sound of the side thrusters reverberated more loudly on this deck as a single, big engine churned the water. Huge rudders shifted tiny degrees with the automatic navigation commands. He reached for a steadying hand as the door jumped back. He teetered and sat back. He'd close his eyes just for a moment.

Adam never felt the first torpedo take the *American Farmer* forward of the engines. The second struck, and he stirred. A third explosion ripped into the jacketed double hull amidships not far from where he lay. His eyes opened.

The *American Farmer* settled foot by foot as bilge pumps surged to life and a klaxon sounded. The overhead deluge system burst into life. At first, Adam thought the blivets had sprung another leak. Then the familiar odor of cordite and sulfur filled his nostrils as emergency lights caught smoke hovering high in the cavernous opening.

He looked at the wide steel deck choked with giant gas tubes and huge supply blivets. He rose to a knee, testing his balance. The deck plating vibrated with a rhythmic lurch every few moments telling him one of the thrusters worked harder than the others.

A ship's system must have failed, he thought, but was not adept enough to know what happened. Bill would know.

"Bill. Oh, Christ." Adam said aloud.

He reached up and hit the intercom for the bridge. "Bill? This is Adam. How you doing up there?"

Silence answered.

"Bill? Come on buddy. Talk to me. Just say something. The intercom's on. I'll be able to hear you."

Nothing.

Just then, a ringing chattered into the sound system throughout the ship. He picked up a bulkhead phone. "Bill?"

"Bill? No this is Kim. Is Bill there with you? Why haven't you answered? What's happening?"

His head filled with cotton. He couldn't think. Hours had disappeared from the countdown clock. "Kim? How'd you get aboard?"

"What?" Kim answered, incredulous. "Aboard? Are you okay? I know you got a knock on the head, but what the hell are you still doing on the *Farmer*?"

"I'm, well ..." Adam felt like he'd awakened from a deep dream-sleep. His head pounded even harder than the thrusters. "I'm staying behind to send the signal manually. Just in case." His words slurred as he wiped saliva with the back of his hand. "The ship's doctor shot Bill. He's hurt bad."

"What? Jesus, Adam. I think we can help you, but you and Bill gotta get to a lifeboat."

"No."

"Listen. The *Emma* sank two hours ago. You shouldn't be there."

"Holy shit." Adam's head cleared a little. "What happened?"

"The Navy thinks an Iranian submarine. It's all confusion just now, nobody really knows. They must've been waiting. The Australian navy was all around there for protection and never knew. She must've sat on bottom for a month." Kim paused. "No matter now. The *Emma* is gone."

"I must have passed out, Kim. I think we have another gas

265

leak. I need to fix it."

"Fix it? What's wrong with you? Wait. You don't know? The *Farmer* took a torpedo, too. One of our subs got it. I wish the goddamn Navy would tell us these things. Did you know a submarine was standing guard?"

Adam's head wouldn't clear.

"Ah, no matter," Kim said. "The *Farmer*'s a hell of a ship but she's not a warship. You gotta get Bill and you to the lifeboat."

Adam calculated in his head. His friend made sense. "Okay, okay. You've got to tell Tom and Sheila. With nearly half our strength gone, the chances of sending the signal that far out isn't good. They'll have to wait before they shoot." He glanced at the countdown clock. Less than three hours to the old point zero. "If we're half strength, we needed to recalculate and let the asteroid get closer."

"Yeah, I was afraid of that. What are we going to do?"

"Let me … think." Adam stared into the huge cavity while sounds of the horns and alarms disappeared into his mind's background. "How badly is the *Farmer* damaged?" His words slurred. "Are we still holding over our point?" He pressed his pounding head against the steel bulkhead. The cold felt good on his skin.

"Absolutely. Not a millimeter of change according to our satellite reads. Tell me what you're thinking."

"If we were damaged, then I've got to assume the laser is damaged. I'll get Bill into the lifeboat. You get the sub to pick him up."

"Bullshit," said Kim. "No way. You both go."

"This is no big deal, Kim. Don't forget this was the contingency we planned all along."

"Jesus Christ, no. Remember, we still have satellite command and control."

Just then the laser system shrieked. Adam looked around. A blue revolving light and a strobe screamed for attention.

"What's going on?" said Kim.

"The laser … I think there's a leak."

"You've got to get off E-Deck. You and Bill get off that ship. Let the Boeing YAL send the signal. Everything in the laser will kill you with the first breath."

Adam dropped the phone and stumbled for the emergency equipment locker. He donned a mask, rubber slicker, and hood. He lurched back and shouted into the receiver. "Got to go now, Kim, to check out the system."

He didn't wait for the reply. Invisible vapor escaped, probably from the PA's meddling. The low and high detectors made for a confusing mass of alarms and lights. The hydrogen fluoride pressure decreased. He checked along the tank's system until he found the valve. The broken handle leaked with a loud hiss. A colorless and poisonous gas, hydrofluoric acid ate everything in its wake. He backed off knowing the protective gloves and hood would be useless in minutes. He wasn't afraid. He just needed to last long enough to get Bill into the little automatic lifeboat.

A cross-feed from a backup system appeared undamaged. He hurried to the control panel dragging one leg and flipped the switch for the backup supply. Too low a pressure wouldn't allow the fine spray of hydrofluoric acid into the deuterium chambers. He watched as the tanks' actuators rotated open and the system pressure climbed. He dropped to one knee. His head pounded. Amber replaced the gauge's red light, then a green light replaced the amber. The blue strobe ceased. The other alarms continued, but the worst of the damage was bypassed.

He rose unsteadily with one hand on the instrument panel and checked the nozzle. The technicians knew far better than he, but most of the instruments showed green lights. Two rested in the yellow range, but not enough time remained to have someone walk him through the system. He dragged a leg back to bulkhead desk and picked up his tablet.

He tapped the keys to the sequencing computer. The *Emma* was offline, of course. For a moment, he thought of the huge, red-hulled containership with its white superstructure and grandly painted American flag. In the *Emma*'s place, he wrote the command to engage his laptop still sitting eight stories above him on the bridge. If for any reason the Tierra del Fuego signal failed, the laser on the *Farmer* would take over the guidance and send the code to the command module's destruct circuit. By that time the asteroid would be closing on the moon's orbit, moving at tens of thousands of miles per hour, and only a fraction of a degree of deflection was possible. He prayed for this to be enough to miss or at a minimum, target the northern icecap.

The deck moved under him as he made his way back to the phone. Halfway there the last laser alarm quieted. The high overhead lights flickered and then died. A generator amidships came to life and the red "Exit" sign illuminated. The fire alarm alone bleated a warning.

The phone dangled at the end of its cord. He pulled off his mask. "Kim?"

"Adam! Shit. Where'd you go? Never mind, I can hear. You must have fixed the laser system."

His words were slow and plodding. "I just turned on the backup supply, and hit the restart sequence button. That won't last long." He put both hands to his head, feeling like he was about to explode.

"Maybe it won't have to. Tom moved the firing time up. He said your system was signaling a fault to the command center. He wants to shoot as soon as the comet is within range, so Cheyenne Mountain's scrambling like crazy."

"Not comet, Kim." His voice slowed, even in his ears. "Asteroid." Sensations on the left side of his face faded. He felt like he'd come from the dentist's office and wiped at his drooling mouth.

Why is the pounding in my head so bad?

"Will there be enough power?" Kim asked.

Adam answered. "Don't know. Never tried changing graphene code before. William Lee might know. Not me." Adam wearied of the struggle. "Need to rest a minute."

"Okay, okay. I'll let Tom and Sheila know. You and Bill get to the lifeboat launch now. It's automatic, so board and just hit the button. I'll give the Navy a heads-up."

Adam slid to the floor. He forced clarity into his thoughts. "We both know the answer, Kim. That little boat only does five or ten knots. Even with thirty hours of fuel ..." The simple calculation overwhelmed his mind. "Listen, Kim. I'm pretty sick. I think you already got the report, didn't you?"

Kim hesitated. "Yes, I did, but ..."

Adam wondered what his friend could possibly say. "Don't worry about it. Tell Julius I'm sorry I can't give him back his ship."

"Fuck the ship. Get to the lifeboat...."

Kim's voice grew distant. The echo chamber of the huge container hold vibrated with loud clanks and squeals. Adam thought the torpedo shot must have damaged the steel plating. Ripping sounds reverberated as the ship twisted and torqued widening the gap in its hull as it fought to maintain position.

Adam gentled his head to the deck as the phone slipped away and hung by its cord.

Tell Julie I'm thinking of her. Remind Katherine about the paid-up college fund. Take care of yourself, Kim. Things are going to be bad for a while. Can you help Bill?

Adam said none of this aloud. As pleasant endorphins circulated and relieved the pounding headache, his brain eased its struggle. The klaxon sounded far off. His vision swam a last time under closed lids. The pain seeped away like a fleeting memory.

"... calling *American Farmer*. This is the *Virginia*, over." The high overhead speaker crackled and repeated, over and over again. Adam never heard.

Chapter 36

The Ushuaia International Airport, Tierra del Fuego, Argentina lay five miles away over the rockiest and roughest terrain on the planet. Two companies of the 101st Airborne Division crowded the tiny spit of land to protect the Boeing YAL, a KC-10 fuel tanker, two C5A transports, two F-18 fighter jets, and a pair of F-22 long-range interceptors. The soldiers dug bunkers and foxholes around the airfield against three times as many crack, heavily armed Argentinean and Brazilian marines. An angry consortium of twelve South American countries protested in the United Nations against the US invasion of the lonely outpost.

Tom watched Sheila's eyes fill with tears as she turned down the CNN News broadcast volume.

"First we come uninvited, and now this? Is it true?"

Tom said, "We need to get the Boeing YAL launched."

"The *Emma* is gone. The *Farmer* is barely afloat. The YAL can only aim the signal. And now, an astrophysicist claims we always planned to bring that thing south. You're CIA. Is that what was planned?"

"That's a rumor," Tom said, waving his hand as if to dismiss nonsense. "We always planned the asteroid to miss."

"Right. Of course. When you had two ships and could send the signal a million miles into deep space. What about now?"

"Now," he said, his breath escaping. "Now, we're counting on a little luck."

She shook her head. "Others maybe. Not you and Adam. Your minds don't think luck. Tell me what the politicians and scientists cooked up. I deserve to know. Plan B's calculations send the asteroid into the Arctic ice cap. Right? Is that true?"

Tom's teeth tapped rapidly. "It's been changed."

Her eyes widened. "Who changed it? Where does it go now?"

"I don't know," Tom said. Of course he did, but could hardly say anything.

Sheila turned to the tent flap. "Well no wonder we've got company."

Two circling contingents of sleek fighter jets from a half-dozen South American countries orbited. No one believed the US ambassador's speech that ISIS controlled the asteroid's flight, not the United States. So far, no orders were given or shots exchanged.

"And if we can't control it, where does it hit?" She was up and pacing.

"Virginia, North Carolina, South Carolina." His voice trailed off.

"Oh Christ," she said, striking the tabletop with her small fist. "With half our strength gone, where can we send it?"

"The angle means it comes closer before we can pulse the guidance—"

"*Where*, Tom?"

"A thirteen-degree divergence, given the angle—"

"Tom? Please."

He needed her to stick with him for just a while longer. "South America. The scientist is right. Buenos Aires, Montevideo, Asuncion. Maybe we can guide it to the *Farmer* if she'll stay afloat long enough."

Sheila dropped her head.

Tom said quickly, "I grant you it's not a good choice, but it's all we got." Another lie.

Sheila watched the barren landscape through clouded plastic tent windows. The cold sun kept the horizon lighter than the deep, frozen blue over their heads. As invaders, she and Tom faced life in prison if Argentina got to them first. If the Argentines didn't bother, she didn't want to starve to death when winter returned. Their food could only last a few months.

She wiped at her scar. "You know bringing that damn thing into this hemisphere is our choice and it's not right."

Tom didn't answer.

"Adam is dead on that fucking ship. How did all this go so wrong?"

He cringed. She never swore, and he needed her to hold together for a while longer. "There are a lot of people who'll be making sacrifices in the coming hours, Sheila."

Her anger boiled to the surface. "I know that, goddamn it. You

271

don't think I know?" She turned to him with dark fury and a clenched fist. "How could they get to the *Emma*? What's up with that? Who the hell is in charge of security, anyway?" She looked at the silent White House phone with its hotline into the presidential bunker. "Tell me."

"Please, Sheila." Tom breathed through his open mouth, knowing she might already suspect the truth.

"No, Tom. A three thousand by two thousand-mile landmass in North America is less than a speck in the universe. How could Rahim Tajalli calculate with such accuracy?"

"Let it go, Sheila."

"We're the most powerful nation on the planet, and some third-rate country with a wacko physicist murderer and half-dozen obsolete submarines sneaks in and kills the two ships about to save us?" She turned on her husband. "You're a goddamn sailor. How did they do that?"

"I don't know," he said. Despite the cold, sweat beaded his forehead. "We'll be lucky if we have the chance to find out. The *Farmer* is still afloat, you know." He counted on the *Farmer* surviving until the end. The code was loaded. Adam never questioned the changed column of figures.

"You know what the tsunami in Japan looked like, right? Whole cities swallowed, then swept back out into the ocean taking people with them." Sheila's mouth set in grim fury. "That ship represents half power. You and I know how close we were with everything at peak output. Now we have a derelict ship, an untested algorithm invented to break an unbreakable code, and the goddamn Air Force with thirty-year-old equipment. Are we all just crazy?"

Tom needed to slow her down, have her concentrate on the task only minutes away. The old code no longer mattered. The new one was loaded and ready. "I don't know," he said. "Administrations come and go. They have their own agendas, but we have our jobs to do."

She paced at the tent opening. "You're telling me Washington makes the most selfish choice in the history of mankind—"

"We don't know that," Tom said, his voice rising.

"Oh, yes we do. You just loaded a different algorithm. Didn't you?"

Tom looked away.

"You're still working for the CIA? Goddamn it, Tom. You are. You know you are. Our politicians want to minimize damage to America. What the hell was wrong with concentrating on farther north? We had a better chance to miss completely, or maybe hit the Arctic. That's what Adam wanted but apparently everyone's political career is too important. This is all true, isn't it? Now, we are going to kill the southern hemisphere."

She softened her voice. "Tom. Baby. You know this is bullshit, right? The US is going to kill a couple of other countries, hundreds of millions of people, most with brown and black faces, to give itself a better chance. We've sacrificed our national integrity on someone else's back."

"It's a Sophie's choice, Sheila."

She gripped the tabletop. "No, it isn't." She spoke in wide, spaced words. "We did this, and we should pay. Not others. God might judge us kindly, Tom, but the world will not. We'll be a country of international criminals. Pariahs. You and I are the only survivors of our team. *We* will kill these millions of people. Do you understand? *We* will be the greatest mass murderers of all time, and not the Rahim Tajalli, and not ISIS." She faced him, her rock-solid body shaking with anger. "Why doesn't this mean anything to you? You and me. Adam's the lucky one. He's already dead."

"This will be okay. The innocent will not die. I promise."

She looked at him, incredulous. "How do you know that? You can't know that."

"Because, I know, Sheila. We'll be okay. The faithful will be okay."

She looked at him, trying to see behind the mask. "How, Tom? How do we go from being the world's biggest mass murderers to 'everything's going to be okay'?"

He turned away as his irritation grew, not from frustration but fear. He'd worked for this moment since the day he and Adam sat in the Pentagon coffee shop. But without Sheila, the victory would be hollow. She must understand the destiny of reward was theirs. She needed to agree, and he must convince her.

She looked up. "Did we at least get everyone away from the coastlines?" When he didn't answer she said, "What will happen to the island nations?"

"It's all guesswork for now," he said after several moments at his computer. "Let's just do our job."

She reached out for him. "I love you, Tom, but we're not universal soldiers. We have to question. We should've questioned more—"

"No, Sheila. Not questions. Faith."

The computer screen at her desk dinged. She watched him, a query in her eyes as she touched a button.

"What is it?" he asked, his forehead wrinkling.

Her smile faded. "The Brits got back to DC about the effect on the world tilt. No catastrophic changes."

His face remained anxious. "But the climate will change, right?"

"There's so much more at stake, why are they worried about rain patterns?" He didn't answer. "The desert might need to start handing out umbrellas. What does it matter?"

They were looking at one another as the first *thump* sounded. "What's that?" she whispered.

Thump. Thump.

"Bombs," he said. "Or, missiles."

The tent flap flew back. A young lieutenant stood there. "Sir, ma'am." His eyes shifted wide. "The airfield is under attack."

Tom and Sheila ran out of the tent and to the edge of the rocks. A few miles away, smoke rose over the airfield.

"Oh, my God. Someone fired a shot," Sheila said in a low voice.

Two American F-22 fighter interceptors on cap released intercepting rockets, but were overcome by the sheer numbers of missiles and fighters. Both fell under the onslaught. Several squadrons of small jets popped over the horizon and dove at the airfield.

Sheila took his elbow. "The YAL. Where's the Boeing YAL?"

From the distance, with all the smoke, neither could tell what burned. Just then the huge Boeing YAL parted the gray and black billows and lifted into the sky. Swirls of dark vapor formed great rings off each wingtip. The sound from four huge turbofan engines caught up seconds behind the climb-out. The big KC-10 tanker lifted off a moment later, and almost immediately, a tiny silver jet rolled in behind. A quick burst of light from under one wing and the tanker, full of jet fuel, exploded in a furious fireball plowing into the flight line. Ugly sounds rolled up the mountainside to the command tent.

Sheila slipped her hand into his.

An American F-18 released a missile and shot down the attacking jet. Two more small jets rolled into its place and fired missiles. The big Boeing 747 YAL exploded, mixing black, greasy smoke with puffs of white clouds.

"Oh, God, Tom," she said.

Machine gun and rifle fire sounded from below them. The lieutenant ran toward the shooting as the first *crump* of mortars fell.

As the last of the dead American jets dropped into the bay, troop transports circled to land while others dropped paratroopers. The ground fight was immediate and horrific.

The first rounds sparked against the rocks and ripped the air above Tom and Sheila's heads. He pulled her back to the tent. The White House line blinked. "Tom, look. Answer it."

Shouts outside, and more firing. At the same moment, the high-frequency communications line crackled. Another machine gun opened up nearby. A loud explosion sent rock chips and sand against the tent's sides.

The overhead speaker broke in, the voice oddly calm amongst the chaos of battle and death outside. "Tierra Command, Tierra Command. This is Boyer at Cheyenne Mountain, Sealift Command. Come in, please."

Tom ignored the call, his world moving too fast. He needed a moment. A mistake now would be disastrous.

"We've got to tell them the Boeing YAL has been destroyed," Sheila said.

"No. Let me think."

"Yes," she said. "Answer Boyer. Hurry."

The radio crackled again. "Tierra Command this is Boyer. Are you there? Over."

Tom's breaths came in rasps. He looked toward the sounds of guns, then back at the bank of radios. His hand pushed on the pistol in his holster. He needed to send the code now, while he still could.

275

Hitting South America wouldn't destroy them, only anger them into a war footing. The US could not survive.

"For God's sake, Tom." Sheila pushed him out of the way and hit the transmit switch. "Command here, go ahead, Boyer. We're under attack."

"Ah … attack? Ah, geez. We're too late. Didn't you get the White House call?"

Tom said nothing as he brought his computer power up.

Sheila hit the radio button again. "Negative. Stand by." Rifle fire closed in on the tent. She pulled the table microphone toward her, watching Tom. "White House? Tierra Command is under attack."

"Understand, Tierra Command. Pakistan mission control confirmed Mauna Loa Observatory earlier report the asteroid is in two pieces."

She looked at Tom. "Did you know this?" She looked at his hands typing, readying the commands, saying nothing.

The White House continued. "One piece of asteroid is in the basket. NASA JPL analysis is preliminary, but they advised both asteroids will glance off the atmosphere. The laser shot is not needed. Do you copy? Stand down and surrender to the Argentineans. Do you copy?"

She reached for the button, but Tom knocked her hand away. She looked at him, surprised and frightened.

The speaker crackled. "The JPL is confirming and the president is waiting to announce. Do you copy the asteroid, both asteroids will miss?" The man's voice was excited and pitched high.

Tom pulled the laptop toward him, and rapidly picked at the keys.

"Tom? What are you doing?"

"Shut up, Sheila. Please."

"This is over," she said. "We've got to tell our soldiers to lay down their arms. We can go home."

She turned to run outside but his iron grip stopped her. He hit the computer key for the remote command on the *Farmer*.

"Tom, don't do that. Let me go," she said, her eyes wide and startled.

He watched the screen as a tone sounded, confirming the

connection. "This is for us, Sheila."

"What are you talking about? What's wrong with you? We don't need to do anything. Everything's going to be okay. Just like you said." She looked at the nearly imperceptible nod of his head. "Cancel the command. Oh, God, what are you doing?"

Tom hit the encoder to begin sequencing for the transmission.

A commotion sounded on the ridge just below the tent. A pistol shot, then voices shouted orders.

"Tom stop." She pulled at his grip. "Let me go. If you send that to the first asteroid, the second might slingshot. Who knows where it will go?"

"I know," said Tom.

Tom could see in his mind's eye the *Farmer*'s giant machinery approaching fever pitch with photons fighting one another to be free of their chambers.

"Tom. Stop."

He hit the computer key. "Activate," he said aloud, as if the action needed a voice command.

She screamed and pushed at him to hit the computer's off button.

He grabbed up her other hand, his eyes remaining fixed on the digital count. Somewhere outside moon's orbit at point zero, the laser reached into the void of space.

"Please, baby. Don't bring that damn thing down here. We can go home. Please." She moved to stand in front of him, shaking loose his grip and taking both his shoulders to plead. "We need to get our soldiers to lay down their arms. Men are dying."

His eyes dropped from the clock to Sheila as his arm snaked around her. He pulled the pistol from his holster and pointed at the side of her head. He never heard the round fire.

The high-frequency radio crackled and a woman's voice spoke. "Tierra Command? This is the president calling. Hello?"

Tom shrieked and slammed his fist down on the microphone, again and again. The switch crushed open. He read the remote readings. Adam's destruct circuit opened, the guidance rockets fired.

Six thousand miles away, the presidential bunker and a hundred other nations listened to shuffling sounds inside the tent.

Tom pulled a thermal hand grenade from his briefcase and sat on the floor next to Sheila. He cradled her broken and bleeding head in his lap, pulled the pin, and closed his eyes. His last words resounded through the airwaves.

"I'm so sorry, my love. *Allah Akbar.*"

Chapter 37

Augustus Pignataro, exited the terminal's doors with a canvas bag and scuffed leather satchel over one shoulder. He hurried to the aircraft parking spot, a limp evident in his gait.

"Here you go," he called to the copilot standing near a bright-polished aluminum business jet. "Last of the samples."

"The weather's coming up," the man said, accepting the box. As if in answer, the plane's wings shuddered when a gust blew over the ramp.

Even though only late August, the tiny settlement anticipated the first snowfall to mark the end of visitor season.

"Why not spend the night?" Gus said. "You're carrying back our most precious cargo, you know." His dark eyes laughed.

The copilot shook his head. "I understand you're a lonely old man, but you've kept her a week too long already." Marty's eyes filled with his own merriment. "Besides, school starts on Monday, just like here in Lake Harbour."

A pretty blond woman wearing a Blue Jays baseball cap stopped a few feet away. "What's this? You're lonely?" She carried a small box bound for the cargo bay, and touched Marty's cheek with her free hand. "Hi, Marty. I just don't think I'm appreciated around here."

Marty smiled back. "I can take you away from all this. He's always been kind of an unappreciative, snotty little kid."

"Ouch," Gus said and took the box from her. "That hurts." He found a secure spot inside the baggage compartment.

Marty withdrew an iPad from an inside pocket and tapped in a command. "We'll need to stop in Labrador City for fuel. We've got a pretty good headwind with the Arctic front coming in."

Andrea smiled at Gus, and squeezed his hand. "I'll move her along. She doesn't want to leave either." Both men watched as Andrea walked away. She shook her head and glanced back. "Dirty old men."

They both laughed, and Gus spoke first. "How's the company doing? The news tells me the world still hasn't quit blaming us. Not all that surprising, I suppose."

Marty sighed and checked the security of the baggage hold. They walked to the airstairs. "Oh, there's been backlash, for sure. But Kim is really doing well. The US has a ways to go before we can climb out of the hole we dug, especially since every country knows they could've been a target just like South America. Of course, no one anticipated two asteroids."

"Yeah," Gus said. "That must've been a surprise to Tom and Sheila." He tried to grab back the lightness of the moment before, but without success. "I'll bet the three of us talked out a thousand scenarios, and never once thought the solar basket had a shadow."

"You've probably heard the Russians claim they warned you about a second comet."

"Asteroid, not comet, and if they did, word never got to me. Maybe Tom knew somehow, but I didn't." Gus sighed and looked at Marty. "Of course, I was pretty much out of things there at the end." He gripped his friend's shoulder. "Thanks."

Marty nodded. "You're welcome, but I didn't do anything. I was just along for the ride."

They watched the water's surface and tiny whitecaps for a moment.

Gus said, "You know, it's not every guy who gets rescued by a nuclear submarine. That must've been very cool."

The two watched as small snow clouds skittered aside to let the afternoon sun have its moment. "Uh-huh. So cool, you slept through the whole thing."

"I was lucky the sub had a real doctor on board." Gus wiped at his left eye. The surgery saved his life but the lid would always droop a little, the eye water a little, and his grin remained lopsided. He'd come to like the goofy look.

Marty said, "If you've got to ride out a tsunami, underwater is the only way."

Gus nodded. "Amazing only the US got the brunt of the blame. I mean, we deserved it for our 'choice,' of course, but—"

"Old ground," Marty said. "Quit beating yourself up and leave it to the academics and the apologists."

Gus exhaled. "You're right. I'll be second-guessing myself for the rest of my life."

Both turned their heads toward the cockpit as the captain turned on the electronics and the aircraft's outside lights came on.

"Look's like Frank's getting ready," said Gus. "Are politics settling down?"

Marty considered for a moment. "It doesn't seem like the president's done with Iran. You recall she made it pretty clear what would happen to our enemies. I think the Iranian moderates are actually enjoying the new freedom."

Gus nodded. "And of course the Israelis were happy to wipe the desert floor with the Rahim Tajalli."

"Yes. I'm pretty proud of the Texas lady in the White House," Marty said. "She stayed the course, even when it got ugly. Of course the decision, her Sophie's choice, will haunt her to the end of days."

"That's too bad."

"Yeah," Marty said, "Considering she didn't have a choice. How was she to know? I've got to admit though, she tracked down every one of the characters in that conspiracy to fat-finger the guidance numbers."

"And," Gus said, "she took full responsibility in front of the UN. Takes a big person to shoulder the weight of a lot of selfish people."

"She got reelected, you know. The last president of the old United States."

Both men paused until Gus summarized their mutual thoughts. "Nothing good comes from killing one another. Maybe we learned something."

"Maybe," Marty said. "But then again, you always did see the bright side." Marty picked up a tiny rusty screw from the ramp and handed it Adam. "Toss this for me, will you? The country's not going to recover for a while. You know that, right? Most of the others recalled their ambassadors. Argentina, Brazil, and Uruguay still won't come to the peace table. No one's fired a shot in a couple years, but it's still hurting a lot of people. On the upside, Syria's new government is friendly toward us. Halim is doing great, by the way. He trounced the Muslim Brotherhood in last winter's election."

Gus nodded, pleased. "Yeah, I heard. I wish I could congratulate him personally." A lopsided glance. "Did the company

281

help?"

"It's against the law to use foreign money in a Syrian election. But Kim and Julius found a way without breaking any rules." Marty looked around at the bleak landscape. "Do you like it here ... I mean, at the end of the world?"

Gus knew Marty thought this isolated town a poor choice. "I like it more now, of course. But even in the beginning, it wasn't so bad. I missed seeing Julie, and helping rebuild. It's hard to sit on the sidelines. You know I can't go back, right? Fatwa is only one radical away. And there's plenty of them out there."

On cue, both women stepped from the airport store, sharing something funny. Gus smiled at the image. "Julius still happy?"

Marty nodded. "He loved stepping down and being elected chairman of the board. Oh, yeah. Almost forgot. Brad Benchley and Bill Haverford said hello. Brad will be running this year in the shortened election cycle. Senator or something. And Bill said to stay the hell away from guns."

Gus laughed. "Me? He's the one that shot me, for Christ's sake. His memory's going."

"Yeah, yeah."

"How're his ..." Gus's voice trailed off.

"Doing good. He's up and walking. Doctors are telling him to take it easy. He claims he'll be back on the bridge this time next year."

Gus smiled and said nothing.

They both watched Andrea and Julie stop to talk to a townsperson. Brad and Bill were two of only six who knew Gus's true identity. Adam Michaels, venerated and excoriated, died in the South Atlantic when the *Farmer* was lost in the aftermath of the shadow asteroid's strike. The submarine crew and the doctor believed the men they rescued were the *Farmer*'s captain and a crewman. Bill considered the evil waiting for Adam once his identity was revealed, so instead, he identified the unconscious man as Sam Hardy. A man. Just as he coordinated the submarine rescue and dash for safer waters, Bill started Adam on the road to his new life.

Marty touched his shoulder. "How're you doing? All right?"

Gus turned to look at him, saw the concern on his face. "Once in a while, I get down a little. I feel bad about the deaths of so many. I feel bad about Sheila and Tom."

Marty said nothing.

"I know, but he was a friend once, and a good guy."

"He cost the world millions of lives," Marty said. "Canada and the East Coast were pretty much decimated for five miles inland. We were lucky the captured asteroid was small. We still lost over a million people on the eastern seaboard alone. Tom Connecelli was a terrorist, plain and simple, so get over it. He left us with a world that can't decide who to blame, jihadists or the Great Satan."

"Al-Qaeda and Rahim Tajalli are the mass murders, not us. We made bad decisions, for sure. The last one was a world-class screw-up. But even that will be debated for the next hundred years. Just like Hiroshima and Nagasaki last century. One day the world will come to know we really had no choice. Once we passed point zero—"

"I know, I know." Marty placed his hand on Gus's shoulder. "You've got to let go one day, or it's gonna eat you alive. Consider that the new USA, Canada, and Mexico are back stronger than ever. "

Gus nodded and breathed deeply. "I just hope we can be as gracious in our new prosperity as we are now in poverty. Because one day, we will come back prosperous. We don't know any other way."

"Every nation gets knocked off its pedestal eventually."

"You're right," Gus said. "It's good we refused to take the South Americans to the woodshed. Somebody's actually used their brains in Washington."

"That would be your Congressman Brad Benchley." Marty zipped up his leather jacket. "But you mean in St. Louis, right?"

"Right. Old habits die hard." Gus slipped a letter into his consigliore's pocket. "Security violation, don't say it. Give this to Grandfather. It's typed and not signed. He still in Honolulu?"

"Yeah," Marty said with a laugh, his mood lightening. "Acting as if he doesn't have a care in the world while he and Kim kick world-commerce ass. You know his airplane can be in Labrador City tomorrow. If you want ..."

"No. No, thanks. Maybe next summer. Four years in hiding isn't enough."

"Well. Your grandpa could use you. The humanitarian programs alone ..." Marty stopped. "Anyway, McCaffrey Shipping's doing a heck of a lot of good for a lot of people. He told me to let you know, the chairman seat's waiting whenever you're ready."

Gus sighed. "Tell him thanks, but the answer's still no. But give Kim and Bill a raise."

Marty nodded and fell into silence until he squinted an eye at Gus. "You know Miranda's getting married to Dick Roberts, right?"

Gus smiled at his lifelong friend and confidant. "We get the news up here."

Marty harrumphed. "Good, 'cause I pulled all our investigators off her last spring. She's on her own now."

Gus nodded as both men watched the horizon. "Good."

"You're right it's good," said Marty, "'cause if it were anything else, I'd have to kick your ass."

"I said, I was good." Gus laughed. "Look. I love my wife. Nothing will ever change that. I only wanted to make sure—"

"It's done," Marty said. "Complete. Get on with your life." Marty put on dark glasses against the slanting sun under clouds on the far horizon. "And Julius says to tell you no more reports without Andrea in attendance."

Gus laughed and held up his hands. "All right, all right. I've got it, Mr. Callaway. I'm in total agreement." He turned at sounds of footsteps.

"What's so funny?" Julie asked, running and hugging her father's arm.

"Your uncle Marty is a very funny guy."

"Oh, I know," said Julie, grown tall and lovely. "He makes me laugh all the time."

"Really?" Gus said, turning Marty's way. "This guy?"

"Really," Marty said and accepted the package from Julie. "I'm a very pleasant person, sir. Your niece is a terrific judge of character. You should know that fact."

The pilot stepped into the Citation's doorway. "Mr. Callaway? I'm sorry, sir. We need to move it along."

"Okay, Frank. Thank you." Marty adjusted his ball cap. "I guess that's us."

Julie hugged her father around the neck. "I'm going to miss you, Dad—ah, Uncle Gus."

"Me, too," he said with a catch in his throat. "I'll be in the audience in June. Count on it." Marty raised an eyebrow. "In the back. I'll watch you walk the stage and meet you up here the week after."

The airstair closed while Gus and Andrea walked to the edge of the tarmac. He slipped his hand in hers as the Citation's engines spun up. A tiny face appeared in a round window and waved. They both waved back.

"You okay?" Andrea asked as the jet taxied away.

"Sure." He gripped her hand as small birds lifted from the water's edge

They watched as the airplane took the far runway.

She pushed her arm through his. "And Miranda? Is she okay, too?"

He hung his head. "You never cease to amaze me."

"Remember that, in whatever small part of your pea-brain still remains."

He smiled and kissed her lips. "I love you, you know."

"I know, but that doesn't matter just now because I'm hungry."

The roar from the runway made both turn to watch. The jet accelerated, lifting easily, and banked over the wide bay. High wisps of clouds edged a sky dissolving from blue to gold.

"Who's cooking?" he asked.

"Your turn."

"Last of the fresh veggies, then? Going to be a long, cold winter."

She laughed. "Oh, yeah. I can't wait."

"Me, too," he said. "Me, too."

The End
Levant Mirage
Thanks for reading ~ Oliver

About the Author

Oliver grew up on military bases throughout the country. Like all boys, he played good guys and bad, although he usually favored the good. Coaxing him into an afternoon of baseball or hiking the Southern California hills didn't take much unless a book got in the way.

When the time came for his rite of passage, Oliver and his best friend Herb joined the Marines to become officers. Herb left school early, even though those were the days of limited options. Not long after, Oliver stepped into sweltering heat on the tarmac not far from where Herb had died.

Thirty one men flew the helicopters in Oliver's small gunship unit. They spent days and nights over the mountains and towns trying to keep the world safe for … well, that's not really true, is it? The real reason any of them ever went into those mountains at night for an emergency medevac meant an injured buddy. Some of them, Oliver never knew existed.

After his war, Oliver traveled on to grad school and spent a while wandering. Lots of vets seem to do that, fighting their war all over again. Some found their way back, others did not. A nice, electric model typewriter replaced the old Smith Corona portable. If you read the short story "Synonymy" in A Stellar Collection published in 2013, you caught him during that period of his life. He taught on the reservation in New Mexico and spent some years with the cops, the feds, and even flying commercially. All the while, the writing never stopped. The Smith was traded for a Zenith and a Mac, and then a PC that still travels at the bottom of his duffel. He wonders sometimes if his old Smith Corona manual is at the bottom of someone's closet in Bangkok.

Marsh Island and Blind Marsh, published in 2013 and 2014 by the late and wonderful folks of AEC Stellar, New Orleans represented cooperation and friendship among peers, and his first break in the world of literature. Pearl River Publishing replaced AEC after its demise for Levant Mirage and later will host Oliver's Joshua Tree in January 2016 and later, Bequeathed. The boutique publishing concept is yet another grand experiment for authors not already under the thumb of someone else's expectations. Memorable characters and a great story are not necessarily the sole province of the acclaimed or the big house.

Other books by Oliver F. Chase
Short Story Anthology
"Synonymy" in A Stellar Collection (2013 AEC Stellar, New Orleans, La, USA)

Novels
Marsh Island (2013 AEC Stellar, New Orleans, La, USA)
In the style of Craig Johnson's "Longmire," and with the gritty acerbity of James Lee Burke's memorable characters, award winning author Oliver F. Chase takes us for a ride to remote Marsh Island, Louisiana by way of Las Vegas, the Bahamas, and Mexico. Phil Pfeiffer returned from the Gulf War with a broken back and a bad taste in his mouth. Out of rehab and uniform, Phil tried to live the quiet life of a private detective tracking wayward husbands and skip tracing for a local bail bondsman. When a widow hired him to investigate the death of her husband in a Mexican boating accident, people started dying. The widow later discovered her husband's photo in a celebrity magazine and Phil is again pressed into service. The trail fizzled, yet people continued to die. When the celebrity is suddenly lost at sea, Phil tracked the disappearance to a Bahamian island. Awaiting him there? Deadly sharks and the authorities with a charge of murder, and the widow is no closer to finding her husband.

Blind Marsh (2014 AEC Stellar, New Orleans, USA)
Phil Pfeiffer struggles with the demons of lost friends and missed opportunities only to spiral into the depths of depression. The lovely Las Vegas lounge singer from Marsh Island appears one late night to hire Phil as her bodyguard. A Mafia boyfriend inexplicably abandons her to a high stakes clash of international terror and she must protect herself. Phil finds himself in a wild west shootout and a plot to steal a billion dollar industry designed to bring America to its economic knees. Phil is faced with a choice between his own life and that of the killer. He chooses to take both.

Note From the Pearl River Publishing Group, LLC

<u>Levant Mirage</u> is also available in most electronic formats. Please check with your favorite retailer. You may contact Mr. Chase with concerns, comments, and requests for signed print copies at prpg.llc@gmail.com.

Mr. Chase is often featured as a guest speaker at writer's clubs, book signings, presentations and library groups. Please contact Pearl River Publishing for his availability and schedule.

prpg.llc@gmail.com

If you'd like a chuckle, check Mr. Chase's "Take on Life" at www.oliverchase.wordpress.com. Oliverchase.net reveals upcoming books and tours. Check him out there, too.

Coming in January 2016

Joshua Tree

by

Oliver F. Chase

A meteoric political rise awaits the dynamic son of a California field laborer and an iron worker. Winning election after election, the timing is right, the sky is the limit, and the talk is about the nation's first Latino presidency. The national media announces the birth of a new Camelot, casting both a young senator and his alluring wife in the image of the bygone Kennedy era.

Just when life seems the most promising, a lovely senate aide goes missing. Both husband and wife fight rumors, but far more is at stake than a simple political career. The mystery and the publicity ebb until an unwitting fisherman stumbles upon the decomposed corpse of the aide in San Francisco Bay. An autopsy reveals she died four months pregnant as the uproar and suspicion darken the couple's dreams.

When an inexplicable failure of the continental electrical grid cripples America, the very system the Senator proposed and supported, panic spreads and vultures circle. The country holds its breath as the fate of a nation teeters on the precipice, sidelined against the forces of greed and avarice.

Friends of the Author

A Dangerous Element by Gregory S. Lamb

An American covert operation to destroy the nuclear enrichment program at Natanz, Iran goes bad when a virus is discovered in the facility's closed control network. Former combat pilot, Colonel Mark "Coolhand" Reynolds holds the key to unraveling the cast of shady characters involved in the operation and cover up.

http://www.amazon.com/Dangerous-Element-Gregory-S-Lamb/dp/1940820103
http://gregorylambpdxauthor.wordpress.com
Find Me on Facebook:
https://www.facebook.com/greg.lamb.1612
https://www.facebook.com/LambPDXAuthor
Twitter:
https://twitter.com/GregorySLamb
http://gslambpdxauthor.webs.com

The People In Between by Gregory S. Lamb

Kiraz Nora Johansson and her twin brother never
knew their mother who died while giving birth.
By invitation of a family friend she travels to Cyprus
and discovers her family's past. Through a history
that was nearly lost to her and her troubled brother,
she learns what it means to love and becomes
forever tied to the Cypriot people and their
unforgettable island home.

http://www.amazon.com/dp/B008HTEG6A

Amazon Author Page:
http://www.amazon.com/Gregory-Lamb/e/B008IFYOYW

Relic II: Resurrection by Jonathan Brookes

Fact and fiction collide in this high-tension,fast-paced sequel to Relic.
A baby is born; its mother dies during childbirth.
 The race is on to claim guardianship of this orphan,
whose genetics are a relic of a lost race.
In a perverse twist of evolution, this one
child could unravel 30,000 years of Homo sapiens
 dominance of the Earth.

http://jonathanfbrookes.wordpress.com

Coming October 2015

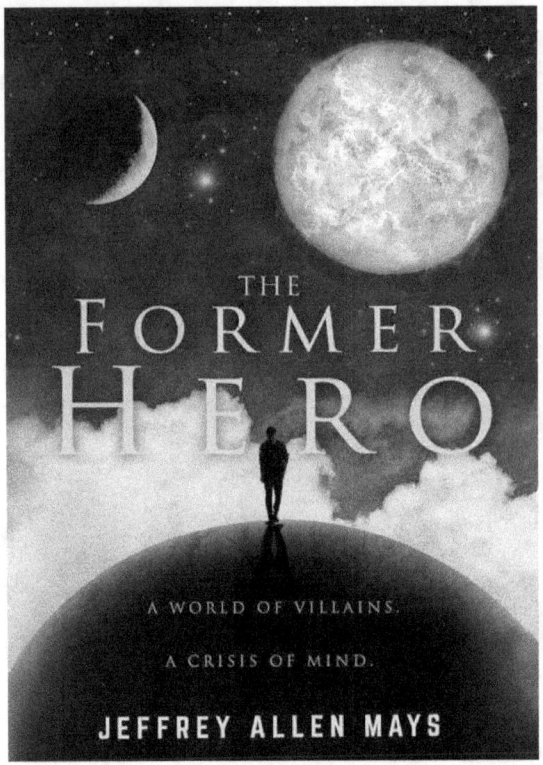

The Former Hero By Jeffrey Allen Mays

Award winning, literary and intellectual feast-a multi-genre, tour de force. Chapter by chapter, it alternates between poles; adventurous and thrilling one moment, intimate and human the next, set in a modern city troubled with terrorism and government corruption one moment, and spinning the legends of history the next. Narrating in measured, stolid prose one moment, and rollicking in experimental, stylized storytelling the next, and soaring in the poetic heights after that.

http://jeffreyallenmays.com/

Available now at Amazon and the from the author

http://www.theminimumyouneedtoknow.com

http://www.infiniteexposure.net

http://www.johnsmith-book.com

http://www.logikalblog.com

http://www.theminimumyouneedtoknow.com

http://www.infiniteexposure.net

http://www.johnsmith-book.com

http://www.logikalblog.com

Pearl River Publishing Group

www.ingramcontent.com/pod-product-compliance
Lightning Source LLC
Chambersburg PA
CBHW060540180626
46817CB00002B/651